THE BOOK OF LIGHT TRILOGY: BOOK ONE

Tree of Life

by
Sarah Joy Green-Hart

ISBN: 9781723954498

Affectionately Dedicated To:

My mom, who never clipped my wings,
my sister, Britta, who insisted I give this story a chance to fly,
and my sister, Jenice, who still teaches me about the light.

Strong women who have carried themselves
with grace amid suffering.

I love you.
XOXO

Prologue | The Year of The Conquest

FLAMES FROM THE city grasped at the night sky, fueled by the flesh and bones of hopeless innocents. The president watched the destruction through a haze of smoke, his mind flooding with self-condemnation as he rubbed the quarter in his pocket. A Kyrios member had given it to him as a "reminder of who we are to trust."

The Kyrios plotted for years, gaining control through a masterful manipulation of the system. Over the decades, they legislated their dream, brainwashing their adherents with propaganda and the rhetoric of politico-religious extremism.

The conspiracy theorists had been right.

During their most recent late-night video conference, the president and the Kyrios attempted to come to an agreement.

"You spit on the foundation of our country," the Kyrios claimed. "We will not allow this nation to become godless."

With a scoff, the president had mustered all the professionalism he possessed to refrain from laughing in their stupid, superstitious faces. "Our responsibility is to uphold the will of the people who elected us, not to force our personal beliefs on them."

"You've been warned. God will bless our efforts if you refuse to repent."

The call ended, and the attack that followed created a national disaster of unprecedented proportions. In a few days, it brought the nation to its knees.

The righteous contents of the so-called Book of Light defended their treason.

Justified in the rioting of their followers.

Justified in their act of war, despite declaring themselves a people of peace and love.

Justified in their claim to regard the innocent while slaughtering the innocent.

Using all remaining forms of communication—which were few—the president announced to the people and faithful military men and women of the nation that they must relinquish their freedom to save their lives.

It broke his heart.

The secure locations reserved for his use were reportedly destroyed. Taking his personal security and staff members, he fled to the countryside and took refuge in a forest. This couldn't be a permanent solution, but at least they were out of the fire. Now, he stood at the edge of the woods, stunned.

On the most frightening day of their lives, he was too wide-eyed and fearful to console the handful of humanity huddled behind him. No amount of public speaking experience could have prepared him for this.

He swallowed hard, clenching his trembling hands into fists. "Stay unified. We will survive this night together. It'll be all right. The trees will"—the statement was idiotic, but he had to say something—"they will protect us."

They could only watch, horrified, unable to ignore the cries of their unfortunate fellow-patriots who found no refuge in the woods.

One | Post-Conquest: 217

JESURUN'S MOM KISSED him, covering his face with tears as she stroked his brow with soft hands. "Your father will find you someday," she said. "He's the only one with golden buttons and black boots who you should ever trust. Do you understand, Jes?"

"Yes."

"And Jes . . . Honor the trees. They protect the oppressed. Their roots are your roots. Understand?"

Jes didn't understand, but he nodded.

Looking into his eyes, she licked her trembling lips and sang.

"The moon is new, so we hide.
We lie in wait, preparing to rise.
In the earth, we plant our roots;
Prepared to sprout beneath black boots.
We are the earth, we are the earth,
We hide in the womb of night.
Peacefully unified, stand for the truth,
And kick back against the black boots.
Rise and be born the mighty Unified."

This was their gate's song. They sang it while they worked and while they played. They sang it around fires, when they were sad, and when they were happy. They sang it loudest after the first cries of a new baby. It didn't mean anything to Jes, but it sounded pretty.

Clinging to a blanket with one hand and a bag of food with the other, Jes lay in the hole his mother had made in the ground. She covered it with sticks and leaves, then left. Not until her soft sobs disappeared did he finally release the blanket to touch her tears on his cheek. Rubbing them between his fingers, sleepiness soon overcame him.

* * *

As the sky changed from black to blue, vehicles pulled into Jes' gate and flooded the air with gunshots and the screams of men, women, and children. It went on for what seemed like hours. He consoled himself with thoughts of happier times. Last night even.

Only yesterday his mother was smiling and warm, as always. Her licorice-black hair had brushed his face as she kissed him goodnight. Her soft voice caressed his ears with "I love you." It was just yesterday, wasn't it? What day was it now?

Without explanation, smelling of night air and vanilla, she woke him and, with dirty hands, put him in this hole at the forest's edge, outside their gate.

Now, here he was.

After the shooting and screaming stopped, Jes waited, nibbling on the food he'd been given. His body ached. Too cramped in this hole. He had to get out soon.

As the sun fell beyond sight, Jes pushed the camouflage away and crawled out of his hiding place. The bad people must have gone away by now. Draping the blanket over his shoulders, he carried the bag of food as he approached the gate and came upon the slaughter.

Not a soul of the dead answered his cries.

He sat down against a house and poured every drop of his innocence into the little blanket until the rumble of vehicles drew a gasp from him and hardened his tears. He had to get out of there.

The blanket fell from his shoulders when he ran, but he couldn't stop. His side ached, and his lungs pressed against his ribs with each breath. Jes ran until the new moon swallowed him into the womb of the night. There he would grow and be born again, but maybe not in the nice way the song spoke of.

Two | Post-Conquest: 232

SUNLIGHT FILTERED THROUGH the fresh spring leaves and shone into the loft through its only window. Horace held Hesper's precious lavender sachet to his nose, the shadow and light dancing across his face. Even though he had calmed down since she arrived, his little whimpers and sniffles of suffering troubled her emotions. If only his mama, Deirdre, would hold him instead of sitting in the corner with her sewing basket, staring.

Glaring.

Never mind. Deirdre was not a gentle woman. Her arms were unlikely to be comforting. At least the lavender seemed to help.

Hesper pushed the leg of his deer-skin trouser over his knee. While stable, the fractured tibia still required attention. She filled her wooden mortar with soft, fresh comfrey leaves and ground them with a pestle as the distressed child shed quiet tears. He needed a distraction while she worked, and she had just the thing.

"In our own land, many years ago—"

Despite his pain, the boy lit up. "My favorite story, Hesper."

She smiled. The Story always worked for children. "The Unified and the Meros lived in one nation," she continued. "The Meros grew hostile toward our ancestors for their love of science and toleration. They set communities ablaze, flushing our people out of their homes to murder them in broad stone stree—"

"Why did the Meros do it, Hesper? Why do you think they destroyed it all and chased us in here? Were science and toleration very bad?"

The question took her by surprise. She had told him The Story many times, but he had never asked for those details. "I read whatever books the hunters can bring to us," she said. "And based on what I have read, science and toleration are good things."

"We do not even study science the way they used to," said Horace. "We can't!"

Deirdre bristled at that and broke from her silence. "Listen to you, mixing your words together like a Meros brat! 'Can't,' he says! We may be the Unified, but our words must never be."

"Yes, Mama."

"Pure speech creates a strong nation. That is wisdom from the ancestors, and you know it quite well, boy."

"I do." He shrugged a shoulder. "I meant to say that I do not understand why we must hide when we are so different from our ancestors. Maybe we could be friends with the Meros now."

"Ugh! Why would you want that?" Dierdre said. "They are hateful, evil creatures who do not honor humans any more than they honor trees. I would spit on a Meros sooner than I would accept friendship."

After Deirdre had her say, Hesper opted for the simplest answer. "I am sure they have a reason for hating us, Horace, even if it is not logical. Everyone has a reason for what they do. However, I am curious about your reason for trying to jump to your friend's loft and falling to the ground, little man." She eyed him with false sternness.

He pointed a finger at her. "Hesper, if you scold me, I will run and hide and cry like the Unified ancestors. Then you will feel bad and leave me alone like the Meros left our ancestors alone!"

Such a good-natured, smart boy.

"And when you come out of hiding at last?" She leaned in and winked. "I will snatch you up the way they do, but I will tickle you instead of kidnap you! Explain how you are going to run from me with a broken bone anyway!"

Horace giggled.

With her hand, she scooped moist, ground comfrey from the mortar and gently applied the herb to the affected area of Horace's leg, careful to not drop any on his bed-pelt.

Only a few moments later, Horace blurted, "You know, Hesper, I want to go out and feel the sunlight and see a Meros."

She could do without seeing a Meros, but how good the sunlight would feel out in the open. She had visited a few sunny clearings in her life. They were far away from the community, though.

"Only naughty children and hunters leave the trees. It is a serious thing to be a hunter, and many of them never return. Try to remember that."

"Listen to Hesper," Deirdre barked. "You certainly do not listen to me about this!"

Hesper smiled at the boy and laid a cloth over his shin, then she carefully pulled his trouser leg down over it. He did not need a wooden splint if he was a good boy, which he was. She wrapped the leg with buckskin and secured it with rags. "Rest well, Horace."

Tomorrow, she would return to apply fresh comfrey, so she would need to harvest more in the morning. Maybe Adahy would be home with ice to alleviate the swelling, too. Unlikely but possible.

Hesper shouldered her bag and rose to her feet. "Feed him good broth." She handed Deirdre a small leather bag of dried stinging nettle. "Cook this in it. And keep him off his feet, of course."

Dierdre stood. "You have such a touch. That boy was screaming. I was so scar—" A rap at the hatch in the floor interrupted her. "I am here!" she called.

The wood panel opened on its leather hinges as Adahy's hands and bearded, bronze face peeked over the floor. He climbed into the loft and offered an obligatory bow of his head to Deirdre before sharing a smile with Hesper.

"Do you have ice today?" Hesper asked.

He frowned. "You needed ice?"

"No. Not until now." She gestured to Horace. "Poor fellow tried to leap to his friend's loft and broke his leg."

Adahy whistled. "Horace, you're fortunate to be alive—and to have such excellent care." He winked at Hesper, burning her cheeks.

"He is taking it well," Deirdre admitted. "Horace may be reckless, but he handles his failures with dignity. I suppose he should receive praise when praise is due."

"He is a fine boy, ma'am." Adahy slid the bag off his shoulder and set it on the ground. The bright red poppies Hesper had beaded on its flap last winter still looked lovely. Whenever she saw him, she assessed her work, always pleased that it held up so well to the hunter's life.

The sack collapsed on itself as he drew out a circular wooden box, pyrographed with swirls and flowers. He set it on a small table and lifted the lid to reveal a creamy-golden wheel of cheese, wrapped in muslin. Deirdre left it to dig through a basket of sewing—for payment, no doubt.

It was the loveliest wooden box Hesper had ever seen. She traced its pyrographed designs with her finger.

"It is a well-made one, isn't it?" Adahy said. "I thought of you when I saw it."

The smooth surface of the lid whispered under her calloused palm. "The markings are interesting."

Deirdre offered Adahy a pair of moccasins and a handful of geodes. He fit the items into his bag and, with a nod to Hesper, left the loft through the hole in the floor.

"Left the hatch open!" Deirdre huffed. "Such a man. It has always bothered me that he mixes his words so often. He is probably the reason my boy does it. They all look up to him, those young ones, and he refuses to concern himself with setting an example with his speech." She grabbed a knife from shelves on the wall behind her. A knowing look on her face, she pointed the knife at Hesper. "He is a stig. Not a doubt in my mind! You had best bear that thought in yours."

Adahy had been bringing them supplies from the outside world for years, but Deirdre regarded him with suspicion? Hesper had never heard anyone suggest such a thing before now.

Deirdre opened the box of cheese and sliced the wheel in half. She set one half aside on the table. "He is too wealthy to avoid marriage, and I pity the woman who gets him. Oh, the uproar when he is found to be a stig! I will be the first to fight for his expulsion." Again, she stabbed the air with the knife.

The hatch was still open.

Hesper kept her voice low. "He has been among us for several years and not one woman has accused him of touching her. He has exceptional self-control. That, I think, is an uncommon virtue among stigs."

Deirdre's hard face broke with a laugh. "Do you ever have a bad thing to say, Hesper?"

Hm. Did Dierdre have any good things to say? "Not of people with his character."

"Let us consider the possibility that very few women would complain if he touched them." With a wry smile, Deirdre replaced the lid on the box and handed it to Hesper. "I hope you remain this trusting and innocent all the days of your life."

Hesper stuffed the box into her bag as far it would fit.

"You be still and obey your mama, Horace. Are you listening to me?" She knelt beside him and stroked his hair.

"I hear you, Hesper. Come kiss me."

She kissed the top of his head. "My little husband." In a few years, he would be too old for her to kiss. She had better do it more now.

* * *

After being in the warmth of the loft, the night's coolness shook Hesper. She looked up with hope for a clear sky beyond the treetops. One star stood out with a faint flicker, nestled between the sway and flutter of the leaf-cluttered sky she had been born under.

"Searching for stars?"

Adahy stood nearby, and because it was always a pleasure to see him, she smiled.

"Yes." She glanced his way, then returned her eyes to the sky. "Always an obstructed view."

"It's torture for you, isn't it?"

"Not that bad." She shook her head. "I am usually content. Helping others to heal and savor their lives is one of the most sensible purposes for my existence, and yet I feel a small pang inside of me when I think of a great world I will never see because of a hatred none of us know the reason for."

Adahy leaned back against Dierdre's tree, unwrapping a resin-like ball of candy. "Hesper, the danger that comes with the beautiful things in the outside world isn't worth it. I have yet to find a wonder that compares to the forest, but even if the forest were not here, your friendship is better than anything I've encountered out there." He smiled and put the candy in his mouth. "Would you like one?" The question came with the spicy fruit scent of his breath.

"No. It smells good, though."

Her friendship was better than anything in the outside world?

Her heart rate and busy mind required all her attention. Pride and nerves must be handled promptly. Gratified pride caused division. She must forget what he said, but it felt so nice, how could she?

Adahy scrunched and opened the candy wrapper a few times. "I, uh, I waited to speak with you and overheard your conversation. I appreciate your friendship, Hesper. Very much."

"You heard her talking?" Hesper closed her eyes. How embarrassed he must be.

He chuckled and stood up straight, tucking the wrapper into his bag. "No. Not much. I only cared about your talking. I heard that much clearer, even though your voice was softer." Hand placed over his heart, he said, "Very courageous stand made, Hesper. Tactful. Well done." He rustled through his bag and drew out and held a small wooden box, tied closed with white string. "Bring this to your mama and papa for me. It's a gift. I hope you all will like it."

Hesper took it, careful not to touch his hand. "It is a nice little box." She stroked the edge of the smooth wood with her thumb and gave it a quick sniff. Adahy's queer, amused expression brought a half-smile to her lips.

Several yards away, the community fire whispered and crackled, and a few birds chirped to each other over Hesper and Adahy's heads. The lofts, held by the branches above them, creaked with the steps of Unified families. All the sounds of home and love, combined with Adahy's presence and attention, made Hesper feel too good to think of anything except pleasing herself. It was time to go home.

"As for Deirdre," Adahy said. "I do not blame anyone for wondering about me. I would, too. Considering that I came here as an outsider, I am amazed more people do not speak of me with suspicion."

"I am amazed anyone does," she retorted, placing the box in her bag. "No Unified is an outsider, regardless of the community they came from. Do not let Deirdre's opinion unsettle you. Life has been difficult for her, and she does not seem to know how to feel better. Her judgment comes from her perception, not your actions."

He shifted the strap of his bag higher on his shoulder. "Why do you suppose no one asks me if I am a stig as Deirdre suspects? Why have you not asked me? I arrived with no proof of anything. I might have fled from my community in shame and come to bring it here. That happens, you know."

Deirdre's ears heard as well as her tongue spoke, and both parts of her were too close.

"Walk with me?" Hesper asked. They walked a few paces past the roots of Dierdre's tree before Hesper said, "Do you want to be asked if you are a stig?"

"Absolutely. That way, it will be an outright challenge to my honesty if anyone speculates about me." His smiling eyes remained fixed on her as he ducked beneath a branch.

"Very well. Are you a stig?"

"No. Never was and never will be."

"Now we have that settled, I will tell the whole community!"

They laughed together and ended their walk beside the sprawling oak that supported Hesper's loft.

"Oh! I just remembered." Hesper took the bag off her shoulder and set it on the ground to dig out her treasure. "I have been carrying this so I would have it when I saw you next. You are here one moment, then you disappear. I have to be prepared at all times." She held out a bottle. "To repel bugs. I am sure you are out of it, so I made this for you as payment for the dandelion roots I requested."

"I was out of it. You're right. But this is worth more than a few roots, Hesper."

"I would not have that mortar and pestle or lavender without you. This repellent does not begin to repay you for that. Hunters are heroes, my friend. You have been a special hunter for my family. With your friendship, more than your gifts."

He smiled. "I will bring roots the next time I come home. Have a good evening."

The warmth of contentment and longing flooded her chest. Why did he have to be so beautiful that her throat ached at the sight of him? "May you have a good evening, too, my friend."

Taking hold of the limb above her, she pulled her body upward and took to the branches in a climbing-dance she had been performing since she could run. Some in the community used ladders, but Papa felt it was dangerous in the event of a Meros night-raid. Most argued that the Meros could set them ablaze without climbing a single ladder.

"Yes," Papa would say, "but they do not, because night-raids are not only for killing."

He had seen night-raids before. They ended abruptly when Hesper was about five or six years old, so she did not remember much about them.

Hesper's loft was not more than twelve feet from the ground, though the oak stood tall, one of the sturdiest in her community. Her loft was the same. Papa cared for it well. So well, in fact, that he had quit hunting several years ago to repair others' lofts, too. Hunters traded for Papa's services with luxury items such as tools, nails, and cups. Having been both a hunter and a builder, Papa held to the belief that building and repairing lofts served his family better than hunting. Trading with hunters provided for all their needs without the risks.

Hesper entered her family's tidy loft through the hatch in its floor. Despite their small family size, they lived in an extravagant home compared to many other Unified. At approximately ten by sixteen feet, the loft was worthy of their sprawling oak and required two windows for light. Costly but necessary furs and hides lined the floor and walls in the winter and early spring. Hesper sewed smoked deer hides together every five years, then she and her brother, Tane, would wrap them around the boards of the structure to protect the family and their home from the elements.

To the right, the family kept a stand with a basin for washing dishes, a low table, and several shelves of boxes containing dried food and nuts as well as cooking tools and candles. Papa's bow and arrows, hatchet, dagger, and assorted copper knives hung on the wall.

To the left, deer hides hung from the ceiling to conceal Mama and Papa's sleeping area. Tane's and Hesper's sleeping areas, similarly arranged, were on the other side of the left half of the loft.

Mama sat in the middle of the room, sewing a pair of leg protectors. Smiling, she looked up. "I thought buckskin would be better than birch bark." Her fawn eyes glowed as she held up her project for Hesper to see. "Your papa's shins seem more battered by the birch protectors than by the branches these days."

Hesper kissed Mama and pulled the box of cheese from her bag.

"What a box! Where did you get it?" Mama asked.

"Adahy brought it while I was tending to Horace, and Deirdre gave it and half of the cheese as payment for Horace's care."

Mama set her sewing aside and rose to take the box of cheese to the table. After smoothing her black hair, she busied herself with gathering the night's meal from the shelves. Slices of acorn bread and dried meat on clay plates made for the usual light evening fare of the Unified. Mama added dried blueberries with a guilty grin and poured water into two tin cups which Hesper took to the table for her. "Why only three plates? Where is Tane?"

"Tane is staying with Tangi and his family tonight," Mama said. She set a knife inside the opened box of cheese and sat by the table.

Hesper joined her just as the hatch swung open and Papa hoisted himself into the loft. He drew up the rope connected to their candle-bowl and sat beside the lit candle to remove his leg protectors and give his shins a good rubbing through the deer-skin trousers.

Mama smiled. "Welcome home, Avriam."

Papa grunted as he sat, then patted Mama's hand. "Dear woman."

This was their way every night. Papa always rubbed his shins and called Mama a dear woman. The ancestors had said that routine ensured security, and so far, it worked well for the Unified.

The family consumed their food in weary, amiable silence until, midway through her berries, Hesper remembered Adahy's box. She hurried to her bag. "I almost forgot. Adahy sent this for you."

Mama accepted the box, stunned. Papa was slicing a piece of cheese when Hesper introduced the gift, and now he sat frozen mid-slice. Mama and Papa exchanged a queer expression.

"What? What is it?" Hesper asked.

"I will speak with him now." Papa gave one last press of the knife, removed the slice of cheese, and stuffed half of it in his mouth as he slipped down from the loft to the branches below.

"What, Mama?"

Mama took the cheese knife in hand and cut the string around the little box, then removed the lid. The fading light made it difficult to see, so Mama held the candle beside it. There, in the palm of her hand, lay Hesper's future.

"Salt," she breathed. Salt usually came in little cloth bags, though. Perhaps this did not mean what it normally meant.

Mama smiled. "And beautiful salt, at that. Look how fine and gray . . ." She took a pinch and felt it with her fingers. "Still a bit moist." She gasped. "Oh my, he has really invested in this, Hesper."

Hesper touched Mama's arm, staring at the salt. "Mama, did you expect this?"

Pleasantly smug, Mama shrugged. "Possibly."

Hesper covered her watery eyes. Why was she crying?

"My dear girl." Mama crooned, touching Hesper's face. "You are blushing?"

Hesper took their plates to wash them in silence. Time to think awhile. Or not. Not thinking about it might be better. Her unsettled stomach and pounding heart troubled her, so she grabbed the seasoning box for ginger root to grate into a cup of water. The hatch opened. Hesper jumped and whirled around to face Papa, clinging to the water basin's stand.

Papa grasped her arms with his thick, calloused hands. "Adahy has formed an attachment to you and would like to make you his wife."

A quick, deep breath chilled the back of her throat. "Of course, Papa. It would be an honor."

Papa's smile nearly split his face in two. "He will visit with meat at midday tomorrow. I suggest you mentally prepare for this."

He washed his face in the bowl of water by his and Mama's bed before tucking himself away behind their curtain, where he shuffled about and plopped down on his mat of bear fur with a tired groan.

Mama toyed with a few blueberries on her plate, thoughtful, then she sat back and whispered, "Hesper, marriage to a hunter can be frightening. They travel far and do business with the Meros under the protection of a precarious and unofficial agreement with them. He will be gone often, and you will wonder if he might not come back. It will keep you up at night, holding your babies tightly, weeping."

Her brow furrowed. "He will keep secrets because hunters do not want to cause fear. They want to return to a home that has not seen the horrors they have—not even in your mind. We need peace to be unified." She popped the last of the blueberries in her mouth. "Just remember, if he keeps secrets, it is out of love. I learned to trust those who know what the outside world is like." A knowing smile crept up on her face as she chewed the last of her blueberries. "Still, you will be a wealthy woman, dear child."

Hesper's smile did not agree with the tears on her cheeks. "I do not care for his wealth. I will be a fortunate woman with that man beside me, and I never want him to wonder if I agreed to marry him for his possessions."

"You think you hide how you feel so well, but we all knew you loved him. Sincerely. I am sure it was no secret to him, either." Mama reached across the table and patted Hesper's hand. "Go to sleep. I am staying up to finish these leg protectors."

Hesper obeyed and laid on her bed-pelt, surrounded by shelves of wooden boxes, a few books, and her frame drum in the corner by her head. She twisted and turned, trying to find a way to be comfortable with her full mind. No amount of shifting or wiggling could help, so she stared out the window and focused on the breeze-tossed leaves for a distraction—it failed, of course.

Moments ago, she did not expect marriage in her near future. Now, in a week's time, she would be a married woman.

Why had he withheld his intent and declaration of affection in favor of gentle hints which might have been the actions of a mere friend? Strange behavior.

The Unified communities across the nation attempted communication with each other on a large scale only once, two hundred years ago. Their ancestors sent a letter from this community to the next, passing it around the nation in hopes of establishing rules to ensure Unified survival. Of course, people were hiding, so who knew whether the letter reached everyone or not? But many of the groups were found, and while the letter seemed to be effective for the basics of their culture, two hundred years later, hunters often had members of Hesper's community laughing until they cried as they regaled them with stories of bizarre Unified practices witnessed elsewhere. Houses on the ground? Tamed animals? Men without beards? Women with cut hair? All unheard of in this area of the country.

Therefore, when Adahy came along with different customs and ideas, it was a challenge but not a shock. He had entered the community and requested they accept him as one of them, for he desired a new home and a new family. The Unified accepted most who claimed to be one of them unless they showed evidence of wickedness. So, the old men and women of the community questioned Adahy, and in the end, each announced their belief in his goodness.

The sharp fellow earned a reputation for quality hunting and became an asset to the community. He even brought in a reading primer to teach anyone who wanted to learn to read. He was Hesper's hero from the day they met, and as a skilled hunter and a good man, he never proved himself unworthy of the title.

What had she done to deserve the attention of such a person?

A dream of the day they met haunted her often. The dream was never about him, rather, it was about the event that brought them together. She would probably dream it again tonight after thinking so much about him.

Turning on her side, she scratched at a knot in the wall. The dream would be just that. A mere dream. Dreams could not hurt her.

Three | Post-Conquest: 232

MAMA'S URGENT WHISPER woke Hesper. "Up, child! Adahy is here with elk meat! It is almost cooked."

Adrenaline surged through Hesper's body as she scrambled to her feet and pulled the hide curtain aside. "Mama! Why did you let me sleep so long?" She had not had the dream she expected, and that was always a good thing, though it would have gotten her up earlier.

Mama peered at her through the hatch opening. "I knew you would not be able to fall asleep." She grinned.

Hesper rushed to the water bowl and splashed its coldness on her face and neck. "I should have been helping you, Mama," she scolded. Was she scolding Mama or herself? Both, perhaps.

"Do not worry. I explained it to Adahy. He will not judge you for sleeping late."

"You explained that I was too giddy to sleep? Oh, Mama!"

"Do not be silly! The red clover tea has been steeping overnight. Send it down to us!" Mama disappeared below the loft. The hatch dropped with the squeak of its leather hinges.

Loose sweet red clovers floated in the pitcher of golden tea, which fit perfectly in the candle bowl. Hesper lowered it to the ground by its rope, then descended the tree and landed her steady, bare feet on the forest floor.

Greeted by the smell of meat and applewood smoke, dancing to the sound of crackling flame, she smiled. The sweet wood almost always meant a celebration. Mama even brought out the salt for the special occasion, shaking it vigorously over the iron pan of sizzling elk and wild onions.

Seated by the fire with Papa, Adahy cast his eyes on Hesper and stood. She bowed her head in greeting, and he reciprocated the gesture. Without a word, they sat together.

At any other time, they interacted with relative ease and sense, but now? She would never get her hormones under control around pheromones such as his.

Papa straightened up. "Adahy, here is your bride. In one week, we will have a ceremony, and Hesper will live in your loft. You will be unified at last."

"I will make you a garment for the event," Mama said.

"Thank you, Theia. It will be an honor to wear garments made by the best seamstress in the community."

"If I am, it is only because of the needles and thread you get for us, Adahy."

A gentle smile filled his eyes with affectionate light. "We all play our part." Turning to Hesper, he said, "If it pleases you, I will bring chicory flowers for your hair on the day of the ceremony. I've noticed that when I bring them, they often end up in your braid, rather than mashed under a rock or in a pot over the fire."

Hesper's face warmed. Especially appealing against the grass after a rain, pretty, periwinkle chicory flowers were a vain interest of hers. They had their uses as medicine and nutrition, but they were beautiful, too. For that reason, she rarely requested them. It did not seem right to ask for more, knowing she was too weak to resist the pleasure of decorating herself. "You are observant."

Adahy winked. "It's okay to enjoy things." He drew a leather cord from his bag, threaded through a piece of metal. A betrothal token. Careful not to touch her, he placed the cord over her head and let the cool metal rest at her collarbone. The round, silver piece featured the profile of a woman's face with an inscription reading, "In God We Trust."

"A step toward being unified once more," Papa said. "This is the chief thing, Adahy. You, who came to us without, will now have a family. And it is high time, too, at thirty-three years of age!"

Twenty-one years old, strong, healthy, and capable, Hesper would be a part of supplying Adahy with the family he needed and deserved. However, any woman in the community could do that. Pride grew from individualism, selfishness sprouted out of pride, and selfishness birthed disunity. Their ancestors' many maxims concerning division rushed through her mind. She must remember that marriage was a privilege, not a right.

Adahy bowed his head. "It is an honor to be unified with your family, Avriam."

Papa clasped Adahy's shoulder, and Adahy wound his arm behind Papa's and clasped his shoulder in return—an affectionate exchange for only the dearest friends. Papa released Adahy to take a piece of meat from the plate Mama offered.

"I regret that our whole family is not here for this occasion. We allowed Tane to stay with Tangi last evening, and he has not come home." Looking to the west, Papa's eyes narrowed. "We have been too busy with this joyful business to go searching for him so far into the western wood."

Mama extended the plate of meat to Hesper and Adahy. They each took a piece and began eating while Papa spoke.

"Tane is passionate about whatever he does," he continued. "He is fiercely loyal to the Unified and shows a propensity for hunting. If only his behavior were consistent."

Mama sprinkled salt into the pan, shaking her head. "As girls, we were daily reminded that if we left the forest, the Meros would kidnap us, touch us, and give us their mark. If we escaped from them, we would be forced to live on the edge of the Unified community—a pariah—never permitted to marry because we had been made impure.

"Now, it is not mentioned as often. I suspect it is because the night raids have ended. I wonder if it would help to daily remind our children again." Mama wiped her cheeks. "I can think of nothing crueler to do to a woman than rob her of the most useful function her body offers to the Unified: new people! It is terrifying, even to me, and I have never seen a black X mark!

"Ever since he was a little boy, Tane has been sensitive about how women are treated. His indignation is now greater than his love for unity. I understand the anger, but I worry. He grows more bronzed by the day." Mama stared into the fire as a familiar muted grief hardened her features.

What happened to the women who were kidnapped and why they were taken remained a mystery. Slavery was mentioned from time to time, but if that was all they wanted, why women? Men were killed, women were taken. Hunters knew the reasons, but they kept silence. Nevertheless, the idea of the Meros monsters' touch kept young women's minds in the forest more often.

In recent years, men outnumbered women, and sometimes there was no one to marry. Men might even leave for another community just to find a wife, or, like Tane, they might devote their lives to the Unified cause, rather than Unified strength.

If Tane had something as valuable as a womb, he would never risk his life for such a foolish reason.

Papa's eyes darkened. "Despite our admonishments, it is clear Tane continues to leave the forest. He claims to honor our ancestors' goal, to honor his people, to honor peace, but he disregards wise counsel.

"I am too poetic from my time as a hunter in the outside world, but, as I see it, a Unified man must be a sturdy tree with many healthy branches, boasting protective leaves and roots that dig deep into the earth." He scooped near the rooty ground with fingers spread out and curved. "In a sturdy tree we build lofts, and in lofts, we build safety to have a family, and in a family"—pointing upward, he shook his fist—"we unify ourselves so that we may be free from Meros oppression. Free to roam in the open. Free from hate."

As if to embrace freedom, Papa's arms opened wide. "One day, we will be so many, they will not be able to push us back or intimidate us! It gives me joy to think on it." His hands fell to his lap. "Though, I fear I will not see it in my lifetime."

Things would change soon, and the Unified would be released from oppression. Any day. Maybe even now? Sometime this afternoon or tomorrow, they would receive news that the Meros had given up their hateful policies. What a wonderful thing that would be.

The beautiful trees gave Hesper peace and kept her safe. Strong, rough trunks. Gentle, fluttering leaves. Faithful, useful, and fruitful, the way humans should be. She did not want to live anywhere else, but the privilege of leaving without fear? What a gift.

Mama scooped a fresh batch of meat from the cooking pan and onto her serving plate. "Tane claims he wants to join the Earth People to build families in the outside world with other brave Unified," she said. "But he does not understand peace or love, so how can he do it?"

Papa's countenance wilted with disgust. "I fear I have done this. I let him be a boy for too long and encouraged his hatred toward the Meros."

The scraping of Mama's spoon was followed by a child's playful shout in the distance. Slices of cooked meat waited to be served from her plate. She squatted beside the cooking pan and dropped in several small slabs of raw elk. Tossed on top of the meat, wild onions sent up a cloud of fragrant steam with a loud sizzle.

"We are not the only influences in his life, Avriam. His hatred is fueled by others. He is eighteen and able to choose his course. We have taught him love, but he hates the Meros more than he loves anyone. Do not blame yourself."

"It is never a child's fault when the flaw of the parent comes alive in them," Papa said.

"This exemplifies the danger in Unified leaving the forest to become the Earth People." Adahy stretched his legs out in front of him. "They claim they want to blend in, build families, slowly integrate the Unified into the Meros world." He leaned forward, his voice growing urgent. "However, I have seen them in action. It's a rebellion that encourages behavior like Tane's.

"Young people leave the forests and follow the leadership of the Earth People to act out violent crimes the leaders themselves will not commit. Vain defiance resulting in the imprisonment and death of many Unified people, including women and children."

"Truly?" Papa grunted and chewed on his food awhile, his eyes adrift on an unsettling current of thought. "I imagined the birth of an uprising by means of this peaceful movement in time, but it is too soon to allow anger to foment. The war will be premature, and the Meros will destroy us. Again."

Shaking his head, he tossed his hand in the air to shoo away an invisible pest. "Enough of politics! Afton!" He reached for the man passing by. "We have betrothed Hesper and Adahy at last! Have meat!"

* * *

The feast of elk and wild onions spread to most of the community before Papa finished his boasting of the match. However, by midday, the joy faded, and he glanced to the west more often.

"Theia, let us take the rest of the meat to Maddex and Lana."

Packing the last of the meat in a small wooden box to take to Tangi's family, Mama said, "We will leave you two alone to enjoy your good day." She kissed Hesper's forehead as they left.

Others from the community sat beneath their lofts, eating meals at their own fires, chatting and laughing over their work. The fragrant wood smoke and scent of meat drifted through the air, weaving itself into the comfortable, quiet sound of peace and family in the forest.

Hesper chanced a direct look at Adahy, which he met with unabashed admiration. This would not do. She could not bear it. The betrothal token would be a good distraction.

"This says 'In God'—I have never heard this word. Is that right?"

"In God we trust. You have it right. It is currency from the Unified ancestors. The number there"—he pointed—"is the number of a year as they once measured them. This is from one of the years your ancestor was in office. The man who ruled the country during the war."

"Is it really? How did you get this? What is God?"

A spark of zeal energized his movements as he shifted his body to face her and crossed his legs. "God is a great spirit who made the world, including people," he whispered. "In the past, the Unified and Meros alike called on God to honor It and plead for help."

"Spirit?" She grimaced. "I have read about spirits. It is difficult for me to accept the reality of something I cannot see. The Unified ancestors were too intelligent to believe such a myth."

He laughed. "They did, though. In time, the Unified ancestors realized they could not prove the existence of God through scientific methods, so they rejected It. In the outside world, they say this is why the Meros rose up and won their war against the Unified. God favored Its believers."

The being, who supposedly created the world, granted favors in war? Aided one group of Its creation against another? That sounded too human and foolish for something wise enough to make a beautiful and complex world.

"If this is true, it helps me to understand a few things that go unexplained about our history," she said.

"How so?"

"I have never understood why the war happened at all. If a spirit is involved, anyone might speak for It and make all manner of claims. Perhaps that is what the Meros did. People seem most passionate about things they believe, rather than the things they see. Passionate to start a war, perhaps." Hesper frowned, brushing a fleck of something off her foot. "Like Deirdre. Without any evidence, she believes you are a stig. No facts, no proof, but all the certainty."

Adahy pondered that. "It defies logic. People will gather to the voice of an invisible authority in a man's mouth—or their own mind."

A breeze redirected the applewood smoke westward. Wood shifted and sent a spray of sparkling ash into the air. The sparks faded to black, rendered harmless. Hesper rose to gather cordwood from beside the tree. "Do you believe there is a god?"

"Yes."

Interesting. "You are intelligent," she said, feeding the fire. "If you believe It, I will give it consideration."

The statement awoke a warm, loving expression in Adahy, so beautiful that Hesper longed to search the lines of his jaw and brow with her hands. To trace every facet of the dear, smiling face as she would the winding paths of the green metal beetle in an ash tree's sapwood.

Too silly and poetic.

"For you, the coin is a betrothal token," he said. "I suggest you not explain 'God' if anyone asks. Many do not know of It, and often those who do are hostile toward the idea."

"I understand."

"Good." He nodded. "Listen, my friend. There's something I want to ask you that is unrelated to God." His eyes dimmed with his mood.

Hesper dusted off her hands and sat with her back turned to the fire so she could look at his face. He was so uncomfortable, glancing away, then turning back.

Finally, he said, "I need to know. You and I are friends, and we have shared our minds before. Please, be honest with me without fear. Do you want marriage? You have feelings for me and you care about me—I know all of that—but marriage is something else entirely.

"If Avriam is pushing you into this, I'll have nothing to do with it and will handle things honorably without causing trouble for you." He leaned toward her, nodding. The intensity insisted she believe his words. "I will be your friend forever, and I will wait if you are not ready. I would never force you into my loft or bed." Raking his hand over the ground, he snagged a twig and spun it around with his long fingers as he studied her face. "Do you truly?"

"Oh, yes," she answered. Nothing in the world sounded better.

He squinted a suspicious eye and ended his scrutiny satisfied.

"I could tell you didn't know the box was salt. How did you not know?" He held a small invisible box to his ear and shook it. "If you had shaken it, instead of sniffing! You are always sniffing at things!"

"It was not in a bag! And sniffing is a useful skill. As a hunter, you should know." The air smelled of Meros spices as Adahy uncrossed his legs and stretched them out in front of him. He must have been to the market earlier. "Either way," Hesper said. "Let us be fair. You gave no indication of an interest in marriage before this."

Genuinely shocked, he cried, "No indication! Is that so? It wasn't obvious?"

She shook her head.

"Without touch, how could I have done things differently?"

"Words." Surely, he did not need to ask. Such a simple answer.

"Is that how it's done? Words? So straightforward. I should not be surprised, considering the source."

"What else is there? Words and deeds." She grabbed the pitcher of honey-golden clover tea and filled a tin cup. "Would you like some?"

"Yes." He accepted the cup in her hand. "As for me, I knew how you felt without your saying a single word. You blushed like a sunset whenever I talked to you." He flashed a cocky smile at her. "You usually calm down quickly. I figured I was doing a good job if you were twitterpated and easy to soothe at once."

"If you are so skilled at hiding that the powerful survival instinct of the deer and elk cannot stand against you and recognize your silent intentions, I do not know how I could be expected to."

"Yes, but I don't bring flowers to an elk! I've left salt for deer, though."

"Stig!"

Adahy clicked his tongue and clutched his chest. "I'm wounded! What happened to the brave woman who stood up for me to Deirdre the Fierce yesterday? Now you accuse me of adultery with deer?"

Hesper laughed and held her cheeks.

Adahy's open smile drifted into something more serious. "Let me try my hand at words, then." He passed his eyes over her face several times, then cleared his throat and said, "I never considered accepting your affection, because I am often away. My life is complicated. But one day, I looked at you, and I realized that if you were to marry someone else, I'd have to leave because I could not bear the loss." He scooched closer, his face inches from hers. Speaking low, he continued, "You inspired me to open my heart. Until I met you, it had been unyielding to anything that tried to affect it.

"You were only a girl when we met. The affection I felt for you was different from what it is now, of course, but you did something to me, and you may never know just how far-reaching the effect of your love is."

The fire was making Hesper's back too warm. Adahy was making her face too warm. Trapped between two fires of different types.

People did not speak that way here. Too many fine words for one person might make them proud. Maybe they spoke that way among the Meros, and he had picked up on their manners.

Nevertheless, he meant what he said, but what did he mean?

To open his heart. Strange, violent metaphor.

Opening the heart meant death.

However, he spoke of a change in himself, and change would come from the mind.

She did something that changed his mind and made him more open to new thoughts?

Openness to new thoughts. That was what an open heart must be.

His words made sense now.

Maybe.

Whether they did or did not, the experience awakened her mind in a way, she was sure, his hands never would. Though, the meaning did not move her half as much as the fact that he was close enough to be smelled when he spoke.

How long had she been lost in thought, fiddling with the moss between them? She started and laid her hand on her lap. "You always smell good," she said, laughing at herself. "Like spices."

"The market." He chuckled. "The Meros love their spices, you know. They keep their clothes and bedding in drawers with cinnamon sticks, anise stars, and cloved apples. Sometimes pine. As a matter of fact, I often trade pine to the spice man to get spice for other communities who don't all have these lofts to take care of with nails and practical things—the tree house choice is far costlier. If we would live on the ground, we could afford wonderful things like clocks to tell the time and pre-jarred honey. Anyway, I handle the spices a lot." He drew up a knee and extended his arm over it. "And you, my friend, smell of wild, rooted goodness, healing and nutritive. Always a faint smell of ginger and mint about you. Holding your strong healing hands will be the most sensational experience of my life."

She could not bring herself to look at his face, but the tenderness in his voice made her smile.

"So, are those the kind of words you mean? To tell you I want to marry you?"

Judging by her dry mouth and self-consciousness, yes? Her voice cracked when she said, "Those would have indicated something more than friendship." She cleared her throat. "Though, I meant words such as, 'I am interested in marrying you. I will be speaking to your papa soon.'"

He laughed a strong peppermint and lavender laugh.

Only Adahy made her think crazy thoughts about laughs having a scent and feelings a flavor. "You have strange, impractical ideas about life. You make me think of poetry too much."

"Yes, I know." He waved his hand with an air of mock flippancy. "My goal is to make you as poetic and silly as I am. On the day we are married, I intend to completely ruin you."

Hesper gasped. "If my parents knew how stiggishly you talk . . ."

Adahy laughed. "Not to be obsessive about your lovely blushes, but I'm sorry if that embarrassed you. It was not my intention."

"Not embarrassed. I have strange, poetic thoughts, too." She rubbed her cheeks and laughed it off. "Shall I share one with you?"

"Yes. Absolutely."

"When someone has a non-traumatic injury or complaint, such as a lump on the head, I focus all my attention on lumps or headaches, and stroke at them through the air. It draws out the swelling and fluid and alleviates the pain almost every time."

"Really? I've never noticed."

"All the herbalists and healers do it. People do not usually notice it because it is subtle."

"Hm!" he bobbled his head, thinking. "The human mind is powerful. I should not be surprised."

"That is not the strange poetic thought, though," she said. "I have wondered if I might communicate feelings that way. If the body responds to my focused thoughts, perhaps it will respond to focused feeling?" She drew up her legs and hugged them, rocking a little. "I have never tried it."

"That's not strange. It's a magnificent idea. I like it. Why not? Try it," he said. "Try it with me."

What? No. No. No. Yes.

He closed his eyes. "If I look, I might give us inaccurate results. Let us see what I feel."

"I feel silly!"

"Well, don't!"

"Well, fine!" She placed her hands near his head, then forced her lids closed. Breathing out the silly feelings, she smothered a giggle and focused on her care and respect for him, then pressed it through her limbs and out of her hands. The thoughts flowed, a stream of clean water, speckled with sunlight. When she opened her eyes, the thoughts were painted on Adahy's face. His teeth lay bare in a grin, like a patch of Bishop's Lace in a sunny clearing. "I felt it," he whispered.

Heart racing, she said, "Truly?"

"A stream of warm water and light"—he opened his eyes—"washed over me. Completely calm."

"Just the way I felt it!"

"It worked, Hesper. It did. That will be useful to you someday." He sipped at his tea and set the cup down. "Should I try to give you my feelings now?" Eyebrows raised, he held his hands up, wiggling his fingers. "It might help you."

What a beautifully terrifying idea! But his impish grin made her too nervous.

"It's all right," he laughed. "I can show you in other ways."

* * *

As the day wore on, Hesper cooked meals and they talked about her work and Adahy's experience in the outside world.

For a time, they discussed a book about dragon mythology that they had both read despite the Meros trade restriction concerning books for Unified. Adahy tried to find books for them whenever possible. According to him, the Meros wanted the Unified to be illiterate and uninformed. It was risky to be caught with a book in his bag. Nevertheless, he sneaked in several books, including the primer he once used to teach many to read.

The lack of work for the day made Hesper uncomfortable. Surely, they were being lazy, discussing mythical creatures and feeling feelings while other Unified saw to their responsibilities to the community.

Just as she rose to scrape Mama's dirty iron pan, Adahy reached out, though he did not touch her. "Hesper, I deal with so many cranky, disgruntled people every day. I'm delighted to take time away from work and spend it with someone as pleasant and honest as you are. You're doing a service for me. Don't feel guilty."

If it made him happy, it made her happy, so she seated herself again, pushing the dirty pot out of her mind.

* * *

Even as the cool evening seeped into the forest, Mama and Papa had not returned. Woodcutters and herbalists were returning from their day's journeys, and only a few stragglers lingered on the forest floor.

Adahy took a great breath and sighed it out. "I'm thrilled, Hesper. A week is too long now that the decision is made." He stood and grabbed his bag. "But we ought to part ways. I will inquire after Theia and Avriam. It's odd that they haven't returned yet."

Hesper stood and bowed her head, smiling her gratitude. She must compliment him, but her courage failed. He would leave! He could not leave before she said something kind to him.

Would she say something poetic and foolish? Perhaps he would think it was silly or lacking in sincerity. Maybe this would make it harder for him not to touch her. Would it?

Just do it.

She pulled words out of her fear and opened her mouth to let them fall where they would. "You are the most handsome man I know, and you are very wise, and your eyes are like the stars."

There. She said it.

A few moments passed, feeling more like minutes. She focused instead on the fine quality of her beaded poppies on his bag.

"Very poetic, my dear friend. Lovely of you to say." His words stroked her ears with the softness of milkweed. "You know, no one has ever mentioned whether touching hair is allowed."

"My hair?"

"Your hair."

"I think you would feel your conscience too well."

"Not a bit. I'd come nearer and kiss your face, but that will have to wait. I promise the stars in my eyes will always be there to see clearly. No more of this treetops-in-the-way torture." He kissed his fingertips and tipped them toward her, then walked away.

She steadied herself with a deep, cleansing breath before leaping to the first branch of her tree and climbing to the loft. She sat for only a few minutes to ponder and gush over the day's events, then the hatch opened, and Mama entered, followed by Papa.

Something was wrong.

Four | Post-Conquest: 232

MAMA DROPPED TO her knees in front of Hesper. "This morning, Tangi and Tane said they were going to the clearing in the east, and they have not returned." She wiped tears from her face. "They should be in a loft somewhere. Anywhere!"

Hesper reached out to hold Mama and hug away the sharpness of the fear. Mama, the ever-present comforter had held her many times. This was the least Hesper could do. Hesper turned her face to kiss her.

"Wife!"

Stunned, Mama stiffened and pulled away to stand and face Papa. "Husband?"

"Your rambling will do nothing for Tane." Papa spoke half to himself as he paced the floor. "Those boys have probably made stigs of themselves in a Meros home on the ground. Our enemy troubles us enough, and we do not need trouble from our own. If Tane returns unharmed, his venture will have been a waste. Experience is the only thing that boy does not have. Perhaps it will drive the truth into his dense mind." Papa slapped his own head.

"In the meantime, we will not speak of him. If he never brings his rebellious, wandering feet back to us, we will not utter his name again. One less impediment to unity."

Mama's confident gaze melted into sorrow. She threw herself on the floor, face to the wooden boards.

In the past, Mama and Papa had a fair number of disagreements. Many frustrating moments for Mama, and justifiably angry times for Papa, but never had Mama offered herself with the plea.

"Avriam, I beg you not to sacrifice your son for unity. I offer you the plea. I will do anything that you ask of me. Do not abandon our son." She took a long, congested breath and shuddered it out. "Do not dishonor the wisdom of our ancestors who gave us the plea to stir compassion in those with power in the community."

Papa stood, erect and unyielding, while Mama, vulnerable and broken, waited for him to relent.

"You are stronger than I am." Her hand jerked forward, hesitated, then took Papa's foot. The other followed. "I must obey you, but I beg you not to require something so bitter and painful."

Papa's posture did not alter. Clearly, he had no intention of responding in a receptive, traditional manner.

If Papa would just touch Mama's head, speak Tane's name—console her.

Hesper's eyes stung at the thought.

He would not give in. So, Mama did.

She stood and shuffled wearily to her place behind the deer hides. The dull light made Papa a mere silhouette in the middle of the loft. Still as Hesper was, the force of her heart's pulsations made her body sway involuntarily.

If she went to bed now, it would be over in the morning.

No. This would never be over.

"Papa," she whispered.

The floor of the loft creaked and hide brushed against hide. He must be looking at her.

Tears blurred her vision as she stood. "I have something to say to you." How weak she sounded. "You are in error to speak to Mama that way. Mama has proven her worth as a human. She possesses the blood of Unified leaders, which is something you do not have." Her voice grew stronger for this step. She would not retreat.

"Hesper, no." Mama called out from behind her curtain with a choke and a sob. "Quiet, girl. Go to bed."

"I am a woman, not a girl." Hesper inhaled through her nose and exhaled through her mouth. Her voice belonged to this declaration, and she must not say it quietly. "Mama opened herself to receive and give life to the Unified people through her children. She is the epitome of feminine strength. You have dishonored her and her reasonable grief, and I am ashamed of it."

Had the loss of his children finally broken Papa's mind?

"Something bad must have happened to Tane, your son. He would never join the Meros, so what qualm do you have with him?"

"Child!" Papa barked. "Who has given you life? Yourself? Have you done it?"

"No, sir. I am living it and using it to speak. Who gave Mama life? Was it you, sir? No!" Her voice crumbled into tears. "You have wronged her and our ancestors in doing so. This is not the way of the Unified. You speak of the shame Tane brings to us, and now you shame us with your hard mind."

"First I shame our ancestors' wisdom." Papa tossed his hands in the air. "Now I shame the Unified with my resolve! Tell me more. Pour more shame on me! Shame for keeping you in a safe, warm loft. Shame for bringing you up into adulthood. Shame for my work and devotion to our people."

Hesper stepped toward Papa, reaching. "You yourself taught me that we speak honestly and respectfully to all. It honors their humanity. You do not even honor her humanity, much less her noble birth and motherhood. You have taught me how we must latch on to peace in every circumstance, shunning deep anger that will cause us to hate or behave irrationally. Peace makes unity, turbulence causes division. Are those not honorable words you have said to me and now forget?"

A rap on the loft's hatch startled them both.

"Who is it?" Papa's cold voice chilled Hesper.

"Adahy!" he called, almost cheerful. "I'm here to see Hesper. I'll be gone for a few days, and I want to speak with her before I go."

"Go, speak with him," Papa whispered.

Hesper wiped her face and strode past Papa to open the hatch. Adahy stood at the foot of the tree, waiting for her. Trembling, she lowered herself to the branches and climbed down to meet him. His voice had been so happy, but when she saw him, concern had stolen the stars from his eyes.

Hesper led him a few paces from the oak where she rested her forehead against the bare trunk of a loblolly pine and touched its comforting roughness. Her thumb resisted movement in a spot of tacky resin.

"Papa is angry with me," she breathed. "Adahy, he might even postpone our marriage if he thinks I am unfit to marry."

"A verbal agreement is binding. The elders will not allow him to back out of a marriage arrangement so easily. I won't allow it."

When he spoke with certainty, he had the ability to convince her of almost anything.

His voice laughed. "Maybe he will be anxious to get you off his hands now."

"I cannot stand by without doing something. Papa will not allow us to talk about Tane until he returns. Tane is dead to us as Joram was."

"I'm sorry, Hesper." His hand rested near hers on the tree trunk. "Regardless of Avriam's shortcomings, I am grateful you were born to a man like him. He loved and cared for you with the same ferocity with which he rejects and scorns your foolish brothers, and it has served you well as a person. Hold on to that knowledge."

Hesper faced him and pressed her back to the tree. Her mind and heart raced one another to a place far from reason.

"I have high regard for your sense of justice, dear friend, but for your own good, you must calm yourself. Will you calm down?"

A few quiet moments passed between their forest-shadowed faces. Adahy's presence nourished her like deer bone soup. Still, something lacked. The hardy, satisfying experience of human touch. The meat and salt of the soup.

"Hesper, listen to me. Your emotions will settle because you are able to make it happen." His voice, soft and quiet, calmed her. "You are strong that way. You sting with nettle, but imagine the jewelweed a wise woman such as yourself has grown alongside it."

Weak and shaky, a laugh wiggled its way out of her. "The antidote to a nettle's sting. Often grows nearby. You are clever."

"I try." He chuckled. "Remember, please, peace and safety are in your loft, guarded by strong, gentle trees. You are home and you are with me, and you're in the forest, which means you are safe, and you can relax . . ."

The water and light sensation came from him now, just as it came from her earlier. Tears subsided as she wrangled her feelings into submission. "How did you do that?"

"A trick I learned from you today, and something I learned from a sympathetic Meros quite some time ago." He shifted, sliding his bag farther up his shoulder. "I love you, Hesper. I will see you in a few days."

They bowed to each other, and Adahy ran to the west on noiseless hunter's feet, as always.

Now, back to Papa. To the argument that would not go well. Hesper's first time defying him. If only the god Adahy spoke of were real. It would be nice to imagine that a powerful being would hear her cry for help. Help to find Tane.

Upon entering the thick black of the loft, she set the hatch in its place with a hope that Papa had gone to bed. When the silence settled, his voice, sharp and short, emerged from the darkness

"Did he touch you?"

What? "No. No, Papa, of course not."

"If that is so, I am forced to believe you spoke poorly of me. Why else would you step away from the loft? You had business you wanted either unheard or unseen. Since Adahy is too honorable and you are too honest for me to insist he touched you, I must believe the only other possibility." Papa slapped her face. "Your brother has brought enough shame to us today," he growled. "You will not do the same. Go to sleep."

The sound of Papa's feet crossed the loft to his bed. He laid down and settled beside Mama, leaving Hesper dumbstruck in the shadows. Like the crack of a tree branch she trusted to hold her up, Papa's patience ended. His desire to punish Tane unleashed him on the innocent with the discrimination of an injured badger. Hesper charged to her bed-pelt and laid down. Her wet, stinging face contorted with anger, but she would settle her emotions. She was strong that way.

An involuntary whimper came up with a sob, and she shoved it down. Hard. *Adahy, hurry home.*

* * *

He had to go now if he intended to return in time to be a part of the wedding preparations. Hesper had been dealing with her father's temper all her life, and she would be okay. He had to trust Avriam and trust the culture. It was the Unified way.

Unity without meddling.

Out of the woods and to the west, he waded through tall grass. The faint sugary scent of evergreens blew his way. He dug a lemon-spice drop out of his bag and popped it into his mouth.

Hesper often had her recurring nightmare after troubling experiences. It might be good to be around for her to talk to tomorrow morning—just in case. Maybe staying for one more day would be wise. He stopped to consider.

The lemon candy coating had dissolved. Soft, honey-sweet spice crunched under his teeth.

This had been a good day. That would balance it out and spare her the troubling dream. She'd be okay.

He carried on walking.

Hesper's brother, Tane, on the other hand, was a zealous bonehead. Tane was with the Earth People. Absolutely. He'd been doing their work, climbing their ladder, gaining authority in their ranks. Often out in public, sometimes dressed in Meros clothing to fit in, he was always up to no good.

Couldn't the Unified be content with peace in the forest for now? Peace so near he could almost kiss it. These stubborn Unified folks would push the Kyrios and their military too far and destroy themselves. The Kyrios and law enforcement wardens might back off for a while if the Unified would bide their time. Not that hiding was the solution. They must rebel against the oppression someday, but not now.

Past the tall grass, he stood on the abandoned dirt road that would take him home. Instead, business called him three miles west, where he'd find a place to sleep for the night before running his errands and returning.

Back to chaos. Back to the corruption of the outside world. For his people's sake. For the Unified.

He couldn't kiss peace, but he would kiss Hesper, and that was close.

* * *

Hesper's small hands scooped a mess of burnt-orange evergreen needles into a pile. With a snap, she broke off a bumpy stick doll from the tall, dead pine and named it Cassia.

Just as she laid Cassia in its prickly, dry bed, the crunch of footsteps turned her around. Hesper screamed and backed into the low-hanging branches. Twigs scratched, leaves shook and fluttered against her face and arms as she flailed her way out of them and took in the sight of the beardless man who startled her. How strangely he dressed, wearing a hat and stiff black clothes with gold buttons as shiny as his boots. He had to be Meros. Unified did not dress that way.

She had snatched up a kit the day before and felt a tiny heart thundering inside its warm, furry little body. Now she knew how it felt. Her heart seemed to be beating just as fast, and her shaking legs would not allow her to run.

"Hesper." The man, hunched over, clutched his chest with one hand. He reached out with the other. "It's Joram. Do you . . . do you not recognize me? Do you remember . . . remember m . . . me? It's been a year." A thin smile. "I often played with you by that pine." He collapsed on the ground, losing his hat, and rolled to his back.

Only then did she identify the features of her older brother, Joram. Her legs loosened, and she ran as if through thick mud. Her childish hands fumbled with the silly gold buttons, and in a fit of frustrated rage, she ripped them off to pull the coat away from his body. Several puncture wounds in his chest put him in grave danger. The bleeding did not seem too bad, yet.

"Bullets go right through." Joram gasped, pointing to his injuries. "Right through."

Bullets? Her tiny hands could not cover them all. Could she lay her body over them? Sit on them? Something to stop what bleeding there was? Impossible.

Normally, she refused to accept the title of Little Girl, but she was all too aware of her mere six years now.

Herbalists and midwives had been training her for only a couple of months, but they had taught her a few things. She now knew about a large patch of yarrow at the northern edge of the woods. Soldier's woundwort! That would help him! She could never get there and return in time to save him, though.

Twitching and jerking, Joram grabbed her arm. "Get Papa."

Right. Papa. Papa! Her heavy legs wobbled and shook as she ran to the east. Where was he? Stopped beside her oak, she listened for his hammering. After a few moments, the faint pounding began, filtered through trees and distance. She closed her eyes to hear better. North-east.

Papa was working on someone's loft when she found him. Her screams and pleas meant nothing. He would not come, and Mama would not go without Papa's permission—something he would never give.

"He is one of them now." Papa hammered a nail into the loft. "Forget him and make peace with the loss."

Hesper knelt and placed her face on the forest floor, coughing on the detritus she inhaled as she wept. If Papa's feet had been planted on the ground, she would have clasped them with her little hands. Even the use of that desperate custom did not change his mind.

Joram was off-limits. The Meros were the enemy, having taken the Unified's country and prosperity and forced them to run for their lives. If someone betrayed the Unified, they did not deserve the safety their people had worked to establish.

Jaw set, she looked to the north. Joram's human papa might disown him, but Nature could not disown its own. Yarrow might save him, but going so close to the outside world at her young age might result in severe reprimands and punishment.

Was it worth it?

He was probably dead.

But what if he was not?

I must do what I can. He would die if she thought only of herself.

It took all her focus and strength to push her legs through the invisible sludge that made them heavy and slow. Determined to overcome it, she pressed on to the edge of the woods and snatched a handful of white yarrow tufts, which she mashed in her hands as she ran, turning them pink with Joram's blood.

When her little legs brought her to his side, he lay in the arms of a bronzed, deer-skinned stranger who spoke soothing words, encouraging Joram to be still. Pale and glistening with sweat, Joram looked past the stranger and gave Hesper a blank-eyed smile before his body quaked and exhaled for the last time. The stranger twisted around to see her. Adahy.

"Whoa! A kid. He knew you?" He set Joram down.

Hesper dropped the mangled yarrow to the earth. "He is my brother."

Adahy's compassionate expression drew out tears that she wiped with the back of her spicily-fragranced hands.

"Here, c'mere." He reached for her.

She collapsed into his arms, a great bundle of heaving sobs. "Papa will not help . . . he will not . . . because Joram became Meros."

A tender touch tucked stray hairs behind her ear. "I will take care of your brother. Go home to your mother."

* * *

Cold with sweat, Hesper awoke from her dream. It came when she was too miserable to resist the unhappy feelings it gave her. How nice it would be to have a recurring dream of how she met Adahy if it were not related to her brother's death. She turned to her side and scratched at the knot in the wood.

Peace. Calm. Closed eyes. The rhythm of her breathing.

After enduring fifteen years of this, she learned to manage. Mostly.

Five | Post-Conquest: 232

MORNING TWILIGHT CALLED to herbalists to begin their day ahead of almost everyone else. This was the hour to cherish the forest; the time for gathering herbs would come later.

Herbalists sniffed at things the way Hesper did. Lovers of healing, plants, and soil, who began their days breathing foggy air and washing their fingertips with dew.

Some went for long walks to look for new herb sources for their community's medicinal and nutritional needs, and others bonded with the forest until the dew evaporated and their treasures dried enough to pack up and take home.

When Hesper awoke, she washed her face, slipped on her moccasins, and headed out. Her dark thoughts insisted she stay home, but the Unified needed her. Shirking duties would not be loving.

She learned that from Papa.

A few herb gatherers wandered toward the east. Right now, she needed to be alone. To the west, then.

Abundant with blackberry and raspberry bushes, the western border was a delightful retreat during berry season, but at this time of the year, Hesper wanted the leaves. Even though they were especially important for the women of the community, precious few took advantage of the western border's gifts due to its proximity to the outside world—particularly, to a road.

The high grass outside of the forest sparkled with dew, and a thin morning fog obscured the view beyond the abandoned dirt road. A rabbit couple chased each other through the open field, bending the grass in whirls and curls as they went.

Well within the safety of the forest's borders, enjoying the peace and quiet, Hesper nibbled dewy chickweed a few yards away from the berry bushes. A family of deer meekly walked by, and she smiled at the elegant creatures as they flapped their tails and rotated their ears, considering her.

A distant human cry caught her ear. Something to monitor, though nothing she had not heard before.

It was getting louder.

Shouts called her to attention and startled the deer family, who darted into the woods, bounding past her, eastward.

Scrambling to hide behind a birch tree, Hesper fell to the ground and scraped her shin on a fallen branch. Sucking in a sharp breath through her teeth, she grasped at the pain, then whipped around and pushed herself up into a squat to sneak a look past the birch.

Two men in Unified clothing chased a young boy of no more than eight years. They had to be toying with him, making a game of it like a bobcat with a rabbit, because a boy could not outrun those men unless they allowed him to. One of them stopped running and hurled a rock. "Dirty theist!"

Tane.

The rock struck the back of the boy's head and sent him to the ground hard and fast. Tane and Tangi froze. After a long, horrible moment of silence, Tangi approached the boy and leaned over to see his face. He shouted something to Tane over his shoulder, then charged and shoved him backward.

Instead of retaliating, Tane put up his hands and stepped away. Tangi glanced back, and, as if seeing the child twice made the decision for him, ran to the north.

As Hesper stood, Tane fled to the west of open plains, roads overgrown with tall grass, weeds, and crumbled mounds of old Unified cities. Hot tears rolled down her cold cheeks. Tane chose to leave a dead Meros boy at their feet and ran away to avoid the carnage. Her mind raced through images of massacre and billowing smoke rising from their leafy haven. She knew enough of their history to imagine it quite well.

Even now, hunters brought reports of forested areas going up in flames from time to time. The Meros did not seem to care for the land or the people in it as long as their actions rid them of Unified.

As she turned to go, movement on the road caught her eye and drew her back. The boy was alive? He touched his head, crying. Hesper twitched forward with the desire to run to him but caught herself and leaned her forearm and brow against a tree trunk, panting.

He was not even an enemy, but a child—a victim of hatred as much as she.

The fog had lifted, and the white of twilight melted quickly into gold. How vulnerable she would be out there. Nevertheless, she stepped out of the woods and sprinted through the dewy grass to the boy. She swiped water droplets from her arms and knelt to turn him onto his side. Hesper's nose and throat twinged with the scent of blood.

Wide with fear, light blue eyes streaked his dirty cheeks with tears. His mother would be thankful for the return of such a beautiful face and hair as soft and white as corn silk. If Hesper showed kindness to the child, the Meros would leave her community in peace and require nothing more of them for penance.

Even if they did not, she must do the right thing. *Right is right.* She would never have peace if she allowed him to die for her negative thinking.

"Don't hurt me. I won't tell," the boy said in a small voice. "I'm not mean to Gentles."

"I would never hurt you. I am here to help." Hesper put her legs out and elevated the boy's head and shoulders on her shins. "Try not to be afraid."

The bleeding required immediate action, so she dug in her bag for a pouch of powdered yarrow and poured some of it into her hand. With a firm bite and yank, the cork of her waterskin popped out. Mixed with a swallow's worth of cool water, the yarrow made a paste that she pressed against his wound. The boy's blood seeped past her hand.

He fell asleep. Fainted? Died? Was she too late? Deliberation had killed him. The bleeding must stop! Stop now! Through gritted teeth, she repeated, "Stop, stop, stop, stop . . ."

It slowed. Clotting. Clotting. Yes!

She lifted her hand a little, waiting for the blood. It did not come, so she released him. The Meros were probably able to do more to help him than she could. He needed the care of his family.

If she followed the road, it was likely she would encounter a Meros to give the boy to—terrifying thought. She picked him up and headed south-east. Somewhere, a mama cried for her child, a papa fretted, a brother or a sister were lonely and confused. And in this little boy's mind? So much fear. She could bring them peace and heal their hurting.

But what was more important? Her own conscience or the feelings of those who loved her?

Who was more important? This child or her family?

She paused to consider. Neither?

Feelings must not determine values and actions. The need determined those things. The child was not of less value simply because she had not developed a deep and loving relationship with him. The child was everything. Preventing a death took precedence over avoiding mere grief. Perhaps, she might dodge both tragedies.

The boy awoke in her arms. "Where are we going?" he murmured.

"I am trying to take you to your own people."

He stared at her for a few seconds. She smiled to reassure him that she was friendly.

"I'm Tom," he said.

"Tom, how far away is your home?"

"A little ways. Over there." He pointed the way they were heading. "I was with my mother. She goes all over the place for her job. She's probably home already, getting people to look for me."

"Why did those boys chase you?"

"I saw 'em sneakin' around Cowslip Gate and pointed 'em out, and the law enforcement wardens who were with us shot at 'em! I thought that was mean"—he scowled—"but they musta thought I wanted that to happen, 'cause when mom was busy talkin' to somebody a little later, I went to look at a flower in the crack of the sidewalk, and the Gentle guys jumped out of the alley and grabbed me." He grimaced. "My head really hurts. Have I got a big bruise?"

"How did you get away from them, Tom?"

Tom reached for Hesper's neck to inspect her betrothal token. "I just wiggled and screamed and kicked and bit and did whatever I could until they got me outside the gate." He released the token. "When I got free, I tried to run back into the gate. They blocked me, so I headed home. I knew someone would come looking and help me. I mean, I'm my mom's only kid, and if somethin' happened to me . . . Well, it would be a national *disaster*!"

"National disaster?" The extreme statement made Hesper smile. "That is pretty bad!"

"Yup. My mom is one of the Kyrios. A Reverenced One. She knows God. If I died, it would be bad!"

God. That word again. "You have lost some blood. Relax."

Hesper ran and walked at intervals for some time. Maybe east was not the best choice? Were they going nowhere? It did not seem abnormal for a boy Tom's age to know where he lived, but maybe Meros children were different? Less aware of their world?

By the time a dark mass appeared in the distance, the dew had evaporated from the grass. To the north, Hesper's forest with its tall dead pine landmark remained in sight. Did it curve to the south in the east? Perhaps the darkness ahead was a part of her forest. A dead end.

As the sun continued its ascent, the weight of the child wore on Hesper and the light hurt her eyes. However, hope awakened as the indistinguishable form began to take shape into what had to be a Meros community.

The community appeared to have been built into a once-great city like those spoken of in Unified elders' stories. Much of it mixed with two-hundred-year-old rubble, a low, jagged skyline of ruins and decrepit buildings.

Preceding the ruinous city, a much nicer community beckoned from the right with well-kept buildings and vivid colors. A fence, topped by thorny, spiraling, metal wires, separated the community from the ruins as well as the grassy plains and forests surrounding it. Men patrolled the fence, dressed in black clothes and hats that resembled what Joram wore on the day he died.

The prospect of meeting the Meros in their outside world, and the sight of strange, unfamiliar buildings that were built on the ground, prodded Hesper's heart to higher rates than she liked. She had to be strong and not face them with fear, or she would seem angry and dangerous.

Tom drifted in and out of consciousness over the journey and was, unfortunately, unconscious now.

"Tom, speak well of me to your people," she whispered.

One of the men behind the fence brought a big black stick to his eye and pointed it at her. This was no mere stick—she had never seen solid black wood before—but whatever it was served a sinister purpose.

"Come closer!" the man shouted.

She hesitated, but obeyed, walking toward him.

"What're you doing with that boy?"

"I found him on the road. Hurt. He told me where he lived, and I carried him here. I only wanted you to take care of him and . . . and let me go."

Another man reached for a box hanging at his hip. He brought it to his mouth.

"Contact Reverenced One Chandler. A Gentle brought young Mr. Chandler home."

To the left, several yards away, a great entryway opened, and a tall woman emerged, flanked by two men. Her black uniform and demeanor threw Hesper's mind into chaos. Black uniforms stood on her side of the fence now.

This was not good.

Those hated gold buttons.

"My name is Trinity. What's yours?"

Hesper abandoned the gold buttons and focused on Trinity's eyes. "Hesper."

"Hesper, you have my son. Set him down and back away slowly."

Disoriented by the flurry of activity, Hesper reached out to give Tom to his mother, but Trinity held her arms at her side, unwilling to accept Tom directly. Hesper set the boy on the earth at his mama's feet. One of the men accompanying Trinity stepped forward, picked up Tom, and returned the way he came.

"We will take care of him," Trinity said, her tone cordial and gentle. "Come with me. We have a place to care for people, and I'm guessing that you could use a drink of water and some peace. Just a little rest, perhaps?"

The field to the north called for Hesper. If only she could get to the forest. What a glorious, liberty-filled, free, sprawling prison. Guarded by trees, not fences or men with black clothes and gold buttons.

"I do not wish to comply."

She must not. Why would she? Maybe she should. How far was it? When did she get here? Why? How might she . . . Her thoughts, incomplete and illogical, rushed into her mind too fast. She stepped backward, shaking her head.

"Hesper, your people will not accept you again. You are a little bird that has fallen out of its nest and been touched by human hands. Come with me." She advanced a few steps. "We have sick people who need help from a kind person such as yourself. You are a woman of medicine, aren't you?"

How did she know that?

No! Reason over feeling. Truth over whim. The woman used poetry of birds as a deception. Her words were not based on the true state of things.

"It's too late, dear Gentle. Come with me." Trinity beckoned with a grasping motion, reaching to ensnare the little bird in her palm.

The community looked an awful lot like a cage with its fence.

Not this bird. You will not keep this bird.

Hesper crouched to the ground and opened her bag, careful to avoid sudden movements that might startle the Meros watching her. A knife would be the best thing, but she could not conceal it properly. Besides, would she truly kill someone? She needed something else.

Keeping her actions concealed, Hesper fumbled through the bag until trembling fingers found the cool metal box of needles. Sliding it open, she selected a suture needle and replaced the lid. With the box in one hand and the tiny weapon hidden in the other, she said, "I have something very precious for you." Her arm quivered, causing the box to rattle in her bloody palm. "I will give it to you if you will let me go."

Needles would mean nothing to the Meros, but if they took it, not knowing what it was, she might have time to run before they discovered the deception.

Instead of accepting Hesper's offer, Trinity lunged forward and clamped icy fingers around her wrists. Hesper attempted to wrest herself free, kicking Trinity in the shin twice before receiving a flash-of-lightning strike to her bruised face.

Hesper's heart sank, her hope was failing, her mind, clouding. She struggled to free her wrist, yanking and wriggling like a worm on a hook. The needle box fell from her hand.

The deception failed.

She failed.

Hesper growled, "You are a bad person." Teeth pressed together, she thrust the suture needle from her free hand into Trinity's arm. Trinity screamed and released the vicious little bird.

No cages, Meros.

Hesper took flight but glanced behind her to see Trinity signal to someone with a jerk of her head. Hope overtook fear, pushing her to move faster, her feet barely connecting with the earth as—*BOOM*—nerves shattered, and weakness surged into her joints. A scream sliced through the steady rhythm of her breathing. Her own scream? Hands held over her ears, she fell to the earth.

Thick fingers grasped her arms, pressing them against her ribcage as they lifted her to stand.

A man.

Touching her?

Screaming, she twisted around, hunting for a vulnerable place on the enormous boulder of a body. But he was protected by clothes as thick as buffalo hide. Beating on his metal-covered chest hurt her hands. The moment she allowed a thought of tiredness to enter her mind, he shackled her wrists and placed her over his shoulder. Her desperate, vapor screams were lost in the open wide spaces, surely dissipating long before the forest could hear them. She screamed nonetheless.

Trinity followed, brooding over her needle wound. Lips to Hesper's ear, she hissed, "Milk-faced atheist."

The entryway closed with a decided *clack*. Behind enemy lines, it became clear that the Unified elders spoke the truth. All her life, Hesper had heard the truth.

Six | Post-Conquest: 232

HESPER'S TEARS FELL at the heels of the man who carried her. Carried her with hands, arms, and a body. The senses awakened by him, and his by her. The connection made, regardless of her will against it. That was the worst part.

She was no longer pure.

With renewed effort, she elbowed the man in the back of the head. Flailing her free limbs and wiggling her torso, she pushed against his arms, but he limited her legs' range of motion with a tight hold.

She could smash his stones . . . If she slipped down enough to get between his legs from behi—

Hard, blinding, pain struck from the left, like slamming her head on a tree branch. Which way was up? Down? Where was Trinity? The big man? Hesper struggled to regain her sense until another strike came from the other side. Her knees and wrists met the road without gentleness. Had he dropped her? At least she knew which way was up now.

Scuffling, tromping black boots passed. No moccasins, no bare feet, no help. Body tense, ready to run. Trapped.

Trinity's high-heeled shoes clicked their way into Hesper's line of sight. "She's going to get her head screwed on straight, right here, right now." Her foot slammed on Hesper's fingers. Hesper screamed and pulled her shackled hands to herself.

When she and Tane were younger, they had fist fights. She knew the feeling of a blow, but never a blow given when she couldn't fight back. It stung so much more. Maybe she could run. Maybe. She struggled to her feet but fell over something and onto her belly. A few ineffective gasps for air triggered panic. As Hesper pushed up on her elbows, Trinity's foot pressed on her back, grinding in the heel of her shoe just enough to hurt.

Click.

Hesper's stomach twisted.

"Officer, pull down her trousers and give her a whipping she won't forget," Trinity said, her voice smooth and stoic. "They're rarely uppity once they've had their cheeks exposed and kissed by metal. And next time, cuff an apprehended Gentle behind their back!"

Surrounded by foreign chaos, an outburst of laughter startled Hesper, followed by a child's voice, piercing through the din. So many Meros! Nothing familiar.

Black road. Throbbing fingers.

She still had not achieved a deep breath.

Sad, green grass at her right, well-trampled.

Someone grabbed Hesper's feet, and another pulled down her trousers to expose her. She screamed and pushed up to pull away, but Trinity's foot shoved her down against the hard road. Something struck cold, leaving a line of burning pain across her rear. Gasping with maddening, too-short breaths, she clawed at the flat, black surface of the road, scraping her fingertips and the heels of her hands. They struck her again. She grunted and squeezed down a cry.

They are not monsters. They are people. They are not monsters. They are people.

A man's yell stood out in the noisy swarm. Air rushed into Hesper's mouth and past her throat, stretching her lungs. Finally. She relaxed and rested her cheek on the cool road and wept aloud. Black boots approached and did not pass by. Hesper pulled her hands into herself lest the boots step on her as Trinity's heels had.

"Is this really necessary, Reverenced One? Are you drunk?" Despite an angry tone, the clear voice carried a gentle, balanced gravel under the surface. This would be okay. She would be okay.

"David." With a final shove of her heel into Hesper's back, Trinity stepped away. "Just the man I need. Here. For you. You're good with the young ones."

Tears cascaded down Hesper's face, collecting in great droplets that hung off her chin as she looked at her apparent rescuer. David inclined his head toward her, frowning. "Pull her pants up, Officer Burns."

"At Her Reverence's orders," Officer Burns said.

"Pull her pants up, Burns."

Someone tugged Hesper's trousers over her rear and released her feet. She pushed herself off the ground and stood. Surrounded by people and a fence, fleeing with shackled hands would be futile and fatal.

Clad in black uniforms and brightly colored dresses, people passed in every direction. Some looked at her, some did not. Others wore pitying expressions, while a few scowled. The pungent, overbearing odor of pine tar and sweet spices had escaped her notice until now. Comforting and disconcerting at once.

David faced Trinity, tall and straight, shoulders back, wearing the same kind of uniform as everyone else, though he had more colorful metal pieces. Just another Meros. She could never fight him off, but if his soothing voice proved to be a lie, she would die trying.

"Does she need Guidance?" David asked. "Whose is she? Earth Person?"

"I told you! She's yours if you'll take her. Definitely not an Earth Person. They show up at our Gates with rocks, and you think they're suddenly going to send someone to do a good deed? If she's from the nearby community, they don't have the sense to build homes on the ground, much less sneak into a base for nefarious purposes."

She thought the Unified were stupid? Call them ignorant, call them weak, call them ugly, but stupid? Without sense? No! Hesper glared at Trinity and spat on the ground. "We honor the trees as our ancestors did, and they had enough sense to survive your war, skeleton-woman."

David stifled a laugh.

Trinity shifted her glare from David to Hesper. "I considered shooting her on the spot, but she struck me as your type: full of spirit. You seem to like being insulted and shoved around by girls. I know you said you wouldn't take more . . ."

David shook his head. Strong words swam in his eyes.

"Take her or I'll put her on the block!" Trinity barked. "She's pretty and strong enough to get a fair price." She slid her hand along Hesper's braid. "On second thought, Vincent might appreciate her." Seeming to stroke Hesper's head at first, Trinity clenched her hand shut around a fistful of hair and yanked, twisting Hesper's neck and pulling at her scalp. Hesper yelped.

Trinity snorted. "You know he likes long hair and women who squeak."

"Well, that explains a few things. You always were a squeaker, Your Reverence."

"I'm sure I have no idea how *you* would know. I kept my pants on 'til it was legal, thank you very much. The only squeaking in our house came from you, man-whore."

David quirked his eyebrow as though he thought the statement absurd, then produced a surprising, breathy laugh that ruddied his face. "Oh, that wasn't *me*, Reverenced One, and I think we have a different definition of 'squeak,' but out of courtesy for the young lady here, I'll refrain from titting your tat." David took a quick look at Hesper. "You said she did a good deed? What's that about? Where did you find her?"

Trinity released Hesper's hair. "The piece of chalkstone was carrying Thomas. He's got a huge gash on his head that she felt obligated to turn into her problem. And look what she did to me!" She pointed out the offensive red dot from Hesper's needle. "Granted, it looks small," she admitted. "Being as thin as I am, it nearly went through my arm. The needle was curved! She must be a medicine woman or something. They're the only ones who carry those."

David's eyes fell on the wound and, flashing with fun, turned to Hesper. Hesper had seen that look in the eyes of many a young boy with mischief on their minds. Even though most of his conversation had been fairly detached and cool, there was no mistaking that spark of fun.

A troublemaker.

The side of his mouth tipped up in a half-smile. Troublemaker or not, David's pleasant clean-shaven face did not frighten her the way it ought. Hands tucked harmlessly in his pockets, he tilted his head and bounced on the balls of his feet a few times. "What warranted public exposure and beating an innocent girl's rear end with a baton, Reverenced One?"

"Consider it Guidance. I'll leave Acclimation to you. She gave us far too much fuss, and since she stabbed me with a needle, I was in no mood to put up with wildcat crap. Decide, Dave!"

David twisted his jaw and sighed. "I'll take her."

"Such an altruistic hedonist," Trinity snapped. "Don't pretend you don't enjoy it. She's a little dirty, and she's been crying, but I think she's pretty under the disheveled hair and stinking hide. If you don't care about that sun-deprived skin of hers. Small chest, too, but you've never minded that."

"Sun-deprived. Right. Does she have injuries requiring attention?"

"I doubt it. I didn't even hit her very hard and she screamed like a little girl."

David scowled. "She almost is, Reverenced One."

"Her? Twenty, maybe?"

"Young enough to be your daughter. My daughter."

"Point understood, and the point is quite dull. She screamed like a little boy, then. Sound better?" Strutting away, Trinity called over her shoulder. "You can take care of her. I'll give the Kyrios your reason for not attending the meeting."

They were alone, surrounded by people. Hesper waited for David to speak because . . . what could she possibly have to say anyway?

"Look at me," David ordered.

They might force her to go places she did not want to go, they could pull her trousers down and beat on her, but it was not obedience. They could not make her submit in her mind. He was not her friend for one good deed.

She shook her head, sharp and short.

"Look at me," he said, softer. He took a firm hold on her jaw with both hands and tilted her head upward. Even though the motion did not hurt or feel forced, it was not a mere suggestion. "Look at me?"

She sniffled and turned her eyeballs away from his to the point of pain.

"Well, you are a lovely thing, aren't you? You okay? Anything hurting? Besides your heart?"

She glanced hopelessly about at the sky, grass, his black uniform, the shining gold buttons—anything but his face. What a pleasant scent he carried with him. Fresh leaves with lavender, lemongrass, berries, and—he slid his hands up the sides of her head, through her hair, wiggling his fingers around her scalp.

She chanced a look up while he was distracted by her head. His expressive brow and the structure of his cheek bones reminded her of Adahy. He had a generous, though not-too-large nose, and even with a serious expression, his approachable persona was strong enough to overcome her hatred for the rigid uniform and gold buttons.

She wanted to like him.

David's childish cobalt eyes caught her staring and wrinkled softly at their corners as he smiled. An unexpected sob rose in her throat, and she gulped it down with a conspicuous tremor.

He tucked her hair behind her ears and sighed. "Well, the good news is there's no blood. Small knot. We should ice it. She hit you on the head pretty hard. I've never seen Trinity act that way in public. You must have made her pretty mad, sister." His laugh verged on a snicker. "Well done. I've been trying to pull that off for years. What's your name?"

"Hesper," she whispered.

"Hesper, answer honestly, did someone send you?" He studied her face, and she took great pains to keep her focus on him. He must not be allowed to perceive weakness.

He looked away from her cold, silent stare, tongue poked into his cheek. A dash of amusement slipped across his lips as he turned back to her. "Honesty really is best while I've got you. You don't want to deal with the Kyrios' methods."

She shook her head.

His left eye twitched and narrowed. "You just decided to be kind to your enemies and bring Tom home? Or are you one of the innocents who didn't even know we exist? I've met a few of those, too."

First, she shook her head, then nodded and tried to stiffen herself against the trembling. She wiped her wet nose on her shoulder.

He smiled. "Give me words, please."

"I knew you existed, sir. I was just trying to help the little boy."

The tight shackles dug into her wrist and would not slide down no matter how much she wiggled her hands.

"You're polite." He drew his head back in surprise. "How refreshing. I've never met an Earth Person concerned with being polite in similar circumstances. Are you familiar with them?"

Hesper nodded. "My brother. They say he wants to be an Earth Person. I do not . . . I do not know much. They are supposed to be peaceful, but . . ."

"They rarely are. That's the problem. Your brother's young, I suppose?"

Hesper struggled to swallow past tears and congestion, offering a weak hum of confirmation. "Younger than I am." Something trickled down her nose and lip. She swiped it with the back of her hand. Not blood.

"You come from the nearby community to the north-west, I assume?" David asked. "One of those groups that live in the tree houses? Anyone there encouraging others to join the Earth People?"

Would he kill her if she was? Hesper shook her head.

"Honey, take whatever's going on in your mind and toss it out. You're fine. You're doing great, and I'm not mad or displeased in the least. Everything is perfect between us. Okay? Friends. I want to be friends, and I'm as honest as can be. At the moment."

Like a dose of lobelia, his voice released her tension. She took a deep breath.

Just a few deft motions and a jangling of metal and David had the shackles loosened enough to relieve the discomfort of her wrists before she even knew what he was doing.

"You see, when your people step outside of the forest and call themselves Earth People, they tend to be a bit dangerous and quick to obey their cowardly elders." He tucked something into his pocket, still focused on her. "That's why I want to make sure you're not one of them. Understand? You're not in trouble."

Tears toyed with her, so she hung her head to hide them.

Mercifully, he allowed her to look down while one of his hands still held her face. "Hesper, you'll be all right. You will make it, and I will do all in my power to help. You'll live with me—"

Revulsion sparked confidence. She met his eyes and hissed, "I would rather skin your back and use your hide for trousers than live with you." Before thinking it through, a gob of spit flew from her mouth and splatted on his uniform, just beneath the colorful metal pieces. He watched the spit dribble down his coat.

So did she.

Like a foolish child might strike a fire with a stick, she lashed out with personal contempt. His temper would flare now, and she would take the brunt of his anger if it gave her the right to be bitter toward him. He took his hand from her face.

Hit me! Hard as you can. I have bee—

He giggled. The giggle rolled out of his chest into his mouth as a laugh. Nothing about this amused her. Nothing about it should amuse him.

"You Gentle girls think of the best insults and threats on the spot," he said as he wiped away laughing tears. "You ladies spit better than any man I know, too. How long had you been saving that loogie up?" He extended his soft-looking, strong hand with long fingers like Adahy's. "Come with me, Hesper."

Lessons from Papa stumbled through her mind. Deep anger would make her irrational. She had to shun it, but she could not. She could not go with him.

David's warm, gentle hands clasped her shoulders. Leaning eye-to-eye, he spoke as if to a stubborn child. "Okay. Two choices. Easy way or hard way. Easy is walking alongside each other. Hard way, I'll have to hoist you over my shoulder like a sack of wiggly, long-legged potatoes." His expression laughingly pleaded with her not to bring it to that. "As a gesture of good faith, I'll remove your handcuffs."

He took a small ring of oddly-shaped metal pieces from his waist. Keys? She had once read about keys in a book, but these did not much resemble the ones in pictures.

Though his eyes narrowed, and he watched her with obvious distrust, he used a key to remove her bonds and slipped them into his pocket. He did not expect her to behave but released her anyway?

"I prefer the hard way," she answered darkly.

He leaned back and looked her over. "Okay then."

She barely made the decision to pull her arm back to punch him, when, quick as the swoop of a hummingbird, he preempted her, grabbing her wrist. His peaceful, sleepy voice and relaxed demeanor had lulled her into overconfidence, and the quick move shocked her.

I am an idiot.

Doubtless, overpowering and forcing her onto his shoulder would be easy, but when she resisted, she caught wind of his weakness, written on his face and in the grip of his fingers.

He was too kind.

Unlike the buffalo-hide bully with Trinity, David did not relish violence or manhandling her. Admirable, certainly, but not above exploitation. Hesper resisted his grip and pulled at his fingers with her free hand. He allowed her to jerk him around but moved little more than an oak in the breeze. Such a maddening, placid manner! A little amused even!

Sweat dribbled down her forehead and hot back. It was no use to wear herself out further if this was all she could manage. Maybe she could at least dislocate something on his body. With one more good yank on his arm, she screeched in his face and stood, glaring at him as the cool air came and went through her lungs with heavy breaths.

David considered her. Disappointed? In what? A tinge of shame passed through her mind. He had saved her, and she treated him this way? Yes, she treated him this way, because none of it was right. Not even him.

Perhaps he was disappointed by her inability to put up a good fight. She was ashamed of that, too.

"You're strong and self-restrained," he said. "Control yourself until we get inside, okay? Then you can scream and cry as much as you want. Punch a wall, tear some pillows, kick a dog or something. Do what works for you." He stared beyond her, thoughtful. "Though, I'll have to get a dog first."

She growled. "I intend to kick *you* where—"

David tightened his hold. "Blast it, Hesper. I don't want to treat you like a sack of potatoes. You've had enough of that for today. I'd rather treat you with respect—the way I prefer to treat a woman."

He released her hand and she fell to the ground. The impact of the fall jolted through her body and into her head. Before she could scramble away, a shadow darkened the sunlight, and her spark of hope clouded over with his sudden, imposing nearness.

Kneeling, he leaned in to speak. "Hesper, listen to me. You don't have to resist. It may seem right to do at the moment, but you will soon understand that reason serves better than feeling in this circumstance.

"The Unified are logical people, and you know how important it is for your survival as a nation. That doesn't change just because you are out here, rather than in the forest."

His voice lullabied her anger, dousing the heat in her face. She unclenched her fists. He moved closer. "It is more important now than ever, and your ability to reason will give you strength to look past the differences between you and me for your self-preservation and peace.

"I'm only a man, nothing more and nothing less. I have no power over your mind." He tapped her forehead. "But you do. You're safe, and I'm safe for you. Your emotions are balancing themselves because sound reason rises to your aid. Do you feel that?"

His warm hand alighted her shoulder like a friendly phoebe bird. The tears on her cheeks dried with a breeze. She nodded, regretting it immediately.

"I can tell," he said. "And sooner or later, you will find yourself moving onward in the wonderful truth that you can face anything you fear with a level head. You're listening closely?" He moved away from her ear to look at her face. "Isn't it empowering to think that you can face anything you fear with a level head?"

The soothing expression on his face calmed her. Rational words, spoken clearly and quietly, sanded down rough feelings.

"Rest assured," David said, "I won't hit you, force you, or break your spirit. I grant you a haven." He stopped. "Hesper, look at me."

She had to, so she did . . . after closing her mouth and swallowing. She must have looked like a complete fool.

"You can trust me," he whispered, nodding slightly. "Falling into my arms and my home may be counted among some of your greatest blessings when you look back on this in the future. I say that without a drop of arrogance. Just facts about the circumstance we find ourselves in together."

Her palms stung from the pressure of her fingers. "You are wrong!"

Why had she come here? Why did she do this?

Because life was not about only herself? Life did not belong to only her.

He saw my rear!

David snapped his fingers a few times. "Hesper, focus."

Shaking with rage, or fear—she was unsure which—she hissed, "I will die before I stay here."

No. Her body would stay, but her mind would not.

The phoebe bird hand flew away with a shrug of her shoulders. "Never . . . *touch* . . . me," she snarled. "I will come." Rising, she drew back her shoulders and mustered every bit of detestable pride she had in her. Ugly as it was, she would need it to survive this. "Where are we going?"

Swiping the air with his pointed finger, suspicious, he indicated to the south.

$\mathcal{S}$even | Post-Conquest: 232

A NEW SERIOUSNESS overtook David's demeanor. A tightness in the cheeks and lowering of the eyebrows. He had been patient for long enough. It was time to stop testing him. He smiled when he caught Hesper studying his expression, though the seriousness persisted. Perhaps he was mad at her.

Good.

He had no right to like her. None of these people did.

They approached a dark red brick house with rows of large windows, glinting in the sunlight. How did the Meros live so exposed to the light, everything hot and shining, even in the spring?

David opened the indigo round-topped door and waited as Hesper passed him and stepped inside. Cooked chicken and spices filled the air. A rare meat in the woods.

Her feet sank into a large midnight blue carpet dotted with golden stars around a silver moon. She crouched and stroked the fibers, then pressed her hand into it like a bed of moss.

A dry bed of moss. Lifeless.

The moon felt the same. The stars, too.

Only an illusion.

The dark wood floor around the carpet shone like ice. Smooth to touch, but not slippery.

David had been watching her. Expecting impatience, Hesper threw a wary glance his way and found nothing contemptuous. He didn't seem to mind—even smiled a little. She stood and lifted her chin.

The long, horizontal mirror on the wall before her reflected a pale, dirty face she had never seen so well. It did not belong here in all this order and cleanliness. It belonged with the trees, the wolves, the pebbly brook. She lowered her chin.

Was she . . . wild?

"This is the entrance," David explained. "A place for people to hang their coats."

A tall, brawny, older woman bustled herself around the corner, looking to David with a frank and sensible face. "Sir! We have a guest?"

"Lorelei, take this young lady to Anise."

"Yes, sir."

Going to someone else? David's presence gave her safety more than danger now. She took a deep breath and searched for peaceful feelings. No. She must never feel peace.

Never.

"Whoa." He grasped her shoulders. "Hesper, it's all right. Anise will help you get the sweat washed off and give you a chance to recuperate, okay? Relax. You're safe. I promise. If anything happens to you under my care, I vow to allow you to kick me where you intended to earlier."

"I do not want that. I want to stay with you."

What was she saying? Why was she letting him know she was afraid? Hesper's hot face meant blushing cheeks. Knowing her face showed her discomfort made it worse.

His hands in his pockets, he bounced on the balls of his feet a few times and rocked back onto his heels before settling with a small sigh. "Lorelei, I'll take her. Bring an ice pack and a snack to Anise's room . . . and something better than water. Electrolytes and all that."

"Yes, sir."

To their right, a large doorway led into a long path with clear walls. David pointed it out. "That leads to my brother's room, and this door next to it is the parlor. We're taking the stairs, however." He smiled.

A mess of paintings in enormous gaudy frames filled the walls from eye level and upward until the stairs opened into a spacious hallway of doors. They stopped at the second door on the left.

David knocked softly. "Anise."

A waft of cinnamon fled the room when Anise opened to them. A black X marred her cheek. It was strange how much everyone dreaded it, yet it was such a little thing. A little thing with heavy meaning.

A striking figure in white, cloaked in thick black hair hanging at her ankles, the tall and slender Anise had the features of a fairy-queen from the dragon book Hesper once read.

"You again?" she said to David, smiling.

Hesper caught a wink and smirk pass over his face. Clearing his throat, he said, "Anise, this is Hesper. She's been through a lot this morning and needs some tender loving care."

"She's young." Anise frowned. "Well, of course, you're so good with the young ones. Come in, dear, won't you?" Anise extended her flawless hand, palm down, fingers reaching out in firm invitation.

Hesper had never seen a hand so delicate and smooth, and as she took it, she half-expected it to fall apart like a dying lily. The blood from Tom's head on her own hand did not appear to disturb Anise in the least.

The door closed behind them as Hesper and Anise stepped into the room. Beside a window, a raised bed of shimmering emerald material glittered in the sunlight. Cinnamon sticks hung from sheer pale green ribbons tied onto either side of the glossy, purple wood at the head of the bed.

Anise inspected Hesper's hair and scalp. "Well," she said, appraising her with a keen eye, "we have minimal work ahead of us. You're well-groomed for a Gentle, but I can tell the day has worn on you. We'll start with a bath. This is a bathtub." She gestured to the tub in the corner. "I'll get soap to wash with, shampoo to . . ." she trailed off and gathered the mysterious items as she named them, lining them up on the edge of the tub.

"Why do they call us Gentles?" Hesper asked.

Anise glanced over her shoulder. "Gentles?"

Did she not realize she was saying it? "Yes."

"Oh, ah, well, because they say we must be treated gently to keep us happy. You know the story about when war came? When they left us all alone in the wild places, they called us the Gentles because they thought our tears demonstrated a weakness to be pitied." She smiled. "That's the legend anyway. The facts behind the legend are a mystery to all of us."

"If they treat us gently, why did they pull down my trousers and strike my rear and my head and—" Hesper looked away. It was worse than being touched. Worse than being marked. If anyone tried to expose her body again, she might . . . she might kill them.

"Is that what they did to you, Hesper?"

"Yes."

"Surely, not David."

"No. He stopped them, I think."

"That sounds more his style." Anise smiled and began unraveling Hesper's frazzled braid. "I'm sorry you went through that. You will find that gentleness is the rule in this house, and you have little to fear."

Anise turned a knob in the bathtub, unleashing a steady flow of water from a spout. She felt the water a few times, adjusting the knob often, then turned to Hesper, delighted. "I bet you've never bathed in warm water with soap, have you?"

"Only rivers. Warmed water in the loft . . . rarely."

"Now, let's see." Anise took a few steps toward her. "We need to get those old skins off and clean you. So . . ."

Hesper scowled and backed away, bumping into the door behind her, the knob jabbing into her lower back. "Why? Why must I wash?"

Anise clasped her hands. "Well, dear, Gentles don't bathe frequently, and the Meros prefer for human odor to be minimal. Additionally, you are dirty and sweaty. I think you will find a bath to be a refreshing comfort." Revelation passed over Anise's face. "I'll step out while you undress and come back once you are covered in the water. Sound all right?"

Hesper stepped out of the way as Anise reached for the doorknob and opened it. When the door closed, Hesper leaped into action, bounding for a window. Glass prevented her from jumping through it. Maybe it would break and . . . The fall would be too much. She would be seriously injured at best, and they would see her and snatch her up, immediately.

Trinity . . . Hesper's knees weakened. Leaving David would put her in Trinity's hands.

Anise called through the door. "Ready, dear?"

Hesper's heart, already beating too fast, felt as if it would crack her sternum. Quickly, she undressed and got into the tub, leaving the betrothal token atop her pile of hides. The water continued to rush out of the spout. The wall behind the tub, flat and dry, gave no clues as to its source. Where would they get all this water and how was it getting into the house?

"I am in the bath," Hesper called out.

Anise entered and opened a large chest between two shelving units and gathered from it a small bundle of richly colored fabrics, which she laid out on her bed. Gliding over to Hesper, she turned off the water and set a towel on the floor as she explained the use of washcloths, soap, and shampoo.

"Any questions?" she asked.

So many. "No, ma'am."

"David doesn't hate body hair the way most Meros do. He's"—she tipped her head, frowning with thought—"shall we say, pleasantly earthy? Most of the time they wax the hair off nearly everything except the head the day a Gentle arrives. You're quite fortunate to land yourself in this home. So, if you've ever heard rumors of that, you can dismiss them." Pointing, she said, "I'll be sewing over here if you need me."

Anise sat at a contraption in the corner of the room, humming a tune. She pressed a little box on the floor with her slippered foot. It lit up and began humming along with her as she drew bits of cloth through it.

A hard knock on the door startled Hesper into reflexively covering her chest with her arms.

"It's Lorelei," Anise reassured her.

A small tray with a big blue bag, a plate of colorful food and a glass of lilac liquid passed from Lorelei to Anise. Anise set the tray on a table beside her bed. "Bath first." She smiled and returned to her corner. "Did you need ice for something? Were you injured?"

"My head."

"We'll get this on the spot as soon as you're out and dressed."

Hesper would knock over every little bottle and bar on the edge of the tub and spit on it if it were not so pathetic to do so. She scrubbed her skin sore, angry, hating that she liked the sweet smell of the soap—that anything felt good at all. She grabbed the thick, white towel and dried her face, breathing the scent of spices in it and summoning rage to stomp the swell of emotions.

Not Adahy. Not now.

When?

Sentimental thoughts had to be squelched in favor of clarity and wisdom if she ever wanted to see him again. Even if it was simply to apologize. She understood Tane's passion now—his hatred. This was a darkness he could not help but raise his fist to.

Rage would not serve her well here any more than sentimentality or despair.

Anise rose. "I have clothes for you, and a toothbrush. I'll fetch them." She laid a fluffy, green garment over the back of a chair near the tub. "Judging by your teeth, I'd say good hunters introduced you to toothbrushes."

Hesper dried herself, put on the green garment, tying its belt around her waist to hold it on, and faced Anise's mirror.

"Something the matter, dear?"

She had to ask? Hesper raised her voice as she said, "Yes. I have been kidnapped and taken away from my betrothed and family! Shall I wail and sob to prove it to you?"

Taken aback, Anise froze, blinking rapidly. Surprise melted into sympathy. "I wish I could do something for you, Hesper." Her delicate hand combed through Hesper's hair. "David and I met at an auction."

Hesper scrunched her face. "A what?"

"A place to sell things. An auctioneer puts an item on a pedestal for everyone to see, and he asks who would like to buy it. They take turns offering money, bidding for the item, and whoever offers the highest amount, pays it and purchases the item to take home. Understand?"

"Yes."

"David came to purchase an antique map," Anise said, "and I was on the auction block before the map."

Hesper's mouth fell open. "You? They sell people?" She had heard of Unified serving as slaves, but not that the Meros sold them like possessions.

Anise stared into her memories, then into Hesper's eyes. "Yes, dear. David happened to know the man who seemed intent on purchasing me. It troubled him because that man purchased several Gentle women in the past, but he was not kind. He chained them and kept them for entertainment like dogs. David outbid him, bought the map afterward, and we left.

"Later, seeing that he was a kind person, I begged him to let me go. He sat with me and helped me understand the potential repercussions of that action. Besides the punishment he would face, in the event of an escape, Law Enforcement almost always raids nearby forests. They imagine the Gentle will flee to a community. Their extreme reaction serves as a deterrent for the community-minded Gentles as well as sympathetic Meros who might attempt to release Gentles before they're marked." Anise gestured to the X on her cheek.

Most women did not attempt to go back after being marked. Until now, feeling the violation of being made impure and no longer eligible for marriage among the Unified, Hesper did not understand that. Not really. Was the forest not enough?

No. Maybe it was not.

"Why?" Hesper faced the mirror and leaned her forehead onto the cool surface. "Why do we matter to them so much?"

A light touch traced up and down Hesper's back. "It's been so long, Hesper, I wonder if anyone knows. They give reasons of religion and our allegedly rebellious natures." She offered a wan smile. "It took time for me to believe David, but when I did, he hugged me and let me cry and told me about *nepenthe*—anything that makes you forget your current sorrows." The light touch became a gentle hand, flat against Hesper's shoulder blade. "He became my *nepenthe,* and we learned to love and respect one another. He's quite good at making me forget things I've lost."

Hesper had so many questions that she would have to reserve for David. Anise, brainwashed and addled with hormonal reactions, accepted what she wanted but would not admit to wanting.

Anise selected a round, purple bottle from the shelves in front of them and sprayed a fine mist into the air.

Hesper sniffed. "It smells like roses and wet dirt."

"Yes, a little, doesn't it? If you want it, you may have it." She put the bottle back and selected a burgundy dress from her bed. "This one." Returning the other dresses to the chest, she asked, "How have you discovered the smell of roses in your woods?"

"Hunters brought them."

"Ah, I see. Any particular hunter?" Anise gave the burgundy dress a shake for its wrinkles, displaying a coy smile.

"My betrothed." Hesper emptied the words of meaning in her mind. Clearing out her feelings, she embraced numbness. Betrothed was only a word. "He brought roses to my mama because she sewed things for him."

Anise paused, her hand on Hesper's shoulder. She gave a light pat. Silence passed, not needing or wanting to be disturbed with more details.

"So, it, uh—the dress wraps around," Anise said. "As long as the length is right, this will be perfect for you. I'll close my eyes if it makes you more comfortable."

Hesper removed the green garment she wore, and Anise encircled Hesper with her arms to wrap the dress around her pale body as Hesper pushed her arms through the long sleeves. Like a whisper on her skin, the dress slid on almost as if she were not dressed at all.

Anise opened her eyes to tie a large bow at the side of Hesper's waist. "This dress never fit me properly. David has an eye for size, but he missed with a few. I kept them around to alter later. Now I'm glad I never got to this one." She caressed the sleeves down to Hesper's wrist. "Well, it's lovely even with the sleeves a bit too long." She stood behind Hesper, her gentle hands resting on her shoulders as they looked into the mirror together. Hesper's white skin stood out in contrast with her black hair and the burgundy fabric.

"I say, you remind me of a Watchman's Hollyhock," Anise said. "And look! Without the braid, your hair is curling up some. So thick and wavy."

Hesper felt the ends of her hair, just below her waist. A few faint bruises on her face reminded her of Papa's slap. Or was it Trinity's? Both, perhaps. She would take any amount of Papa's slaps if it meant she had gotten home to be near his hand.

The offense looked silly now.

She looked silly now.

Who are you now?

She was a silly girl with a bruised face.

A stick doll dressed in rose petals.

"About this hunter. What is his name?" Anise sat on the bed. "Come. Sit."

"Adahy."

Anise's mouth hung open as she stared into nothing.

Creaking across the floor on her bare feet, Hesper picked up the betrothal token and slid it over her head. She pressed the coin's coolness against her skin and sat on the bed.

"Does . . . David know about him?" Anise asked.

"No."

Anise bit her lip, her brow lined with concern. "Officially betrothed then?"

"Officially. Since yesterday." Oh, the emotion burned her chest and throat. It would not go away. Where could she go to just cry? To be alone and weep. Anywhere! Somewhere.

The door was just a few steps away. The forest was not even a mile to the north. So close to freedom, and unable to get to it.

"Anise, is there any way to get out of this?"

"Oh, my dear, my dear." Anise took Hesper in her arms. "May God be gracious to you. The only way out is to follow the light in your mind until you're no longer here because you're there." She reached up and tapped Hesper's temple.

Stiff and unresponsive, Hesper allowed Anise to hold her. *May God be gracious to Adahy.* It certainly had not been gracious to her.

Eight | Post-Conquest: 232

HESPER HAD EATEN the snack they provided for her and iced her head. Now, Anise led the way downstairs. At the bottom of the steps, a blur of red whipped around the corner and slammed into Hesper.

Dressed in red trousers and a red coat, a tall woman slathered on a thick smile just in time to conceal a full withering glare. Eyes trained on Hesper, she called over her shoulder toward the room she had just exited. "Well, David, she's adorable. Have you played with her yet?" A false smile could not hide such thick contempt. It was unlikely she wanted the contempt hidden to begin with. "And, my, my, she's a wide-eyed one. That'll be fun, hm?" Without waiting for an answer, the woman mumbled something about "owl eyes" and clacked away in high-heeled shoes.

"That's Evelyn," Anise whispered. "A very unhappy person. Don't let her trouble you." She gestured for Hesper to go into the room in front of them.

Hesper halted in the threshold. A honeyed-rose aroma overwhelmed her, and the room's rich colors of blue, gold, and blood-red were a wonder to look at. A large aged map hung on the wall with shining fern-green dragon illuminations along its edges. To Hesper's right, the statue of a blue woman with several arms stared through large, black, painted eyes, wearing an unusually placid expression when considering the skulls around her neck and her cherry-red tongue sticking out. Hesper touched one of the statue's hands. Her eyes watered. A cold, lifeless thing made her feel?

"Hesper, are you all right?"

Wrapped up in the wild colors and interesting features near her, Hesper had been ignoring much of the room, including the other person in it.

David stood by a table. His black hat hung off the back of a chair, leaving his shock of wavy brass hair exposed. His curious expression toyed with amusement.

Of all the things to be disturbed by, the fact that he saw her rear bothered Hesper the most. The mere hint of a dress, hanging on her body, made her feel exposed.

She crossed her arms in front of her chest as David gestured to a chair, smiling. "Come sit with me."

Hesper narrowed her eyes. As trustworthy as he seemed, trust would lead to attachment, and she must not do that, or she would believe lies as poor Anise did.

A few books and a pen lay before David. An exquisite spouted pot, painted with vivid birds and pink flowers, sat on the table to his left. A small cup rested on a plate to his right. Hesper sat in the chair he had gestured to.

"You look lovely," he said, seating himself.

Sincerity rang out in every word, but even stigs could be genuine. *How shiny his hair is.*

"Lovely is weak. I am not weak."

"Is it?" He set his pen down and leaned his elbows on the table, resting his chin against steepled fingers. "Loveliness has twisted my arm behind my back and brought me to my knees when strapping young bodies and vigorous minds couldn't sway me in the least. I can't say I've ever equated loveliness with weakness. It's quite strong, just in a different way." Pen wobbling between his thumb and forefinger, he said, "You can be the kind of strong you value most while still being lovely."

"Fine."

"Hesper, how are you managing?"

"You saw my rear, sir. It bothers me."

David dropped the pen and sat back in his chair. "Understandably. Listen, I have seen many rears in my life. Many." He laughed under his breath. "Some have been quite nice, some have been frighteningly not, but when I saw your poor derriere, my only thought was that it should not be out. While that doesn't unsee anything or give your pride back to you, I hope it helps to know that your rear means nothing to me. You pain and perception of your dignity do, though. Let's talk." He waved his hand over his books and pen like garbage to discard. "This can wait. I have the oversight of a section of the country. I have to review and . . . Well, you don't care about my boring business." He scrunched his nose and pushed his work aside. "Right now, you're my business."

His business? Hesper's face flushed, and her temper ignited. "Sir, you have been kinder to me than I ever expected a Meros man to be, but I do not wish to be your business."

He whistled. "You're a strong-tempered woman, aren't you? Here, before you spoil that silk dress." Producing a white cloth from his sleeve, he said, "We never use those for anything. Military personnel keep one around the left wrist, just peeking out. A reminder of our service to God and Its messengers or something like that." He tried to laugh as he offered it.

She set her jaw. Let his devotion to God to wipe his own tears when she kneed his stones and escaped.

He left the white cloth in the middle of the table, patted it, and sat back. "I'd prefer you not be my business, too, sweetheart. However, they execute Gentles who are not spoken for within two weeks. If you reject me, your strength and fine features will sell at an auction and secure you a home somewhere—that much is true—though whether it will be with someone who will call you 'darling' and mean it?" He shook his head. "I can't guarantee that.

"You might wind up with a fine sap—I mean chap . . . like me"—he winked—"who will let you impose your spirit on him, but you might not."

"How can you do this?" she whispered. "How? How can you know this is wrong, and hate it, but still do it?"

His fingers drummed out a steady cadence for only a few seconds, then stopped with the gentle slap of his palm on the table. "This is not the system I want; it's the system I have to work with. I do what I feel is best in the circumstance I am in."

"I will never go home, will I?"

David brought his chair around the table and sat with her, knee-to-knee. He slid the white cloth closer.

She ignored it, allowing the tears to fall on her lap.

"Hesper, some of your people come to the Meros and find relief from fear, appreciating the security," he said. "Others find that life is easier here and learn to enjoy their lives with us in time, and some join us of their own volition, preferring this to the forest. You will find your own reason to make peace with your situation."

"*Nepenthe?*" she asked, sniffling.

He delayed his answer, surprised, then said, "Yes, *nepenthe.*"

This time, she took the cloth when he offered it. "I cannot find *nepenthe.*"

"It's understandable to feel that way, but, darling, what if you were to find it? Imagine that."

What would it be like? What would bring it about? David? She eyed his uniform and gold buttons. He appeared too good when compared to the people who trapped her here. If only they were in the forest and he was Unified. What excellent friends they could be.

If only.

But they were here. Would he help her forget?

"What are you thinking about?" he asked, barely above a whisper.

"Your words."

"You were. I knew you were." He smiled. "How do my words make you feel?"

"Calm and quiet."

He nodded. "You want happiness and contentment, and you can find them here, too."

Maybe, but she should not have to. Her face twisted with tears. "Sir, I want to be in my loft. If I cannot have my home, all the pleasure you have to offer will never compensate for what I have lost."

His watery smile said more than words could. "I'm sorry, sweetheart. Meros laws are different from the laws of the human heart. Gentles have to stay."

She slapped the table. It hurt more than she realized it would. "Stop calling me that. I am Unified, not Gentle. You will find me anything but gentle if crossed as my ancestors were."

"You're right"—his eyes flitted to her hand and back to her face—"I spoke carelessly. Did you hurt your hand, Hesper? It's bruising."

"No."

"Did Trinity hurt your hand?"

Hesper twisted her jaw and answered with a glare.

An eyebrow curved. "I'll take that as a yes. Everything move properly? Wiggle your fingers and all that?"

"It's not broken," she said. "Do you have comfrey or arnica?"

"Arnica. I'll have it brought to you." He checked something on his wrist. "I have to go soon, Hesper, but before I do, I need to know if you're married."

"What would it mean if I am?"

"It would mean I won't marry you myself. The Kyrios aren't concerned with marriages they can't sanction, but I am. They won't allow me to keep you here unmarried for more than the two weeks. I suppose the papers can be signed without consummation to follow."

He shrugged a shoulder. "It's no one else's business, after all. Maybe it can be worked out."

"Marry?"

"'Course." He frowned. "Say, your face just went from cream to wine and back to cream in two seconds. Such a reaction! Do you need a drink of water? What did you think I'd do with you?"

"Make me a slave." The lack of hesitation surprised her. The answer was stupid. Why would he go through all this for someone he was going to use as a slave? He would not. How could she have thought so?

"Slave?" He laughed. "Some serve as slaves elsewhere. However, that's not how I see marriage . . . or women."

Slavery might be better. "I am . . . was to be married in one week's time."

"You poor, sweet woman." He shook his head. "I'm sorry, Love. Our policies favor order and consistency over mercy, even to merciful people like you." A far-off look overtook his usually strong presence of mind. With a few blinks, he came out of his thoughts.

"Thirsty?"

"Yes, sir."

He stood and passed behind her. Hesper studied her fresh, clean hands. So foreign and strange. A brief clink and a gentle wooden tap passed over her ears, but she did not care what it was. David would not hurt her.

He seated himself and poured a golden-pink liquid from the spouted pot into the cup. "Spiced rose. Lovely stuff," he said. "I meant to pour you a cup earlier, but you needed to talk more than you needed tea, I think."

Staring into the liquid, Hesper said, "Why did you stop them from hurting me, sir?"

"Oh, that. Well, I was heading to a meeting. While screaming is not uncommon around here, I felt I needed to follow yours." He sat back, crossing his ankle over his knee.

Hesper wasn't cold, but the warmth of the tea's steam on her shaky fingers soothed her. "Why?"

Surprise raised his eyebrows, then thought lowered them. "Because you're a human? Because I hate public humiliation? I don't know."

She studied his face. "I am uncertain about you."

He grinned. "As you should be."

His buttons caught her attention again. She had almost forgotten about them for a while. "Whatever your motive, you treated me with respect and asked them to cover me. You have my gratitude."

His hair really was shiny. Come to think of it, Anise's hair was, too.

"Give the tea a try," he said.

Hesper took the delicate little cup and sniffed. It smelled like peace. Peace? Her thoughts were turning to poetry. Peace had no aroma. She sipped it. Tangy, floral, spicy.

"Do you like it?" He touched her shoulder.

A nod was as much as she would give him.

"I'm pleased to hear it." He glanced at his wrist. "You're pleasant company, Hesper, and I'd love to spend more time with you, but I have a mess of boring old people who require me to be useful to them in a few minutes." He strode around the table to gather his books and pen. "When you're ready, someone will show you to your room, and I'll be around to see you later.

"I've contacted my brother about a few necessities. He'll pick them up from the market and be home tonight." Books cradled on his left arm, he spun his hat around his right hand and stood in front of her.

"Why is your hair so shiny?" she asked.

The hat stopped spinning. "Shiny!" He crinkled his nose and gave a lopsided grin as he positioned the hat on his head. "Uh, well, have you seen yours since you washed and dried it? It's as lustrous and enticing as the Koh-i-Noor diamond."

"From washing it, then?"

"Possibly?"

Hesper stood slowly and handed the white cloth back to him.

He pressed it to his nose and inhaled. "Thank you. I'll treasure it for the rest of my life." A wink and a smile bade her farewell.

Alone with her cup of tea and its whispery steam and a soothing *tick, tick, tick* from an unknown source, Hesper tried to heal her mind with comforting thoughts of home.

* * *

David engaged the ignition of his car and pulled away from the house. No time to walk to the Bastion today. Every Gentle tried to escape at least once, and it was imperative that he be there when it happened. The promising interaction with Hesper secured nothing. He must be home as much as possible until he had her heart anchored in his hand.

Until now, he'd had no intention of taking more Gentles, but his heart went out to Hesper when he heard her scream. So young and overwhelmed.

Then she spat on him! That stirred his heart right out of pity into a longing to give her an enthusiastic kissing.

He had never attempted to woo a betrothed woman before, or a woman so fresh out of the woods. This required a moderate level of formality and distance. For now. Too much physical affection would clam her up. He might have the tastiest handful of yum-yums in the world, and a wild deer would still want life more than treats.

However, Hesper's woodsiness wasn't the biggest challenge. A young buck waited in the forest for her. Some poor Gentle fellow considered himself the luckiest guy in the woods just a short time ago. Now the darling girl would never be back to love him and have his babies.

I'm sorry, buddy.

David had to be better than the other guy, whoever he was. At Hesper's age, he had to be better than her mother and father, too.

Tall order.

He was in excellent shape, whipping guys twenty years younger when he took his turn as Military Instructor.

He checked himself in the rear-view mirror—not bad-looking. He winked. Plus, he had the skills. He snorted and laughed at himself.

You've also got a hemorrhoid, stud muffin.

Though he had never had trouble gaining the affection of women he wanted, assuming Hesper wouldn't be an exception might be a mistake. She submitted to light hypnosis when they met. In the parlor, however, she strode up to resignation and acceptance, teetered on the edge, and tumbled backward. She often regarded his uniform just as he thought she might be trusting him with her subconscious mind. It must be a hang-up for her. He'd try to alleviate that next time they spoke.

A conflicted girl, Hesper carried a strange mixture of nerves and confidence. It couldn't be a fun way to live. Though it probably put her on edge enough to work in her favor if the average person wanted to manipulate her.

Fortunately, David wasn't average in this area. She needed to be brought to a place of peace. If he could help her get there, he would. She swayed with his suggestions, bending under his influence, but a brand-new stiff bit of cloth required time, effort, and a little steam to get to favorite-shirt comfortable. If she didn't take well to steam, he'd give her more time. *No problem. All the time in the world, sweetheart.* He smiled.

Hesper's emotional response to the Kali statue intrigued him. The moment carried an electric weight he felt from across the room.

One legend of the dear goddess of destruction told of the time when she resisted the control of ignorant thieves who had ideas about how she operated and thought they could manipulate her with the offering of an innocent monk.

She manifested herself and slaughtered them.

An interesting omen if ever there was one. Perhaps he should apply his skills with a lighter hand. An honest hand.

Pianissimo, Mr. Charmy-Pants. Soft and true.

Hesper demanded his help when he stepped out of his house that morning. For a split second, that scream, a shattering crystal vase in a sun-flooded room, struck his nerves and loosened everything that held him together.

Whether either of them wanted her to be his business or not, she was. Despite her defenses, they clicked together like a loaded magazine and pistol. In time, they'd chamber a round, aim for the sky, and pull the trigger. The moment would probably be unexpected and glorious. They were meant to know each other.

Or he was just nuts.

No kidding. Did he really have to tell himself?

David parked the car in the small lot beside the Bastion and flopped his head back against the headrest. Hopefully, his work in the jail would go quickly. Another of those young Earth People waited for him, accused of assaulting an officer.

David often got crap from the Glorious Ones because he wouldn't use violence when handling Earth People. Yes, well, when they used violence, they didn't get anywhere. Unified men were tough folks who responded to honesty and held up well to pain.

If he ever got his hands on one of the jokers who organized the Earth People's efforts, though, he'd probably be willing to resort to violence. It was as if they intentionally fed their young to the military while eluding law enforcement themselves. In the name of Unified patriotism, the scumbags sent zealous Gentle kids to commit crimes for them. While the Kyrios were willing to send specialized forces after mongrels and dissidents, none dared organize a concentrated effort to hunt down the Earth People's ringleaders. It was ridiculous.

One cigarette before dealing with the Kyrios. David rolled his eyes. Maybe two.

Hesper even touched Kali's face . . .

He had to get home to her. Just one smoke.

Nine | Post-Conquest: 232

ANISE STOOD IN the hallway chatting with two other women. A button-nosed redhead with green eyes and freckled candle-glow skin broke away from the group to hug Hesper, then held her at arm's length. "I'm Jade."

Hesper's eyes flooded. "Hello."

Brushing a wavy lock of auburn hair from her round face, another woman said, "I'm Dulce. We're pleased to meet you, Hesper. Though, believe us, we know what you must be going through."

Resting a lithe arm around Hesper's shoulder, Jade walked her to the others. "Pretty soon you'll feel like this is your new community and you'll be nearly as happy as you were before."

"As close to being happy as you can be," Anise amended.

"Oh, and David is just great." Jade squeezed Hesper's shoulder. "It may seem weird to be married to a man with more than one wife at first, but you get used to it. He's good at helping us forget."

"Married." Hesper uttered the word, painfully cold in her gut and chest. "I did not realize. He . . . he married all of you? He is a stig?"

Anise laughed. "No, no, dear. In this culture, the wealthy are encouraged to marry multiple Gentle women. To them, it is acceptable and moral behavior. David has remarkably few compared to others."

"We're rescues," Dulce said. "I was at the end of my two weeks. The local law enforcement wardens brought me to the base for execution. David stopped them and agreed to take me. I will always be grateful, no matter what challenges our situation presents."

"Trinity bought me as a gift for David. They sold me for only fifty meras because of my freckles!" Jade scoffed. "Fifty! A girl with missing teeth went for two hundred, and she had to go with this mean-looking man with a waxy mustache and a woman's butt." She stuck her tongue out and gagged. "Have you seen men with women's butts? It is so, so, so, weird."

Hesper's pulse quickened. "This is wicked," she whispered.

Anise opened the door behind her. "Let's go to my room, shall we ladies?"

The women filed in and seated themselves on the green bed while Anise locked the door. Facing Hesper, she said, "We must trust that the god who knows and sees all has a bigger picture of morality than we do."

"If it helps you," Dulce said. "They told me the Book of Light is filled with wisdom, and the Kyrios will access it regularly for complicated matters. It contains nothing indicating marriage to multiple women is wrong."

Hesper sneered. "The Kyrios? Whoever they are, they lack skill in critical thinking."

"Never openly criticize the Kyrios, Hesper. Keep it in your mind." Anise tapped Hesper's forehead gently. "They govern Theocracia as the human hand of God. Trinity is the incumbent Chandler Reverenced One, and David is her brother, so he is a successor and has the responsibility of taking the seat after her. We must learn to hold our tongues and show reverence, even if we do not agree."

"I respect what deserves respect," Hesper answered.

"I hope for your sake that you deem the Meros way of life worthy of respect." Anise's grim smile felt like a threat somehow.

Hesper raised her chin. "I will never respect this marriage matter." A horrible thought struck her. "Does David come to your rooms at night?"

"Yes, dear," Anise said, "he often does."

"And thank God he does!" Jade cried. "Anyone who pities me for being married to that man can suck an egg, 'cause I have no complaints. Anise is his favorite, though."

"How can you stand it?" Hesper spat. "I could not!" It did not trouble the women that their husband walked away with their kisses still on his lips, only to be rubbed off on the next woman in a few minutes. She was no sentimental silly, but this level of detachment verged on the deranged.

"If I loved David, I would be jealous to the point of murder," Hesper declared. "I will not fit here. I refuse to."

"We find a way, Hesper." Dulce shrugged.

Enough. The ladies were kind, but . . . "I need to urinate."

"We refer to that as needing to use the bathroom," Anise said.

Ugh. Poetry for urination? "I need to use the bathroom."

Jade jumped up. "To the left! I'll help you find it!"

Inside? These people are disgusting.

"No, I will go by myself." Hesper slipped into the hallway before Jade could insist. The door clicked as she closed it. She waited a moment, and when Jade did not follow her, breathed a sigh of relief. Scanning the dimly lit hallway for unwanted company, Hesper scampered to the staircase.

With the volume of Papa's hammer, Evelyn ascended the stairs in front of Hesper, slowing when she sighted her and her so-called "owl-eyes"—something Evelyn could not seem to keep her own eyes away from. Evelyn's white-spruce face, lined with past-laughter, carried a warmth that refused to come out. Her eyes, reminiscent of Mama's maple-syrupy ones, glistened with the cunning of a snake's.

"Good afternoon, dear. What's your name?"

"Hesper," she whispered.

"Ah, Hesper. Were you going to tour the house?"

"Oh! No." Hesper clenched her dress in her hands. "I need to use the bathroom."

"It's that way, darling. I'm shocked that no one showed you. Come."

Evelyn passed by and Hesper followed her to the other end of the hallway, just short of a second staircase. "Here." Evelyn pointed to a door on the left. "I hope you sleep well tonight." She smiled with a confusingly sincere warmth. "You can't trust Meros men, so lock your door." Her brow knit with concern. "David'll be in your bed before you can say, 'what do you need, Your-Almost-Reverence?' and there won't be a thing you can do about it. If it's any consolation, he's usually gentle . . . and generous." Evelyn entered a door across the hall and closed it behind her.

Would David do such a thing? No. Why would he be cruel after being so kind? But this was not her world; anything was possible.

On wobbling legs, Hesper sneaked back to the stairs she was familiar with and hurried to the first floor. Empty and silent, the room invited an escape, but how could she ever cross the distance between her and the door? She had to try. One anxious step forward built her confidence. After a few more paces, boldness wavered, and a jagged bolt of fear shot through her limbs.

Keep going.

Give up.

You might succeed!

Not now.

Even death is better than sharing a husband!

They will catch me.

KEEP GOING!

The doorknob broke her internal debate. The door opened.

Hesper whirled around and ran up the stairs to the safety of the hallway. Breathless and tingling with adrenaline, she dragged her feet to the bathroom and opened the door.

She stared.

What was this place?

* * *

Jade led Hesper to a room with bare walls where the sun poured in through uncovered windows, sparkling on the slick floor like a puddle of light. A pile of charming, colorful decorations and pretty things lay on the currant-and-cream bed covering.

"May I help you?" Jade asked.

"I need to be alone," Hesper said.

Jade touched Hesper's shoulder. Her smile, sympathetic and sincere, made Hesper's face burn. With a hug, Jade left.

Embroidered golden circles edged the bed cover. Like David's buttons. Joram's buttons.

You are not a Gentle, you are not a Gentle.

They would not make her cry. She would persevere. The blood of Unified leaders coursed through her, demanding her courage rise to this occasion. Screaming a growl, she pushed the things off her bed—no, not her bed!

She did not want their pretty things. Their unnatural garbage. Did they think her favor and pleasure could be bought with trinkets and finery? Never! Her affection was hard-won and skillfully kept. A steady, consistent man could do it without a single gift.

At the window, she watched the world of black uniforms outside. The colorful houses would have been a beautiful sight if this were not a prison. Face pressed to the warm glass, Hesper strained to see farther east. The entire community bowed in reverence to an enormous stone building in its center. Bland and ominous when compared to the white and red homes with their bright doors, its purple pennants snapped and flapped in the breeze: the only splash of color on the monstrous thing.

The forest's leaves whispered in her mind, wondering where she was, why she betrayed them, why she chose the glaring sun over their shade.

She did save a boy's life. Perhaps that would be sufficient consolation. Life was not just about her, it was about everyone, but selfishness came so easily.

Turning from the window, she considered the room's warm colors. All cold. All the things provided to make the room attractive, splayed across the floor. The bed promised a softness far beyond the thickest moss, but it meant nothing if she had to share it with someone who laid naked in beds with others. Nothing would ever seem warm away from her cozy little loft. Nothing would seem warm without . . . Mama. Mama was forever lost.

Hesper had been innocent—so innocent, she did not know it until now. The forest and the people in it were saturated with the blessed simplicity she could not find in herself anymore. Baked in the sun, wiped dry with the touch of Meros hands, and thinking poetic foolishness to process the pain, she floundered in unwanted knowledge.

She grasped at her chest and placed her head between her knees. Shivers became whimpers that evolved into tears, and the gentle rain from her eyes grew into a storm of heaving sobs. She collapsed on the hard wooden floor. It did not matter who heard or saw her. At best, they would take pity, at worst, they would end her suffering. She was a Gentle after all.

She slammed her fist on the floor. It was stupid, and it hurt, but she could endure a little pain for her own foolishness.

Because of her actions, Mama and Papa would hurt.

Adahy would hurt.

Her chest hurt.

She struck the floor again and again, growling until her voice broke into pieces in a violent cough and slowly decomposed into a quiet, burning stream of tears. No feeling apart from sorrow, no thought of anything beyond grief. Her crumbling wall of strength fell on her as debris, suffocating her. She walked in the suffering of her ancestors when they fled to the wilderness to survive the war. Like a deer with an arrow in its lung, it may run for a little while, but eventually . . .

Air. I need air.

A warm hand rested on her shoulder. A voice.

Frantic, Hesper crawled across the room. She whirled around and pressed her back against the wall, flinging her arms out, fingers spread and gripping its smooth, flat surface.

David sat on the ground, too far away, crisscrossing his legs. "I'm here for you." He held his hands out, palms up. "You're going to be okay. This won't last forever. Is this new for you?"

Hesper shook her head and swallowed hard, blinking away tears. She had to break free from this feeling. Each breath hurt her chest and squeezed her heart. *Not enough air.* "My fingers tingle," she gasped. "Am I dying?"

"Nope. You're alive and well and everything's going to be okay," he said softly, crawling over to her. Then, lighter and thoughtful, "You know, a little bit of light does a lot in a dark place." His words plunged into the ice-covered lake of fear she had fallen into. He still smelled sweet and tart even as she drowned. The warmth of his voice grabbed her numb hand and pulled her toward the surface.

She fought to listen. *Focus.*

He continued, "You are a bright ray of light. Even in a dark spot, you have the advantage because you can shine the darkness away. Do you see?" He touched her hand—physically, this time—and without knowing why, she grasped it. He did not pull or insist. Only a tiny movement invited her to come nearer, so she did. Kneeling, she leaned against the safety of his chest. No stiff uniform or metal buttons this time. Only a soft shirt. *So soft.*

Hand on her back, he uttered a soothing, "Shh."

Slowly, her body relaxed, and she took a deep breath as the pain subsided. He should not touch her, but it did not matter. The warm breath passing over her hair settled her emotions.

The smell of spices always comforted her because it followed Adahy wherever he went. Now, she would have to find comfort in the scent of David.

Ten | Post-Conquest: 222

DURING THE DAY, Jesurun counted on cities to beg for money, and if he was lucky, he'd land a cot in a homeless shelter at night. On not-so-lucky days, he rested his head wherever he could. Few people raised concerns, even fewer bothered to ask questions, so he carried on largely unchallenged—no challenges he couldn't escape easily anyway. Most people didn't care enough to do anything when he ran from their help.

Once in a blue moon, he let a person or family take him in for a few days or weeks. Sometimes they taught him stuff, and sometimes he got work for money. Other days, he learned how to protect himself, mastering many of the ways to make sure someone never got up again. Ever.

One chilly autumn evening, he staggered into a barn and climbed the ladder to the hayloft, where he flopped on prickly bales of hay. A few hours later, he awoke to the friendly face of another boy.

The boy called, "Pops! There's a kid up here!"

A man poked his head into the loft. "Sure 'nuff." He took his hat off and rubbed his head. "Hey there, son. What's your name?"

Jes stared at him. This farmer was too nice. He'd pin Jes down and try to adopt him. Jes knew the type.

The farmer beckoned and Jes followed down the ladder and through a swarm of curious hens who clucked around his feet. A friendly golden dog nosed him a few times and stuck his snout into Jes' palm. He giggled quietly and gave the dog a quick scratch on the head as he followed the farmer up the stairs to an open porch and entered the farmhouse. The warm kitchen smelled of wood smoke, coffee, spicy sausage, and maple syrup.

"Kimberly! We found a boy in the hayloft. He looks starved half to death. Can we do somethin' for him?" The man shrugged and seated Jes at the table. "I dunno where he came from. He won't talk."

Kimberly approached Jes and bent over, smiling, her hands on her knees. "We'll fix you a nice meal and give you a warm bath. How does that sound?"

Kimberly smelled like lilacs. Her warm brown eyes loved him the way his mother's once had.

"Who's that?" A raspy voice choked out from another room.

"We don't know, Dad. We found him in the hayloft," the farmer answered.

"You don't say. Lemme see 'im."

Kimberly and the farmer exchanged concerned glances, but led Jes to the old man, nearly grown into his worn chair.

"Come 'ere, boy. What's yer name?"

The smell of the old man's bucket of tobacco spit nauseated Jes. *You smell bad. I don't like you.*

"What ails ye? Are ya stupid?" He grabbed the boy's arm and yanked him forward.

Jes gagged at the smell and started to cry. If he cried, the farmer and his lady would feel bad for him and get him out of there quickly.

"He's a blundering idgit, that's what he is. What're ya gonna do wit' 'im?"

"I s'pose we're going to feed him and try to find out where he's from so we can bring him home," the farmer said. "He probably has a family worried about him." His merciful, firm grip pulled Jes away.

"Come here, big guy." Kimberly placed her gentle hand on the back of Jes' head and directed him to the kitchen.

No one managed to get a peep out of Jes all day. They let him spend the night and planned to bring him to the local market to ask if anyone knew of a missing boy.

Bull. Nobody's gonna haul me around a market askin' people 'bout me.

Snug under a colorful patchwork quilt that smelled like Kimberly, Jes shared a bed with the couple's son. Except for the old man, this was the best place he'd found in five years.

He'd met men like that old guy before, and he knew what to expect from them. He couldn't think of any reason worth going through *that* again. Of course, the old man might have an "accident." Jes was good at planning accidents. *No one suspects a kid.*

As Jes neared sleep, the door creaked open, broadening the hallway moonglow in the room. The hunchbacked old man crept in with the added clunk of his cane. He wrapped a cold hand around Jes' left arm, and his bony fingers dug into his bicep as he led Jes out of the room. "If you scream, I knife ya," the old man whispered, his mouth sticky with spittle.

* * *

Jes returned to the bedroom to put on his own clothes and shoes. The farmer's son lit a candle.

Not now! "Go back to sleep, kid," Jes said, tying his shoes.

"Kid? How old are you?"

"Ten."

"I'm older than you," the boy said, perplexed.

Jes glanced back at the boy and snorted.

"Anyways," the boy threw his blanket off and swung his legs over the edge of the bed. "I should've said something. I'm sorry. I was just glad it wasn't me this time. Did he hurt ya' bad?"

"Hurt? Nah. It's nothin'. Some sickos pay good money for that stuff. It's bought me a few meals. You shoulda charged the old prune. He won't be botherin' you again, though." Jes finished tying his shoes. "Tell your mom I think she's pretty and smells nice, will ya?"

"'Kay. You leavin'?"

"I'll be in big trouble when they find the old guy."

"Grandpa? What'd you do to him?"

"I didn't do nothin' except give him what he deserves . . . in the neck."

Eleven | Post-Conquest: 232

THE MUTED SUNLIGHT comforted Hesper. Though, the curtains that softened the light had not been there the night before. A thick, oily scent hung in the air. Someone crawled onto the bed and touched her arm with soft, cool fingers.

"Good morning, beautiful."

"Jade," she rasped.

Jade touched Hesper's arm. "I heard you had a rough night."

Yes, she had a rough night, and no one could entice her to speak about it. She had no sensible words to explain those feelings.

Her hand felt strange. Uncovering it, she found it had been carefully wrapped with white cloth. A bit of some sort of balm reached beyond the edges of the bandage.

"David did that." Jade pointed. "Arnica, he said. He wanted me to spend the night in here with you in case you needed anything. He was worried about your meltdown. He thought you might be distressed to wake up to him, though, so he got me."

"What is a meltdown?"

Jade grinned. "It's like melting butter. You were solid and put together, and then you weren't. I did your room up for you. Hope that's okay." Jade looked around, considering her masterpiece. "You can change anything you want. I won't be offended." She pointed to the wall behind Hesper. "I gave you a present, too."

Hesper craned her neck to see a painting of her woods hanging on the wall with the dead pine tree standing out above the other trees. "Did you make that?"

"Mhm. Do you like it? It'll take some time for the paint to dry. I was painting when David came for me, and I finished in here while you slept."

"It is beautiful. That must be what I smell."

"Oils. They have a stink about them, don't they?" Jade giggled. "I'm so glad you like it. I would love to teach you how to paint! You could paint one for me, too!"

"How did you know those were my woods?" Hesper pushed the blankets off herself.

"I guess David's nephew talked about where you found him. That was really nice of you, you know."

"Tom is his nephew?" Hesper asked.

"Remember? Trinity is David's sister." Jade grinned. "Do you want some breakfast?"

"Well—"

"Okay. You have to do something first." Jade gripped Hesper's shoulders and looked into her eyes. "You have to open the chest they got you, 'cause it's driving me crazy!"

Her silly face and desperate grip concerned Hesper. Was she a lunatic? "Chest?"

"Over there." Jade pointed to the right. "Cole brought it with him last night after you fell asleep. David delivered it." She frowned and shook her finger, mimicking David. "I've been ordered to 'let you open it for yourself.'" Judging by Jade's pleading green eyes, the wait had been torture.

"Who is Cole?" Hesper scooched off her bed and plodded over to the large chest, a dull cedarwood box with copper-colored hinges.

"Cole is David's brother," Jade said. "He's been gone on business, but he's back on the base for a while."

A familiar, sweet, spicy smell greeted Hesper as she unlatched and lifted the lid—almost stronger than the cedar. She would never escape it, would she?

"*This* is my favorite part of getting gifts from David!" Jade said. She dropped to her knees beside Hesper and took in a lung-bursting gulp of the fragrance. "He has an eye for size and excellent taste."

The box contained the epitome of flawless order, with fluffy towels and featherlight gowns, neatly folded and packed together, while boxes, bottles, and trinkets filled in the nooks and crannies.

On top of it all, a cool, orange ball with neat rows of cloves stuck into it, and another ball that seemed to be made solely of cloves. What they had been stuck into was hard to say, but it was dry and small now. She held it to her nose. An apple?

"Cole does all the folding and arranging for him," Jade said. "He does a nice job. It's sad to ruin it, b-u-u-u-u-t . . . you really need to look at what's in there. Now! Please?"

"Oohing" and "aahing" each item, Jade entertained Hesper more than anything in the box ever would. Though, it was difficult to show indifference to the crisp, white paper and box of pens.

"Such nice things, Hesper! I bet the box of paper and ball-point pens are really something for you!"

"Nice? Yes, they are nice things." Ashamed, Hesper tucked the paper and pens under a dress to forget how much they thrilled her. Nothing should be thrilling. It was a mistake to attach herself to anyone here. She must control herself. But . . . No. She must.

"He is so good to us, Hesper. Before long, you will forget this seemed strange at all. He gives us quality time and affection. Gifts are just a nice thing he does. He never uses them to replace himself."

"What happens if one of you has a baby and he favors the mother?"

Jade laid a towel on the edge of the tub. "Oh, we're not allowed to have children, so that won't be a problem." She turned on the water and plugged the tub's drain.

"How is that possible?" Hesper asked.

"Only Meros women are allowed to have children with Meros men. Evelyn is the child-bearing wife and Anise is the first. They say I'm the favored one, but I think Anise is, so far."

Hesper waved her hands and shook her head. "No distractions about favorites. Babies. Tell me. How can it be prevented?"

"They issue prophylactics to prevent it. David might explain it to you," Jade said, too casual. "If a Gentle does become pregnant, it'll be taken care of. If it's a big problem, it'll be taken care of forever."

Prophyl—what? A problem? Taken care of? Were they talking about the same thing? Surely not. "Children?" Hesper asked. "Are we talking about being pregnant with a child, or is this poetry for something else?"

Jade lapsed into a series of choppy movements, averting her eyes.

"Are you well?" Hesper took a few steps toward her.

"Yes, I'm fine. Your bath is almost ready. Will you need any help preparing for breakfast? It's in"—Jade glanced at the clock—"twenty minutes. When the short hand is on the number eight and the long hand is on the number twelve."

"I will be ready."

Jade's sunny disposition returned. "See you later." With a quick wink and smile, she opened the door and made her exit.

A bath every day could not be healthy.

Hesper sat on her bed and put her face in her hands for one more cry.

Being here could not be healthy.

Twelve | Post-Conquest: 232

COLE LIFTED HIS chin over the pull-up bar.

Eighteen. He lowered himself.

David had a new girl.

Cole pulled up. *Nineteen.*

The guy who swore off more wives had a new girl.

Surprise, surprise, surprise.

Twenty. Done.

He lowered himself to the floor. David had come to the exercise room earlier and finished his preferred eastern methods ten minutes ago and now sat on the floor with a cup of water, running through a series of annoying behaviors over and over. He scratched at the lotus tattoo on his arm, closed his eyes, furrowed his brow, scratched the back of his neck, made a statement about something to do with self-hypnosis for kicking nicotine, then repeated the process all over again. Normally, his quirks and the differences between the brothers didn't bother Cole—except for the orange eastern bathrobe and harem pants David often wore. Those would bother Cole forever, but besides that . . .

Today, however, whacking David's head with that giant wooden lollipop *gada* mace he liked so much was a satisfying thought.

David had called yesterday while Cole was working. Out of uniform, trying to handle a dispute between a market shop owner and a Unified hunter, Cole wasn't about to stand there with a military communicator to his ear for a half an hour while David blathered about his latest find. He got the stuff David wanted, came home, folded it pretty-like, and crashed in his bed.

Hands on his hips, Cole finally snapped. "Why did you take a new Gentle, Dave?"

Eyes closed, brow furrowed, David asked, "It's your business, how?"

"And *she* was *your* business, how? Take care of the women you have! You've already got a blasted harem. Not to mention, I'm the one who digs your women out of trouble in court. Unless they let me study the Book of Light, I've got nothing new to help you. You know they won't. They've rejected my request five times. I'm tempted to appeal to it someday. Just to see them squirm."

David opened his eyes. "Your religious awakening hasn't done much for your compassion and mercy score, has it?"

"I'm quite compassionate when it's—"

"They were going to give her to Vincent, Cole."

Cole paused. "Okay. Trinity said that?"

David nodded once.

"It's hard to watch women go to him," Cole said.

"I don't watch if I can help it." David downed the rest of his water. "Officer Marotz showed up here late last night."

"Not Marotz."

"Oh, yes."

Cole cringed.

"Sobbing. She'd been dealing with this for months before taking the risk to get help. That's what I get to watch. I'm not interested in being directly responsible for Vincent's taste being inflicted upon someone."

"He doesn't do it to everyone."

"Just the ones he likes," David said, quietly. "And he'd like the new girl."

David knew what he was talking about with people and their nature, much to Cole's indignant chagrin. His frustration settled.

"Okay."

"So glad to have the approval of Boy Genius." David stood and put on a t-shirt. "Remember how Jade was? A total innocent. It's the same with this one. Something drew me to her. I need her. She needs me."

"Sure. Savior of the innocent, hope of the defenseless, David Chandler, the—"

David laughed. "Ooh, is that jealousy in your pocket, or are you just in dire need of a woman?" He waggled his eyebrows. "You'd better judge me harder, baby, 'cause I can't feel a thing. I do what I feel is right, even if it makes people think I have a savior complex."

Cole put up his hand and turned away to start another set of reps. "I have no use for a woman, and I'm not jealous of the prison you've made for yourself in the least."

"I think she's from one of the communities you've worked with. North of here."

"Doubt it. None of the women there are stupid enough to leave."

"She was helping Tom. She had a noble reason for what she did."

Cole's stomach hollowed out and sank. He had been about to take the bar. Instead, his fingers grazed it as he let them fall to his side and whirled around to face David.

None of them would do it. Not even for a boy. They were logical, cautious people.

Why had he let himself care about them? It wasn't worth the stress.

Yes, it was.

Absolutely.

It was worth it to care. He could only hope that if the new girl was from a community he worked with and she recognized him, she wouldn't try to kill him in his sleep. She wouldn't succeed, and she'd lose her life.

He grabbed his glasses from the weight bench and put them on his face. "I'm calling it quits early. I need to pray."

* * *

Scrubbed and dried, Hesper put on the thickest dress in the chest. Nothing felt as safe as hides, but it was better than the whisper-soft dresses that made her feel naked. With a glance and curl of the lip at the perfume bottles David had sent, she reached for the door just as someone knocked.

Dressed, refreshed, and emanating a rich, peppery-sweet fragrance, a giddy Jade held something behind her back. "I have a gift for you." She held out a heart in the palm of her hand. "It's a rhodonite. You don't have to take off your other necklace. Anise told me what it was, and I think two is fine."

Jade hung it on Hesper's neck by a silver chain and clasped it. "Where I come from, they say rhodonites are for friends to share with each other, and its energy helps you to balance your mind and focus when facing a challenge." She placed a hand on Hesper's shoulder. "I hope it helps you."

The cool weight of the stone rested in the center of Hesper's collarbone even as the warmth of the gesture washed over her. She tried to turn her lips upward, but they twitched and fell. What a kind woman Jade was; a presence to rest in.

"I'm sure there's a reason you're here." Jade leaned in and kissed Hesper's cheek. "We have to hurry, or we'll be late for breakfast."

Hands laced together, Jade and Hesper descended the stairs to the left and rounded a corner to the right, entering an enormous room with ceilings as high as Hesper's oak. A window spanned almost an entire wall and permitted enough light to make the shining dark wood glimmer like water. The quiet, richly colored room provoked the same euphoric, breathless awe Hesper felt when standing amid a group of red pines. Blue and white plates and colorful bowls, filled with fruit, adorned a long, shining table.

Jade elbowed Hesper, gently. "Life often looks better in the morning."

Evelyn stood by David's side as he spoke with a strange man in the corner. David's eyes snagged on Hesper, and with a smile and a quick appraisal of her appearance, he approached, hand extended.

Unexpected heat cobwebbed through her cheeks. David had touched her, held her, and seen her with her wits pouring down her face. Still, he did not take advantage of her weakness. He covered it, just as he ordered Burns to cover her nakedness. Releasing Jade's slender hand, Hesper almost accepted his warm offer but simply could not bring herself to do it. Quickly, she pulled her hands back.

David's smile spoke of respect even as it laughed at her decision. Sometimes, his facial expressions were too complex to understand. He smiled, and that had to be good.

Near to her, he whispered, "You're fine, honey. You don't need to be embarrassed or feel guilty, okay? Your hand seems to be improved. I'm glad." Speaking aloud, he said, "I'd like you to meet my little brother, Cole. Boy Genius. He works closely with your people. An expert in customs and laws—both Meros and Gentle. He's been to more schools than I've been to restrooms." He laughed. "Mother always loved him best. Cole?" David beckoned to his brother, who spoke with Evelyn in a darker corner of the room now. Cole's tall, slim body stiffened, and he held his face as if nursing a headache. A sneeze echoed off the walls and ceiling, ushering in a period of awkward silence.

"Is he unwell?" Hesper whispered to David. "I am quite good at relieving headaches."

"I'm sure you are." A half-smile slid onto his lips. "Trinity thought you might be a medicine woman. Seems she was right?"

"I'm sorry. Excuse me." Cole's high, nasal voice came as a surprise. Still holding his face, he passed Hesper with great, noisy strides, a breeze of market fragrance drifting in his wake.

"Is it just me, or did that smack a bit of foppery?" David asked no one in particular. After a few moments of silence, he shrugged. "Well, he's a big boy. I'm sure he's fine." He stepped past Hesper and kissed the corner of Jade's lips. "Thank you for being so good to Hesper last night. I owe you." Waggling his eyebrows, he winked and slid his hand across her waist as he moved on to the table.

A bit unsteady, Jade approached Hesper and stood beside her to whisper, "I said it before, I'll say it again"—she tittered—"anyone who pities me can suck an egg."

Lorelei served a breakfast of eggs and toast to go along with the fruit on the table. Some of these fruits were unfamiliar, all were out of season, and most were sprinkled with different shades of brown spices, smelling of special days in the forest. Hesper followed Jade's example and scooped fruit onto her plate. After a taste of a sliced apple, her hunger awakened. Wedges of sunset, chunks of bright yellow, little purple fruits that burst between her teeth, green slices speckled with black seeds, and blueberries. She ate, heedless of those around her. The new flavors sang in her mouth the way books had sung in her mind, the way soil and plants sang on her skin. This was . . . this was . . . eating a paradise.

Poetry? Poetry for eating?

"Whoa."

Evelyn's voice?

Whoa? Hesper's heart sank. Were they looking at her? She lifted her head.

They were.

"I told you you'd find things to enjoy here." David took a bite of his toast. "Carry on and let the woman enjoy her food." His lips twitched upward. "She's hungry, and goodness knows the fruit options are limited in the woods."

Evelyn cleared her throat. "Have you had sex with her yet?"

David shot a look at Hesper. "Evelyn, if you attempt to humiliate her again, the two of you will be trading rooms."

Evelyn clanked her fork against her plate and said, "Is your new toy still going to see the doctor?"

"Not a toy. No, dear." He frowned at his egg as he dipped his toast into it. "I'll be spending time with my brother. He has to give his report to the Kyrios and successors, and then we're—"

"Well—"

"Must you persist in this interrogation?" He raised his voice through a mouthful of toast.

"You've got the corner on that market, I suppose?" She sneered. "Yes. I must. I don't want you to catch a disease from her and pass it to me."

He stared at her in disbelief as he brought the napkin on his lap to his lips. The chair creaked as he leaned back with a charming smile and cold eyes. "Did you intend to give me the opportunity to pass things along to you anytime soon, Love? I have my own concerns in that area, and I might need a rain check 'til you've had a checkup." His smile darkened. "No, Hesper won't be seeing the doctor today, and no, you may not take her yourself!" He took a bite of a sunset wedge. "You may, however, go shopping if you'd like."

"I think I will."

* * *

The ladies showed Hesper the garden behind the house. The apple tree alone impressed Hesper. She parted from the women, bunched up her dress, and climbed the squat tree. It felt like home. Sort of.

Delighted, Jade gathered up a fistful of her own dress and joined Hesper with some help. "Whew! I'm out of practice!" She shifted around to get comfortable and smacked her head on a branch.

Hard.

Silent, she blinked a few times and Hesper grabbed her arm to steady her.

"Jade, are you all right?" Dulce asked.

Jade smiled and waved the concern away. "I'm fine. I'm fine." She touched her head. "Maybe not. A lump! It's huge."

Hesper felt the spot. No blood. Jade was right, though, a big lump had formed. Hesper cupped her hand over the lump and stroked through the air, conjuring good thoughts and energy, pushing it out through her hand, soothing the inflammation.

Grief, love, hope, and devoted affection scrambled through her mind like a pack of panting, tumbling wolf cubs. Not her own feelings. Jade's?

"What are you doing?" asked Jade.

Hesper took a breath, startled.

Jade touched her head. "It's smaller. Did you do that?"

"Your body did." Hesper shrugged. "It might be sore later, but it looks better."

Anise and Dulce gawked at her.

"It is common for healers in my community," Hesper explained.

Anise raised her eyebrows and smiled. "Well, it certainly seems a helpful skill! I'd like to hear more about it sometime." She turned to Dulce. "Let's walk while the girls enjoy the tree." Dulce and Anise continued on, discussing petunias.

The "girls" did enjoy the tree. Jade seemed unbothered by the hard hit, turning her face to the sky with closed eyes. Hesper felt like that whenever she got into full sunlight in the forest. Warm and friendly on her face, she could not keep herself from closing her eyes and sighing at it at least once or twice. She had never seen someone else do it, though.

"Do you miss your mama?" Hesper asked.

Jade lowered her face and turned to Hesper with a sad smile. "I try to not think of her. When I need a mother, I go to David."

"How can David replace the woman who gave birth to you?"

Jade did not smile this time. "He doesn't, but he's comforting and warm and listens well. He's been through a lot of crazy stuff, but he hasn't let it make him bitter. He let it make him . . . motherly." She laughed. "That sounds so stupid. Especially since he also turns me on just looking at me. Motherly and sexy is a little weird. Maybe my brain is sick." Jade's creamy skin blanched. She puffed a breath and opened her eyes wide. "Listen, I have to go."

"Are you well?" Hesper asked.

Jade lowered herself to the ground. "Oh, I don't know. It comes and goes. I'm getting sick or something. I need to rest."

If Jade's injury was worse than expected, she might need help. "Jade!" Hesper scrambled down the tree.

"I'm fine!" Jade waved Hesper off and hurried indoors.

Hesper ran to the door and swung it open. Jade stopped.

"Really, Hesper, stay outside." She turned around. "If I throw up, I want to be alone. It's so gross." Off she went and disappeared around the corner, leaving Hesper alone in the doorway.

* * *

When Hesper caught up to the women, Anise welcomed her with an arm around her shoulder. "Did you leave Jade by herself?"

"No. She needed to go inside. She felt ill."

"I've noticed that. She's sick lately. She should see a doctor, but she's doesn't trust them."

"Why? What do they do?"

"She had a traumatic experience, that's all. Doctors play a part in carrying out the law as much as they help sick people to heal and be well. The law Jade broke required Medical Justice. They had to remedy her situation. Now Jade is sensitive."

"She really ought to toughen up. It's a wonder she's lasted this long." Dulce's soft voice came across hard.

Hesper dared not look at her, much less glare. "I need a book of the laws or something," Hesper said. "What did she do?"

"Nothing you need to worry about. It's not your responsibility and never will be unless you keep secrets."

No! Enough with the hiding. "Not good enough, Anise."

Anise's face set into regret. "She was pregnant, Hesper. It's not allowed."

Hesper shook herself free from the women. "What a stupid rule! Jade told me about it. Sick, perverse people!"

Anise took Hesper by the shoulders. "Don't say that so loudly, dear." Her urgent whisper caught Hesper off guard. "You'll find yourself at the law's mercy if you do."

Hesper challenged Anise with her eyes. When Anise did not back down, and her jaw set in an unfeminine and unexpected way, Hesper's eyes fell. Surely Anise had seen horrors that Hesper never had. The counsel of an elder almost always held value.

Anise released Hesper's shoulders. "Let's walk and have a little more time to pretend that life is beautiful."

The women walked in silence for several moments, but Hesper could not stand leaving the conversation alone. "What did they do with Jade's baby?"

Anise sighed, exasperated. "Dulce, I need to speak with Hesper alone." Dulce's eyebrows twitched, but she headed back to the house without complaint. Anise's gentle manner froze over. "They got rid of it."

"How could they get rid of a precious baby?"

"It's nothing to worry about." The frozen look disappeared, and a false, almost-convincing smile took its place. "Look at me, child. Jade tried to keep it a secret, but the law required David to bring her to the Kyrios when he learned of her condition. Considering the fact she withheld the information, they were merciful." Anise nodded as if trying to convince herself. "Cole stood up for her and managed to talk them into a less severe consequence.

"When you and David are married, he will be responsible for pregnancy prevention. You will be responsible for telling him if you think you may be pregnant. It's unlikely." She turned toward the house. "You're better off pretending you don't know this. It was unfortunate, but it was Jade, not you. Don't let worry get to you. None of us can afford worry."

Could they afford loyalty and sympathy? Were those too costly? "I am not worried. I am disgusted."

Anise laughed under her breath. "I understand, dear. There's even less room for that. I've had enough of the outside for now."

Hesper glowered as Anise walked away and entered the house. She grabbed and ripped a fistful of larkspur from its stem and threw it on the ground. Riding on indignation, she assessed her circumstance with a few quick glances. David's garden came to an end about four yards away. After that, open, mowed grass reached all the way to the fence in the back. A forest waited just beyond.

David's home appeared to be the westernmost of a long row of large houses. All the roads, people, and businesses carried on in front of the row. Besides a few guards, no one could see behind David's house. The ladies were inside. David occupied himself with his brother.

Interesting. A timely opportunity.

She was just mad enough to try for the impossible. Yards away and facing east, the guard would give her enough time to make for the fence without being seen. She hiked up her dress and sprinted to the edge of the property where she grabbed the sun-warmed metal fence. The small rhodonite necklace and her betrothal token hung with equal weight against her collarbone. *You took this chance, and now you stop? Hesper! Go! Go!*

Adahy had said she inspired him to open his heart. She did not fully understand that until now. Love bound her to this place as much as it called her away. Her heart opened so wide to fit everyone into it, it broke. *It is breaking. Right now.*

She vented a growling, frustrated scream. The fence shook with a metallic rattle when she spun around and threw herself back against it and slid to the ground.

Unless Jade went with her, Hesper's plans meant nothing. Jade's wound needed to be healed, and it would never be healed here. Hesper turned to press her face against the fence. Only a dash away from freedom. The clean air blew through the forest's leaves. They still whispered.

She and Jade might become a community of their own.

Rising, she wiped tears away and brushed off her dress. Hopefully, no one noticed her, so she could sit somewhere and stare into nothing for a while, rather than face scolding or punishment. She traipsed back to the garden path, toward the house, heavy in mind.

Smoke. She sniffed. Not wood smoke this time. Tobacco smoke.

Few people in her community smoked tobacco. Cigarettes cost a good deal of money. They sometimes smoked mullein, skullcap, or lobelia, but the odor of tobacco still lingered in her memory.

David's voice came from the direction of the apple tree. He stood beside it, cigarette in hand. "A little flushed?"

Hesper's legs weakened. Finally, a benefit to these impractical dresses: hiding the infernal knee-shaking that started back when she saw Joram in a Meros uniform. Though, she had been around David enough to know he was quite astute, with an eye for details. If he saw her knees shaking, she'd never regain her confidence.

"I was—"

"Trying to escape?" he asked, amused. "You know that's frowned upon, right?" His eyes laughed at her as he brought the cigarette to his lips and took a long drag, waiting for her reaction.

"Is stealing people frowned upon?" She gasped and looked at the ground, fidgeting with her hands.

"Yes, it is. Unless you're a Gen—Unified." He chuckled. "Let's go inside." With a final puff, he dropped the cigarette and ground it under the ball of his foot. He held his hand out. She had to go with him but was most certainly not going to be friendly. It would be hypocritical for her to accept kindness from him after trying to escape.

"I'm not trying to get fresh with you. I figured you needed support. I startled you."

Why!? Why does he see everything? "I can walk."

David smiled. "Okay." He extended his arm behind her and escorted her inside the house without a touch or word about her slowness.

"Have a seat." A short echo of his voice reverberated off the walls and ceiling of the dining room.

She obeyed, and he sat near her at the table. "Did you . . . Did you have any traumatic experiences with the Meros before this, Hesper?"

"Why?"

"Just curious. I'm sorry if I cause you fear that makes you shake. That's pretty intense. I'll try to be more considerate." He gave her a double take. "Do you realize your face is remarkably expressive? It's lovel—strong. Quite strong. Not lovely. I have no idea what I'm talking about."

His sassy simper almost snuffed out Hesper's fear. He would not be silly if he were mad at her, would he?

"I enjoy giving gifts in person sometimes, instead of sticking everything in a box, so I ha—" His eyes narrowed. "What? Are you expecting me to go off on you? Yell? Punish you? Force you into your room and lock you in?"

Hesper's head buzzed with a nod. "Yes," she whispered.

He smiled. "Don't do it again. It's fine. Rather endearing. Quite the scream you have. It may have been better than the one you delivered to my face when we met. Quick feet, too. I'll have to remember." He pulled an item from his uniform pocket, wrapped in smooth paper and crinkling with his touch. He set it on the table and pushed it toward her. "It's chocolate. Ground with stone and shipped in from overseas. Hard to get! They say it's worth the money and effort, though. Cole loves it—especially when it's spicy. Strange man." He leaned back, resting his elbows on the arms of his chair. "Have you heard of it? Chocolate, I mean."

"Heard of it. Hunters brought it in occasionally. I have never tasted any." She touched it, then regarded the colorful metal pieces on David's coat. "Am I not in trouble?"

"No." His mouth twisted as he frowned. "I see you don't believe me. I don't think you'll do it again, so I'm not overly concerned." He stood and set to unbuttoning his uniform coat. "Besides, I'm not sure I would have had it any other way. There has to be at least one escape attempt. After that, you'll fall madly in love with me and never want to leave my side." He put the coat on the back of his chair and sat. "So, we're on to the more pleasant part now, hm?"

She scowled. "Are you being funny?"

"Apparently not!" The golden laugh appeared, far shinier than his buttons would ever be. His young, sensitive eyes danced often, and he had a boyish way about him, though he was certainly far beyond boyhood.

He tugged the white cloth out from under his sleeve and dropped it on the tabletop. With a few deft motions, like a sleight-of-hand-trick, he removed gold coin-like somethings from his cuffs and let them clatter on the table.

Hesper wrinkled her face. "Why are you fidgeting with your clothes so much?"

"Is that how it looks to you?" He tipped his head and smiled.

"Yes, sir."

"I'm just getting comfortable. These uniforms are stiff as northern absinthe." He undid the top button of his shirt. More relaxed now, he leaned back and crossed his ankle over his knee. "I imagine they're not your favorite thing, either."

David was a handsome man with a pleasing neck and strong forearms with smooth skin, and his hands . . .

She caught herself staring and closed her mouth. They were just eyes. Just arms. Dangerous ones. They belonged to a dangerous man, and she had to shut this out and be stronger than her impulses.

David leaned in. "Are you all right?" He touched her.

This time, new feelings awoke with his touch, filling her with wide-eyed, trembling hope. Hope for what? She moved away and clenched her hands and teeth against the pleasurable sensation.

You are weak, Hesper.

"We need to talk about all of this." The chair creaked as he leaned back. "What are you feeling?"

"Nothing," she said much too fast.

He squinted an eye at her and placed his hands on the table, palms up. "I'm pressing this matter. You are far too direct a person to feel whatever you're feeling with no outlet. Hesper, take my hands."

She shook her head.

"Why not?" He smiled. The window permitted sunlight to streak across the upper half of his face. His mouth spoke in the shadow. "Does it matter anymore? The first touch has passed, and now we move on. Let's move on, sweetheart."

"Why do you want to hold my hands?"

His fingernails were so clean.

"Well," he said, "because we'll have to be married if you're to stay with me. I'd like the opportunity to win your affection and make this a happier story than it is now."

"You want me to like you?"

His shivelight smile whispered sunshine in dark places and bolstered the light in her mind. The light Anise told her to look for. There it was. In his mouth.

A loud affirmation. "Yes. Yes, I do. I want you to like me, Hesper. Very much. Even if we were not in this situation, I would wish for it just the same. Will you give me a chance?"

Hesper's heart doubled its pace and became much too obvious. She couldn't ignore it, but why? She had had a quicker heart rate before, but nothing this overwhelming. Not while feeling . . . good? She felt good? "Why do you think I must hold your hands to grow to like you?"

"Fair enough. Let's just say that it helps, and I don't know a soul who doesn't enjoy it." His soft laugh made her want to smile.

"What if I wanted a baby?"

He grew melancholy and sat back. "That can't be. I'm sure you've already had that explained to you."

"Why not?"

"It's against the law. We'll discuss this once we're married." He sounded more like the David who challenged Trinity now. Cold.

"What if I told you I am half Meros?"

"That would be worse for you. Besides, that's a lie."

"You deserve to be lied to if you think this is right. Do you have any natural affection for your own children?"

David's eyes sparked with anger before his face went dead. "Who said anything about thinking it's right?" Licking his lips, he tried for a laugh and landed on a sorrowfully amused smile. "You go straight for the jugular, I see." Weighty silence hung over them. His shirt rustled as he shifted in his seat.

"I was harsh. Even to my enemies, I must speak with control and tolerance."

Puffing a humorless laugh, he said, "I assure you, I'm not your enemy. You're human, and you have concerns and passions." Gentle eyes examined her face. "I will never deny you that. You don't have to be a mindless stoic in my home."

She was ashamed of herself as he gathered his coat and the other bits and pieces of his uniform and walked away. Lenient and kind as he was, interacting with David felt like trying to dam a river with her hands.

She released a sigh of relief.

David stopped.

Her breath hitched. He was coming back.

"Hesper, will you hear me out?" He pulled a chair away from the table and turned it toward her. "I'm doing the best I can in a system that is royally screwed up." Seating himself, he pointed. "If you tell anyone I said that, I'll have to give you more chocolate. Up your nose or something." He grinned. "Sorry. Trying to be funny again . . . and failing." Fingers drumming on the table, he sighed in such a frustrated manner, he had to be angry. The drumming stopped abruptly, his palm pressed onto the table.

"If you can find the strength to open your heart to someone you don't trust, I promise I will not make you regret it. I respect you and your feelings, and I want to approach on your terms to the best of my ability, given the circumstance. I believe the way to your heart is through here." He touched the side of her brow. "Everything is through there, of course, though not in the way you, particularly, need. I don't know what that courtship will look like, but I am up for the challenge."

Slowly, her eyes drifted upward to his. "You have earned my friendship, sir."

He smiled. "If you're comfortable, you can call me David. Any time."

"David." Her face stung, so she looked away from him. I know you see it," she said. "I blush. It is less embarrassing if I let you know that I know."

"Why do you think you're blushing?"

"Am I not?"

"'Course you are," he laughed. "Will you tell me why?"

"I do not know."

His fingertips, like cool drops of rain on her cheek, turned her toward him again. "Aw. Yes, you do. Anger? Frustration? Embarrassment?" His smile was so like Adahy's. David did feel more like a comrade than an enemy. Someone who sympathized and cared. Like a . . . human.

"I feel like grass," she said, her voice hoarse. The words were a relief—almost a pleasure—that she would soon regret. The feeling painted a picture in her mind and stirred up sensations she could not describe without . . . poetry.

"Your hope that I will like you makes me feel that you are running through the grass, rousing a glittering cloud of fireflies inside of me."

Smiling bewilderment enlivened his face as he flopped back in his chair and giggled. Traces of the giggle lingered in his voice as he said, "Who's wooing who here?"

"I think you are trying to woo me."

A slow smile worked its way into his lips. "Yeah, that's what I thought, too. Bested while playing my favorite game. The moment you said that, I tell you, my insides quite exploded with flappy-flying creatures. Maybe they're fireflies, too. Though you haven't gone barging into my grass without invitation, as I have yours."

He took her hand. "You're both fascinated and frightened by all the fireflies, I think. Is it even possible? Are they really glowing, or are you imagining it? Is the glow fake? Am I just baiting you? And, above all, what are you supposed to do with them?" He kissed her hand and held it between both of his. "Honey, you don't have to pretend to be okay with everything. I hope I can draw sunshine from your eyes and bring roses to your cheeks for good, but even if I don't, the moonbeams and lilies are equally enchanting."

The roses, warm with summer heat and prickly with thorns, bloomed into her cheeks in a new way. Her breath caught as she mentally scrabbled for her resolve and self-control before it let loose and she acted irrationally.

"We're going to be all right," David said. "If this were a song, I'd say we have a major seventh chord on the horizon." He reached up and cooled her cheek in his palm. "I don't expect you to understand it now. It'll make sense eventually."

In a short time, his strong, smooth hand had been with her through enough fear to last a lifetime. The masculine touch both cleared and clouded her mind.

David drew back. "I'm leaving this conversation here," he declared, "because I'm on the verge of going moony." He fanned himself, batting his eyelids. "I can't have you taking advantage of me in my emotionally weakened state. Also, I have a meeting with the Kyrios in an hour, and I'm too old to deal with them after being charmed out of my senses without a nap in between. I'll be in my room if you need me. Otherwise, stay out of trouble, will you?" He gave her one more wink and a smile and left her alone.

She would probably be married by the time another realistic escape opportunity arrived. Relationship consummated, body possessed, and the first pleasures lost . . . or gained. At the thought, she trembled inside, burning with hatred for the feelings David stirred up in her. Feelings she admitted. Awful, horrible, wonderful feelings that were nothing like hatred. Truthfully, she was okay with that.

But Adahy.

She was not as strong as she thought she was before someone truly challenged her—until someone challenged her love for Adahy. She was lying to herself about her feelings for the sake of upholding the principles that were dear to her.

No. Worse!

It was not about principles. It was about her pride in upholding them. Only pride.

At least she was being honest with herself now. It was not hard to become a stig, after all.

Just think of those babies.

David's gift still waited in front of her. He had the chocolate wrapped in brown paper, like a dried leaf, and tied with white string. She pulled the string, and the paper came off with little effort. The next layer, a sheath of shining silver, crinkled as she pulled it away from the dark brown bar. It smelled a little earthy, saccharine, and reminiscent of cedarwood. Sweet and bitter, the chocolate melted over her tongue with unrivaled smoothness. Better than maple sugar.

It was good.

It was very good.

But it was not *nepenthe*.

Thirteen | Post-Conquest: 232

HESPER ENTERED THE honeyed-rose room and touched the blue woman's hand as she passed. It was only art, but it gave Hesper thoughts of fresh herbs in her hand and soil on her fingers, filled with the life-giving energy she experienced while supporting laboring women as they birthed their children. The intoxicating light of human freedom.

This room felt good. Still, good feelings could not protect her from herself, though she wished it were so. All wrapped up in goodness, she crashed. She had allowed David to manipulate her feelings, rather than fighting to the death, and now she did not deserve Adahy.

Maybe manipulate was not the word. He did seem genuine. Still, he handled her feelings and turned her mind and affection toward him. It did not have to be malicious to be manipulation.

She squeezed the blue woman's cold, hard hand, trying to milk comfort and support from it. It offered no motherly warmth, only strong silence. Sometimes strong silence was preferable.

Right and wrong, loyalty and perfidy all mixed together. Could she make the wrong place the right one by doing the right thing? Could she love her enemy and heal without discrimination? It would never bring her back to Adahy, though. That wrong would never be right.

Where was the light? The outside world was supposed to be a place with so much light, but it was nothing compared to the darkness of her tormented conscience. She had nowhere to turn to for relief. She would just have to live with it.

She closed her eyes to still her mind.

Adahy's laugh sliced into the silence, startling her. His voice, given to him by the forest, rang out with the camphorous strength and mild coolness of a pine. It brought so many memories to her. David's voice followed, warm and boyish.

Dressed in loose trousers and sweat-drenched shirts, David and his brother entered the room glowing from physical activity with energized smiles and breathless laughter. Cole left the room the moment he saw Hesper, but she had seen him, too.

The most ridiculous thought came into her mind. Adahy?

Hesper's eye snagged on the drawing of a pink flower on the side of David's exposed bicep.

"Well, hello." David's jovial mood blossomed into a comfortable tenderness.

Was he . . . happy to see her?

"I headed to my room for my old-man nappy-poo when Cole lured me into a match, claiming it would energize me better than a nap. Not sure if it's worked. Guessing not, 'cause he thumped me this time." He laughed. "But excuse me, Hesper, my brother's rude. It's just his nature. I'm going to have a chat with him."

David followed Cole, calling for him before he had even stepped out of the room. "What is your problem, Cole?" In the foyer, he continued with a softer voice. "I've never seen you behave so rudely, and that's saying something! Are you allergic to Gentles all of a sudden, you boob?"

The men's footsteps and bickering faded away and disappeared into another part of the house.

Adahy was no stiff, baby-faced Meros man. The elders approved him. He had proven himself. Cole was not Adahy. She just missed him and saw what she loved where it was not, just as she felt love where it was not—where it could not be.

* * *

Hesper slept through much of the afternoon. The dream of Adahy and Joram began repeatedly, but she woke up in the middle of it each time. Considering her situation and anxiety, the dream was to be expected, but it played out in an unusual way. More aware of the fact that she dreamed, adult Hesper tried to get through to little Hesper who broke the twig off the tree, called it Cassia, and laid it in a bed of orange pine needles.

It is okay. It is only a dream. You are not truly living this. Move away from it. Forget about it.

On the dream's third attempt to get through, just before little Hesper would see Joram in a Meros uniform, four hard knocks roused grown Hesper from her sleep.

Neck and back slick with sweat, she sat up and looked around trying to remember where she was, to understand the lines of gold light and shadows streaking the room.

The door rattled with another four knocks.

"I am here," she slurred.

A man's voice called through the door. "Yes, I know."

She rolled off the bed and opened the door. Cole waited, hands behind his back, shoulders squared, his bare chin up and feet together. His hard appearance softened when he saw her. "I apologize for my rude behavior earlier, miss."

Cole's gold buttons were shinier than David's. Cole was taller, too, so it was harder to avoid them. She lifted her head to acknowledge his words.

His face grew cold. "I've been assigned the task of fetching you for dinner. I hope you will come." His fingers wiggled, and he reached up to adjust his tie.

She shook her head as if to decline. "I will be there shortly."

"I've been asked to escort you." He cleared his throat and held out his arm.

"I can walk without that."

Smothering a smile, he drew his lips into a hard line. Either he demonstrated a disgusting measure of contempt and arrogance, or he struggled to stifle friendliness. She slipped past him into the hallway. "Why did you smile?"

He chuckled. "You may have caught on that the Meros are fascinated with the psyche. Psychology is emphasized in our education from a young age. Whether we're discussing law, history, culture—anything."

He gestured for her to walk with him. "While my work is in law and culture, my understanding of psychology bleeds into that work. That being said, it's a pleasure to see a Gentle adhering to the moral customs of her people. I expect you'll be an interesting case." He paused. "I wonder how long you will hold up."

"I have been forced from my customs more than once here. Why do the Meros do that? Is it intentional?"

"Yes, miss. The Meros use mind control and varying levels of hypnosis, and, uh, other methods, occasionally. It's subtle but potent." He pulled at the white cloth under his sleeve. "I rather enjoy watching Gentle minds break as much as David delights in putting them together. An interesting business: deconstructing and rebuilding the psyche."

"Why do you not like me?" she asked. "What have I done to earn your contempt?"

He cast a couple of quick glances at her. "Are you always this direct?"

She reached for the end of her hair behind her back. "Direct?"

"Asking uncomfortable questions of people who you hardly know."

"I did not know it was an uncomfortable question."

"Hmph." His eyes swept over her. "I have no dislike for you, miss."

Her chest ached. How could Adahy be here? Adahy would not do this. Adahy would not lie. He would see her and tell the truth right away. He would not insult her and say the rude things Cole did.

"Are you related to any Unified?" she asked.

A few steps ahead, one hand tucked into a pocket, Cole spat, "Why would you ask such a thing? I'm no mongrel. The idea is offensive to me."

"Are you always this direct?" she retorted. "Offending people you hardly know?"

He faced her and smirked. "*Touché.* Fair enough."

Emboldened by the neutral response, she persisted. "Are you? It might offend you to be related, but are you? Because you remind me of a man I know. Your voice, even. Do you have another brother?"

"We can talk about this another time." Cole strode away to the dining room.

David rose from his seat at the head of the table and came forward to greet Hesper and kiss her forehead. It did not bother her as much now that his affection felt real and less threatening. The pleasant feeling from his touch, though resented, still was pleasant.

"How do you feel, Love?" His hands held her face, smoldering through her principles. She swallowed and cleared her throat. "I am well enough."

His eyes seemed to will her gaze to meet his own. With pursed lips, he studied her face, stroking her cheek with his thumbs, close enough to smell.

She sniffed. It really was a good, fruity, fresh smell.

Melting into his hands would bring her relief. Safety. Warmth. Love. All the things she had lost. If she leaned on him—such a simple thing—he would put his arms around her, and she would let herself love him, forget the tension, and rest.

Rest in light.

He must stop looking at her.

She needed air, trees, freedom. She might go crazy trapped inside these walls, away from thoughts of everything except David. Closed off—

"Are we going to eat or make out?" Cole snapped. "If the latter, kindly take your prey elsewhere so we can eat without throwing up. I haven't got anyone properly Stockholm syndromized or hypnotized—whatever you've got going on—and I'd rather eat food, honestly."

"I am well," Hesper insisted.

David ignored Cole, communicating affectionate disbelief with his eyes. He swiped Hesper's almost-tear away, then he let her go and returned to his seat.

"Brother dear"—David placed a napkin on his lap—"it comes down to understanding a few things about the female psyche and acting accordingly, not hypnosis or syndromes." Staring at Cole, David bit his bottom lip, winked, and said, "Don't blame me for your ineffective neanderthalic charm. We don't all need tricks to be likable. Maybe you should appeal to the Book of Light about it, the way you've been dreaming. Perhaps it will assist you in balancing religion with agreeableness."

Hesper groaned internally when Cole sat at the end of the table beside her. As Lorelei served their meal, Jade leaned in to whisper, "Make sure you cover your food in case Cole has another allergic reaction to you."

Hesper cracked a smile, but Cole made her too uncomfortable to let herself feel it.

"Miss Hesper, how do you like it here?" Cole asked.

"I hate it." She stared into her soup. She might even hate *him*.

"Is that so?"

"Yes."

"David is fond of you, you know. He's a good man, my brother."

"I know he is."

He cleared his throat. "David says you arrived only yesterday." His eyes alone darted toward David, who was preoccupied in a conversation with Anise. When Cole directed his attention Hesper's way again, he burned with an uncomfortable focus and fire that she did not appreciate.

"He's gifted at manipulating people to stir up affection and garner loyalty." Cole twirled a spoon in his hand as he spoke. "I've never seen him succeed so quickly. You've adapted to our customs quite well. It's almost as if you wish to stay. No escapes? You're just going to sit here and take this?"

Hesper scowled. As if she would tell him.

As if he wanted answers.

He wrinkled his nose and pasted on a maddening condescending smile. "I enjoy watching Gentles run." He paused, eyes sparkling with amusement. Waiting to see her reaction? "You know what I think? I think you're smart and trying to earn trust to get out of here."

Hesper held her spoon in her soup and stared hard at a floating carrot. "Or so he trusts me enough to let me help with food preparation."

"What's that supposed to mean?" Cole held his spoon half-way between the bowl and his mouth, glaring at her.

She shrugged. "Enjoy your soup."

"In your position, respect will do more for you than smarts will, miss."

* * *

Jade opened the door next to David and Evelyn's and turned on a light. With a match, she lit a sort of stick on a small table in the corner.

"Incense," she explained. "Juniper and geranium." Seated on a mat on the floor, she beckoned to Hesper. "What did you do all afternoon?"

Hesper knelt. "Nothing. I slept and thought."

"I painted. Want to see?" Jade stood and half-skipped to an easel facing the window. Smiling, she invited Hesper to approach. The painted child's fat, freckled face glowed with life. So real, Hesper wanted to touch its wild curling wisps of fiery hair. It bore a striking resemblance to Jade, but David's eyes were unmistakable.

"Is it you?"

"No. It's a picture from my mind." Jade bit her lip as she considered her work.

"It is beautiful," Hesper said.

Jade lit up. "Really? I'm glad you think so. I named her Merrily."

"A good name."

Jade's lively smile died and went stiff. "Anyway."

Now. Now was the time to ask. "Are you afraid to leave?" The question earned a fleeting frown from Jade. "What do you mean?"

"I tried to escape."

"I know." The heaviness lifted, and Jade laughed. "David and I watched you from the dining room. He caught me going to my room and started talking to me, and we wound up in the dining room just before you did it. He expected you to make a run for it. I didn't think you would, but he insisted your body language told him otherwise. Then you did it! He shouted, 'a-a-a-a-a-and she's off!' and hummed music for you to run to."

He WHAT? "I want to be offended." Hesper laughed.

"Don't be offended. It's funny."

"Why do you want to stay here?" Hesper asked. "Do you want to leave? I stopped because I want you to go with me. Will you go with me, Jade?"

Jade sobered. "No, Hesper. I'm married. I love David, and he loves me, and I want to stay with him. I have nowhere to go. No one to love me out there." Her delicate hand swept Hesper's idea away, toward the window.

Hesper loved her. Was that not enough? Of course not. Even love from a married Meros man sounded better than being a pariah. Up and down, indecisive, losing her mind in a sea of hormones, feelings, thoughts, anger—all on the edge of unity. Hesper took Jade's hand. "I . . . I love you."

Jade uttered a squeak of sympathy and kissed Hesper's cheek. "I'm going to stay here because I believe it's what God wants. I gave my life and hopes to It so that It'll flow through me. Whatever happens, I'm in Love's hands."

Swallowing hard, Hesper managed, "I do not understand what that means, but, somehow, I do understand what you mean."

"For now," Jade said, "we should enjoy the good moments. Have you ever played chess?"

* * *

After Hesper learned the basics of chess, she played against Jade several times. Jade won each game, because, allegedly, Hesper sacrificed rooks too readily.

Later, as twilight melted into darkness, Jade put the board and pieces away and crossed the room. *Click.* It went dark.

"It's a full moon tonight, see?" She cast a crazy, smiling glance at Hesper, gesturing to the window. Then Hesper lost her to the glow. Absorbed with the moon-splashed world outside, Jade did not speak for several minutes, like a child, fascinated by the activities of adults, expecting life to be happy. Hesper stared through the window at the gray world. How did Jade see anything else?

"The moon is my favorite thing in the whole world," Jade said, at last.

Hesper slid off the bed and sat on the floor beside her. Jade put her arm around Hesper. "You're crying."

Hesper smiled. "Am I?" She wiped her eyes. "Do you always make everything wonderful?"

"No." Jade giggled. "The moon does that. Anything is better dipped in silver. It nourishes the good in me."

Silver, not gray, silver.

Jade rested her head on Hesper's shoulder then fit their fingers together, placing their hands in Hesper's lap.

"Tell me about your home," Jade said.

After a long time of talking about life and experiences, Jade fell asleep relaying the story of her first kiss. David gave it to her when she was ready for it—only when she said she was.

"A gift wrapped in a smile and arm-ribbons. A comfortable, hot, sweet kiss, like a mugful of drinking chocolate made with cream."

Which made sense to Hesper without much thought, even though she had never experienced a kiss or drinking chocolate herself. Just the idea and sound of the words reminded her of David.

Hesper stroked Jade's short, blazing hair and admired her freckled shoulders awhile before waking and helping her into her bed.

The streets would be abandoned now, and David was asleep. The odds might be in her favor if she chose to flee, but she did not have the desire to do it. Besides the fear of David losing his temper, what about Jade and her baby? That alone made her chest ache.

David had said Hesper had to be spoken for within two weeks, perhaps she stood a chance of convincing Jade to leave before she ran out of time.

Fourteen | Post-Conquest: 232

HESPER SLID THE token over her head and deposited it in one of the envelopes David had given her. Adahy's dear name condemned her, scratched across the envelope in black ink. She held it to her chest and wept in her hand.

No more of this nonsense.

She slid her sleeve under her nose and swiped her eyes with her hands. This people, their god, their laws, and her loss must be faced with dignity and strength—beginning with Cole. He might reject the idea altogether, but she would face him as an equal in her mind.

If she could escape with Jade, she would. Until then, it was time to make peace with the moment, while maintaining hope for Meros humanity and Adahy's courage and loyalty. It was the only way to stay alive. While giving up the token might be a piddly symbolic gesture to bolster her strength, if it worked, it was worth it.

* * *

The hallway to Cole's room glowed with diffused moonlight from the long window on the right. The door at the end of the hallway was open, and the room was dark. Perhaps she could just leave the note? No. She needed to talk to him. Darkness did not have to mean he was not there. She lived in moderate darkness much of her life, after all.

Moonlight shone through a glass wall, dimly illuminating ceiling-high shelves of shadowy, blue-tinted books. A dark doorway gaped at her from the right. Furs, strewn across Cole's bed, testified to his Unified interests. The hunter bag resting against it, however, spoke of darker, deeper connections.

Bead poppies on the flap. Unmistakable bright red, even in the moonlight.

It could not be, though it had to be. With a quick glance over her shoulder, she tip-toed to the bag and knelt, setting her envelope aside. Hot with rage, she opened the bag, shoved her hand in, and dug out the bottle of bug repellent. *The snake!* She pulled the cork and dumped the bottle's lemongrass and geranium contents on the floor.

I hope every tick and mosquito in the forest finds you and drains the blood from your body!

She did not mean it.

Yes, she did.

Not truly.

Her head. Her lungs. Her stomach. Her insides all bunched up.

A light from the hallway cast her shadow on the floor, followed by quiet footsteps. Petrified, she took a sharp breath and willed her leaden feet to move. Legs and arms trembled in the struggle against her terror as she half staggered to the gaping black doorway at her right. Just as she plunged into the darkness and tucked herself behind the wall, the quick, quiet steps emerged from the hallway. The room she had been in lit up and threw a swath of light several feet into her hiding area. Fortunately, the wall and its shadow concealed her.

Loud steps followed the quiet ones.

David spoke first. "All right. What is it you want to talk about? Can we resolve this, or are you going to beat around the bush again?" He paused. "You smell something sweet and lemony?"

A book slid out of its shelf. Skin whispered on paper, pages fanned and flipped.

"Your new Gentle . . ." Adahy's voice. Cole's voice.

The book clapped shut.

"Yeah, I figured that's what this was. It's all you can think about."

"I th—"

"What?"

The book slid back into its place with a gentle *thunk*.

On the day they kidnapped her, the terrible *boom* knocked Hesper to the ground. Cracking tree branches and rolling thunder startled her from time to time, but the rustling of the envelope exceeded them all. She left it on the floor by the bag!

Cole's voice wobbled. "What have you told her, David?"

"Told her? About what? What is that?"

Stern, Cole's voice came closer to Hesper's door. "About my mission. About me."

"Nothing. Absolutely nothing you didn't hear me say. I swear it. Why?"

"This has been the worst day of my life," Cole muttered.

David spoke too quietly this time. Hesper directed her ear toward the room and struck something with her shoulder. Such a little thing to cause so much chaos. The lights came on, wolves howled in her mind, and sweat dampened her skin. She gasped and scrambled to find the traitorous . . . what? Bumped thing?

Someone was looking at her.

Tears came, regardless of her attempts to breathe them away and cover them up. Quiet ones, at least. What was the use in not looking? She faced the problem behind her with shoulders back and weakness dripping from her eyes.

David stood there, brow knit with sympathy, amusement crinkling the corners of his eyes. Unable to look him in the face, Hesper pulled her shoulders back and lifted her chin.

"C'mon out, Hesper," he whispered. "It's okay."

She took his offered hand, and he led her into the open, where Cole had his back to them.

"Will you leave us alone for a few moments, Dave?"

David sighed. "What's going on, Cole?"

"Give us a moment," Cole barked.

"I'm not going to ditch her with you."

"She and I need to discuss Gentle topics." He shook the envelope.

"Top secret as all that?"

"Yes."

David's eyebrows shot upward in surprise. He took Hesper's shoulders. "Do you understand why he wants to talk to you alone?"

"Maybe."

"Are you okay with this?"

When she did not answer, he held her shoulders a little tighter.

Cole would not hurt her, and she had no reason to fear his words anymore. "Ye—yes. I am okay with it."

One of David's eyes twitched. Still looking at Hesper, he said to Cole, "Listen, you and I know you're harmless, but you be nice— kindness might be too much to ask." He faced his brother and scowled. "Don't scare her."

Cole clicked his tongue and assumed an expression of snarky boredom as he put his hands out. "She's as sacred as the Book of Light."

David squeezed and released her hand, then walked away.

Immediately, Cole's voice crawled out of a deep, dark hole. "Why are you in my room?" he asked, removing his coat and laying it over the back of a large, soft chair a few feet away.

"I hoped you would deliver that to my community for a hunter I know." She paused. "Your coming startled me, and I did not think things through, so I hid. I am not here to do anything wrong."

Except to dump out his repellent. What a waste.

With the envelope in one hand and the token in the other, Cole wavered between kindness and pride. The deliberation passed between his jaw and eyes. A flicker of tenderness, then a twitch of his jaw.

A flicker.

A twitch.

A flicker—

The twitch of his jaw.

"Do you think my years of hard work and schooling have brought me to the prestigious career of a delivery boy?"

He removed his hat and tossed it to the side. What had appeared to be very short hair, was long hair tied up on top of his head.

Hesper's mouth went dry. "No. No, sir. I hoped you would do me this favor when it is convenient for you. I would appreciate it, though I know you do not like me." She looked up. "Or do you? You still look familiar."

"You're seeing things."

The truth. The horrible truth.

"Yes, I am," she whispered, choking on her words. "Strange things that make my heart pound. Impossible things."

Cole snickered. "I know what you're doing, you realize. You hope that the fellow this belongs to will take it as a message and come to rescue you."

Twisting his mouth as with a bitter taste, he said, "I'll deliver it. Only because I know this hunter quite well, believe it or not. He told me, just yesterday, of his impending marriage and described the virtue and charm of the young lady. His praise was not without merit, I see." A lifeless smile curled up on his face. "I'm sorry we took you from him. It will grieve him to know you're with us. Are you sure you want to return this?" He held the coin out. His tone, cold and hard, pressed on Hesper's courage. "I assume it's a betrothal token."

"Yes. Return it. He will need it again someday."

Cole shook his head. "Knowing him and what he said of you, that's not likely."

Hesper choked a sob back. "Return it. It is just another lie."

All the cold hardness melted away with his long, quiet sigh. "Are we understanding each other, Hesper?"

She clutched her chest. The sobs would not come out. Only in.

"Will you allow me to explain?" He stepped forward.

She stepped backward. "You lied to me. To all of us. When I saw you at my door to take me to dinner, I could not believe Adahy would do this. You acted so stiffly Meros, it gave me enough doubt. I refused to accept that you were a traitor and a spy. Poetry about you prevented me from accepting obvious facts."

Adahy was only a pervert looking to try an authentic milk-face before buying one at an auction. A liar with no affection for her, duping her, making a fool of her.

But she had felt his love.

She had felt his love?

Yes, she did.

She did.

"I hate poetry!" she cried. "It is the only way to explain things anymore!"

"Hesper, please sit before you hurt yourself. I'm still the man you have known all these years."

"I will not hurt myself! This dress does not make me weak!" she shouted. "Faithfulness to your personality cannot atone for this any more than a dagger through the heart can heal the wound simply because the dagger is pretty." She spat on the floor. "I want to say horrible things to you. Things I would be ashamed to say. I cannot. But I am thinking them."

Cole put his hands in his pockets and said, quiet and steady, "I welcome your thoughts."

"I cannot mean them, though I want to. I want light. I just want the darkness to go away."

"Say words you do mean, Hesper. No matter what they are or how wise or foolish you think they sound. Sometimes the truth gives us light. Light doesn't ride only on kind words."

Fine. He asked for it.

"I feel an ache in my body"—she grasped at her chest—"when I think I would have married, given children to, and offered myself to a stranger. You're a wolf who lurked about, waiting patiently for a little deer to grow, fatten, and fall upon your teeth." She covered her mouth. This was crude, inappropriate, and bitter.

"Go on, Hesper."

"Wolves have no regret," she whispered, "because they are wolves, and they do what is natural to them. Like you, Meros."

"Those are words you mean?"

Did she? Did she mean them?

She stood in his house, expressing painful words and weeping in his presence. He allowed her to berate and accuse him without retaliating, even though he could. Both were vulnerable in their own way. It spoke well of him.

"Hesper, I respect you and your feelings about this."

Affection and repulsion mixed together in her mind. She only loved his memory, not him. Like the body of a dead loved one.

Like her own character.

He was not the only traitor in the room.

"I must address my own weaknesses," she said. "I have been untrue to Adahy. Since you are Adahy, I must tell you, even though I am so angry I would sooner strike you." She wiped her tears, as angry with them as she was with him. "I allowed myself to be touched and to have feelings that are new to me. Hardly gone for a day and I show my lack of integrity. In this way, I do not deserve Adahy."

With as much humble pride as she could muster, she lowered herself to the ground to take his feet. "My plea is for forgiveness that I do not deserve. I am no better than a stig. If you grant me your forgiveness, I am at your mercy."

He seated himself by her head, leaving his feet under her hands. "You must feel this guilt strongly, Hesper," he said, "to believe that you have done something so awful that the plea seemed appropriate when asking for forgiveness. My God, why would you be asking me for forgiveness, my friend?

"If I say I forgive you and touch your head, you will get up and run away when I want you to hear me." A deep breath. "Listen, I kept your people alive. I went from community to community, learning of you and reporting to the Kyrios on your strength. My research may have been the only thing keeping them from wiping you out. They want you gone for religious and economic reasons.

"And the Earth People are becoming such a problem, the Kyrios were going to put an end to it all, which they could, because this base contains a mere fraction of the Meros army. There are more Meros soldiers than civilians. Well-trained, with weapons your people don't know anything about.

"The Kyrios see what I see, and I saw a dangerous force with unexpected weaponry and excellent intercommunal communication. That made you far more mysterious than they were willing to chance. Especially knowing how effectively your people have warded off the rogue attacks of armed civilians. My action bought time for the Unified." He slid his feet out from under Hesper's hands and rested his head beside hers.

"I am not a stranger," he said. "Becoming your husband was precious to me. My love for you is sincere. Once I determined to marry you, I refused to even shake hands with a woman. I have been completely yours here as much as there, and I need your forgiveness for lying and putting you through this."

He was not the same. This could never be what she had hoped it would be.

He placed his hand near hers. "You have done nothing wrong. I am open to you, Hesper, for anything you need or want." He touched the back of her head. "As I've always been, with or without the plea."

Hesper and Cole sat upright as David strode in and lurched to a halt. Hands in his pockets, David bounced on the balls of his feet. "Ah." A twist of the jaw. "Should I be troubled?"

"No, no." Cole stood and faced him. "A Gentle custom. That's all."

Hesper rose and turned away to wipe her face.

David grunted. "Uh-huh. I'm familiar with it. They try to use it when they get arrested sometimes. I see someone's been spitting. I'm pretty sure I know who it was." His eyes flickered toward Hesper.

"I am well, sir." Hesper bowed her head to Cole out of respect, and Cole returned the gesture. She charged toward the door, her vision blurring, sobs rising, and she almost made it out of the room before crying. Instead, she broke down against the wall and let David hold her.

Cole could die for all she cared.

Oh, but the memory of Adahy. She cared. She cared.

Fifteen | Post-Conquest: 232

TWENTY MINUTES UNDER a screaming-hot shower and David was finally considering getting out. He was up to work out before sunrise, as usual, but his mind hadn't been in it. Trinity called to demand he get "his Gentle" to the doctor and to summon him to a mid-morning meeting concerning a natural disaster in his jurisdiction. He couldn't focus after that. At least he worked up a sweat and went through the motions. That was worth something. Right? Right.

His life had never been free of drama, but since Hesper arrived, the illusion of peace had all but disappeared. Jade was acting strange, his cold war with Evelyn turned hot, his own conscience started shooting brimstone and ash all over the place, and small as it was, his tattoos were itching and burning these days. Just one more thing to deal with.

It was a strange comparison, but Hesper's coming kind of felt like the old days when he wasn't legally permitted to have sex because he was a teenager. He'd find a hiding place and take his girl of choice there, and a senior officer or some other individual with a blasted flashlight would find them *in flagrante delicto* and send them running like a pair of yowling alley cats. He ran home yanking his pants up more times than he could count. Hesper was a flashlight that washed out his boldness. Those eyes saw everything, it seemed. She never closed them even when she closed them.

He turned off the water and yanked his towel down from the shower door to dry himself. With the towel wrapped around his waist, he stepped out of the warm stall and onto the cold tile floor. In front of the mirror, he inspected the in-shower shaving job, twitched his pecs, flexed his arms, then twisted his torso to look at the tiny, itchy chapati tattooed at the base of his neck. He got it at the same time as the lotus on his arm and couldn't remember the act of getting either one. When he first saw it, he thought it was a moon, but the colors weren't right. Chapati was delicious, so chapati it was.

Only a drunk would get a friggin' flatbread tattoo.

He used to laugh when he thought of it. As he got older, it bothered him a little more for some reason.

Out of the light, cool colors of the bathroom, and into the dark wood and sapphire damask of the bedroom, David went for his drawers. Evelyn faced the mirror by their bed, putting in her earrings.

The colorless, unimpressive sunrise blazed bright white through the sheers as the house resurrected with early morning rituals. Doors opened and closed, faucets ran, laughs tinkled down the hall, mincing female feet pattered, and occasionally, a shriek of delight added an exclamation point to the often-delightful polygamous prison sentence.

"You think she's pregnant again?" Evelyn asked.

David opened his top drawer. "What? No."

"I do. You need to be more careful with the poor creatures."

"I'm meticulous concerning the care of those dear women. Her pregnancy baffles me to this day." He pulled up his boxers.

"Of course. You're David." She misted perfume on her neck. "God forbid anyone accuse you of being careless or abusive."

Excuse me? "Careless? Never. Abusive?" He strode across the room to stand in front of her. "Have I hit you? Denied you affection? Withheld anything you needed? Food? Water? Freedom? Time to talk? Anything?"

"No."

"Have I divorced you for your affairs or taken a baseball bat to your boyfriends?"

Evelyn's lava-red lips hung open. No more magma to spew? She wouldn't hold his gaze now, and that was a bit disappointing in a strong woman like her.

He nodded. "I don't think we've ever loved each other, Evelyn—that's not why we married—but we could've been good friends with excellent benefits."

"Benefits." She snorted.

"You backed away from lovemaking"—he pointed—"not me. And if you ever try to claim it was because I was selfish, or refused, or inept, or bland, or whatever your bitter mind is thinking up these days, you know full well you'd be lying."

She pursed her lips, tucked a strand of hair behind her ear, fiddled with her neck, buttons, earrings. After living with him for so many years, she had trained herself to keep a blank face to avoid assessment of feelings she wanted hidden. A useless effort. The woman was a veritable treasure trove of tells every day. The face should've been the least of her worries.

"Uh-huh. You aren't denying it. So, let's not attempt to insult me there. There are so many other things you can insult me about, accurately." He frowned. "Hey. Look at me. You're no shrinking violet. Don't be intimidated by a man in his underwear. Man up, woman!"

What a beautiful, hard person. They were just incompatible, and it brought out her worst and made her unhealthy in her heart. Such a pity.

"The abuse is in having so many wives, David."

"Anise was my first wife, Evelyn. No one made you marry me. They made me get married, but no one forced *you*." He took his uniform from his closet and began dressing. "Besides, you have your own men. You just can't marry them. Nothing's keeping you from changing your mind and picking someone else." As if she'd pick one of her lovers. Marriage to a Kyrios successor meant prestige and wealth. Period.

He considered her, buttoning his dress shirt.

"Anise was the second wife," she said. "You and I both recognize that, even if the Kyrios don't. The rest of us were mistakes."

"Not mistakes. Letting Brock Sweeney have Anise for his sadistic thrills would have been a mistake. Letting Vincent have Hesper for his twisted, dark idea of pleasure would've been a mistake."

"So, why is Owl-Eyes so special to you?"

David pressed the top button of his shirt through its hole. "I don't know. She's not exceptionally attractive or affectionate. She's kind of weak in a way."

"She's got something. Something you need."

The couple stood on opposite sides of the bed, staring at each other while David put on his cufflinks.

"You know, I want to love you, Evelyn. I don't want you to be unh—"

"No, you don't. You don't have the guts to love someone who knows you well. Go play with your new toy. Give her a good time, and those thoughts will pass. See you at breakfast."

* * *

David rounded the corner into the dining room. Hesper sat at the table with her head bowed on her arms. She was sinking. Her heart was breaking. This garbage with Cole made the whole thing a bit more complicated, too. Especially since he needed Cole to take her to the doctor today. If she couldn't handle it, regardless of Trinity's orders, it would have to wait.

Lorelei bustled out of the kitchen to set the table with silverware and a basket of fruit as other members of the household trickled into the dining room.

He needed to talk with her. Alone.

"Hesper." A light touch on her shoulder. "Come with me?"

Hesper lifted her head and reached for his hand. *Strange.*

His heart rate accelerated, and his stomach flipped. *Like a dumb kid.* He accepted her strong hand without a word and led her through the foyer to the parlor.

"You're tired," he said.

"I am."

"Will you sit?"

"I might fall asleep." She blinked rapidly, shaking her head.

"What happened last night? With Cole. Something drastic. I mean, you chose to take my hand today. You clearly didn't rest."

She released his hand. "I'm sorry. I was half-asleep. It was rude to just grab your ha—"

"Nope. Flappy-flyers. Right here." He touched his chest. "Remember? They went all over the place. Not rude at all."

She laughed.

"You laughed! She laughed. You laughed? Have I made you laugh before this? I don't think I have."

The familiar bloom diffused through her cheeks. "I do not know."

"Cole said you requested he return your betrothal token to the hunter you were to marry."

"Yes, I did. You said he worked closely with them, so I thought he might help."

"Brave move when considering how rude Cole had been to you. I would have expected you to go to me or Anise about it."

She frowned. "The thought never occurred to me."

"Eh, I guess it makes sense. You're direct. Why would you think of adding a middleman?" David smiled. "Cole said he's doing it, though. It all just seems a little weird. He's acting strangely."

"Nothing is wrong anymore. I have accepted my situation. Your brother was kind enough to help me see it through."

She wouldn't look at him. Was it just her way, or dishonesty? No fidgets, tics, or trembling were manifesting.

David narrowed an eye and nodded. "Uh-huh. Well, that makes the next topic of discussion easier on us both, I hope.

"An important meeting with the Kyrios came up last minute, but you still need to see the doctor to make sure you're healthy. I got a call from Trinity demanding I get your health confirmed immediately." He cringed. "I won't send you alone, though. I've asked Cole to take you this morning. It's the only appointment the doctor has available for the next few days. I hope you don't mind. It's not ideal, but it's better than Evelyn." He lifted his upper lip and bared his teeth in mock terror.

"No, sir. I do not mind. I trust your judgment."

He quirked a half-smile. *Trust.* "Good. If you get a clean bill of health, we can marry any time you'd like. No longer than two weeks, as I said. Whenever you're most comfortable and ready, day or night, we'll settle it, okay?"

"Okay, David."

She didn't seem beat down now. She did in the dining room, but not here, alone with him.

I wonder . . . "Hesper . . ." He laughed at himself a little. "May I kiss you? Be honest. I won't be mad at you if you say no, and I won't make you regret it if you say yes."

Gray moonlight eyes turned his way and inspected his own with alarming intensity. Then they shifted to his lips as if considering them. He didn't want a kiss, necessarily, just trust. Only to be closer to her and have her trust that he wouldn't hurt her.

"Not my lips," she said.

"I wasn't thinking of a particular part of you. Just you." He smiled. "So, that's okay with me."

Hesper stiffened, watching him with the owl-eye look Evelyn liked to make fun of.

Her neck was satin in his palm.

Even then, her eyes persisted.

He gently pressed his lips on her jawline, warm and smooth. Just a kiss on the cheek basically. Almost.

Okay, a low kiss on the cheekish area.

High kiss on the neckish area.

Same thing. Right? Right.

Perfectly still, she drew in a few slow deep breaths. Breaths of self-control. David almost laughed at that. He drew back and couldn't help smiling. Hesper had closed her eyes, and a quiet, euphoric haze lingered around her face. Her lids fluttered and opened, first looking up, then down, then somewhere in the middle, and—bless it all—she giggled. A breathy giggle.

"That was very respectful," she said. "You have my gratitude."

It was, wasn't it? Overall, this was a moment he could be proud of. It had a subtle touch of spice, but little gestures often carried heavy weight, especially for someone like Hesper who'd never been touched with romantic intentions.

"Pish-posh. Gratitude for me? You have *my* gratitude, dear lady."

"For what?"

The feel of soft skin under his hand and mouth, her involuntary, vulnerable tip of the head to offer what his lips asked for, the glow of pleasure on her face.

All that, yes, but something else, too.

"Trust. I won't abuse it. If you ever want to try my trust, let me know." He winked.

* * *

Cole kept a respectful distance as they walked the road to the doctor's office.

This silent walk would kill him. So would this disgusting doctor's appointment. He had half a mind to simply snatch Hesper up and get her off the base. Forget the risks! It would thrill his soul to see her running free right before they shot him.

"What is the place with purple pennants?" Hesper asked.

Thank goodness she was talking.

"The Bastion of Holiness. The Kyrios and their employees work there. It's also a jail. Underground."

"Does David work there?"

"Yes, ma'am."

They stepped into the doctor's office where a brown-haired woman greeted them with a bright red-lipstick smile. "Honored Senior Officer Chandler," she said.

Cole lifted his chin to acknowledge her. "Gwen."

"Exactly on time," Gwen said. "The doctor will see you immediately, Hesper."

Cole turned his hat around and around in his hands as Gwen came out from behind her desk and gestured for Hesper to follow.

"You are not coming with me?"

He gripped his hat. "No. I'm just an escort. It wouldn't be appropriate for me to go in there." He spoke as loudly as he could without yelling. Maybe if Dr. Kratz heard who brought Hesper, he wouldn't try anything with her like he did with the rest.

Gwen led Hesper beyond a door and returned without her. The electric typewriter tapped away for several minutes, stopping for Gwen to take care of other patients coming in for their appointments. The minutes passed, and Cole finally took a seat to wait without fidgeting.

Gwen leaned over and fiddled with something under the desk, coming up with fresh lipstick. "Did you bring her to the base?"

Cole resisted the urge to roll his eyes. This woman knew nothing of subtlety, and man, he hated the bright red lipstick trend.

"No. She arrived Sunday morning. I returned to the base on Sunday night."

"Oh, so she's your brother's?"

Shut up, Gwen. "Yes, that's right."

Gwen laughed. "Your brother falls in love with any Gentle he meets. If you used him on your mission, he could charm the Gentles right out of their woods and completely end the conflict if you weren't so set on your method."

What in blazes did the doctor's receptionist know of his 'method' or mission?

"Charmed and subjugated Gentles doesn't mean the end of the conflict."

She shrugged and brushed a bit of hair behind her ear. "You would know, I suppose." Gwen made a ridiculous show of fanning herself with her hand and undoing her blouse's top button.

The conversation ended with a tasteless comment about Cole's single status.

And Cole's cold shoulder.

Several people arrived during the wait, seating themselves and reading or conversing. The appointment seemed abnormally long. Dr. Kratz's voice warbled through the door occasionally, but nothing louder than that until twenty minutes into the appointment.

Hesper screamed.

Cole stood, took a few steps, stopped. No. He couldn't. It wouldn't be wise.

Or would it?

It was just an examination.

Oh, Hesper.

She screamed again. The doctor's shout followed it this time. Muffled, indistinguishable words flew on the other side of the wall. Cole took a few great strides toward the examination room, but the knob wiggled and shook, stopping him, until Hesper swung the door open and flew out in the fashion of a frantic squirrel. Cole caught her arm as she stumbled over his foot and stabilized herself.

The doctor, an old, bald, mustachioed man with bushy eyebrows, came behind her, bloodied on his nose. "You can tell your brother, based on questioning and an extremely limited examination, she's got a clean bill of health. Blood tests will be ready by tomorrow, though, so he'd best not bed her 'til afterward. Just in case." Dr. Kratz scribbled something on a piece of paper and handed it to Gwen.

"She is very ill-mannered. You'd better teach her quickly before she bites the wrong person." He pointed to his face. "So, if Successor Chandler is distressed by the minimal physical, he'd better come with her to a different appointment to keep her in check while I do what I need to do."

Hesper's jaw dropped. "I am not a baby, and he is not my husband. Meros or not, he will not touch me there. And neither will David!"

"Are you willing to die for your lady parts, milk-face?" the doctor hissed. "No Meros husband will touch you there if I haven't!"

Hesper's face glowed red with indignation.

Cole put on his hat. "Doctor," he said, "you have overstepped your bounds by your unnecessary insults and crude language. She is the property of the Chandler household, and my brother has the right to accuse you before the Kyrios for the maltreatment of his property. I advise you to change your abusive manner toward us. Come along, Hesper."

Cole opened the door and Hesper passed through it. He lifted his chin and his eyebrows to Dr. Kratz—a silent threat before leaving.

Cole observed Hesper unnoticed for a few minutes. She never glanced at him. It seemed unnatural. Deliberate.

He'd lost her forever.

Such a nice day. Sunny, breezy, and totally ruined by that thought.

David did seem to like her. He handled her just-so and quite delicately. *My God, I want to kick him in the face.* Fifteen years! Fifteen years she'd known Cole, and David the sultan just about had her heart in a day. David would handle her right. He would care about her past traumas. He would be loving and patient with her in her frustrations. He would hold her when she had her bad dreams. *No. No. I can't watch it happen.*

He cleared his throat. "What are you thinking, Hesper?"

"You people are sick to send women to that kind of . . . thing."
Her face twisted with emotion. "Doctors are evil."

Sixteen | Post-Conquest: 232

WHIMPERS DRIFTED DOWN the hallway. Quiet, quiet . . . But real. Hesper's hand froze, curled around her doorknob. She listened.

A shout. Crying.

Down the empty corridor, the noise led her to Jade's door, where she pressed her ear to the glossy, cold wood to hear the heated conversation.

"Please! David, don't let this happen again!" Jade's voice.

Evelyn, sharp and unkind, crushed Jade's words. "You let this happen. You didn't tell us. All we ask is that you tell us."

"What business is it of yours, child-bearer? That's all that separates us. You're allowed to have children, and I'm not. Stop acting as if you have authority over me. I married *him*." Jade's anger sounded unnatural for her light voice.

"Evelyn." David's voice now.

Someone cold grabbed Hesper's arm. "What are you doing?"

It was Anise.

"Listening." Hesper tried to jerk her arm away, but Anise held tightly.

"It's none of your business."

"Yes, it is."

"It's Meros business."

Hesper craned her neck to give Anise a good view of her scowl. Kind and well-meaning, perhaps, Anise still was not her mama and never would be. Hesper had been probed, prodded, and pinched, and her patience now reached its threshold.

"No, it is my friend's business." Her face settled into stone as she turned the doorknob. Anise lunged for Hesper's other arm as the door opened, but she was too late. She released Hesper and stayed in the hallway to pace.

Jade lay on the floor, clasping David's feet while Evelyn ransacked the room, looking behind things, under things, in things. Jade sat upright when the door opened. Her magical face, so transparent with its feelings, turned to Hesper, coated with tears like a window on a rainy day.

David crouched and took her face in his hands. "Jade, Jade, you have to understand. There's nothing I can—"

"Call it a miracle, David. Let's go away for a while. We'll come back with the baby in Evelyn's arms."

Choking on his tears, David caressed her face with impotent passion as if trying to take and keep her features in his own care. Brow to brow, they wept together.

"We'll just do that," she squeaked. "Then . . . then you can have a baby, and no one needs to know it was mine." She smiled, hoping, wishing, doubting. "I won't even talk to it. You can sell me, give me away, shoot me in the backyard. Just don't. Please, don't."

Evelyn's searching came to a halt, and she now noticed Hesper. Pointing to the door, she yelled, "Get her out of here!"

Before Hesper could protest, fingers dug into her arm and yanked her out of the room. It took a few moments to get her bearings and understand who was pulling her around and scolding her.

It was Anise again.

"For your own good, don't meddle with the affairs of the Meros! You'd best understand this right here, right now."

Someone else said that once. *Trinity!*

"Right here, right now? Get my head screwed on straight? Is that what you mean? I *meddled* with their *affairs,* while they have *destroyed* my life." Hesper tried to tear away from Anise's icy grip to no avail. Instead, she shoved her chest with her free hand.

Anise's jaw dropped.

What? Did she think Hesper was as placid and settled as the other brainwashed brides?

"Your god sees none of this because it is not a real thing. You cannot trust something you cannot see to defend you, you must do it yourself! You are so far from that truth that you are willing to be a coward and force others to be one, too!" Finger pointed in Anise's face, she growled, "You have no courage, loyalty, or desire for unity with your own people. Traitor!"

"You really don't understand the situation you're in, or how deadly this game can become. You're being foolish, Hesper!" Anise tightened her grip and shook her. "Accept the warmth and love you're offered. This is the only place you'll find it. I choose to survive as our ancestors did. In this way, I'm Unified."

"Passive unity. Selfish unity!"

This must have been how Tane started. Passive resistance to the Meros was outrageous. *What am I becoming?*

The door opened behind them. Anise released Hesper and stepped back, averting her gaze. David closed the door and leaned back against it as the shuddering groan of a laboring mother poured out of him. So far, he had been only pristine, now his field-of-wheat hair and straight-as-a-pine carriage failed under the uncertain wave of tragedy.

"Hesper"—his desperate whisper made her uneasy—"you need to stay out of this and leave Jade alone. She's not in her right mind."

"I will not," Hesper said.

A frowning smile answered her. Hands stuck in his pockets, he passed by and headed toward the stairs to the dining room.

Evelyn emerged from Jade's room and slammed the door behind her. With a quick sneer for Hesper, she strutted after David.

"Hesper," Anise said, taking her by the shoulders. "I know what you're thinking. You are doing quite well here. David is smitten. Do not ruin your chance of a good life. Stay out of that room. It's against the law for a Gentle to disobey her Meros husband. You'll endanger your life."

A fair warning.

Hesper grabbed the doorknob. "He is not my husband yet."

Jade lay on the floor with her hands clasped, muttering under her breath.

"Jade."

Wide-eyed and tearful, she sat up. "I'm pregnant, Hesper."

"I heard that. What is going to happen?" She knelt on the hard floor, knee-to-knee with Jade.

"Jail tonight and a trial tomorrow." Jade took a fistful of her short red hair and squeezed. "Hesper, I can't do this. I would rather die. It hurts my heart."

"Can David stand up to them? Defend you? Convince them they are wrong to do this?"

"Oh, Hesper. It just doesn't work that way." Jade's hand, sticky and warm, grasped Hesper's. Pity shone in her eyes. "No one can change the law. Cole talked them out of a much worse penalty last time, but what can he do now? They'll never hear him."

"Does it matter if no one will hear him? Or is it the trying that matters?"

Jade shrugged and shook her head. Hopeless. She had lost hope already.

"I stand by the truth that my feelings should not determine who I help," Hesper said. "I care about you, Jade, but even if you forbid me to try to help you, I am interested in saving your baby's life, too. They are not able to forbid me, so I will persist."

"That sounds nice, Hesper. You can try if it makes you feel better. Just remember, you're going to suffer for something that's not going to happen. They can't do anything to stop it. Mongrels are mongrels, no matter who loves them."

"Humans are humans!"

Hesper would live without company, love, pleasure or hope for anything more as long as she lived where kindness was the rule—not gentleness.

"I am not equipped for this world. It is a place of nightmares."

"You are," Jade said, "'cause you're here. It's not a mistake. You know how I said that the moon makes everything wonderful? You are your own moon, Hesper. The sun may be on the other side of the world, but the moon is kind enough to reflect it for us. Sunlight is still here. That's the reason I like the moon so much. It's my example."

"I want to think about a way to help you." Hesper stood. A battle against injustice was best begun while the passion was fresh. "Your poetry is nice, but you are in trouble. I am going to go fig—"

David had been standing in the doorway. Hesper's body jerked, and her heart jumped with the surprise. This was, quite possibly, the worst trouble she'd ever been in. Maybe if she left quietly . . . As Hesper slipped by him, he squeezed her hand but said nothing about disobedience or consequences. As a matter of fact, the squeeze seemed thankful. The door closed behind her, shutting David in with Jade, leaving Hesper alone with her thoughts.

Seventeen | Post-Conquest: 232

LIGHT FROM THE full moon painted Hesper's room blue-gray. What had begun as "resting her eyes" to consider her course of action became the rest her body demanded. She traipsed down the hallway to Jade's door. The scent of Jade's incense lingered in the empty room, but she was gone. Hesper's stomach sank and growled.

A dark thing had happened. People had taken away a woman because she did not want them to destroy her child. Thinking it through that way stabbed Hesper somewhere deep and intangible. Things would not look better in the morning. Not this time. Adrenaline surged through her, weakening her knees and hands. A frantic, wild desire to escape pushed her down the hallway and stairs.

Fearless, placid, and ready with many hands to do the work before her, the blue lady of the honeyed-rose room caught Hesper's eyes and thoughts. She stopped at the door to stare.

If a statue could inspire a desire for competence and a sense of loyalty, why couldn't Hesper do the same? She and Jade were kin. They were of the same people, and the Unified had to remain unified or they would lose their identity.

If Hesper steeled herself against the fear of death and pain, she could plead with those who had a voice to speak for her in the outside world. Death would come someday, and pain was just pain.

Perhaps Cole . . . He knew their laws and he helped Jade before. She whipped around the corner into Cole's wing. A small, warm light emanated from his haven. He was awake.

Good.

Bad.

Awful.

No. Good.

She proceeded through the moonlit hallway and stopped at the door, where she lingered in the shadow near the light of sight, breathed deeply, and stepped over the line.

Cole faced his window, away from her. Loose, brown hair hung to his shoulders and he appeared to be reading a book beside a small light that kept the room dim but warm and welcoming. Hopefully, he was unaware of her presence. At least until she was ready.

Unmoving for several minutes, barely breathing, she watched him as he turned his pages. Notes of music expanded, filling the room, touching her emotions like the call of a loon. Her heart swelled, and the music caused a trembling in her, much as Adahy's box of salt had. If only the music gave her courage as much as it gave her heartache.

Why was she even here? The madness she felt in the hallway had passed. And if Cole could do something about Jade, surely, David would have talked to him about it.

Perhaps she only wanted to see Adahy, a piece of home.

Perhaps her motives were selfish.

Perhaps she would never trust herself again.

Cole stood and mumbled something to himself, then chuckled as he sauntered to his bookshelf and slid a thin, dark green book back in its place.

Hesper half-hoped he would see her as he rolled a ladder to the next shelf with a careless hand, though she almost completely hoped he would not.

"Sir." Her voice wavered.

With perfect calm, he whirled around, glasses low on his straight nose, an open book in his hand. "I wondered when you would speak up. It's still sir, even though you know who I am?"

"Do you know what has happened to Jade?"

He clapped the book shut. "No. Tell me."

"She has been caught withholding her suspicion of pregnancy, sir."

"This is the second time," he said, exasperated.

Hesper jumped in quickly. "I do not know what your feelings are on this, sir. I only ask that you be willing, if there is anything in your law that permits it, to defend her."

He said nothing.

"Sir, it is too bold of me to ask, considering our situation and my ignorance. I have seen the grief of a mother who has lost her child. My own mama. I cannot bear not to try to help, and I believe Jade would try for me. I promise to do anything you require of me for your efforts." She bit her lip and winced. "You forgave me, after all."

"Your loyalty is fierce, Hesper." He smiled. "I will see what I can do, but not because of your plea, my friend. You owe me nothing. When is the trial?"

"I do not know. Jade is gone already."

"Are you certain she's pregnant?"

"No, but everyone else is. I must have missed something while I was with the doctor."

"I wonder why the man didn't tell me. I spoke for Jade last time, and we decreased the severity of her punishment. He must assume there's no way out of it now. I give him a hard time about these things, too. Maybe he's ashamed." He crossed his arms and stared at the ceiling. "If Jade would have told them, they would simply sterilize her. Since she concealed it, her life is on the line." He closed his eyes. "Come on, Jade!"

"Sterilize?"

"A procedure that makes it impossible for a woman to have children. Long ago, the Kyrios banned major surgical procedures in the belief that they caused more harm than good—except in this circumstance—so it's a last resort. After two pregnancies, concealed or not, a Gentle woman will be sterilized. Of course, if it's been two *concealed* pregnancies, she's usually going to die." He shrugged. "No need to sterilize a dead woman."

Somber after such an explanation, Hesper cleared the horror from her throat and rasped, "The outside world is worse than any nightmare."

Cole chuckled and put the book back. "You are more right than I hope you will ever know." He crossed the room to stand in front of her. "Listen, I don't know what I can do. Jade's a special person, and you've felt that, too. I hope I can—"

"Me, too." She stepped back. "Sir, as grateful as I am for your forgiveness, I do not feel I can forgive you. If that changes anything, I beg you to reconsider for Jade's sake."

"I'll stand with her. Don't worry about that."

That was all she wanted. Hesper bowed and turned to leave.

"Hesper."

"Yes?"

"Normally, the entire family is to attend a trial, but you're not a Chandler yet. Even if . . . if David insists you come—and he might, because it's the law—I strongly recommend that you feign illness."

"Lie?"

He sighed, flopping his hands to his legs. "Absolutely. If I can't talk them into mercy, their methods of execution are difficult to watch. They'll require you to get your X and make a vow to God. You won't be permitted to simply step outside."

"It is kind of you to look out for me, sir, but I am capable of taking care of myself. We do not all have a god to call on for help. I am strong enough for this."

His face carried so much doubt. "Hesper."

"What?"

"I am going to take a chance that you will hate me more than ever after this, but I beg you not to allow guilt to harden you. Feeling that you have done wrong and never truly cleansing the conscience may lead to a host of mental illnesses." He gestured to her. "Don't let those precious healing hands of yours clench up too tightly. It would be a tragedy."

These hands had done good things and touched many of nature's wonders. Now they were clean and softening. Ridiculous and useless. Hardly precious healing hands.

"There are times when tragedy is necessary."

* * *

Early in the morning, Cole awoke from a short sleep, bathed, dressed in his uniform, and headed to the dining room for an early breakfast. David sat in his usual place, picking at his food.

"Have you slept, Dave?"

As if waking from a dream, David's tired eyes widened and sparked with life. "I'm sorry. I can't believe I didn't tell you."

"I already know. It's fine."

"Who—?"

"Hesper."

Tender fondness swept over his face. Then worry. "I couldn't sleep." He rubbed his brow into wrinkles. "I've never been irresponsible with Jade—I swear it—and she would never be unfaithful. I'm at a loss." He hung his head.

Cole sat at the table. "I'm going to defend her."

David picked up his napkin from his lap and dropped it on the table. "Stand up like a man and let me hug you."

Eighteen | Post-Conquest: 232

THROUGH THE BASTION'S paper-and-ink business of the foyer, the Chandlers followed the blood-red carpet to the Judgment Room. Many had gone up the stairs and through these doors on their feet. Half of them were then carried to the back door and never seen again.

Golden chairs graced the bland, gray stone platforms with a supercilious air. Behind them, a large alcove, separated from the room by a copious curtain of red velvet. The sacred place where they kept the Book of Light would kill the unworthy soul who entered. It was common knowledge that guards were unnecessary because the Book would protect itself. No one dared to sneak in for a look.

Jade stood in the middle of the room with an officer acting as a guard.

Years of scrubbing and disinfecting after executions left numerous bleached patches on the stone floor. Cole and his siblings grew up with its strong fumes, eyes watering from their youth.

"God, I hate it here," Cole mumbled to David, slipping his hand into a pocket for a licorice hard candy. He avoided trials on the base whenever he could. The more he was away, lecturing in universities or training law enforcement warden hopefuls, the better.

"I don't blame you. We don't have good memories of this place."

Cole tucked the candy into his cheek. "That's putting it nicely."

"It's rare that I don't get through to Law Enforcement Councils elsewhere. They're intimidated by the family name." He shook his head. "The Kyrios know me too well. I'm trying to be positive, but whenever I'm in this room I see Mother cutting Uncle Mark's throat and dropping him in his own blood." He swallowed hard and pointed to the spot. "I wanted to speak up, but I couldn't. Now I can speak up and make a difference, but the odds are stacked against us. I'll go insane if I have to see another family member die that way. Especially if they have Trinity perform the execution."

David patted Cole's back. "Whatever happens, I won't blame you, and you shouldn't either." His eyes burned into Cole's consciousness. "Cole, promise you won't lose your mind. Jade wouldn't want it, and neither do I. You were eight years old when that crap hit the fan, but you've been through training now, you've performed more executions than you can count, you know how to turn off the emotions. Even when it's someone close to you."

True. He did. His emotional response to his uncle's execution prompted Mother to send him to Early University "for his own good"—a high honor that he was worthy of but didn't want.

Half of each year he was schooled away from his family, taking advanced classes and enduring physical training beyond anything typically required of military children. Besides education, the university's goal was to take gifted individuals and make them into killing machines. So, he learned to control tears after witnessing and performing an indecent number of executions. Mother got what she wanted.

He completed school and childhood within four years and entered his specialty education at twelve. Everyone except Cole was impressed with that. It was nothing more than youth wasted because he mourned—an overreaction to a healthy expression of grief.

"I believe in you, Cole." David adjusted his tie. "If anyone can find a loophole, it's you."

"It's entirely contingent upon their willingness to see it. Plenty of loopholes and possibilities, but their minds are closed."

Cole left David to talk to Jade. She smiled as he approached. "Did Hesper talk you into this?" she whispered.

"No. She requested my assistance."

"You should be nicer, Cole. The two of you would be so cute together! I can't believe you were going to marry a Gentle. When I heard she was betrothed to Adahy, I just . . . I just! Oh, my God, you scalawag!"

Cole smiled. She had such a clear mind, filled with happy thoughts. "That would take some doing at this point." His lips curved upward without smiling. "I'll do everything I can for you, Jade. Excuse me."

The room echoed with his footsteps as he made his way to David, who stood near the doors with his wives huddled around him like frightened chicks with a mother hen. Hesper stood apart, though, and Evelyn never looked like a frightened chick, no matter how near she stood.

"You have to trust me, Dave."

David squinted. Obviously, he already didn't understand, but after three decades, he knew better than to question Cole if he said such a thing.

"I'll try."

"Did you know he was doing this?" Evelyn hissed.

A subtle eye-roll. "Since this morning."

"And you're letting him?" she scolded. "Jade's beyond defense at this point, David. This will look bad."

David cleared his throat and caught Cole's eyes. "He's a big boy."

Several minutes passed before the Kyrios arrived, late and casual about it, of course. The Reverenced Ones, clad in black uniforms, wore large bronze medallions engraved with the Kyrios' symbol of a circle and five downward rays. Trinity led the way as they filed in from the door at the right and sat in the chairs on the lowest platform.

The two Glorious Ones came behind them and took their seats of honor, a step above the Reverenced Ones, dressed in white tunics, also embroidered with the symbol of the Kyrios.

Vincent had been one of the Glorious Ones for the past ten years. Upon his mother's mysterious death, he fell into his position as if it were a comfortable sofa. This whole trial business almost always appeared to strike him as a nuisance that interrupted the true duty of any male Glorious One: fathering other men's children.

"What is the first of the two charges, and against whom are they directed?" Vincent's deep voice, rich and clear, carried an undercurrent of boredom.

First? There were two? Cole glanced at his brother with a questioning look.

David frowned, confused.

What did Jade do? Did she attack someone? Jade would never . . . Cole raised his hand. "Glorious Ones, I wasn't notified of any other pending charges against the accused. I request the second charge, and all alleged evidence pertaining to the same, be withdrawn from today's proceeding until a later date."

Well, this was stupid beyond belief. As if they would delay the trial for him.

Vincent quirked an eyebrow.

"Glorious One, I've chosen to defend Jade because she is a woman of virtue." Cole pushed up his glasses. "I intend to do whatever I can, even if it means making a fool of myself with requests such as this."

Vincent's equal in authority, Ariana, responded with her high, lilting voice. "We are glad to hear of your Gentle sentiments. We will have to remember."

Gentle sentiments. Please! A pathetic jab Ariana threw his way now and then to make him mad. "I have human sentiments, Glorious One."

Ariana sniffed. "We are not inclined to delay this trial or any part of it, for your lack of information or preparation. The Kyrios are not at fault for counsel's deficiency. We will proceed."

Evelyn stepped forward. "The first charge is second offense concealed pregnancy of a Gentle, Glorious One. Directed against Jade Chandler."

"And the second charge?"

"Witchcraft." Evelyn passed a large envelope to Ariana who opened it and pulled out a thick green rope of braided silk with a single knot in the middle.

Cole blew out a long, quiet breath. Witchcraft didn't get mercy. Never. Not ever. No one dared defend a witch. Their reputation would be destroyed. *Jade, why?*

"What is the witchcraft involved with this?" asked Vincent.

Evelyn explained, "She held it to her heart and repeated a spell in hopes that it would prevent a forced miscarriage. We have an anonymous witness."

"You called on the forces of evil to protect the mongrel in your womb, Jade?" Reverenced One Minh asked.

Such a Minh way of wording it. Newly appointed as a Reverenced One on the council of the Kyrios, she was possibly the most sincere and religious of the bunch. That would change before long.

Jade lifted her face to them. "No, I call on no forces of evil, I called on—I don't know what."

Vincent leaned back in his chair. "Does the defense have anything he could possibly say?"

"Firstly, reconsider the terminology," Cole said. "These practices are no longer associated with a living entity, evil or otherwise. Mere superstition. Tradition even. We don't need to make this into witchcraft, Glorious Ones."

"Semantics, Cole." Vincent chuckled and scratched at his head, shaking his graying black curls. "You're too professional to reduce us to an argument over semantics."

"Not Cole. Senior Officer Chandler," Cole corrected. "As an expert in the customs and laws of the Gentles, regarding the 'who' she invokes, I'm sure she doesn't know. I've been to her community in Section Twenty-Five, and this is a common custom to prevent miscarriage. I believe it has origins in the nature worship of her ancestors, which has since been eradicated from the community, though some of its traditions remain."

"Unsatisfactory. Witchery is in the roots, and witchcraft it remains." Ariana gave a flippant wave of her hand. "Anything she does to take control of her own body is witchcraft, Cole. A means by which God's will may be bypassed. More so if she participates in an activity with direct connections to witchcraft, no matter how ancient the custom's origins may seem."

Ignorant, stupid, closed-minded—Cole bit his tongue. "I propose we find out if she actually called on any forces of evil as Her Reverence"—he gestured to Reverenced One Minh—"suggested she had."

Vincent rubbed his face and sighed as he shifted to lean on the arm of his chair. "Jade, what is the spell you repeated?"

Was he ever not bored? Maybe when he had Trinity in his bed.

Almost cowering, Jade looked to the floor as she answered. "Held fast in this womb, planted by love, child, grow into a beautiful flower." She swallowed hard. Her voice shook as she continued, "Nature will bring you to us safely with good health, sound in body and mind."

"Are there any further arguments to delay justice, Senior Officer Chandler?" Ariana asked.

"No, Glorious One," he said, "I don't impede justice. It is evident Jade never called on forces of evil. She called on her baby!" He took a moment to look at each Kyrios member. Not a single softened face among them. "She may have broken the law, and ignorance of the law is, of course, rarely an excuse, but she wasn't ignorant of this law, and clearly didn't realize her action would be considered a violation. Consider it mere positive thinking or a form of self-hypnosis. This activity has never been seen as witchcraft by anyone else."

Vincent stood. "Are you quite finished, Cole?"

Cole faked a smile and collected himself to speak with restraint. "Senior Officer Chandler. It's Senior Officer Chandler. You speak of my professionalism, Glorious One, but where is yours?"

Vincent raised his hands in surrender. "Nevertheless, nothing you have said will sway us, *honored* Senior Officer. Not concerning witchcraft."

"So, you've reduced justice to something worse than semantics. You've reduced it to mere opinion, Glorious One?"

Vincent laughed and exchanged an obnoxious delighted glance with Ariana. "Oh, dear, dear, Senior Officer Chandler. Interpretation, not opinion."

"Semantics," Cole snapped. "What's the point of this trial? You knew about the charge of witchcraft. Why not kill her and have it over with? What's the point of allowing her to have a trial if your unchecked opinion is the only thing you need?"

"Unchecked opinion?" Ariana cried. "Are you insulting us, Cole?"

"Chandler!" he barked. "Do you *feel* insulted, Glorious One?"

Ariana threw a concerned glance at Vincent, who raised his hand and pressed it down a few times as if that would tamp down the tension.

"Senior Officer Chandler," he said. "You know the law as well as—if not better than—most of us here. Give us a solid, legal reason to declare a proven witch to be innocent."

"I've said what I've said, and it's worth consideration."

They claimed to have a great book of wisdom, yet no one brought it out. No one ever proved they had an informed opinion.

Vincent laughed. "I assure you, we have heard—"

No, no, no, no, no! David was going to be livid after this.

Tough.

Cole crunched down on what little remained of his licorice candy. "I appeal to the Book of Light."

"The Book—Cole," Trinity leaned forward as if to stand, then caught herself. "You've lost your mind."

"No, I haven't. It's a logical step for a lawyer who's dealing with a trial before the Kyrios. It's the most sensible thing I've done in a long time."

"We built our society on the principles of God's Book of Light. It is the skeleton of Meros Law. You'll ruin your reputation with this move," Trinity cautioned him. "It demonstrates a lack of faith and trust in the words of God, and I suggest you let go of it. It's a direct affront to the Glorious Ones."

"Was that supposed to be an argument? Sounded like a desperate regurgitation of freshman law classes . . . Skeleton? We have it wrong. It's the heart and flesh, the blood. It ought to be taught in law school. It's a big book, I suspect, considering the laws we have. Do you believe our ancestor's hard-line interpretation of principles covers the nuances of achieving true justice? Jade's pure heart may stand as justification before God. I insist."

"You may not appeal," Ariana spat. "We know what it contains. It declares that no witch is pure of heart."

Cole folded his arms. "How oddly specific. I want to see it. My professional integrity demands it, and my conscience will not rest if I've not seen it in black and white."

Ariana addressed Vincent. "Let's bring this to a close. We're wasting our time."

Pathetic. Instead of taking a legitimate, legal request seriously, they were brushing him off and painting him as the fool. Not today, Kyrios.

"Very well. I appeal to God. I request a week of daily prayer, seeking God's will concerning access to the Book of Li—doesn't this sound stupid?" He tapped his forehead. "I must request a week of prayer concerning access to the book our laws are built on? During a trial? This should be standard practice."

He'd seen many injustices and horrors in his time as a lawyer, but nothing before this had pushed him over the edge into the unknown of appealing to the Book of Light. Sure, it was insulting. Maybe they needed to be insulted. As a matter of fact, they did need it, and it was about time.

Quick and sharp as lightning, a dark mood descended and sat in their midst. The haughty, sanctimonious forms in their gold chairs remained still, except for the slightest shift of arrogance.

Cole planted his feet and straightened up. "Since God is the Creator of all, and no Meros or man of any nation, including Theocracia, has played a part in Its creation, only God Itself may refuse the appeal. I have *Meros Law* in my personal library if anyone wishes to verify my claims concerning the authority of God. Though, I'm sure we might find it in the Bastion library as well."

David whispered, "Cole, this is going too far. You need to stop."

"I appeal to God," Cole repeated. "I have a point to prove."

Vincent broke off a quiet conversation with Ariana to address him. "We cannot allow this behavior in the Judgment Room, Senior Officer Chandler. If we give in to this, it would not speak well of us or the god we serve. Conduct yourself in a reverential manner, or we will be forced to apply disciplinary action."

Disciplinary action could be anything from a fine to execution.

He would earn their contempt no matter what he did. At least one way was honorable.

"I . . . I appeal to God." Now his fate rested in God's hands.

Ariana's delicate face broke with a scowl. "We must consult with one another in private. Excuse us." The Kyrios made their regal exit to the right.

Expecting David to charge, Cole whirled around to face it. David stormed over to him and spat a harsh whisper, "Cole, what are you doing? No one appeals to God. That's ludicrous. They're going to think I was privy to this, it's going to reflect poorly on all of us!"

Cole anticipated this response, but not with quite so much anger. "How can our system be safe for the Meros people, seeing the Kyrios aren't willing to appeal to anything beyond their own opinions, David?"

"It doesn't matter!" David cried, eyes wide and voice much higher in tone than it had been in a long time. "The system's flaws can't be remedied in a single trial! You screw around with them too much"—a sharp stab of the finger toward the golden chairs—"and you're going to lose any standing that might allow you to make a positive change!"

Cole scoffed. "My standing is based on my bloodline. They can't do anything about that."

"Are you kidding?! It'd serve you better to think of the blood in your veins that keeps you standing and *breathing*, genius!"

Okay. The coward had a point. It wasn't the only point to make, however.

"You're afraid. You run on fear instead of hope. You'll save someone if it gets you off, but won't risk your own blood, water, and spirit to save anyone!"

That was harsh. He'd take it back if he could, but he meant it too much.

David shook his head slowly. "It's too late now, I suppose. Even if you retract your demand, the damage is done."

Jade's firm touch calmed Cole's agitated spirit. For the first time in a long time he was free from Hesper's love, so he gave Jade a gentle hug. There were no honest words to comfort her.

Hesper stepped away from the family and stood before Jade to take her into her arms. It required all of Cole's sense and self-control to refrain from asking David why he didn't comfort his own wife. Sometimes, David was the bravest of men. When dealing with the Kyrios, he was little more than a castrated cream puff.

After a shamefully long thirty-minute recess, the Kyrios returned with composure regained and egos repaired.

Hesper kissed Jade and hurried to her former place beside Dulce as the trial continued.

Vincent approached the family to speak with them. "Senior Officer and Successor Chandler, we are willing to compromise on a prayer for God's will in this matter. However, we have an unconverted Gentle among us. We expect that she will be converted soon, so we're willing to allow her to take her vow and receive the mark now so that she may be present. We understand that newly acquired Gentles require supervision, and it would be imprudent to send her away."

David joined Hesper and whispered in her ear, she asked him something, he responded, and she nodded.

"Yes, Glorious One," David said. "We'll take your offer."

Cole's insides sank. *Oh, Hesper.*

An officer brought the tray of accouterments required for the black X. Reverenced One Minh rose from her seat and led the officer to Hesper. Minh raised her right hand and said, "Press your palm to mine."

Hesper obeyed as Minh's whisper-soft voice recited the vow in a well-rehearsed manner. "Do you declare your future belief in the Creator and bind yourself to righteousness and honesty before It and these witnesses?"

"Yes?"

Had she ever lied before? It was unlikely.

Minh picked up the wireless tattoo machine from the tray and tilted Hesper's head to the side with her free hand. Hesper jerked away to look at and smell the machine, then glanced at Cole just before he leaned forward to offer her cheek to Minh.

Minh's fingers dug into Hesper's cheek and under her chin, cranking her neck too far as she dragged the machine across her face. It was clearly her inexperience, not cruelty, but lack of intent did not make it acceptable.

Minh stopped and cursed. "Girl, stop crying or you'll ruin the machine!"

Ruin the machine with a few tears? Okay, now that was cruel. Cole whispered, "Stop." He cleared his throat and said more loudly, "Stop!"

The Reverenced One scowled and switched off the machine.

"Give me that thing." He swiped the contraption from her hand. "I can do it better than you anyway."

Minh shot a worried look at the Kyrios, which Vincent quickly alleviated with a few lifted fingers of consent. With an air of hurt pride, Minh retreated and sat in her golden chair.

Cole stepped into Minh's place, frowning. "Hesper," he said softly. "I don't want you to have this any more than you do, but if you're going to have it, you'd best receive it from someone who loves you, so it won't hurt as much."

David tipped his head, his eyes inquiring after things he shouldn't know.

David could wait.

Cole slipped the white cloth from his sleeve and put it over the palm of his left hand. Touching her with his skin would only add to the violation. She rested her head in his palm and relaxed as much as could be expected.

He finished the dreaded black X with care and without tears.

The Unified would see her as handled and impure, even though she was the purest person he knew. So many Unified her age didn't take the rules seriously and sneaked off to have their fill of rebellion and forbidden delights. He'd seen it with his own eyes. Yet this woman held her convictions fast and would be treated like a criminal because of some ink in her face. Ink put there by people who did not want the Unified to be unified. This was one aspect of the Unified culture he could never respect.

Vincent stood. "The intention of this prayer is to seek God's will. Let us kneel."

They all knelt, including Vincent, as he uttered eloquent words to God, requesting God's ear, God's will, and God's power with such a clear, clean, robust voice, it had to be a prayer.

Maybe to everyone except Cole.

Cole knew a few things about prayer. His father prayed. He himself prayed. Vincent only orated. Prayers such as this were common on the base, but answers from God? Not so much. Vincent's words complete, they waited.

The fragile voice of Reverenced One Pierce unraveled the silence. "I testify to the guilt of this woman! She is not worthy. The Book of Light contains nothing that will save her."

"The voice of God through a man," Ariana cried.

That was it. That was truly it?

Cole stood. "Let me see the Book."

Vincent's amusement finally bubbled up into a belly laugh. "Dear Cole, you allow your heart to eat up your professionalism and sense. We access God daily, and you need never fear whether we are doing Its will."

Cole clenched his teeth to tighten up his temper. "Don't insult me, Glorious One. You knew that claim would mean nothing to me before you said it."

"We did, but we haven't the time to find new ways of wording things to please you, *Senior Officer* Chandler. Turning his attention to Jade, he said, "Jade Chandler, you are guilty before God. You have the right to choose the method of execution. Water, blood, or spirit?"

Cole raised a hand. "Glorious One, this is—"

"Spirit," Jade answered.

Dumbfounded, Cole closed his mouth and took off his hat to scratch his scalp, push up his glasses, rub his jaw. Anything to avoid losing his temper further. Was she giving up? This unearthly bundle of positivity and passion was giving up?

"We will accommodate your wishes, Mrs. Chandler," Ariana replied.

"How gracious of you to accommodate her wishes," Cole retorted. "Accommodate a wish of mine, if you please, I wish and appeal to you for her to be imprisoned and her child spared for a period of three months. During that time, I will organize a committee, with the aid of the Kyrios, for the purpose of contacting God."

Destroying the child in three months would be an uglier process, but if waiting might save Jade . . .

"Your appeal is denied," Vincent answered. "Isn't it clear God has denied her? Adequate contact has been made."

Cole raised a finger, cringing, "Dispose of the mongrel if needs be, but let the time and space be given for a committee—"

Hesper strode to the front to stand beside Cole. Feet planted with confidence, shoulders back, chin up—the pose looked unusual in a dress like hers, but if she were wearing hides? She'd have looked as fierce as a mountain lion. She wore anger like a crown, and it was always beautiful.

She pointed at the Kyrios. "You are sick people! Your minds are sick! Your god is sick! I would call you brute beasts, but even beasts have more honor!"

David rushed to grab her hand and lead her back to her place. She resisted him, managing one more firm point at the council. "Death is too good for you! The soil would spit you out! I hope you live forever with the agony of your conscience and may you never find rest!"

David wouldn't comfort his wife in front of the Kyrios, but he corrected and stopped his fiancé when she stood up for something? Too worried about people liking him to love anyone deeply.

Cole would have stood with her if she were his. Naturally, he would have tried to talk her out of it if it had been planned, but after doing it, she deserved respect and support.

Vincent responded gently, "David, you will have her here daily for conversion classes, beginning next week. I will take the responsibility for her instruction myself. I think we'll get along nicely."

The genuine amusement on his face concerned Cole. He liked her. Too much.

"Considering her kindness to one of our own, and that she is new to our ways, I grant leniency for this passionate behavior. I will do the same for your brother, though he has no such excuse." He eyed Cole as he descended the platforms and beckoned. "Jade, step forward."

Cole caught Jade's arm. Though he rarely perspired due to stress, the situation had dampened his hands. He squeezed her arm harder to keep a grip.

Vincent stood on the floor, level with the Chandler family. "What now, Cole? What shall we do? Shall we have a bit of hand-to-hand combat? Your work with the Gentles has made you quite barbaric these days."

Jade waited, no questions, no wondering. She knew as well as Cole that they were powerless, even though his entire body and soul screamed to do something. If anyone required evidence of the effectiveness of Meros psychological tactics, they needed to look no further.

Quiet surrender to death.

That's what happens when people grow accustomed to allowing others to rule over them. Cole was equally guilty. Reluctantly, he released Jade.

"I request that she be granted the right to the death-light," Cole blurted. What a stupid request. "She has been a true believer, pious through and through, despite this superstitious practice that condemns her, due to her piety, an exception should be made that she may enter the afterlife."

Vincent exchanged a surprised glance with Ariana. Suppressing a laugh, he answered, "Denied. No Gentle has ever been permitted a death-light burning. We'll certainly not begin with a witch. We realize it's distressing, but God's ways are higher than our own."

Vincent touched Jade's face and kissed her forehead, then ordered her to kneel.

This absurd prolongation and the benevolent display of the kiss made Cole's face hot with anger. He cleared his thoughts, focused on breathing, and tried to leave behind the fury. He failed. A livid fever was rising.

Coolness. Calm. Breathe it away. Press it down with a blank mind. Now. Now.

Failure.

He gritted his teeth and bit his fist. He had to put his faith in training and self-discipline. Survival meant flipping the switch on feelings, even if he hated it.

Shut it off. Shut it off. Why couldn't he shut it off?

Vincent placed his hands on Jade's shoulders. "Jade Chandler, you have violated the laws of God and the laws of the Meros. Your punishment, as you have chosen, is by spirit. We the humble servants of God are here and stand ready to reveal Its wrath against unbelieving atheists."

Reverenced Ones Pierce and Minh joined him to tie her feet and hands together and lay her on the stone floor. Trinity handed a long black strap to Vincent who knelt beside Jade and wrapped it around Jade's neck. Without further ceremony, he tightened it.

Cole could whip Vincent in a fight and help Jade up from the ground, but she would still die. The Kyrios might kill him, too.

Cole's death would add to the family's grief and, potentially, result in the deaths of many more in his own family and the Unified. He had to resist his noble impulses.

Dear God, it's painful to sacrifice one for many. One? No. Two. This is the sacrifice of two.

Beyond the heavy thoughts he found to keep himself centered and in control, Hesper's scream filled his heart with ice that spread and splintered through his whole body. Why wasn't David helping her? Anise did much to restrain and little to comfort.

Hesper would never calm down long enough to listen to him. David could do it. He often broke through the barrier of will while guiding someone to calm. His voice worked well for his job, but it was probably not so easy to use when his wife was being murdered before his eyes.

Cole joined his family and waved Anise away. Hesper stopped screaming and looked into his eyes. "Would you just kill me now? If you do not kill me now, I will die like that baby. Even after its mother is dead, it may live for just a little while, but for no purpose and for such a short time, there is no sense in it."

That was not a good sign. If she remained calm, perhaps he could do something for her. He opened his mouth to speak—

"David, you may take her body and burn it," Vincent announced. "Her possessions and whatever she's given to you must be burnt to remove evil influences from your home. Do not mourn her." His hands held out to them, he used his gentle authoritative post-execution voice. "No tears are to be shed for the wicked. In the fear and reverence of God, consider the iniquitous ways of an atheist and her witchcraft. You are warned." He adjusted his tunic and strutted out, followed by the unfazed council of Kyrios.

Hesper's sobs echoed in the great room, disrupting the stillness of the stunned atmosphere.

Many crimes were punishable by death with blood, water, or spirit. None of the options were pretty. It was a shame she had to see it. Unified brutality was emotional, not physical, and despite the emotional trauma Hesper had suffered in her life, she remained an open-hearted woman. It was no wonder she would love quickly and mourn a horrific end to it all in the same manner. The Unified sense of loyalty and justice demanded grief. However, they were accustomed to untimely deaths. Survival remained the priority. Hesper would be okay. Unless this was about principle more than Jade, which was quite possible.

Hesper wrenched her arm out of David's grasp as he tried to draw her away. Cole wanted only to do the natural, human thing: to hold her and be there while she cried. It was the right thing to do, but it might add a terrible insult to a soul's critical injury. So, he stood with her and grabbed David as he passed in the direction of the platforms.

"You go on. I'll bring her home," Cole murmured.

David rubbed his jaw a few times before he waded through his dread to Jade, picked her up, and carried her away, followed by the rest of his wives.

Now alone, Cole placed his hand a finger's breadth from Hesper's head and focused, trying to send all his affection, concern, and empathy through it. There was little to lose in trying, though this was desperation at its finest.

Hesper stopped crying and shook with involuntary, residual sobs. "I feel it, Ada—Cole." She shuddered.

He shouldn't have tried. The warmth from his hand offended her.

"The water and light feeling. I feel it from you."

That? Cole felt it, too. He didn't think she would.

Trembling, she took feeble hold of his uniform coat. Cole sucked in a sharp, surprised breath. *Keep a grip on yourself, man.* No matter how right it seemed, he would never put his arms around her without invitation.

"Forgive me for this." Arms wrapped around his ribcage, she finished her cry as humans should. If this wasn't an invitation, he didn't know what was.

Footsteps echoed off the stone walls.

Vincent.

Cole squeezed Hesper tighter, and she turned her face away from the Glorious One.

"So, Cole, listen. Your behavior today was really something." Vincent patted Cole's back, disbelieving but impressed. "I think you know it. I understand you were close to Jade. She was a lovely creature. However, your work with the Gentles ends now." With a long, silent, steady stare, he forced Cole to acknowledge him.

"Yes, Glorious One."

"I don't think it's healthy for you anymore. I should have you in the jail overnight, but I'm opting for mercy. Your family needs you."

The jail? Yes, well, perhaps that was a reasonable punishment. Cole had behaved in an unacceptable manner, though how could he have behaved any other way when no one else dared to speak up? Someone had to rage against the powerlessness. He couldn't let it know he felt it.

"Thank you, Glorious One."

* * *

The Chandlers tossed Jade's possessions and gifts into a pile, including her paintings and, lastly, her body, David set the pyre ablaze. The stench of burning flesh chased away the sweetness of Jade's drawer of incense, bringing a sick finalization to the ugly ordeal. The smell of an innocent's death. Cole and David watched over the fire for several minutes, saying nothing until Cole couldn't bear it.

"Something has to be done, Dave."

"Like what? Don't be so sure they'll have mercy on you again. No one's that valuable. Guest lecturers are a dime a dozen, and others will rise to wave education's standard. I promise." He took a cigarette and lighter from his pocket. "You may be the best, but it doesn't mean you can't push the Kyrios farther than your worth.

That's why I don't try anything. I'm not worth much to them. I've got a smooth voice and a few tricks. That's about it." David lit the cigarette and tucked the lighter away.

"Unless Trinity dies—you know she's sick—and you'll take her place. You're worth a lot because they don't want me to take that position."

The brothers turned away from the pyre and walked toward the house.

"Don't even think about it." David brought the cigarette to his lips, looking to the west. "I don't need this right now."

Cole wrinkled his nose. "Why not think about it? Someone needs to find out what's happened to the Book." He spun around to walk backward, facing David as he spoke. "I mean, did you see how ridiculously they behaved? Did you really notice it? They don't hear from any god I know!"

David's derisive laugh blew a few puffs of smoke in Cole's direction. "Oh, you know God yourself now, hm?" He snapped. "Did the two of you have tea? Go for a stroll through an ethereal garden of wisdom and spiritual enlightenment? Forget about it." He blew the smoke from his nostrils as he dropped the cigarette and assumed a quicker pace to walk ahead.

Cole crushed the cigarette under his shoe and let out a deep breath to kill the pressure in his chest.

He tried to appreciate the sunshine as Jade would have, closing his eyes and paying attention to the warmth on his skin, but the fire crackling and Jade's treasures popping and shifting in the flames thwarted his efforts.

He hadn't paid attention to the current phase of the moon. Out of reverence for its greatest lover, he hoped it would glow full in a cloudless sky tonight. Jade deserved it.

This wasn't over for him. David may play the coward, but Cole refused.

* * *

Hesper stood in the doorway of the house, numb, watching the smoke. She reached out and squeezed David's hand as he slid by. He glanced at her with a whisper of a smile and passed through. When Cole arrived, she stepped back and allowed him to come in.

"Ada—Cole, do you think it should be raining? This should not be a sunny day."

She did not look at him. The thought of his uniform made her sick, and she had seen enough Meros authority symbols to last for a long time. Instead, she fixed her eyes on the flaming pyre, built near the spot where she abandoned her escape efforts. At least Jade had escaped.

Without conversation or even permission, she spent the day with Cole. The man she once loved would be a proper sanctuary because he was wise and would not bother or hurt her.

By day's end, she still sat, facing the window, willing herself to love the moon as much as Jade did. Cole sat on the floor, reclined against the sofa, looking at a book. Smoke drifted through the air as embers of the great injustice slowly flickered out. By morning, it would be warm but otherwise gone. Hesper toyed with the rhodonite necklace no one noticed or, perhaps, cared to try to take from her to burn.

"Cole."

"Hm?"

"What happened?"

"The wrong thing." He closed the book.

"Is that truly the god you believe in?"

"No, no, it's not."

"Does It judge and kill?"

"It can do what It wants to, but It is just," Cole said. "This wasn't the right way."

"What is the right way?"

"Hm . . . I guess you have to get to know It to find out. God is bigger than this, and you'll like It, from what I know of It." He smiled. "Jade was more of a gift from God than an example of Its wrath. If you can imagine what a god who gives gifts like that must be like . . ."

Hesper rolled the delicate silver chain between her fingers. The tender sting of the black X came to life on her cheek.

"Intervention is required now, and the Book," Cole said, "the Book is the key. I have to look at it."

Nineteen | Post-Conquest: 227

THIS FRIGGIN' COLD spell would not let up. It sneaked past Jes' stolen furs and under his worn-out clothes with the tenacity of a lonely, young housewife. If only he could run into one of them tonight. She'd give him somewhere to . . . warm up.

He managed a frozen smirk.

A few degrees less cold and he'd make it just fine outside. Most seemed to think someone his age likely deserved to be a bum, so he stayed outdoors a lot more since he started looking and sounding like a man.

Fifteen years wasn't that old, was it? Maybe it was. Maybe he did deserve this. He couldn't think of why, but . . . well, it was hard to think straight when he couldn't feel his toes.

Apple Gate looked like a good place to find a nighttime landing spot. Any of these houses might be friendly enough to open its doors. His nose and fingers needed a break from the cold before playing the door-knocking game, so he'd step inside the first open business on his path.

Gentle drums beat their way through the air. Must be a wedding in the woods. Though it would be weird to have a Meros gate so close to inhabited trees unless Apple Gate was an Earth Person community. He looked around. Nah. Earth People never built Gates this big. They kept more trees, too.

It was a good thing for him that the Gentles were so close, though. Just in case. The Gentles gave him a warmish place to sleep a few times in the past.

The light from a general store window in the town circle ahead promised warmth and a bite to eat.

Promises, promises. Lights don't mean open.

It was worth a shove at the handle at least. The door opened with the surprisingly loud jangle of sleigh bells.

He sniffed the air. Castor oil, chicken soup, and a hint of mint. He hadn't eaten since—when was it?

"Good evening, sir!" A clear, friendly voice came from somewhere. An old person. A nice one.

Easy as whore-pies! If he was respectful, old people never suspected he'd steal—

"You look as if you've been walking a long time. I've got a fire in the back and some soup you ought to have. Posthaste!"

Where was the guy? Jes looked around, trying to spot the source of the voice.

A strong hand with swollen knuckles grabbed Jes' shoulder and pushed him forward. A *short* old person. They were sneaky . . . and dangerous when wielding canes or purses.

And shotguns.

Oh! That lady with the knitting needle a couple years back. That was actually super scary.

No matter the weapon of choice, terror was the name of the game when a short person felt the need to attack him. They were easy to miss 'til it was too late.

Jes laughed. "Whoa, buddy. I'll come without pushin'."

Releasing Jes' shoulder, the old man strode ahead and giggled as he disappeared around the corner on surprisingly long legs for a short dude. "C'mon, big guy," he called, clinking dishes and slopping liquid somewhere out-of-sight.

Jes pulled back his hood and followed the old man into a fire-lit room. A pot hung over the fireplace. People who could afford to run a business and have electricity usually had a regular stove, but okay.

A bowl of soup waited on a lace-edged, quilted, brown placemat.

"This for me?" Jes pointed at the soup.

"No, no, no, that's for the dog." The man scowled in the unsettling way of frustrated, angry old people.

Jes looked around. "Dog?" At the table? What the . . .?

The old man giggled. "You got looks but not brains, I see. Yes, the soup's for you!"

Jes smiled. *A friggin' funny guy, huh? All right, old man. Let's be friends—after I knock your dentures out.*

Warmth made his cold hands tingle as he unwound the rags he had wrapped around them. He pulled the chair away from the table and sat in front of the steaming bowl of golden broth, loaded with noodles and dotted with chicken and colorful vegetable bits.

Seated in a chair by the fire, the old man slurped at his own bowl and asked, "What's your name?"

"Jes."

He swiped a noodle off his chin and into his mouth. "Short for Jesse?"

"Nah. Jesurun."

"Quite a name. What's your last name?"

Jes shrugged. "Mom never told me."

"Want crackers?" the man asked, holding up a metal tin.

Jes nodded. He liked crackers.

The old man held the tin out. Jes took it and scrabbled a handful of salty oyster crackers, crumbled them up, and plopped them into his soup. He dropped the spoon a few times—stupid fingers wouldn't work right—but once he got a hold of it, the good soup made his nose and cheeks prickle and drip as it thawed him out. He swiped his nose with his sleeve.

"Where you from, Jes?"

"Nowhere." He couldn't remember where he came from, honestly.
"You have somewhere to go?"

Thanks for the reminder, dipstick. "No."

The old man rose and made his way to shelves built into the wall
to Jes' left and grabbed a couple of teacups. "Like tea?"

"I like anything."

"Ah, good. I enjoy a cup of white tea in the evening. I'll close up
shop and get some tea for both of us."

The old man left Jes alone with the crackling fire and peace.
Quiet. The sleigh bells jangled. Switches clicked. Cash register
opened . . . The soup was almost gone. Just a bit of broth-soaked
crackers and a few broken noodle pieces. Jes shook the remnants
into his mouth.

The old man returned with a handful of silvery dried leaves. He
passed Jes with an "oh-goody" grin and shrug and dropped them into
a kettle sitting by the fire.

"So, who're you?" Jes asked.

The old man poured water into the kettle. "Jones." He burped.

Jes snorted. "Jones. Isn't that, like, a last name?"

Jones straightened up, frowning. With a shake of his head, he said,
"No. Last name's Atwood. So, kiddo, who's chasing you?"

Friggin' nosy . . . "Who said someone's chasin' me? I know I
didn't!"

Jones set the kettle on the table. "Jealous husbands? LEWs?
Thugs?"

"I dunno what the fu—"

"What the heck you swearin' for, boy?" he barked. "There'll be
no cussin' in my house, or I'll throw your bloody rump into the darn,
dimnity, condemnity, poopity-scoopin' snow!" He eyed Jes. "See, I
can swear with the best of them. Don't try me, pith-face."

Did he just say pith-face? What was he supposed to say to that?
Jes considered the words and shrugged. "Okay. Sorry, man."

"My question is a natural one," Jones said quietly. "You look to be a troublemaker, but you seem to have a good heart. I'm trying to figure out what's going on. Who's after you?"

"I've had all of those on my butt in the past."

"What did LEWs want you for?"

Jes sniffed. "What does a LEW want anyone for?"

"If a law enforcement warden wanted you, right or wrong, I want to know why."

Jes pushed away his empty bowl. "I've lost track of the reasons and the times," he growled. "Okay?"

Jones' shiny old eyes swept the floor a few times. "Where's your family?"

I don't see why it's any of your business, but . . . "LEWs or soldiers—I don't know what—killed my mom when I was five, so I've been takin' care of myself."

"Since you were five?"

"Yeah."

"Where's your father?"

"What gives you the right to ask all this?" Jes stood, sliding his chair back.

Jones stared into the fire, rocking in his chair. "You can always leave, kiddo. Gonna go far below zero tonight, though, and most folks in Apple Gate aren't gonna let you in. They want peace."

Jes wasn't ready to leave. Give the old man harmless info for some warmth? Fair trade. "My father was military. I never met him. Mom insisted he'd find me someday. Happy?" He slammed back into his chair.

"I'll teach you somethin', son. I don't care if you call me sir, but as you go on in life, you'll find that if you learn to say 'sir' and 'ma'am' regularly, you'll get further than you would without it."

Bossy schmuck! "Yes, ma'am. I get it. Thanks."

Jones pursed his lips. Shifting out of thought, he grabbed the tea kettle and poured off-colored water into a cup on the table.

"I thought you said it was tea."

"White tea," Jones confirmed.

Jes grunted at the liquid, sniffing it. What was that silvery stuff the old guy put in there? He'd never seen tea like that before. Smelled better than a lot of other things he'd drunk. He survived that, he'd probably survive this, but plants were all kinds of messed up. He'd consumed plants that had him sweating, puking, and hallucinating for days.

"No one's after you?" Jones repeated.

"No, sir. Nobody official. Not that I know of anyway. There's a couple people who probably think I'm after them, though." Jes smirked and took a sip of tea.

"Uh-huh, I see." Jones sat in his rocking chair. "Where you going after you leave here?"

The tea was good. Mild. Hot. Delicate? Yeah, he would use the word delicate for this.

"I don't know yet."

Jones stared at his folded hands, resting in his lap. "You're welcome to stay here."

"Why?"

"Oh"—he sipped at his tea—"'Cause I'm a lonely old man who doesn't know better."

Jes laughed. "I'll stay the night. Sure. Thanks."

They finished their tea, and Jones took Jes to another room farther back in the building. He dug blankets and a squishy pillow out of a cedar closet and laid them out on the sofa, then fluffed the pillow and set another blanket on top.

"It's a bit frilly with all the flowers, but a blanket's a blanket, right?"

All this fuss embarrassed Jes. A spot on the floor would have been enough.

"I ain't complainin', man. I just wanna warm place to sleep. The . . . the uh, pretty blanket's kinda a treat."

Jones grinned. "Yeah, my wife liked things pretty. I never saw any sense in getting new stuff just 'cause I'm not a lady. Our son hated it, though." Jones pushed his hands into his corduroy pant pockets and grew wistful. "He has what he wants now. Simple. Minimal. Joined the military a few years ago in hopes of becoming a LEW someday. He's doing a good job! He's an officer working in the Bastion of Holiness. One more level of training to become a LEW." He licked his lower lip, thoughtful. "Well! Anyway, you need some stuff. You're welcome to a bath. I'll get a few things from the store for you—soap, toothpaste, a brush, and all that—unless you have those things, which I don't think you do."

"I got a toothbrush," Jes said, pulling it out of his back pocket. Sure, it was a mangled, filthy thing, but it worked!

Jones' eyes nearly fell out of his face. "Kiddo, you need a new one."

Jes spent a warm, comfortable night in Jones' home, and the following day, Jones kept him around for odd jobs. With a few excuses and a few 'oh, before you go' moments the day was over. So, Jes spent another night.

A few days into this routine, it was time to think about staying. Jones obviously wanted to keep Jes, but it'd been a long time since he'd let himself be kept—a long time coming. He was tired, and this was as sweet as silk sheets in a Glorious One's mansion. Whatever that felt like.

Jones had a shelf loaded with books about all kinds of things. Jes enjoyed the book about human anatomy best, but he kept that a secret from Jones. During daylight hours, he enjoyed fantasy books with stuff about dragons, princesses, and magic. In fifteen years, he had never heard of anything like it. If he ever stopped somewhere long enough to get schooling, they stuck math and psychology under his nose. Jones' education gave Jes a whole new world to think about. A world where suffering made people into something better and good triumphed over evil. It made him want to do something crazy like . . . sing, draw, write!

However, he spent most of his time sweeping floors, stocking shelves, doing the heavy-lifting and high-reaching. He had a steady job for the first time in his life.

He also enjoyed a pale, dark-haired girl who frequented the store. Her voice, her face, her hair, her lips—everything about her made him happy. Besides liking Jones pretty well, she was the reason it was worth it to leave off living the life of a feral cat to get all tamed. It'd take time and effort, and he hoped she wouldn't up and leave the gate without notice before then, but he'd marry and take care of that girl someday. The idea made him nervous. How long did he have to wait to marry her? Could he get married at fifteen? Wait—what was her name?

Every day, they'd talk, and every day, he'd forget to ask her name. Girls never made him nervous, so why the heck should this one? After a month of this torture, he settled it: he had to get her name and ask her to hang out with him—have tea or something.

I sound like a friggin' stuffed-shirt. Oh, miss, you're so charming. Come over for a bit of tea, won't you? Gag!

The day after he made the decision to ask for her name, a shipment of fruit arrived and Jes had just begun putting them out. The sleigh bells rang and Jes' girl walked up to the fruit. His hand shook as much as his breath as she stood beside him and grabbed a peach and nectarine. She sniffed the peach first, then the nectarine. Gave a squeeze to one and a squeeze to the other. Another sniff, a feel, a rub.

"The nectarines are perfect right now. You might be better off with that if you want to eat right away," he said. With the cost of fruit in the winter, nobody could afford to buy the wrong thing.

She smiled and turned the nectarine over in her worn hand a few times, then held it to her nose for a committed sniff. "You are right. It is."

"Where do you come from?" He threw the question out to stop her from leaving.

A small smile touched her sweet pepper-berry lips. "The earth." She walked away.

What did that mean? Was that a code phrase for being an Earth Person? Did she think he might be one, too? Was he supposed to say something back?

He'd get her name next time.

By afternoon, business slowed, giving Jes and Jones downtime to talk and have a late lunch. "I'll go back and fetch chili from last night, and how about some tea? A sandwich sounds good, too." Jones lowered his bushy eyebrows. "Bacon and lettuce. That feels right—tomato! Keep an eye on the store, hm?" He patted Jes' back on his way out.

Jes pulled out a pad of paper and busied himself drawing a dragon as he saw in one of Jones' books, taking an occasional glance at passersby outdoors. A couple of black uniforms caught his eye after the third or fourth glance: LEWs. Their manner and rifles said they were probably there for Immediate Justice. Jes sneered at the thought. He'd seen Immediate Justice before. It was generally reserved for common people who were so obviously guilty no trial was "needed." They paced up and down the street, gawking at and accosting passersby, letting them go, then doing it all again.

Jes returned to his paper and flipped the sheet to start over. This time he drew a picture of his dark-haired girl, smiling. As he finished the final black curl, a burning sensation shot from his chest to the fingertips of his left hand. The left hand snatched the pencil from his right and the happy girl's face grew wet with graphite tears.

The heat cranked itself up, and fear overcame his fascination. Searing pain ripped through his body and forced a wail into his throat. He swallowed it down and clamped his mouth shut. The last line of the new drawing pierced and sliced through the layers of paper beneath it and went off the edge of the pad, across the counter, leaving a long storm-gray streak. The pencil tip broke off with a snap. He threw the pencil to the ground as soon as his fingers would obey him.

Out of breath, he looked around the store for witnesses. A few heard the commotion, but it resulted in a few laughs and scowls. Nothing more.

He'd drawn the girl being attacked.

No. Raped.

Not something he would draw on his own, or something he ever wanted to see. He might be a criminal, but he refused to be that kind. Until he got strong enough, he'd been on the receiving end of it, and he had no interest in delivering that kind of horror to anyone else.

Swallow these emotions. Kill panic. Crush the feelings. No one could be allowed to see him worried, or they'd ask what was wrong. The drawing had to disappear before someone saw it, or he'd lose everything.

Beyond the window, his dark-haired girl lugged a sack of grain out of the feed mill.

He crumpled the paper and tossed it in the trash can, then he stomped on that sucker. And stomped on it again.

The fire gradually withdrew from his fingers and traveled up his arm, leaving dark markings in the shape of a bear's pad on his palm, followed by a black trail that spiraled upward and retreated into his chest over his heart. His whole back itched.

The marking on his arm looked like a tattoo, but it burned when touched. "What the . . ."

Outside, his beautiful girl still dragged her sack of grain on the ground, but then her face changed, plastered with fear.

Oh, no. The LEWs.

She spun around to drag the sack back to the feed mill, but she'd been spotted. One of them pointed, and the duo rushed her.

Jes stood up, knocking his stool to the floor.

The girl abandoned the sack and ran with life or death terror distorting her sweet face, but they grabbed her before she had a chance. People glanced at her and walked by, trying to stay out of the LEWs' way. How could they ignore a girl's screaming?

Jes jumped the counter, shoved the door open, and sloshed through the gray slush. His breath formed great misty puffs in the cold air, and his heating arm created a trail of steam.

I'm gonna kill 'em, I'm gonna kill 'em.

With the momentum of a thousand tumbling injustices and horrors, he planted a mighty swing of his fiery left fist on a LEW's jaw.

"Paws off her, whore hounds!" Jes shouted.

The so-called whore hound staggered back and let go of the girl who delivered her knee to the other's crotch. Jes threw himself at the first LEW and knocked him to the ground. Straddled over the LEW's torso, Jes hacked at his face with the weight of lead as darkness flooded his eyes and mind.

Jabbed at his temple, the barrel of a gun slapped him back into reality. "Oh, my God," he whispered, staring at his fists, covered in fresh blood. What had he done?

It was over. Everything was over.

"Get up!" the LEW with the gun ordered.

"I lost my mind. Please. She's just a girl," Jes cried, his cold face, wet with tears. *Crying? WHAT! Crying? Cool down.*

Jes looked for the girl, but she'd gotten away.

"Just a girl? She's an Earth Person, wanted for murdering an officer."

The LEW's bayonet knife sheath, secured at his hip, pressed into Jes' leg.

Time for a little insurance.

As he moved to stand, Jes unsnapped the sheath.

Standing, Jes reached out to help the LEW up, but he refused to take Jes' hand. Still, Jes had gotten close enough to grab him and kife the bayonet knife from the unsnapped sheath. Jes placed himself behind the LEW before the gunman comprehended the unexpected move and pressed the knife to the LEW's throat 'til a trickle of blood slid down his neck like watery catsup over the edge of a squeezed bottle with a broken seal.

Jes smiled. Satisfied. He hadn't done anything violent in a long time. It was starting to feel good.

Jones emerged from the store, stomping through the dirty snow. "What . . . What is the meaning of this?"

"Do you know this boy?" the armed LEW asked.

"Yes, he's my son. What's going on here?"

His son? Jes' heart throbbed. He was losing a dad? No, no, no.

"He works in the store. Calls me son the same as everybody else. I barely know him," Jes said.

The LEW frowned, suspicious. "He's at death's door for the assault of a law enforcement warden and Disruption of Justice."

Jones pressed his palms downward in a quelling motion. "The boy has a lot to learn. If you give me a chance, I'll work with him, Warden Cadence."

Warden Cadence wouldn't have it. Jes' handiwork had his comrade crying like a prepubescent boy. That was unforgivable.

"I'm afraid not, sir. Not possible. He's fortunate I'm giving him his choice of execution."

"Those medallions of justice don't do you much good, do they?" Jones said, disgusted. "All your psychology training, and you still can't understand or don't care to help the errors of a boy such as this. His personality ain't right. He's been abused and split down the middle of his soul. He doesn't know who he is or what he should do."

Jes let the catsup bottle cry-baby go, dropped his knife, and raised his hands. "Hey, I'll take it."

Warden Cadence shifted his body, his gun still trained on Jes' head. "What'll it be, son? Blood, Water, or Spirit?" In circumstances such as these, a gunshot qualified as Blood.

"I've already been through them all because of you Kyrios pigs." Jes spit on the warden's jacket—right on his name.

"Look, I'll pay for your friend to see a doctor, I'll give you my store," Jones said. "I'll do whatever. Sirs, let the boy go." Jones clasped his hands together and took another step.

"You're pushing it, old man."

"You old fart, knock it off! You're gonna get yourself killed. This's got nothin' to do with you!" Jes yelled.

"He's breathed into my old sad life and made it all new, sir." Jones put his hand over his heart, eyes watering. "I want to help him heal. Please, don't deny an old man a little joy." He took another step. "Sirs, you can't tell me you've never made any mist—" Jones touched the gun and Warden Cadence backhanded him, knocking him to the ground.

BANG.

A collective shriek flew skyward. Some in the town circle dropped to the ground, others remained standing, watching. A few children cried. The concern passed over like the swoop of a bat. Then nothing. No outrage. No yelling. No one ever did anything.

Having LEWs was better than not having LEWs. That's what drunk bar philosophers who'd lost hope said.

Just be good. Stay out of trouble, and you don't have to worry about the Kyrios, the military, the LEWs. Nothin'.

Yeah, right.

Jes' heart froze and broke into pieces as the old man's blood stained and melted the dirty slush beneath him. A familiar heaviness crept into his thoughts and sat on his chest.

"You killed him!" His body burned, and the bear paw glowed beneath his skin, a swirling liquid flame.

Warden Cadence stepped backward. "My finger slipped. I swear it."

The catsup bottle LEW backed away and pointed. "Charles, look at his arm!"

"Butcher! I'll kill you!" Jes shouted. Tears boiled over and traced a cold path down his cheeks.

Two more LEWs arrived, holding onto the girl—cuffed this time.

Warden Cadence's confidence returned. He smiled. "Ah, there she is. Great. That didn't take too long. A few unexpected casualties, but we're in good shape, gentlemen." He eyed the girl, then turned to Jes. "I have an execution here, then we can be on our way."

Catsup bottle LEW spoke up. "We need to keep this guy. They might want to run him by the Kyrios. He's got something supernatural going on."

* * *

They tossed the girl's violated, beaten body into the wild river. They gave Jes a good roughing up, but he still had use of his limbs. A symptom of the LEWs' remaining humanity, maybe.

Whatever happened, he couldn't go to the Kyrios. He'd rather follow that girl into the river than face those butchers.

Hanging his head, slumped over, bloody, bruised, and cuffed, they underestimated his will to live and his willingness to die.

While they took turns lighting their cigarettes with a single lighter, Jes stomped on the foot of the LEW standing near him and threw himself into the water, giving himself to its merciless current.

He'd survived worse.

Twenty | Post-Conquest: 232

WIDE-EYED, A beardless Adahy stared down at Hesper, his face blue with moonlight. As he moved, wood smoke and fragrant spices escaped his hide clothes and whirled over her face.

Where was she? She propped herself on her elbow. Was he saying her name? Blinking her thoughts clear, she stared at him, understanding nothing until he said, "Let's go!"

"What are you talking about? Why are you here?"

"Getting out—you really should lock your door. David and I will keep an ear open for any word of retribution against your people. We'll move your community to safety. I'll explain the mark to your family."

She scoffed. "Move an entire community for me? Papa would never take me back. I will never be able to get married—"

Cole waved her words away. "There are more liberal, understanding communities, Hesper. Very few, but they exist. I'm going to get you out of here at least, even if you don't go to your family."

"Does David know you are doing this?"

"What does that matter?"

Was that supposed to make the question go away?

He huffed. "Yes. It was his idea." A pause. "After I . . . gave it to him."

"It is irrational," she said. "I refuse to go."

"Are you crazy, Hesper? You have no idea how difficult it is to get this kind of courage from that dolt," Cole cried. He grabbed her wrist. "It may never happen again."

Why would he touch her that way? Oh, right, because he was Meros. She pulled against him and scowled. "I have seen enough death for one day."

He bit his fist and growled into it. "No one is going to die." He tossed a pair of gloves and hide clothes from his bag onto the bed. "Put this on. You'll need it to climb over the fence."

"You cannot do this."

"Excuse me? Don't tell me what I can—" He bit his fist again, then, with a quieter, calculated tone, he said, "Please, don't tell me what I can't do." At the side of her bed, he knelt and took her hands. "If you won't stay, at least allow me to take you to say goodbye. I will do this for you for no other reason than that I love you. I'm not asking anything of you but trust."

Trust? What trust? "Earlier, I was grieving and shocked. You were familiar and a comfort, but—" She pulled her hands away.

"This might be one of your greatest regrets if you don't come with me right now," Cole said.

Tempted, at first, to spit his words back at him, ignore it all, and deny the veracity of his claim, she scowled, then swallowed. He was right. She might regret this forever. Regret if she did, regret if she did not.

She growled. "Very well. Wait outside while I change."

He smiled and looked so much like Adahy, even without the beard, that it made her throat tight. Quick as a rabbit, he zipped out the door.

"This is foolish."

The leather trousers felt so good around her legs. She tightened them with the cords at the side and folded the hem. She opened the door and peeked into the hallway.

Empty.

Voices strained through the walls and space. Light on bare feet, she hurried down the hall and stairs to the foyer.

"Who's there?" Cole interrupted David mid-sentence.

"Hesper."

"Thank God," David whispered. "Hurry up, or you'll return in broad daylight."

Cole darted for the dining room. "Let's go."

"Hesper," David called in a quiet voice, though not a whisper.

Turning, she got a face-full of his chest as he pulled her in for a tight hug—a warm and comforting spot of sunlight after a swim in her dark conscience. Planted in one spot, his hands never roamed, but tightened and loosened gently over and over as if trying to get her closer by renewing his hold.

"Don't let them tell you that you're impure. You are beautiful and loyal, and I consider you one of the few truly holy things I've encountered in my life. I won't forget you, dear girl. Forgive me if I have caused you distress in any way. We'll work it out here if you stay with your family—and I believe you should." A few moments passed in his gentle swaying embrace.

She did not want to let go.

"Say! You're hugging me back." A smile filled his voice. "Forget the white cloth with your tears, I'll treasure *this* forever."

Even if the Unified allowed her to live with her family, she would never be held this way again. No one would marry her or call her holy—whatever that was. Something good? She was a silly person, aching to have things she did not even understand. Comfort and light seemed wrapped up in the sound of 'holy,' though. It felt nice.

Knowing that, she could not muster resentment for the pleasant feeling and David's mysteriously worded affections. This had to be the reason the Unified considered compliments and touch outside of marriage to be dangerous inhibitors to unity. It had the power to turn her into a selfish, hormonal mess. The Unified would never survive if they permitted this kind of attention to individuals on a regular basis. The community would suffer for the individual. Hence the reason selfish, faithless stigs damaged Unified communities.

If the Kyrios caught David and Cole helping her escape, not only David and Cole would suffer, but her entire community.

All for her?

She was not the most important thing—only in her mind.

David released her.

With a willful shake of her head, she said, "I want to be the light that shines through the leaves. Not the darkness in between. Staying there would be the worst way to end this string of foolish choices, but my mama deserves a goodbye."

Hesper joined Cole in the dining room. They sneaked out the back door and slipped into the misty night. Concealed by the flowers, they crawled along the garden path until it ended a few yards away from Jade's smoking pyre.

"We have to wait for the south guard and the west guard to be farther away," Cole said. He dug another hide from his bag and shoved it in his belt. With a quick whip of the head to the left and the right, he started forward. "Run," he whispered.

On light feet, they ran to the fence. Cole swiftly scaled the links, pulled the hide from his belt, and threw it over the thorny wire. He used one hand to beckon for Hesper to follow, then hoisted himself over the wire and landed softly on the other side. Hesper followed and brought the hide with her as she dropped to the ground. They fled into the darkness of uninhabited woods, not even fifty yards south of the base, and ran within its borders, leaving it in favor of the road once out of sight of the guards.

Within minutes, Hesper's breaths came short. Her strong legs could not keep up with her lungs as deep weariness settled into her body.

"What's wrong?" Cole slowed his pace.

"I am hungry and tired."

"Here." He dug in his bag and drew out a pouch of nuts and offered them. "Let's walk while you eat," he said. "You've been missing meals and not sleeping properly. Not to mention the emotional exertion you've endured."

She slipped an almond in her mouth and looked up.

Stars.

How beautiful they were, like small, white snowflakes stuck in the sky.

"I have not gotten to see them uncovered until now. We can stand at the edge of the forest and look if we are brave, but, well, you know how much I have wanted to see them this way." She whispered, "The sky goes forever. It feels safe."

Cole never stopped scanning the area, visibly alert and tensed. "Hm? What does?"

"The sky. The stars."

She had his attention now. "The stars. I didn't think of that." A half-smile softened the tension in his face. "You're seeing them in the open." He looked upward. "They make me feel I'm with God, somehow. How is it that they make you feel safe?"

"It is a big black blanket. What is beyond them?"

He chuckled. "Science isn't our expertise. Some say our souls go beyond the stars when our bodies are burned with the death-light, but even your ancestors never made it that far. They imagined it, though! Centered much of their entertainment around the idea of traveling from galaxy to galaxy. Far beyond any reality they actually lived. Before The Conquest destroyed everything, they made it to the moon and a few planets." He must have sensed her stare, because he turned to look at her, too. "You should see the *aurora borealis* in the northern country. That breaks a heart in the sweetest way."

What was sweet about a breaking heart?

"We are going much too slowly for my sake."

* * *

Entering the forest, Hesper breathed in the aroma: wood, leaves, dirt, and pine. No perfume or incense could ever duplicate this perfect blend of peace and nostalgia.

The Unified buried their loved ones here. These trees grew healthy and strong because her people gave back to the earth in their death. Nothing flew away beyond the stars. Everything remained in the soil to nourish future generations.

She also met her first Meros here.

"Cole."

"Yes?"

"Why are you doing this? Truly."

"I love you, and I owe it to you."

"Because you lied to me?"

He balked at the title given to his deed.

"You do not think you lied? Call it deception, call it treachery, but call it a lie, and you are offended? It was only business, right? Nothing personal," she said. "It was personal to me, sir."

He scratched at his jaw and sighed. "Yes," he said, "because I lied." Only a shadow spoke. Nothing more. Perhaps it was best that way.

"Remember Joram? Remember Papa? Papa did nothing to help his dying son. I cannot stay, Cole. Even if it is the right thing to do."

"Hesper, Joram was a true traitor, or at least an Earth Person. I knew him, and your papa was right, even if cruel."

"You knew him?" So many hard thoughts too quickly. "Does betrayal ever run shallow, sir, or is it always deeper than expected?"

He grunted a little. "Betrayal runs as deep as the roots, Hesper. Sometimes it's farther than you can dig, and sometimes it's shallow and edible. Pull it up, recognize the root, and eat it. It's all a matter of perspective and type."

"I do not understand."

"That's okay. You have more important things to be concerned with."

Beneath the familiar branches of Hesper's tree, Cole leaned against the trunk. "Do whatever you need to. I'll wait."

She grasped the branch—rough and solid. It had its place and was not capable of doubting its integrity and purpose like she was. How precious a branch felt.

She pulled herself up and climbed into the good, warm loft. "Mama," she whispered.

Someone stirred in the darkness.

"Oh, Hesper." Mama scrambled and stumbled but finally reached Hesper and wrapped her arms around her. "Where have you been? You smell of fruit."

Mama smelled of wood smoke, dirt, and wild carrot. Childhood.

"I cannot stay."

"Avriam!" Mama stroked Hesper's face. "Wake up. Hesper is home."

A long silence. Hesper and Mama did not need to talk about the reason because they both understood. Hesper felt it.

"Papa is asleep. He worked hard today," Mama said.

Papa was awake, choking on his pride.

"Mama, goodbye," Hesper said. "I love you. If I stay, people will die. Too many."

Mama grew stern. "Goodbye? You belong here."

"The Meros have marked me, Mama." Hesper cringed.

Mama released her. "What do you mean they marked you?" Her fingers stroked Hesper's cheek. "You will not dare to take my last child from me."

"Mama, I—"

"No. Stay." Mama's dear, raspy hands took Hesper's. "We will do something about the mark."

"It will be there forever, Mama. It does not go away."

"Avriam, come out and demand your daughter stay!" Mama's voice broke. Silence followed. "Avriam!" she sobbed. "Your last child will be gone forever!"

"Enough!" Papa croaked.

Mama squeezed Hesper. "Your Papa does not mean it."

"Kind, wealthy people care for me. I am not being hurt or beaten. I will be okay. I love you, Mama." Without another word, Hesper pulled out of Mama's arms and slid through the hatch, down to the branches.

"Hesper!" Mama cried. "Hesper, no!"

Weak in her knees, Hesper leaned against the trunk beside Cole. "We must go. Now," she whimpered. She pushed herself away from the tree and forced her feet onward, almost walking into him.

"Hesper, stay," he said. "This community needs you. They will adapt. You may be the reason they grow open to women returning. You could be a part of ending the stigma."

They were wasting time. Why did he insist?

"I will get out of your life and never return." He thrust an arm out to stop her from going around him. "You won't have to go on pretending to love me or marry me. I won't do that to you."

"That is not the problem, sir. Marrying you would be less of a shame than backing out of a marriage agreement. Stop harassing me about it. I have told you my reasons. Move your arms."

His disapproval came through in the sound of his breathing. "I can't see your face, but I hear your determination."

That settled it. If she pruned impossible hopes and wishes, maybe she would produce the fruit of peace and life.

Hesper savored the crunch of the forest floor beneath her feet and took each breath with the intention of imprinting the scent in her mind. Her fingers grazed the rough trees as she passed. At the edge of the forest, she wrapped her arms around a birch and pressed her cheek against its coarse, thick body. "I miss the feeling." She closed her eyes. "The peaceful trembling inside of me when I am with the trees." The moment of severance had come. With a kiss, she released the birch and stepped onto the grass. Life in the forest ended now.

* * *

"Fold my hides and put them under your bed. I'll get them sometime tomorrow."

Angry, Cole charged ahead to get to his rooms and cool down. Instead of parting from him as they approached the staircase into the upper hallway of rooms, Hesper stayed at his side until they reached his wing.

"Is there anything else I can do for you, Hesper?"

"Cole, have I done the wrong thing? Anise told me to look for the light in my mind when I came here. I am trying to apply this poetry in a realistic way. I feel I am, but hearing Mama's tears—"

"Hesper, only you can decide if you're doing the best thing. I just hope you're doing the best thing for you. Sometimes . . . Sometimes you have to do what is right for you and let everyone else work around it. Your life is just as important as mine or David's . . . or even Theia's. There's often more than one right choice."

"I am afraid. I am afraid to marry David. I am afraid to live here. I have so much fear."

"Shine that light on it." He pointed to her head and smiled. "Light is good for relieving fear. You'll be okay."

He bowed as a farewell and turned to go.

"Wait."

The "wait" could mean so many things, but Cole's heart rate accelerated, and his breath quickened in spite of knowing that.

"It has been hinted at that David does not require anyone to have a sexual relationship with him. Is that true?"

That was unexpected.

He shrugged. "I don't ask him about his private affairs unless they involve me somehow. But even in his wilder times, he never was the type of man to force a woman into that kind of activity. He didn't need to. Why? Has he done something to make you uneasy about the idea?" *If he so much as put his lips on her—*

"No. No. To the contrary, he has alleviated some of my fears, but if I chose to have that kind of relationship with him, and I became pregnant?"

This would make for a terrible rest of Cole's life. He'd look for a transfer to another base or apply for a permanent position in a university as soon as possible, but first, to give her the facts she needed to brace herself. Uncomfortable as it was, her question was reasonable and necessary, and she, for whatever reason, wanted the truth from him. He owed her.

"Come to my wing?"

The moments of staring deliberation surprised—almost insulted—him.

She tipped her head and frowned. "You took my hands earlier."

Was she serious? Cole breathed a brief humorless laugh. "I was high on adrenaline, begging you to escape when I thought you'd jump at the prospect." He cleared his throat. "You recall that you hugged me earlier?"

"That is not fair to bring up."

"Exactly."

A quick nod. "Okay. I'll come."

"And you'll be perfectly safe, too."

* * *

Cole set his bag on the floor beside his bed and gestured for Hesper to sit in the recliner to wait while he took out his contacts and put his glasses on.

He sat on the sofa near Hesper. This had better be a quick conversation. Talking about David and Hesper together made him want to take a long walk over coals ablaze with the death-light. He'd rather send his feet into the afterlife without him.

Time to shut off the feelings and turn on the educator.

"Pregnancy. Well, there are ways of preventing that, but my research on the different bases around the country suggests there are a lot of Unified becoming pregnant. It shouldn't be happening, but it is."

"That is frightening," Hesper said.

Frightening, true, and uncomfortable. "I have no guarantees for you, my friend. Children of Meros and Unified couples are considered Mongrels. They're not permitted to live. You just do whatever you can to avoid pregnancy." A bleak smile drifted into his lips.

"No one wants to explain the details to me. Why is this so troubling?"

Are you serious, woman? "Hesper, as for me, it's uncomfortable because . . . I want to marry you. Your marriage to someone else, particularly my own brother, and all it entails, is not something I'm enthusiastic to lecture you about."

Her bleak smile matched his own. "I understand. I did not think of that. I am just so scared."

With his finger, he traced the edge of a coffee ring on a coaster near his lamp. Taking a deep breath, he plunged into honesty. "I would be, too. That's a valid reaction. We're going to do all we can to alleviate that." He studied her face: pale, paralyzed, blank. "You hear me, Hesper?"

Signs of an attempted smile crept into her face. "How did you know Joram?"

Oh, that again. "Uh, well, he was as Meros as anyone I ever knew. Showed up and started working as a janitor in the Bastion. Trinity bumped him up for training as a soldier, and he became her assistant in about five months. She can get anything done, that woman.

"Before The Conquest, the Unified had a better system. They kept track of each birth, recorded names, gave citizens identification numbers. Back then, this would never have happened. If he didn't have identification, he would not have just waltzed in and gotten a job, much less joined the military.

"Our system is pathetic. Runs on brute force, fear, and hope." He stopped tracing the coffee ring. "Hope for the Kyrios and military, not civilians. We hope the brutal tactics work as a deterrent to disobedience and dishonesty. Anyway, I'm off track. It may be that the less you know about the Kyrios, the better. So, uh, yes. Joram participated in a few purgings, but . . ."

"What are purgings?"

"It's the killing of alleged undesirables. We don't do them on a grand scale anymore. Maybe a few troublesome communities. Or if someone reports a mongrel, the Kyrios send soldiers to get rid of them unless the mongrelism is rampant. In which case, law enforcement wardens take care of it."

"My brother killed people who were part Unified?"

"It's likely. He went. Whether or not he killed anyone, I don't know. I never went on a purging with him."

"And you? You have gone on purgings?"

A terrible frog foamed up in Cole's throat. "I have."

"How could you do that? How could *he* do that? *You*, I guess I understand, but Joram?" She shook her head. "It is the evilest thing I have heard of."

"I haven't accepted one in ten years. I won't do it anymore. They hate it, because it's part of training, and I have to hand the responsibility over to someone else during my periods as a trainer," Cole said. He cleared the frog out. "They no longer attempt to give me those assignments. This is why they jab at me about having Gentle sentiments." He leaned forward. "Think, Hesper. Why did your mama abandon her children?"

She didn't answer. Of course, she didn't. The answer would be too disrespectful to her papa.

"It's because your papa said 'no.'" Cole shrugged. "The Unified raised her to obey her husband without question, and we're all that way somehow. We act on what we've been taught is right, often without considering that it's not so simple. I killed people, but I believed it was right at the time."

His words made her squirm and screw up her face, but she rose to the challenge despite her discomfort. "That means my brother is doubly wicked. He was taught differently. Why would he try to come home after doing something so horrible to his own people?"

"When you're dying, I suspect you don't care as much what people think of you. He may have had a change of heart. That's only a guess, though." Cole brought his hands to his lap and folded them. Tipping his head, he smirked. "Your papa raised a bunch of rebels, didn't he?"

Hesper laughed a little through the tears. "It seems he did." The laughing eyes faded as if she saw something beyond Cole— something terrible. "Nothing is of value anymore. Nothing. It is all waste. I feel I am standing where I thought I was safe, but the earth around me has fallen away. I am alone on my solid ground." She whispered, "When is *that* going to give out?"

"Hesper, is there anything I can—"

She touched her cheek and winced. "No," she barked. "You can stay out of my way." Standing, she faced the door, completely still. Cole followed her gaze to David, who stood in the doorway.

"David, come in."

"Things not go so well?" David asked.

Hesper rushed past him without a stomp, slam, or tear.

"Her father wouldn't talk to her. Her mother begged him, and he wouldn't hear her. Just now we were talking about how we knew her brother. It went downhill at that point."

"We knew him? Who's her brother?"

"Remember Joe Cuspus? He ran away when she was young. He passed for at least twenty, but their father isn't old enough for that. He had to be only fifteen or sixteen."

"Joe was her brother? A Gentle?" He laughed. "You've got to be kidding. Oh, man. Don't tell Trinity, she'd be mortified. She was so hot for him, it was absurd. Did you ever report this to the Kyrios?

"No!"

"I don't blame you. I wouldn't either. Though, it's pretty important to know that the Earth People have infiltrated the military."

Cole sniffed at that.

David sauntered over to the sitting area. "They shot him, didn't they? Declared a traitor, I think."

"Yep. He attempted to warn his community that the Kyrios were sending a spy. Whatever his political loyalties were, he cared about his family."

"You mean to tell me they killed Hesper's brother because of you?"

"I never wanted her to leave those woods." Cole laid his head back on the chair and began mentally counting the leaves in the pattern of the copper ceiling. "I didn't want her to know any of this."

"About that." David flopped into a chair. "I caught what you said about loving her. At the trial."

David would never turn Cole in, but some things kept best as secrets.

"Oh," David grunted. "Do you ever look guilty. Time to 'fess up, Cole. Let's talk."

Twenty-One | Post-Conquest: 232

SHEETS OF RAIN scraped the earth and crashed onto the roof. Cloaked in silence, Hesper hunkered down in her room, staring out the window at the torrent blocking her view of the base. Always faithful, nature's rejuvenating power had a way with her mind. Her options for experiencing it may have changed, but it would be with her wherever she lived.

In the early afternoon, she laid down to try for much-needed sleep until a soft knock rattled her door.

"Go away."

"No can do. I have a proposal for you." The confidence in David's voice did not match the knock.

"Propose somewhere else. I do not care, and I want to sleep."

"Hesper, knocky-knocky, I'm coming in." David entered in full uniform with a folder. "Okay, my dear, listen up."

She squashed her head with a pillow and rolled onto her side. He knelt on the bed, took the pillow from her with little effort, chucked it behind him, and spoke without skipping a beat. "First off, young lady, show some respect to your elders." He crawled off the bed and stood.

"Respect? I have been through en—"

"Yes, you have. Which is almost entirely the reason I'm here." He softened his serious tone with a slight smile. "I won't pretend to understand your suffering. I understand your reasons, though I've never experienced your situation. However, I've lost my wife and child. Don't you dare think I'm not grieving just because I've kept my chin up. If you recall, Vincent orders us not to grieve. He means that. You get me? He *means* it." He pointed at her. "If he catches wind of us grieving for a so-called witch, we'll have big problems on our hands. My grief must have its place and time."

She was awake to him now as she sat up. She would listen.

He smiled. "Now that we're friends again, I have no interest in acquiring another wife at this time. You're lovely, and if I must, I will. I wouldn't lay a hand on you, though. I mean"—he twisted his face and looked away, thoughtful—"we'd discuss the situation thoroughly. Women have needs as well, and I recognize that. So . . . a conversation would be warranted." Clearing his throat, he continued, "I'd much rather see you given to someone else for all our sakes. The law says a Gentle can't stay unmarried with the Meros for more than two weeks, or she'll be executed. Plain and simple.

"Here is my proposal. I know someone who wants one wife and one wife only. You. Will you have him?"

"What . . . Cole?"

"That's the one."

"He lied to me and betrayed the Uni—"

"He did no such thing, you beautiful woman. Here." He tossed the folder onto the bed, and a few papers fell out of place. "Read these. He may have lied, but he didn't betray." Hands thrust into his pockets, David distracted himself feeling the curtains and inspecting the pattern.

Hesper picked up a handful of the papers and sniffed at them. Slightly floral and something else . . . She read a few but did not need to look far to see the truth. It gave her much to think about, much to forgive, and much to be grateful for.

"Done?" He smiled. "I don't know what he's told you. I only know you think he's a traitor. My nerdy little brother will never get married if you won't have him. I can't have a permanent bachelor disgracing the Chandler name, can I? People will talk." His deadpan expression twisted into an amused grin and wink-wink. "I went through great trouble to get those papers to you, and I want you to consider the evidence. Exhibit A. I need to get those back before someone finds out I've taken them and hangs me by my toes. Have you had your fill?"

If not for Cole's deception, Hesper would not be alive to hold a grudge against him. She stared blankly at the papers, aching to hold them to her chest to cry, but that did not make sense to do.

"Why did he come to us anyway? What did he mean to do with us?"

"Ask him yourself. I'm just here for the evidence." David smiled. "What I will tell you is that I'm sure—no, I'm convinced—he cares about you. He'd leave all this"—he swept his arm before him—"if he could do it without hurting anyone.

"My brother doesn't care for most women. It's a pity because he's a bonny, brawny boy and someone ought to have the privilege of the affection of a snob of his caliber. Losing the woman he cares about—to me of all people—would be unbearable. I dare say one of us would lose an eye or limb over it."

David grabbed up the papers and put them back in their folder. "Hesper, one more thing. Maybe Two. Three—as many things as it takes."

"What?"

"If he had an itch to harm you or your people, what would he care if I added you to my 'harem,' as he likes to call it?" He bounced on the balls of his feet, shaking his head. "He wouldn't. He could also lay claim to you by force. You may be mighty, but let's be truthful, he's bigger than you and an honored senior officer who's expert in fairly wicked psychological tactics and martial arts, as we all are.

"If he wanted to, he could destroy you physically in a heartbeat, emotionally in less than a day, and mentally in a week. Meros law permits him to wed you, bed you, whip your back bloody, and lock you up, but he hasn't—and he won't. He'll just leave and waste away as a scholarly hermit in the wilderness, living on dong quai steeped in dew while he flagellates himself once a day with stolen locks of your hair."

Hesper could not help smiling. "You are his brother, and you are Meros. How can I trust you?"

"Sometimes, my dear, you'll find yourself in circumstances where trust is the only option worth choosing." David turned the doorknob. "Cole's having meals in his room today. See you later."

"David!"

He faced her.

She could not say it. He deserved to know how much she . . . liked him, how she would have been willing to marry him, that it was not a dislike for him that led her to do what she was about to do, but she could not.

He appeared thoughtful, a fragile smile played with his mouth. "I think I know, Hesper." He scrunched his nose and nodded. "I know."

* * *

The rain beat on the window beside Hesper. A low, long peal of thunder grounded her in the present. The first knock received no response. She knocked again.

Cole opened the door. Surprised, he blinked at her with bloodshot eyes. Was it sleeplessness? Eyestrain? Crying? Whatever the reason, his eyes took a deep breath, aglow with delight upon the sight of her.

Adahy.

Tears spilled out, despite her will against them.

He peered over his glasses, his finger tucked inside a yellowed book he held at his side. "Will you come in?"

With a sniffle, she nodded.

He stepped back. "I'm glad you've stopped by." The door closed behind her.

Her lips trembled as she whispered, "I hope you can forgive me."

"Did you say something?"

"I hope you can forgive me," she said.

"Forgive you for what?" He pointed to the soft chairs in the middle of the room. "Let's sit."

As she spoke, she followed his lead. "Judging you. Not believing you. You are the kindest Meros to ever live, and I am no better than bitter Dierdre in the forest, criticizing you without any facts."

He sat, but she did not join him. Instead, she stood, full of feelings she lacked adequate words to express.

"You told me the truth. I saw it. You spared the Unified more than once when the Kyrios were going to kill us. You convinced them we were dangerous, organized, and capable of far more than we are."

"How did you find out I told the truth?"

"David. He showed me the records of your meetings with the Kyrios."

Cole burst into laughter. "Aside from the fact that was incredibly illegal, that was a kind thing for him to do."

"Why do they not send someone else to confirm your reports?"

"It's my baby, not theirs. I've sent a few disguised as hunters— only at certain times—as temporary help to back my claims. They've seen your people training and receiving mail. Things like that. It's up to the Kyrios to decide whether to take my word for it. Until Vince called the mission off, they appeared to."

Hesper lowered herself to her knees and regarded his face, affectionate respect pressing against her heart. "Will you forgive me, Cole?"

"Nothing to forgive. It's understandable—justified even. Sit with me?"

"I feel as though I have been terribly proud, and I need to stay here for a time."

He covered his mouth. Trying not to laugh? He deserved credit for trying. "Please, don't make me feel like a god on a sofa. Come up here. Your kneeling makes me uncomfortable."

Very well. She sat where he requested. "Cole, I have other things to talk to you about."

"I'm listening."

"Why did you come to spy on my community?"

"I went to destroy. Until I met you." The side of his mouth curved up. "I was young and ignorant. I saw the women and some hunters, but I never saw a Unified child. To confuse me further, this child tried to help my comrade, your brother. It touched me.

"I realized that you were people. Real people. Knowing Joe passed for one of us, while being one of them, well, it blurred the lines of prejudice for me considerably. It sounds silly, but it was a profound moment.

"I had just begun my search for God and requested It allow me to experience things that would make my mind open and capable of receiving Its influence. Seems one answer to that prayer was you."

"Cole," Hesper hoped that staring out the window would keep her from crying again. "I will not mistreat you anymore. I am grateful for your kindness to me, and I promise to keep my word to you."

Cole squinted, frowned, then grinned. "Underneath all your straight talk, what is it you're not saying straight?" He swiped his fingers underneath his collar to tug at something. "Dare I ask if you want this back?" Her betrothal token! He took it up and over his head and held it out.

Was he offering marriage again? After all this?

He withdrew his hand. "If I have misunderstood you, I'm sorry. Don't feel obligated. I—"

"You have not misunderstood."

A broad smile. "Well, this is quite something." He placed the token around her neck. "Ten minutes ago, I planned to transfer to another base. Thank God for a snitchy big brother—a blessing for the first time." He held his breath and blew it out. "Hesper, I'm going to be honest. I am desperately fighting an urge to kiss you right now—I won't!" He held up a finger. "But perhaps it will do you good to know how I'm feeling." He laughed uncomfortably and stood. "This is wrong in so many ways, but we're doing the best we can, right? I don't know what I'm saying. This thrills me more the second time around."

"I feel it, too, though I have already been touched, Cole," she said with shame.

Cole sat beside her. "Look at me." Without a touch, he curved his hands around the sides of her face as if holding it. "We are going to do things right. Meanwhile, remember that you have done nothing wrong. You and your heart and mind are precious to me. You are not impure, and I hope I can convince you of that." He wiped his eyes. "I'll get a grip on myself. No compromise for my own self-control issues. No guilt on you for anything."

Picking up his book, he crossed his legs and attempted to read. In two seconds, he clapped the book shut and tossed it behind him. "I'll go kiss David instead."

Twenty~Two | Post-Conquest: 232

THEY WERE TO SAY Cole had gone to his father's old vineyards for a time of reflection. The truth was, Cole had to sneak out under the Kyrios' nose and tie up loose ends in Hesper's community.

He allowed Avriam and Theia to tell him of Hesper's loss. Avriam fell to his knees, ashamed, begging Cole for forgiveness for his daughter's behavior. It was heartbreaking and infuriating at the same time.

The following day, Cole announced that he would be leaving the community. Avriam didn't seem surprised. Almost as if it were the most natural thing to do after losing your betrothed in such a manner.

While Cole packed, Avriam did basic repairs on the loft, preparing it for someone else to use once Cole was gone. After a while, Avriam's nail pounding stopped. Haunted and empty, he held a hammer at his side.

"What is it, Avriam?"

The words seemed stuck in his throat. He opened and closed his mouth several times before gaining the courage to say, "I am full of such regret." He choked up on the hammer. "I have a confession to make."

"Yes, sir?"

Shame softened his face. "I already apologized to you for Hesper's behavior and loss, but she returned home, Adahy, and Theia begged me to persuade her to stay. I would not. I could not bear one more disobedient child, knowing she had been touched. No compromise! Compromise wears down the integrity of a people. But I was wrong. Forgive me." He spat out the request for forgiveness, then broke down into sharp, coughing sobs that wrung tears from his eyes. "You are a better man than I am. I believe you would have married her with the black X, and my pride took that from you." He wiped his eyes and turned away to make himself busy. "You will find a woman who is worthy of your strengths, but I consider you a son and a brother forever. You have been good to my family."

Cole touched Avriam's shoulder. "You are right. I care little about a black X on Hesper's face, but I forgive you. I will not marry anyone else." Cole put his arms around him for a firm pat on the back and a kiss on the cheek. "Farewell, my friend."

"I wish you sunlight, prosperity, and peace, Adahy."

Cole slipped out of the loft and lowered himself to the ground. Falling night pressed itself into the forest. Cole didn't care if the Kyrios knew he had it in for them, but he cared if they caught him showing it outright and ruined his and Hesper's lives because of it. Time to get home.

In the open, Cole looked back for the last time. A quiet smile brushed his lips upward. This place flipped his opinions over to expose them and drove a wooden wick into his heart. It waited to be set alight by an opportunity for revolution—a real one—not a subjugation of the unbelievers. The only way for healthy humans was to live with the freedom to choose and declare what they believed without fear.

David and their mother often said Cole was unrealistic. The claim had little merit coming from a woman who expected children to think with adult logic and a man who believed he could marry several women while maintaining a happy home. Their good father, a simple man, praised Cole and believed in him. He accomplished nothing worth anything to the Kyrios, and his missing finger disqualified him from joining the military to even try. Wise and kind, Dad never declared Cole's hopes to be unrealistic.

If only he were here now.

* * *

Hesper sat in the honeyed-rose room with a book of Theocracian philosophers Vincent had assigned during her conversion classes. Since she could read and take on more "in-depth" assignments, he thought it would be a valuable study for her.

Vincent treated Hesper with kindness. He did nothing inappropriate. Not a touch, not a raised voice. Nothing. A few days into her classes, the thought that Vincent murdered Jade came to her mind less often. His patience when she challenged him the first couple of days earned her respect. She would never respect him, though—only his patience deserved it.

She dropped her books, feigned ignorance, snapped her pencil tips, over-sharpened her pencils repeatedly, and "accidentally" spilled things on him until he no longer permitted drinks during her classes. Since he was not even annoyed by her petulance, the effort wasted her time and energy. Not to mention how dangerous her actions were. How far could Vincent be pushed? The day she stopped her little rebellions, he acknowledged it with a smile. "Now that you're done flailing your indignation about, we can be productive."

Productive meant teaching her to pray.

He insisted on praying in the Judgment Room, but Hesper refused to go. So, he dropped the matter, and they prayed in the classroom. Hesper could not appreciate Vincent's hands raised in worship to an allegedly spotless being. If his hands were holy, they were holy unto himself, not God.

He taught her many things about the Meros, the Kyrios, and The Conquest.

That she must be dedicated to God.

All she did and said belonged to the invisible deity, and by extension, to the Kyrios.

She must separate herself unto the mighty ruler of all as a consecrated vessel of Its love, goodness, and beauty.

Efforts to be spiritual struck Hesper as an attempt to manufacture the feeling of living in the woods. A weak form of it touched her once while reciting a prayer with raised hands.

She had only a few days of classes left, with two days off for marriage. Once the classes were done, she had to read the extra books her literacy earned for her.

A simple thing, this conversion concept. How did they ever determine that someone truly converted to their beliefs? They spoke of conversion as if it were a matter of faith and conviction, but when it came down to it, knowledge, not belief, satisfied them. Which was fine. It made it easier to complete the classes and find peace in her new home.

The ticking clock entered her consciousness. What had she just read? The words went through her head, but nothing stuck there during the last few minutes. *She* had to have better self-control and focus on the words.

How was Mama doing? How was Cole in the woods? He planned on being home today. It would be nice to see him before going to sleep. The clock over the fireplace indicated a late hour, but she did not fully understand the clocks yet. Still, he could be back . . .

Lorelei had left a cup of jasmine tea some time ago. It was cold by now. She clapped the book shut and drank the tea. It was a little warm yet.

Driving rain rumbled on the roof and windows in the foyer. Hesper set the cup down and sighed.

He would not be home.

David had introduced her to spicy-sweet pickles at lunch, and they were on her mind for the rest of the afternoon. Maybe she could crunch a few before bed . . .

Outside of the honeyed-rose room, cigarette smoke ruled the air. David drank and puffed away his woes in the dining room all evening, stuffed in a hollow tree of a house to smoke himself like a slab of meat. She did not judge him, but she did regard him more highly than he regarded himself and hated to see him this way. She hated seeing Papa display anger when he felt fear, too. This behavior had a different face with the same mind.

She had to go through the dining room to get to the kitchen, so she entered with gracious feelings, trying to pretend David was not drunk. Perhaps he was not.

"How are you, my dear?" he asked.

His voice was clear, and he seemed alert and pleasant.

"I am well, David. How are you?"

"Ohhh . . ." He twisted his hand back and forth with a shrug of the shoulders. "Pretty crappy, actually." He gave his cigarette a flick into the tray and took a puff, blowing the smoke through his nostrils.

"Is there anything I can do for you, David?"

Mischief twinkled in his eyes. "Nah. Just take care of your happiness, honey. Let yourself be happy."

"I can do that. I think."

"Say . . . Why're you up?"

"Reading Theocracian philosophy."

He cringed.

"Cole said he would come back today, right?" she asked.

"Yeah, that's what he said." David grinned.

Thunder shook the windows. Storming now? If Cole came home in this, Hesper would be upset. "Do you think he will be reckless enough to try to come home in this downpour?"

"Psh." David's shrewd smile answered for him. "You're planning on getting married tomorrow, right? You think he's going to postpone that for a little rain? Especially with the way you two torture yourselves with this no-touching business." He winked, lazily wagging his fingers in her direction, the cigarette propped between

234

them. "You know that fool came and kissed me because he couldn't kiss you when you agreed to marry him?" He shuddered. "Disgusting. Good thing I'm man enough to take it, but I sure hope he's a better kisser for you."

"Better?" He was obviously kidding somewhat, but . . .

He chuckled. "I suppose if there isn't any kissing before you're married, there won't be any comparisons made, hm? I've never thought about it."

"Jade said your kisses were like a mugful of drinking chocolate made with cream." Perhaps it was too soon to mention that?

"Did she now? I like that. Sounds pleasant. I think I'd kiss that." He flicked cigarette ash into the tray and took another drag. "I'd say hers were . . . berries fresh off a sun-soaked berry bush." He blew out a sigh and forced a smile. "Well, honey, you'll have to report to me on Cole's, hey? I'd say his kiss resembled puppy breath and cheesy noodles."

The front door opened, sucking in a chilly gust of wind and a quick earful of its screams. Hesper ran to the foyer. Cole pulled his hood back and wiped his face with his hands. He took off his cloak and dropped it on the floor, and finally noticed Hesper after he removed the first moccasin.

She approached and picked up his wet cloak.

"I can't believe you're up."

"Reading. Waiting for you."

Cole picked up his bag. "Let's talk. I need a bath."

* * *

Hesper hurried ahead of him. By the time he reached his wing, water already rushed into the tub and fresh clothes waited on the back of his sofa.

"How are your classes at the Bastion?" He plopped his things on the bed.

Annoyed, Hesper grunted. "I hear what he says. I answer his questions. I behave. At first, it was difficult to keep from dreaming of field dressing Vincent."

Cole entered the bathroom. "Normal ladies around here dream of undressing him."

"That is ridiculous!" Hesper dripped oil into his bath. "Why would anyone undress a grown man unless he is near death or paralyzed?"

Cole froze. What did she say? The Unified were too pragmatic about marriage and reproduction for her not to understand what he meant. Then again, maybe not. They explained biology but not presentation or romance. He laughed. They probably had an adventure on their hands.

"You don't understand what that means, Hesper?"

She capped the oil and frowned at him. "Is this more poetry? I am getting better about that."

"No, ma'am! Quite literal. We can talk about it another time. Tomorrow, perhaps." His cheeks went hot. When did he become a blusher? It's not like sex was uncharted territory for him.

You've never loved anyone before, though.

He followed her with his eyes as she returned the bottle to its cabinet. "How do you know where everything is?"

"I have been sneaking around, trying to learn about you."

He shrugged a shoulder. "That's okay. You look embarrassed, but it's okay. How is David?"

"The same. He is up now, drinking wine in the dining room."

"Still? Is Evelyn around?"

"She left the country. That is all I know."

Cole sucked at his teeth. Not good. David suspected Evelyn of affairs long ago, and for her to go so far away? Suspicious. "How about Anise and Dulce?"

"Dulce just lives. Quietly walks around, reads, plays the harp in her room. Anise has not been seen. Her door is still locked."

"That's unfortunate." Cole took his hair down. "Anise reported her suspicion about Jade to Evelyn and David. I wonder if she didn't realize what would happen. That's an awful load of guilt to carry without talking to someone about it."

"I have tried to get her to come out, but maybe another try would be worth the effort. How did things go with Mama and Papa?"

"Avriam knelt to me, begging forgiveness for your disappearance. Before I left, he asked forgiveness for not letting you stay when you visited." Cole's voice cracked. "Your Mama returned the box of salt."

"Poor Mama and Papa," Hesper whispered. She checked the water in the tub, flicked it from her fingers and turned off the faucet. Wiping her eyes, she said, "I rarely cried until I left the woods, Ada—Cole." Sometimes she said his name without difficulty, but other times, she forgot herself.

Too many griefs at once. Time for happy thoughts. "You're pampering me, my friend. We will be married tomorrow. I'm getting all the fire before I've chopped the wood—all these wifely things."

"I show you my affection," she said. "If you think this is all the fire I have to kindle, it is a wonder you ever wanted to marry me." A passion-inducing saucy smile made her the most beautiful being he'd ever seen. She approached the door. "I am also quite good at sewing and patching clothes."

The door closed behind her. *Well, that was confusing.*

Twenty~Three | Post-Conquest: 232

TRINITY SHOVED THE paper across the desk to Cole. He signed his name on a line at the bottom, and she snatched it up to file it away.

Certainly, Cole would have tried to go to someone else for this if he knew Hesper's history with his sister, but why bring it up for no reason? To just say that Trinity exposed her and struck her and stepped on her hand and . . . Maybe she should have told him.

Still, looking at Trinity did not bother Hesper. Maybe because she had Cole with her.

"Do you have any mark or token for her?" Trinity asked, clearly avoiding even a glance at Hesper.

Cole shook his head.

Trinity gave an annoyed lid-fluttering roll of the eye. "Even David, the Ever-Benevolent-And-Gracious, gave his girls piercings."

Cole set the pen back on the desk and stared at Trinity. "You've seen girls on the auction block. They've been owned by so many different men, they're riddled with holes and inked from head to toe. Ownership. I hate its meaning. We don't need that. It doesn't seem in accordance with a god of love."

"Something, Cole!"

"Is she my wife or not? My choice or not?"

Trinity seated herself. "Yes, I suppose it's your choice. I'm your big sister. I've got to do something to bug you now and then." She deigned to throw her gaze at Hesper. "Judging by the looks on your faces, I assume I should congratulate you. I can't say I've ever seen a Gentle look that happy at her wedding." Trinity warmed 'til she was almost pretty. "Be happy."

Cole extended his hand to Hesper. His gentle grasp spoke so many loving, silent words, the thoughts and feelings it elicited overwhelmed her. The sensation of fireflies rising inside of her was not new. David woke that up. She cursed it, resigned to it, cursed it, then honored it. It came with regrets as much as sweetness.

Cole drew her hand to his warm lips, and her mind clouded to such an extent she decided against speaking and laughed at herself. Such foolishness. Blushing would not be so embarrassing now, right?

No. Still embarrassing.

Cole grinned, winked, and led her out and through the dim Bastion into daylight. Farther down the road, David walked toward them, waving his hands in the air. Dark glasses covered his eyes. When they met, his genuine smile forced Hesper to reciprocate.

"Well, fancy meeting you here," he crowed.

"Is your head bothering you?" Cole asked.

David breathed a laugh. "Always. Not much, though. The only plaster last night was in the walls—I swear it—but the sun is too friendly for what hangover I do have—Say!" He gestured to Cole and Hesper's clasped hands. "You went along and took care of business, I see."

Cole squeezed her hand. "Maybe we can have a ceremony with dancing someday. Drum out some songs. Exchange actual vows." He glanced at Hesper, his smile laced with sorrow.

David lit a cigarette. "Party like we're Unified, hey? Heading back home, then?" He waggled his eyebrows and grinned, exhaling a stream of smoke.

"Your eyebrows are losing their head, you hedonist."

"Yeah, guilty as charged." David giggled. "Before you go, whenever you can spare time, we should talk. They're tossing around the idea of an assignment for you in a few months, and you should get a heads up 'cause ol' Vince will probably be looking for prompt commitment. You know how he gets snap decisions out of people."

"Good to know. Thanks."

David clasped Cole's shoulder and clapped it a few times. "Congratulations to you both. Your hair looks especially lovely with those chicory flowers, Hesper." He gave her a wide-eyed, sassy smirk and wink. "And Cole, as usual, you look like a thick stick with hair." He smiled and went his way.

A momentous thing had occurred. Marriage. Hesper married a Meros—willingly.

This might be an unpleasant day. Cole and Adahy might be the same people, but Cole did not act Unified. He carried himself like a Meros man. Would he treat her the way Adahy would have? Her belly grew queasy.

Maybe she had made a mistake—an enormous mistake.

Ginger tea would be nice for her stomach.

Marriage was overrated.

The first day of marriage—definitely overrated.

It was too late now.

Cole opened the door to their home and allowed her to walk in ahead of him.

How pale and flushed she looked in the long mirror on the wall. How could she be both? Her mouth open to plead with him for consideration, she turned around.

"Do we have ging—?"

He took her gently by the waist and drew her to himself.

This was okay. It was not what she expected, but it was okay. Nice, even. She closed her mouth. What did she expect? She had never considered it, really.

He unclasped their hands to caress her cheek and administer several blessedly tender kisses on her lips. It settled her stomach far better than ginger tea would have, even as it unsettled her heart.

This was, most certainly, not a mistake. Tears may have been plentiful, but poetry made a lot more sense since leaving the woods. It seemed the only way to describe her reality right now. It was . . . bathing in hot water, drinking warm milk, and staring into a fire.

She had her answer for David, and it was not puppy breath and cheesy noodles.

He didn't smell like only spice today, but a fir tree. Much stronger than whiffs she would catch in the forest, but what a peaceful, familiar—wait. Why did he stop kissing her? She opened her eyes and sorted a smile out of the emotional chaos. His lazily serene face warmed her. More than anything, she wished he would kiss her again. Still, warm, masculine hands on her face and waist were enough goodness for one person. Overindulgence bred wastefulness.

"I've been aching to get my lips on you for two years." He caressed her cheek with his thumb. "I want to kiss you again, but I don't want to be overbearing."

She smiled. "I was thinking how I wish you would, and that I should not be greedy or indulge myself by asking."

"Our virtues are a little too virtuous." His lips touched her cheek. "You deserve a few indulgences, and I intend to indulge you so often, you'll begin to feel entitled to it."

She closed her eyes, savoring the simple pleasure of his touch— lawful touch. With kisses as soft as mullein leaf, his lips grazed her cheeks and eyelids, her forehead.

It was silly to think, but she could take his hand and touch her face with it all day long. As she reached for his hand, he stopped and pulled his face away from her. She opened her eyes, frowning, aching for his face to be near hers. Was he teasing her?

"Are you crying?" he asked, amused, perplexed. Concerned?

"Is that not normal?"

"If it's not, it should be." He smiled.

Adahy. He was here. It was him—her precious friend.

Hesper whispered, "I do not know what is happening exactly. This is not what I expected or learned about. This must—I will sound stupid—this must be how the sunrise would feel if it were sentient."

"Hesper! Listen to my Unified woman waxing poetic!"

She reached up to touch his smile. He closed his eyes, kissing her fingertips.

"Is there a moon rise, too?" she asked.

His lively, delighted expression startled her.

"Your face!" she laughed. "Is that because of what I said?"

He scooped her into his arms with a rakish grin.

"No more of this treetops-in-the-way torture?" She laughed.

"Ab-so-lutely not."

Twenty-Four | Post-Conquest: 232

SUNLIGHT STRUGGLED AGAINST thick white curtains, saturating them with a warm glow and peeking out through the sides. The muted light rested on Cole's beautiful face. Hesper smiled and sidled up to his body and nestled her cold nose between his jaw and neck to warm it up. The arm she lay on came to life and curled around her. Cole smacked his lips and rumbled out the first of his morning voice.

"So, it was."

"What was what?"

"The most sensational experience of my life." He brought his free hand to where hers lay across his chest and held it. "Holding your strong, healing hands, that is."

She laughed. "I do not know why, but hearing you say that made my heart pound."

"I know." He kissed her forehead. "But"—he kissed her again—"the rest of you killed me, and I went to whatever spirit home the dead go to. I'm dead to any and all sensations experienced apart from you."

A giggle escaped her lips. She stifled it and pressed her face into the pillow.

"Still blushing?" He sounded surprised.

"You know very well that I am!" She laughed and kissed his prickly jaw. "You smell of fir trees and morning skin."

"Morning skin? You've got me there. What's morning skin?"

"Skin smells different right after waking up. I like yours."

"Does it taste different, too?" He aligned his face with hers and kissed her.

She whispered, "This makes me feel—"

"Well, naturally." He breathed a laugh and kissed the corner of her mouth, his hand tracing her spine.

"No." Her throat tightened.

On to her jaw.

"It makes me feel I am a part of nature in a way I never have been before."

Her ear.

"As if I can just—"

Brushing her hair away, he kissed her neck.

"Exist without worrying about anything else. No concern about my purpose or about . . . life or death. It makes things seem . . . hazy." She swallowed. "It is hard to talk when you do that, you know."

He propped himself on his elbow. "Do what?"

"Things that feel nice."

He chuckled. "You are a delightful person to love and be loved by, Hesper."

"I get the feeling I must be doing something strange."

"Not strange. Just perfect."

She eyed him. He spared her feelings, not wanting her to know she was odd.

"Vincent has told me about worship," she said. "I think I have worshiped a flower by touching it gently, worshiped a child by kissing their small head, worshiped a scent by appreciating it." She held his face in her hand and tucked his hair behind his ear. "Is this worship, Cole?"

He appeared thoughtful. "Worship is, by definition, reverence and adoration." His fingertips tickled her shoulder. "I experienced a great deal of reverence and adoration for you even before we married. It seems natural to carry that over into new expressions of our affection and aspects of our relationship." Another kiss for her lips. "Thank you for trusting me, dear friend."

Heat flooded her face. "I think marriage will be hard on my cheeks."

Cole relaxed on his pillow. "Look what I found." He grabbed something near her head. A chicory flower. "We probably have a mess of them all over the bed."

She kissed his cheek.

"I don't want to get up. Ever," he said.

"I do."

"That's too bad. We may need a compromise. I propose we lay here and imagine it, then stay to serve ourselves bed-tea."

"Bed-tea?"

"You know, where you have tea right after waking up? I'll take a strong infusion of your chamomile kisses and an ungodly-sized mugful of your cayenne ones. Keeps sickness away." He frowned. "What? If hot water is the issue, we can take a bath."

"We have probably missed breakfast."

"I'm overcome with grief. I'll take the tea now." He puckered his lips like a little boy.

"My stomach is eating itself," she retorted. "You *should* be overcome with grief."

He rolled out of bed with a great sigh that morphed into a groan, then shuffled off to the bathroom.

On the table beside the bed, the betrothal token and rhodonite necklace lay half in the shadow and half in the glow of sunlight. In this somewhat fortunate turn of events, the reality of a fresh murder still hung over her head. Murdered only a week ago, Jade appeared to be dishonored due to the edict of a tyrant.

No grief.

She'd forgotten. No grief. Hesper had thought David showed a lack of self-respect, but, truly, he grieved in a way the Kyrios accepted. *Poor David.*

Cole strode into the room, clothed and hair brushed.

"Cole."

"Hm?"

"I am sure Jade made friends with anyone. I do not presume to have been special to her. I have learned that I trust and love too fast, and her manner was to ask for love and trust immediately. Though, my concern was one of justice as much as affection."

Cole sat on the bed. "That sounds like her—and you."

"She kept me level-headed during the first couple of days and probably saved my life, keeping me from doing something foolish. She is special to me and the injustice is disturbing." She scooched over and grabbed the rhodonite necklace from the table to look it over, feeling its smooth surface. "How can I preserve her memory, Cole? Is there a way? How can I grieve without grieving? How are you doing it?"

Cole's eyes dulled, and his smile faded.

"Never mind. I should not bring it up."

"No, no." He touched her hand. "That's a good question. Bottled up grief is unhealthy." Gesturing to himself, he said, "I have turned to prayer. Jade was a good friend to me.

"I knelt and offered my emotions to the being who gave me the ability to feel them. I thanked God for allowing me to know someone that was so painful to lose, and I thanked It for a decent sense of justice."

That would not do it for Hesper. Neither would tears. She had cried herself out in the Bastion and did not need more of that.

"David drinks and smokes, you pray, but what is there for me? I have no belief in this god. I cannot turn to It and feel I have done anything lasting."

"What do the Unified do?"

"You know."

"'Course I do!" He smiled. "I want you to think about it."

The Unified buried their dead, grieved, but carried on working to survive. They taught their children the truth: loved ones were gone, and their bodies would decay and become a part of the soil, feeding the trees and plants that ensured the Unified's safety and health.

Jade's memory concerned Hesper. Impotent tears were not as honorable as actions taken to preserve the dead in the earth and the mind of the living.

"You have your afterlife," she said, "and Vincent barred Jade's way to it because he did not allow you to use this death-light, correct?"

"Yes, that's what many believe. The Kyrios create the lightless flame—no one knows how—and sell it for funerary purposes. Her journey to the afterlife would have been in the smoke."

"I will give her a Unified afterlife. I will gather some of her remains and bury it by the apple tree. She will live in the tree."

"That's a good idea for her and for you." He patted her hand. "I'll get breakfast and bring it back. We'll do it after we eat. Sound good?"

* * *

After Hesper honored Jade, she and Cole spent the morning seated on the sofa, looking out on the spring blossoms in the backyard. Lorelei brought them black tea and an assortment of fresh, spicy cookies, but they spent the rest of the time alone. Cole read portions of his favorite books aloud, and here and there they canoodled the day away in a pleasant nest of contentment and cuddles.

Early in the afternoon, Cole took up a pen and a small slip of paper from his desk. "I feel like writing a poem. . . For you."

He held the paper on a book, pen in hand, poised to write, and drew a few tiny circles in the air above the spot he intended to write on, preparing. "My wife is as beautiful"—examining her, he twisted his mouth—"as a . . . as a storm." Neat, sharp, and slanted, his words resembled letters she understood, but they were connected to each other in a way she was not familiar with.

He studied her, leaning forward to breathe in the scent of her hair, then reclined and wrote. "The smell of glory is in her hair."

A light tap on the door interrupted their peace.

Cole focused on the paper. "Come in."

"The door was ajar, otherwise I wouldn't have dared to bother you." David entered the room and stood in front of them. He took his hat off. "Cole, the Kyrios want to see you today, at your leisure. It's good."

"At my leisure?"

"Okay. As soon as possible."

"That's what I thought. What's going on?"

"I guess you'll have to ask them."

"David, are you okay?"

"With what?"

Cole shrugged. "With life and all of its wonders?"

"I'm fine."

Cole quirked an eyebrow. "Okay."

David huffed and swiped at his nose. "Evelyn left. Hired someone to deliver papers for a divorce and left."

"Divorce!" Hesper cried. "How can she do that?" Especially now. Heart racing, she glanced at Cole. Having been so close to someone, how could anyone ever part casually?

"They require nothing of her? Allowing divorce for trivial reasons necessitates counteraction. A man and woman should hold each other and mourn the loss of their unity first. I imagine that you would have very few of these separations if they required this."

Her face blazed with embarrassment. Who was she to make these assumptions and tell people what they ought to do?

David smiled. "You're probably right, sweetheart. I hope you are of that mind forever." He turned to Cole. "You have a warrior of silk, Cole. I hope you deserve her. But watch out, she has a kinship with dear Kali in the parlor." He grinned and finally relaxed.

"Kali?" Hesper asked.

"The blue woman—well, she's often black, but in my parlor, she's blue."

"What is she?"

"Goddess of destruction. Ancient religion. Perhaps you can convince Kali to destroy this whole blasted system."

"Goddess?"

"Female god," Cole explained. "It's not real, Hesper. Only a story."

David snickered. "Perhaps." Looking at Cole, he grew serious quickly. "Sorry. Let's just say that I've not had an experience with either, so I profess an equal level of faith in both."

"This does not make sense. I thought they said the Meros were favored because of their belief in God. Will your disbelief cause your god to turn on you or your people?"

"I don't know. I take that story as a legend to be—" David's eyes turned to Cole again. He stopped, swallowed hard, and nodded.

"Why do you keep stopping when you look at Cole?"

David put his hands in front of him. "I'm a bad influence it seems." Clearing his throat, he said, "I'm the only one my disbelief will destroy, Hesper." He smiled. "And I've made peace with that. But if the nations of the east went on a suicide mission and pulled their ridiculously old nuclear weapons out of hiding to break through God's favor to nail us, I'd stand outside with arms wide open to give the boom a hug before I died—say! Did you catch how that rhymed?" He smiled and sighed. "It won't happen. They hate us, but the Unified once made this the most powerful nation in the world, and the Kyrios shut us off and blocked trade, except for a few select companies and countries. Now, most of them couldn't trade with us even if we wanted them to. They fell apart. They could never attack us." He pointed at Cole. "He can back me up. He's traveled more than I have—hunting for his precious forbidden books—but we've both seen it."

"I'm rambling, though. It's what I do best when facing what I like least."

Cole cleared his throat. "I'm sorry, Dave."

David raised up one side of his mouth in a flippant smirk and snorted a laugh. "We all expected it, didn't we? When Evelyn learned that we couldn't have children, she wanted someone to mother, and I wouldn't have it be me." He set his hat back on his head. "Maybe we could've made things work out if I didn't have the other ladies around, riling her up."

He shrugged and gave Hesper one more look. "Thank you for your concern and pure heart, Hesper." With nothing else to say, he nodded and sauntered off.

Cole stood. "I may as well get this over with."

"What might they want you for?"

"Could be anything. I teach and counsel and do a host of things for them. If it's good news, it's an assignment elsewhere."

"With me?"

"That can be worked out." He took off his t-shirt to get into uniform. "Especially under the circumstances."

* * *

Dressed casually in a black Y-neck shirt and jeans, Vincent welcomed Cole into his office with a warm smile and brotherly embrace. It was unusual to see him like this. He always had a gold stud in his left ear, but his collar bone showing? The gold chain hanging there? This was Vince at home, not at work.

What in blazes was the lech up to?

Vincent's age did not exceed Cole's by more than ten years, but repeated childhood illnesses, work, and war had taken a toll on him, so he appeared considerably older. However, despite his mature look and peppery gray-black hair, his mannerisms and emotional face possessed a pleasing youthful quality.

"It's been some time since we've talked, Cole." Vincent spoke in a less authoritative voice than usual.

"A few days, Glorious One."

"That's business. Unpleasant business. I meant that it's been a while for friendly conversation, one-on-one. Sit."

Cole obeyed and sat in the hard metal folding chair.

Vincent took a small tin and whisk from a cabinet as he spoke. "So, married, huh? I never thought I'd see that happen. You were always so choosy. Even years ago, when we went out looking for company for an evening, you often seemed to spot some Gentle slave girl in the corner. We'd encourage you to make arrangements with her owner, you'd refuse, then turn down every other option available and go home early." Vincent laughed. "She's an impressive woman, though. I'll give you that. Very spirited, but in a . . . subtle way. Perhaps a Gentle wife is the way for me to go. They're more pliable."

"What have I been summoned for, Glorious One?"

Vincent seated himself on the swiveling chair behind his modest, disorderly desk. "Straight to the point, hm?" He straightened a few papers and put a pen in his pen cup. "I have a temporary position for you out west if you want it."

"What is the expected duration of this assignment?"

He shrugged, scooping green powder—matcha—from his tin into a small gold-streaked bowl. "However long it takes. I anticipate up to two years. No more. Care for some? I have another *chawan* in the cabinet." He took up a steel teapot to his right and filled the bowl with hot water.

"No. What does the position entail?"

Whisking at the liquid, he said, "Twenty years ago, they permitted mongrel births. Hundreds of them. We went in with an aggressive purging, and it didn't go over well with neighboring gates. Shook them. Too many 'children' involved." He stopped whisking to look at his drink, then continued. "Which is understandable. It's unsavory. I don't enjoy having them purged for their parents' wrongs, but we can't have mixed nations and cultures."

Finally finished with whisking, Vincent brought the frothy green liquid to his mouth and drank most of it in seconds. "You know how they sent me to the far east to study for my position years ago. I was given this *chawan*." He looked it over, tipping it to see the bottom. "My tutor said that it was once cracked, then repaired with gold— *Kintsugi*, he called it—he thought it would be a good reminder to me of how damaged things, like myself, could be repaired. Scars remain, but with *Kintsugi,* they are honored and make the vessel more beautiful and just as useful."

Time to get to the point. Cole preferred to be home, kissing the Unified woman in his room. He scratched the back of his neck, antsy, then crossed his ankle over his knee. "What are you suggesting, Glorious One?"

Hands clasped on his desk, Vincent said, "I want to practice a metaphorical *Kintsugi*. I like you, but as it is, your relationship with destiny is broken. You're directed toward an early grave. I believe we can fix this before it's too late. Since you had such wild success blending in with the Gentles, so much so that you convinced them to give you a bride . . ." He paused.

So calm. So smug.

"I have no idea what you're talking about."

It was stupid to deny it. Obviously, he knew what he knew.

Vincent's faced scrunched with an amused, disappointed frown. A long, loud snort of laughing disdain rattled through his nose and throat. "Please, Cole. You think we're not aware that you knew Hesper before this?"

Cole took a few breaths to calm down, staring at the gold streaks of Vincent's *chawan*. He lifted his chin. He may have been busted, but he sure wasn't ashamed.

"You're to slip into an area rumored to harbor and allow the birth of mongrels. Get involved with them and earn their trust. Learn who the mongrels and their parents are. Take care of it secretly."

Vincent didn't play pranks, but this had to be one.

"You know I don't participate in purgings."

"You've rejected purging assignments in the past. That's true. This, however, is for you alone. It's different. More calculated and careful." Vincent downed the dregs of his matcha, then set the *chawan* on the desk and pushed it away from himself. "Perhaps this won't be so offensive to your sensibilities." He wiggled his fingers in the air, smiling. "Cole, we are the strongest nation in the world, but the mixing of religions and bloodlines resulted in the downfall of the nation centuries ago. Godlessness was only a part of it. We cannot permit it to happen again.

"Our strength teeters on the edge while Gentles are among us. Their areligious ideas and rebellious attitudes must be weeded out. Allowing us to grow together again would return us to a time of brutal civil war, and we will be a divided, fallen people who no longer honor God.

"We allow marriage and sexual relations because men will do it with or without permission. Now, it's at least an organized, profitable endeavor. Though, I'm certain you see the dangers of permitting mongrelism."

No. He didn't and raised his eyebrows to say so. If Vincent was honest, he would admit that he didn't either. Everything he said sat on his countenance like a mask. He'd learned to shut his feelings off like Cole had, learned to play the game, to distance his mind from his conscience and get the job done. But if Cole ever said that, Vincent would laugh in his face.

Or cry.

Sometimes he wanted to say it and see what the result would really be.

"I'm giving you a chance to reaffirm your loyalty, or we will have to dismiss you from service to the Kyrios."

The Kyrios couldn't dismiss anyone from an honored or successor position. Those who served the Kyrios in that capacity either lived serving the Kyrios or, quite simply, died. Young.

"You can't fight my bloodline, Glorious One—with all due respect."

Surprised, Vincent threw his hands in the air, shaking his head. "Don't look at me! The Kyrios made this decision. Personally, I think it would be a shame to dismiss you when you've just begun a family. Your first wife and already out of work?" He clutched his chest. "You might have to give her to someone else who can take care of her. I mean, I won't judge you for your decision—whatever it may be.

"If you choose dismissal, rest assured, I will gladly care for her. She's quite handsome, bright, nice teeth, trusting on the surface and responds well to conversational hypnosis."

"I don't have a medallion of justice."

"With your education and experience, you've been long qualified for one. You are an expert in the law, a sensible man, and a capable warrior. You will be an asset to Theocracia meting out justice, rather than defending it. Which makes us wonder why you've never broached the topic."

Cole wouldn't answer that question. Vincent knew. What did he need a medallion of justice for if he had no interest in killing mongrels or Unified?

Was killing Vincent worth dying for?

"Given that I've never heard of secret purgings on this scale, I have a few questions." Cole kept eye contact with Vincent. "Will the law enforcement wardens be aware of my mission there?"

Vincent leaned on the table, steepling his fingers, tapping them against his lips. "Local authorities won't be aware, but you have the right to make yourself known to them. Use your head."

"Is my wife permitted to come with me?"

"As long as she is not privy to the nature of the assignment." His lips pulled back, displaying a false smile full of pearly white caps.

"How much time do I have to decide?"

"About five minutes."

He wanted a snap decision. of course. What choice did he have? Death or assignment. "I'll take it."

"Good." Vincent busied himself with drawers and papers. "I'll have arrangements made for a few months from now at the beginning of winter. When all is ready, we will send you, medallion in hand." He stuffed the papers into a large envelope. "Have you seen your sister recently?"

"She married Hesper and me yesterday."

"Her sickness is worsening. Thought you should know. We're going to visit her. You might want to consider it, too."

* * *

When Cole returned home, a ragtime tango poured out of the parlor. David had taken to the ivories again. He hadn't done that in at least a month. Music had always been a healthy, private form of therapy for David, preferred over drinking and smoking. His return to the art meant he was probably trying to pick himself up. Good.

Twenty~Five | Post-Conquest: 232

FORCED RETIREMENT FROM his mission among the Unified gave Cole the freedom to travel and do more of his out-of-forest work, teaching in the universities and speaking at in-depth Law Enforcement training seminars through the summer. Odd jobs popped up for him and his expertise along the way. All told, nothing exciting, except that Hesper came with him.

Watching Hesper experience so many new things made for an interesting newlywed phase. She commanded respect, even from senior officers and wardens. They didn't treat her with the subtle disdain offered to Gentles. Most men didn't take their Gentle wives on business trips, though. Perhaps that indicated special status to the people who met her.

While alone, they read together, and sometimes Hesper prayed with him. Unlikely as it was, Cole cherished the hope that she would someday believe as he did. Who could blame her for not being able to? Her experience had been poor, thus far. Beyond poor: Revolting.

But if he knew her at all, she would overcome her experience and emotions to choose what made the most sense.

Summer passed, and harvest came and went as the leaves fell from the trees. Temperatures dropped and the northern sections of Theocracia expected snow any day. The Kyrios were likely to send for him to discuss the new assignment details soon, so he held his weakness up to God and sought strength more often. He couldn't do what they asked of him, but he couldn't refuse, either. His tenuous position required priority over comfort.

His tenuous life . . .

Blood guaranteed his position of favor and privilege, but David had been correct when he advised Cole to protect his physical blood. Too worked up to acknowledge its veracity at the time, he considered David's advice cowardly. Cole didn't have any room to wiggle in rebellion without risking Hesper.

This morning, he swung his legs out of bed and shuffled over to his window to kneel. Hesper lay in their cozy nest, a rosy glow warming her precious cream-vellum face and her thick black braid crossing the wrinkles and rises of ivory sheets. Her pale hand rested palm up on the bear fur. A wrinkled, furry, lovely mess at peace, sleeping comfortably.

He could shut his conscience off. If it came down to it, he could obey. But Hesper? She would never understand. He would seek solace in God for doing his best in an impossible situation, but Hesper had no such relief for her conscience. Especially when someone else's actions caused her guilt.

He could try to hide his assignment, but . . . what if he couldn't?

Covering his face with his hands, he uttered a prayer. "Maker of all, the Book of Light came from you. We are not meant to be kept from your light any more than we are meant to be dominated by it. As it is, we are both; they keep us from it and use that separation to dominate us.

"Show me the Book of Light in my heart and mind. I have a path to walk that is riddled with potholes made by those who keep the light."

Cole's simple, sage-like father was not regarded as a great man. With no university education and his missing finger barring him from military prestige, he grew up a farmer and vintner. But he knew how to plant seeds and bottle ideas that aged well.

One thing he planted in Cole was the last phrase of any prayer he prayed. Cole used it now. "Be merciful to me, one small piece of Your artwork."

A small arm curled around his lower back, and Hesper's body leaned against his side. Uncovering his face, he put his arm around her and rested his head atop hers. Years ago, Hesper answered his prayer for experiences that would open him to God. God would listen again. Why wouldn't It?

The door rattled with a mighty knock, startling them both.

"If I didn't know better, I'd say that was a law enforcement warden." Cole laughed. "They always knock that way. Come in!"

Trinity's heels clacked across the floor. "Cole, where are you?"

Her illness had progressed over the summer, but that woman was hard to knock down. She clung to life with a grip of iron.

He waved so she could see him on the floor beyond his sofa. "Here!"

"Why in blazes are you on the floor?"

"What do you need, Trinity?"

Bones and parchment skin, Trinity approached Cole with a piece of paper and a medallion. Her eyes, carrying indigo bags wherever they went, wouldn't look at him. "Your flight will be tomorrow at four in the morning. Pack as much as you want, you're the only passengers. That paper has all the information you'll need. If you have any questions, try to figure it out yourself." With a faltered step at the first, she clicked her way out of the room, her ankles shaking in her heels.

"Huh. I didn't expect that so suddenly." Cole stood. "I'd better wash up and pack."

Hesper promptly trotted off to the bathroom ahead of him. She laid a towel over a stool beside their copper tub and turned on the water.

Cole slipped the moccasins from his feet. "Trinity doesn't look well, does she?"

"No, she does not."

He set the envelope from Trinity onto the stool with the towel and undressed to climb into the tub. "Hesper, give me the envelope, please."

She picked it up, gave it a sniff, and handed it over. He opened it and read to himself:

Assignment: Section 26, Pomo Gate
Flight: 4 A.M. November 12th Escort arrival: 3:45 A.M.
Furnishing Budget: 350 ₥
Monthly Salary: 300 ₥

Honored Senior Officer Chandler:

We have secured employment for you as a secretary in the law firm of Attorney Alan Bandello, a former military officer of good reputation and wisdom. Honorably discharged for personal reasons. Housing has been arranged.

Your time frame, as previously discussed, is a maximum of 2 years. By this time, your assignment must be complete. We require a monthly progress report.

Due to the confidential nature of your assignment, Mr. Bandello has been told that you and your wife have been granted a leave of absence and require a change of scenery. Your wealthy grandfather, looking out for your best interests, called ahead to make arrangements for you.

Your moderate celebrity, particularly among those of Mr. Bandello's profession, and the distinction of your name and family, require an alias. Mr. Bandello expects Brock Cartwright. Do not wear your insignia.

You have our confidence,
Vincent Phaiah

Vincent never took the time to write his own letters, so his signatures were rarely the same twice. The alias had to be Vincent's idea, though. A kid named Brock had been Cole's rival growing up. He hated the name.

Vincent always had been and always would be a passive-aggressive bully.

Cole folded the letter and placed it on the ground. Resting his head back on the tub's edge, ready to unwind, he recalled Hesper's presence and opened his eyes. She still stood beside the tub, frowning at him. He raised his eyebrows in a question.

"Cole, why can't you tell me?"

"Read the letter."

She read it and looked at him. "That tells me nothing."

"That was their intention."

"I refuse to go to Pomo Gate if you refuse to tell me."

She wouldn't say that if she didn't mean it or at least intend to put up a hefty fight.

"I understand why you might be troubled by this. Consider that if you don't go now, they're not going to send you later. That will be two years, Hesper. Two years."

"I mean what I say."

"Be reasonable. You're coming with me whether I tell you or not."

"Who will make me, *Brock*? Do you think I am unable to keep silence?"

"What? Oh, come on! I trust you. It's better for you if you don't know. I understand your aversion to secrecy. However, there's no escape from that when you work with the Kyrios. You're a brave woman for taking this—"

"Stop trying to manipulate me. I did not understand it when I came here, but I understand now. You people use certain words and tones to make others think what you want them to think and to create a false sense of calm."

Cole spluttered. How could she think that of him? "I don't do that to you, Hesper. If I ever have, it has been with your consent or to help you settle down. Never to manipulate you. I'm frustrated and taking pains to keep my voice level," he explained. "Between you and me, our feelings, thoughts, and personal lives—we have no secrets. Work is different."

Hesper took the towel from the stool and seated herself in its place, laying it across her lap. She wore a deadly frown and a definite sulk. "Is it bad?"

"What they want me to do? Yes, it's bad."

"Are you going to do it?"

"No. I'm going to find a way around it. I'll mince words with them the way I did when reporting about the Unified. Nothing bad will happen. You have to believe me."

"Do I?"

Point taken. If only he could explain that his life was on the line if he didn't do this. He couldn't. The less she knew, the better. "I suppose so, Hesper. Please, pack. We have to go together. I won't leave you here for two years with David in this state. He's doing much better, but it's a volatile situation, and I'm convinced he has feelings for you that he won't admit to."

"So?"

"So? Do I have to hypnotize you?"

Her face darkened with a clear lack of appreciation for his attempt at humor. She laid the towel over the stool and left the room. Drawers opened, zippers unzipped. She was preparing for the trip.

Satisfied, Cole closed his eyes and sank deeper into the tub.

Twenty-Six | Post-Conquest: 230

SACRED GATE'S MILITARY university acted as a well-educated sugar daddy for downtown bars and dance clubs. These types of busy university gates made excellent hiding places for Jesurun. At twenty, he wouldn't stand out too much, and his build and psychological effect made him an easy choice for some of the low-end bars in need of security.

Jes stood at the door, watching people mingle, drinks in hand. To his left, an annoying persistent little crap-of-a-man tried to pick up a blonde woman and was having a hard time of it. Ahead, a gaggle of girls giggling-drunk on margaritas.

Bored, bored, bored. This scene, pretty typical, bored him to death. Still, he preferred boredom to wandering hungry. But it sure wasn't fun. He did have to plan for the night, though.

If he couldn't arrange a pleasant evening, he'd find the homeless shelter and hope they had room, other times he'd steal or break something to get arrested and have a night or two in jail until his boss bailed him out. His boss had five daughters and three wives, so he preferred to bail Jes out of jail over having him in his home. He didn't need a handsome bouncer twice his size in the house, but he did need him in his bar.

Jes preferred the more luxurious option of getting laid, which usually guaranteed a night in a house or apartment. With chocolate fondue eyes and a friendly smile, he didn't have much trouble seducing a partner. Some old acquaintances used to tease that he got partners with a touch and a glance.

Nah. It wasn't that easy. But close.

The evening wasted away to midnight and he hadn't hooked anybody yet. Too lost in his own head, and not thinking on his toes. He searched the area for candidates and settled on a pretty brunette girl who made eye contact with him.

There. She did it again.

Yep. Going in for the kill. Time to dip that peach in fondue and heat her up.

A few steps into his strut, a short, graying stranger intercepted him. He hadn't even seen this guy walk in.

"Hey, what're you doing here?" the man asked, smiling.

Jes sized him up. Small. Strong. Kind of boyishly cute. Not out of the question for a romp in return for a place to stay. The curves and softness of that brunette were more interesting tonight, though. He'd have to think about this one. "Working," he replied.

"Ah, I see. Where do you come from?"

"I don't see why it matters to you." Jes folded his arms and looked over the little man's head. The girl was losing interest. She was gonna get away.

The man's smile never faded. "Oh, I'd say it matters a great deal."

"Get outta my face."

"Your arm is interesting. I wouldn't wear short-sleeved shirts if I were you. Those tats might get on some people's nerves in a hoity-toity religious town like this."

Who did this guy think he was? "You got brass! Does it offend *you*, babe?" Jes asked.

The man's eyes ripped a hole in Jes and peered right in there.

Jes sneered. "Nah, forget it. Just get away from me."

The man took a step closer—too close for Jes.

"I said get out of my face, moron, or I'll kick your creepy little carcass out the door so fast you'll have to come back in for your skin."

The man sucker punched him. Jes stumbled back into the wall. *Stinkin' short people.*

Regaining his footing and his senses, Jes grabbed a fistful of collar and pulled his left arm back to aim for a nose-breaker. His tattoo glowed, hot coals in the smoky darkness. Conscious of his visible rage and the searing pain, Jes withdrew his fist and scanned the area for witnesses. Sometimes he could get angry without lighting up, but this really set him off.

The strange little man's speed and strength intercepted Jes' retreat. Quite simply, he grabbed Jes in his distracted moment and flipped him over. Folks scattered as the little man dragged Jes outdoors where they took to a wrestling match on the pavement.

"You always glow when you're mad?" the man grunted. "Tell me, how does it feel?" He tangled his arm with Jes' in a way Jes didn't understand. He couldn't break free without causing himself pain, so he submitted. He'd lost a fair fight without one good swing. Maybe this guy would be more interesting than the brunette after all.

Jes gritted his teeth. "It burns."

"Where?"

"Where do you think, midget?"

The man managed a strained laugh, concentrating all his efforts on pinning Jes to the sidewalk. "Its word is a fire in the marrow of your bones. It's up to you to accept that and not let anger control it. It's going to find what it needs and will completely destroy you, but you won't regret it." The man let go of Jes and ran. He had already rounded the corner and gotten out of sight before Jes steadied himself on his feet.

The champion had been defeated.

The bartender flew down the stairs to the sidewalk. "Jes, what happened? I called the LEWs."

266

"I dunno, man. I dunno." He rubbed his arm and shoulder, wincing. "But why'd you go and call the LEWs?"

He'd have to hide somewhere until they left.

* * *

Jes spent a sleepless night in the alley beside the bar, thinking about his thumping and the weird little guy's words. A fire in the marrow of his bones. He sure could use that tonight. *It's gonna destroy me, but I won't regret it.* He puffed a laugh and pulled a few garbage bags over himself for warmth, closing his eyes to stay awake.

Twenty-Seven | Post-Conquest: 232

TIRED SOLDIERS LOADED luggage into the cargo hold as Hesper and Cole boarded the plane. An officer entered behind them and, without prelude, took Hesper's arm and swiped it with an alcohol pad.

"Why?" Hesper jerked away from the officer and looked to Cole.

Cole put out his hand. "Wait, wait." He shot a glance at her name under a measly few medals. "What are you doing, Officer Finch?"

Officer Finch scowled. "The tracking chip, obviously." She held up a syringe.

"No one told us about a tracking device."

Officer Finch pulled a paper from her pocket and shoved it at Cole. The Kyrios ordered a tracking chip because of the potential length of the assignment. They couldn't have him setting his Gentle free or letting her wander off into Gentle communities. Cole looked up at the officer. "Let me speak with Vincent."

Rather than peaceably agree, Officer Finch squinted and cocked her head. No good. Cole sat between her and Hesper while he dug the communicator out of his bag and called Vincent, who didn't answer, of course.

Hand on her hip, Officer Finch's attitude remained firmly in place. "Well?"

"We're not going anywhere. This tracking device is an insult, and I won't take it."

"What is it?" Hesper asked.

"It's a device inserted between the muscle and the skin. The purpose is to keep track of you. It tells them where you are located at all times."

Hesper frowned. "How?"

"Computer World Access System. C.W.A.S. Too much to explain now." Cole stood. "I'm sorry to have troubled you for nothing, Officer, but we're returning to our home."

Hesper spoke just above a whisper. "I will take it."

Cole whipped around and shot her a sharp look. "What?"

"I will take it. I understand why they would want to keep track of me. Can . . . can it be removed?"

"I'm going to speak with my wife alone, please."

Officer Finch tromped away with her syringe in the air.

Cole touched Hesper's knee. "Hesper, you don't have to do this. It's insulting that they would suggest—"

"You must maintain your relationship with the Kyrios to be happy here. We do not need to make them angry over an insult."

After all these years avoiding the Kyrios' full control, his marriage to a Unified woman forced him into their hands. Hesper was right, though. Without being told, she must have recognized the necessity of taking the assignment.

He grasped at his face and pulled his fingers along his eyelids to his nose. With a quick punch to the seat in front of him, he whispered, "Fine." He shouted, "FINE!"

Officer Finch returned with her vile syringe.

"I'll do it," he said.

As long as he didn't contradict Vincent's orders, his position as an honored senior officer required Finch's obedience.

He snatched the packet from her hand. "It's not as if we don't learn how to do this in school. I could've done this a long time ago if I'd known Vincent preferred it." He sat and disemboweled the package. "But no, he chose to do it at the last minute, so I'd squirm. He's challenging me." Officer Finch still stood near him. Cole stopped his work to stare back at the officer. "Officer Finch, your conduct and treatment of me and my wife would not be acceptable even if I were a mere soldier. I strongly recommend you regard me with the respect due to an honored senior officer." He raised an eyebrow.

Officer Finch lowered her chin in return. "Yes, sir."

"I'll take it from here."

"I'll stay to watch, sir," she said. "Unless you want to call the Glorious One about that, too?"

Still sassy! He would have done the same.

He wiggled his fingers through the tight rubber gloves and pulled a small tray from between the seats. "I don't know why you went for her arm. We never do them in the arm," he muttered. "Please, put your hand there, Hesper." He swiped the alcohol pad along the web between her thumb and forefinger and prepped the syringe, then loaded it with its tiny cargo.

"I have never seen you so upset over something this small, my friend." Hesper's gentle hand touched his arm. "No bigger than a grain of rice."

His activity slowed to a halt. He smiled, took a deep breath to deny himself the relief of a kiss, and returned to his business. Pinching the skin, he proceeded to place the point of the syringe within the pinch and punctured it. The plunger slid down with ease, expelling the syringe's contents. With gauze held over the spot, he withdrew the needle.

"Are you okay?" she asked.

"I just poked a hole in you, and you're asking if I'm okay? This makes me sick. Hold this in place, please."

After bandaging the wound, he stuffed the used kit in its tiny bag. Officer Finch ran a scanner over Hesper's hand. The contraption beeped, and the officer slipped a wallet out of her coat pocket for Cole. They saluted one another, and Officer Finch left the plane.

270

                            * * *

Everyone expected Trinity to pass away at a young age. Her health deteriorated steadily after giving birth to Thomas, but no one understood the reason. However, it surprised David to receive a call after Cole and Hesper left in the wee hours of the morning. It made him suspicious. Cole would have thought it suspicious, too. That made it even more . . . suspicious.

Ariana removed the medallion from Trinity's neck and put it around David's.

Was he supposed to feel something? Either about his position or the death of his only sister?

Well, he didn't.

The newly acquired child weighed on David's mind more heavily than anything else. Reverenced and a father in one day. He liked children, but what was he supposed to do with one?

David and Tom stood to the side with Vincent while soldiers covered Trinity and carted her away.

"You realize your sister was one of our most valuable people?" Vincent asked. "You have big shoes to fill, David. Do you feel up to the task?"

"Perfectly. As long as we break the heels off the shoes first."

Vincent placed his hands on David's shoulders and looked him in the eyes. "Are you sure?"

What was Vince getting at? Trying to wear him down, get him to question himself and his abilities. Tearing up the soil to plant a new idea. As if he didn't know the drill.

"Why wouldn't I be, Glorious One?"

"Well, things have been hard for you lately."

"I'm fine."

"I hear you're drinking quite a bit, that Evelyn has run off with someone else, and your favored wife hasn't come out of her room since Jade's trial." Vincent ran his hand along the back of a chair. "So you've resorted to the fat one."

"Excuse me?" David blurted.

"I don't mean to insult you. She's pleasant to look at. My point is to ask what do you need me to do?"

"Nothing, Glorious One. Just tell me where I need to be and when I need to be there."

Vincent smiled. "Very well. Your induction is tomorrow at eleven A.M. We've taken the liberty of packing the boy's things for you. There isn't much." He gestured to the barren room. "Your sister was a rather rigid minimalist. The burning's tonight at seven."

"Thank you, Glorious One."

Vincent swaggered past David and out the door.

Tom appeared to be doing uncommonly well for standing at the foot of his mother's deathbed. David looked down at the fair little boy. "How do you feel?"

"I don't feel anything."

"Not even sad? Nothing?"

He shrugged. "Is Hesper still living with you?"

David smiled. "Yes and no. She's gone across the country with Uncle Cole for a while, but she'll be back."

"I'll be happy to see her again."

"Me, too, Tom. She's a kind lady."

"Pretty to look at."

David laughed. "Are you ready to go, kiddo?"

Tom shrugged and nodded.

David took off the medallion and stuffed it into his pants' pocket. Taking up the boy's bags, they left Trinity's house without looking back, not even once.

* * *

Hesper and Cole stepped into sunny, warm western Theocracia. Section Twenty-Six, Pomo Gate. Cole had been to the area several times, and Hesper had joined him during their summer travels, so they had grown familiar with the area and its pleasant climate. As a seaboard community, the air smelled of fish and seaweed until you went to their markets, which added sweetness and spice to the aroma.

A short, burly man met them at the little airport. His thick, dark suit seemed too warm for the weather, and it showed on his sweaty bald head. Geniality radiated from every pore as he greeted them. "Mr. Cartwright, I'm Alan Bandello. Have we met before?"

Cole shook his head. "No, sir."

Unless Mr. Bandello had met him at a lecture or seen the lone painting in some hallway or another in one of his *almae matres* on the other side of the country, it was unlikely that the old man would know his face.

"Uh-huh, okay, well, I'm delighted that your grandfather called and informed me of your expertise and competence. You will be an excellent help to me. You're overqualified for the tasks I may have for you, but I'm ecstatic about helping a young military couple get away for a breather. I know what it's like, m'boy." He called over his shoulder, "Fellas, get their things!"

"Thank you, Mr. Bandello," Cole replied. "I intend to be an asset to your business for the duration of our stay."

Alan led them toward his white pick-up truck while his men transferred Cole and Hesper's luggage from plane to vehicle. "I have the most splendiferous house for you and your lovely wife—pleased to meet you, my dear." He took her hand and kissed it. "A bandage. Have you had an injury?"

Hesper smiled and hid her hands behind her back.

"The weather here is very nice," Cole said. "I enjoy the climate in the twenties sections."

"Oh, yes. We have magnificent weather here most of the time. Other times, it's hotter than Pyriphlegethon of the Greeks! Still, Section Twenty-Six is the only section I'd dream of living in! Betwixt the fruit and nuts—never mind the ones growing on trees—

and the ocean, there's nothing like it, I tell you. Nothing! And Pomo Gate? Oh, goodness, don't get me started!" He laughed a wholehearted laugh that shook his belly up and down with each syllable.

Alan was like a chocolate muffin; Cole had only to look at him to know he was good.

On his tip-toes, Alan peeked at the luggage in the bed of the truck. "I imagined you'd bring more than this." He swiped the sweat from his forehead with his handkerchief. "If you need anything—anything at all—don't hesitate to ask. I can give you a week before you start working, m'boy, to give you some time to, uh, settle in. Build your nest?"

"Not even. A couple of days."

Alan clapped Cole on the back. "What a man, what a—solid man!" He squeezed his shoulder, then his bicep. "A soldier all through, I see. I think I'll keep you with me if I need to walk anywhere at night—how do you feel about contract killing? There's this lawyer across town . . . Never mind." With a slap on the hood of the truck, he opened his door and climbed in. "Forward ho, young lovers! Homeward bound!"

Inside the truck, there was no mistaking the scents of pastries and sweet tobacco. Crumpled balls of wax paper had been shoved in a cubbyhole of the dashboard. Alan continued his jovial jabbering for ten minutes straight while an ancient dashboard hula dancer wiggled around. Then, "Any children?" A question!

Cole straightened up and flashed a surprised smile. "We're newly married."

"Oh, right. Hoping?"

Let it go, sir. Let it go. "If it were possible, yes, we would be hoping."

At a stop sign, blinker clicking, Alan stared at Cole for a few moments. He swiped at his nose a couple of times before addressing Hesper. "Did the Kyrios have you sterilized, young lady?"

The guts this guy had! Cole jumped in. "No. She's not sterilized. But we'd like to avoid the procedure."

"Hm. You're in Section One? I suppose it's more dangerous there."

Cole smiled. "Does Pomo Gate welcome mongrels?"

Stepping on the gas, Alan said, "Mongrels? I call them children. It's sadistic and cruel to allow them to marry but kill the offspring." Finger pointed, he turned his whole upper body to face Cole. "Do you know why they don't sterilize them right off the bat, m'boy?"

Cole stammered, "Be—because the Kyrios determined . . . that . . ." Time to pull himself together. He straightened his posture and tried again. "The Kyrios determined that the risks of surgery outweigh the benefits. They've proven the operations relied on in the past are responsible for many of the maladies of our ancestors. So, we only use it if necessary, such as in cases where the women prove too fertile."

Alan laughed and laughed and laughed, then, mopping his forehead with the handkerchief, laughed some more. "Oh, son, that's such a funny bit of fiction they've fed us. Nevertheless, apocryphal it remains. As if we should believe a Meros assessment of scientific matters! The real reason, son? The true impetus behind this twisted policy?"

Hesper stared straight ahead, her hands in her lap. No expression except for the wild eyes she always had when taking in new information.

"Affordable, discreet depopulation of the Gentles," Alan announced as if singing an ascending musical scale. "No question!"

Obviously. They wanted the Gentles gone. Everyone knew that. Cole opened his mouth, but Alan placed his vanilla-scented hand directly over it. "Close the maw and let me educate you, my friend. Just let it happen."

Cole's temper was rising a bit, so he wiped his mouth, took in a breath, and blew it out slowly. He slipped a tin of currant-cinnamon pastilles from his pocket and popped one into his mouth. Without words, he offered some to Hesper and Alan.

Loudly sucking on a pastille, Alan leaned forward to see Hesper. "What do you think, dear?"

Cole's eyes widened, and he caught himself clenching his pant leg, white-knuckled. Hesper took it well, though, and didn't skip a beat.

"I can see that they want to get rid of us. I do not understand why, though. They might wish to eradicate some of the behaviors many of us have developed due to their treatment, but if they would stop oppressing us, that might end."

"Ah, but that wouldn't be as fun! Or let them feel superior or suit their goals! Too reasonable! You notice they only take women. They could never manage the men, and ladies are, through their anatomy, more vulnerable to quiet attack. They've got fancy little wombs to mess around with. So, fiddlesticks on the men, let's take the women, get our jollies, keep the strong genes and Gentle genitals away from each other, then we'll get them pregnant and use that means and excuse to destroy those glorious forest people beneath the radar."

Cole cleared his throat. "I have never done—"

"Sh, sh, boy. I wasn't speaking of you. Don't get so defensive." Alan shrugged his shoulders up and down, wiggling his custard-pouch jowls. He grinned. "Loosen up and listen." Driving with his knee, he counted on his fingers as he spoke. "They allow polygamy with Gentle women, forbid the old-fashioned pill form of birth control—and almost any other type—they mandate abortions and avoid sterilization until it looks too ridiculous not to do it—you'll notice that they first look for every possible way to get into that woman's body without cutting her open—then . . . then they got a grip on the prophylactic industry"—he pinched his own earlobe—"what industry there is anyway. Making and distributing the good ol' rubbers themselves! I tell you, m'boy, they are intentionally making bad condoms—I kid you not—I have dealt with many a mixed couple suffering from the trauma of a forced abortion. Some of them experimented with the government issued prophylactics after that. One out of a hundred has a tiny pinprick of a hole.

"It's a long, slow approach, but the Kyrios know folks are watching! Passive-aggressive is the best approach when there's an audience! There are lines that must not be crossed out loud, or the Kyrios' enemies' slow, calculated approach will become a swift uprising of passion. It's chess, m'boy! Don't force your enemy to jump your queen while you're trying to maneuver her to jump their king.

"Plus, they get a chance to make dough in the slave trade and enjoy beautiful women while they do it. The slave trade practically pays for the process."

"You said there's an audience. What audience?"

"The Earth People, clearly!"

Cole couldn't help but laugh. "That seems too complex a method just to avoid the anger of a pest like the Earth People. You believe the Kyrios fear an unarmed rebellion to such an extent, sir?"

"I know they do!" He flicked his nose.

Cole laughed again, incredulous. "Can you give a solid explanation as to how this uterus theory produces the desired results?"

"That's a question we have not yet been able to answer. We don't know what they're doing with these abortions and such, but son, have you ever left the country?"

"Yes, sir. Many times."

Alan squinted. "Uh-huh. Do you know those 'impoverished nations' send aid to the Earth People? By that old 'impassable' bridge across the northern strait."

"The strait that divides us from the eas—"

Alan pointed at him. "Yes, sir!"

Ridiculous! Impossible. The man was a lunatic. "How would they do that? The rest of the world fell to pieces after The Conquest, and we shut them all out. I've seen the poverty with my own eyes."

"Have you now? Perhaps you've just seen the wrong countries? Been in the wrong locations?"

Deemed hostile, some countries no one ventured into. It seemed reasonable to believe the Kyrios' warnings and avoid those regions, but . . .

"Mhm, I can see you're thinkin', boy!" Alan chuckled. "The Earth People are practically invading the northern country! Connect the dots, son, connect the dots!" Alan's devious giggle served as bizarre, comedic punctuation.

"People are watching, so the Kyrios can't order a gargantuan genocide that would toss the table, though the Unified are building alliances and garnering sympathy like caviar and *crème fraîche* for my blini!

"In the meantime, the women—those poor dears"—he glanced at Hesper—"have the Kyrios tap dancing on their self-worth. It's done a-one-and-a-two on the perception of the young ladies. These once-strong women now view themselves as the beneficiaries of a righteous, holy directorate of Gentle welfare and happiness." Alan slapped the steering wheel and honked the horn. He huffed and puffed and honked again.

"I apologize, but it's the truth." He gave Cole a double-take and laughed. "And you're wondering what kind of a lunatic you're working with. I tell you, m'boy, a raving one! A raving lunatic! Some call me a conspiracy theorist, but I will proclaim the truth as loudly as I can. If I'm loud enough, perhaps the Kyrios will hear me, and I'll go down in a boisterous blaze of conspiratorial glory. I hope you'll find it amusing at the least.

"Honestly, I'm sure they watch me closely for my outspoken chatter. If they weren't, I'd be dead by now." He shouted at the dashboard vent, "They want something from me! Hear me, Kyrios? I know you're listening!

"Now, as for why they really want to get rid of the Gentles?" He smiled. "I'll save that for another bout of insanity. The next full moon, I suspect. You'll have to come to me for that. They tie me to my bed when the beauteous *la* full *luna* appears." Clearing his throat, Alan went quite suddenly silent.

The Kyrios were bent on tormenting the Unified, but Alan's hypothesis seemed a bit deeper and more diabolical. Illogical, too. Perhaps he could lay out his thoughts in a more orderly fashion sometime. It would be nice to write Alan off, but the words resonated. It would be simple to prove or disprove these claims about the strength of the Earth People if he obtained permission to leave the country, though proving that abortions and polygamy were being used to destroy the Gentles . . .? Cole rolled his eyes. That was the stupidest thing he'd heard in a long time. It sure wasn't meant for their good, but depopulation? No.

* * *

Pomo Gate centered around a ruined Unified city that contained the bulk of the business district. On the outskirts, a fenced base housed local judges, military, and law enforcement wardens. The rest of the city sprawled low to the ground, mostly residential except for the large grassy square of market booths. Just as they passed the booths, Alan slowed and pulled up to a fine home in a well-treed neighborhood.

"Here's the palace. It belonged to me and my wife. Bought and paid for," Alan explained. "When she passed away five years ago, I didn't see the need to stay. It was too much for one old man, but I haven't had the heart to try to sell it. Too many good memories there.

"I've rented it out a few times, but I'm fussy about who! Just pay for your utilities, and I'll keep a hundred meras of your pay each month. Deal?"

Cole smiled and took the previous conversation off like a coat. "A generous one, sir."

Alan's workers pulled up behind his vehicle and, quick and efficient, carried Hesper and Cole's luggage into the house while they stood in the yard chatting with Alan.

"I have a car for you to use until you've acquired your necessities, Brock," Alan said.

"That's kind of you, Mr. Bandello. Thank you."

"If you'd like, I can drive you over to my humble domicile, four doors down, to pick it up."

"I'll walk there in twenty minutes."

"Let us synchronize our watches. It's about nine o'clock." He twisted his earlobe and flicked the tip of his nose. "Yes, twenty minutes is just fine. See you then. It's the blue house with my name in front of it." Alan hopped into the driver's seat of his truck and drove away.

Cole took Hesper's hand and they followed the stone path to the door. The last worker smiled and waved as he rushed past them on his way out.

After touring the house, they exited through the back door where they stood on a terrace and looked out on a yard filled with mandarin and mulberry trees. The place had been tended well.

"You smell those?" Hesper asked, taking a deep breath. "I have never smelled that."

"The citrus doesn't grow by us. Much of the fruit we get at home comes from other places." He pushed up his glasses. "Quite the tale he tells, hm?"

"Mr. Bandello? I do not understand it all. A lot of words he used are words I do not know, but I understood he thinks they are intentionally letting women get pregnant so they can justify executing them somehow? Correct? Meros men bringing us in because they can, not realizing it is so the Kyrios can kill us without drawing too much attention."

"Well done. That's the gist. Enlisting hunters in pursuit of pleasure. It's a far better method than mere loyalty. No one would be loyal to the Kyrios if they weren't afraid or promised a reward."

"You think it is a tale?"

He squeezed her hand. "Let's just say, I have a lot to think about."

Twenty-Eight | Post-Conquest: 232

CRUMBLED, BURNT PYRES dotted the grounds in tight rows. Soldiers laid Trinity atop a fresh pyre, cloaked in red velvet. David stood among the Kyrios, holding young Tom's hand while the assembly sang a dirge.

> *The soul whispers to God in death,*
> *Accept me, Great One, I pray.*
> *Upon the flaming pyre, I rise,*
> *Rise to see Your face.*
> *Not by the spirit, nor by the water,*
> *And not by the blood.*
> *By the death-light, the lightless flame,*
> *Through Your Glorious Ones.*

Vincent extended his arm, lifting the death-light for all to see. The miraculous lightless flame held the loyalty of believers across the nation. The Kyrios claimed to harvest it through a spiritual experience in a place of power in the afterlife. Since no one knew of any natural explanation, the Kyrios' story stood as the most likely.

Not hot, not bright, the death-light acted as a drain in a sink, swallowing light around it like water. Its destructive capabilities matched that of natural fire, but if it set you ablaze, you were bound to lose bits of your soul until it was put out. Some years ago, a man had burnt a bit of his finger with it and he was never the same again.

People paid a fortune to have the death-light for deceased loved ones, and it was a right for the military, but most Meros civilians did not have fortunes, and some were unwilling to become soldiers. Even if they did, if their loved ones happened to be Gentles, they were out of luck. Only the wealthiest could afford eyeglasses, cars, indoor plumbing . . . the afterlife.

Now, more than ever, the idea repulsed David. The thought that Trinity would be in the afterlife, but Jade wouldn't. . . That wasn't the kind of spiritual atmosphere he wanted for eternity.

Vincent set the pyre ablaze and all waited for the moment when Trinity's soul would begin its journey to the afterlife in the smoke.

Ah, there it was.

The smell of human flesh. Going into the afterlife was always a bad-smelling affair.

As the dark flames engulfed Trinity, the crowd dispersed, but David had to stand watch 'til only Kyrios remained. Tangled in the smell, the sound, and the all-too-hypnotic movement of flames, he fell into a pensive mood that bordered on black. Despairing thoughts of the afterlife and of his present life consumed his mind.

Could he escape? Retire. Leave in the night and never return? Maybe start a new life and marry a normal woman from a small gate. He almost married a small-gate girl once . . .

Whatever he chose to do, the Kyrios would hunt him down with astonishing speed. He'd seen it done before.

Medals, badges, missions accomplished, successful and efficient opportunities for the delivery of justice, and even a few humanitarian efforts got shoved under his belt. A legacy worth leaving, a history to be proud of—or so they wanted him to believe.

As things stood, being a charred body on a red velvet pyre would be the greatest honor he would receive, but like his sister, he'd be a nobody in his heart.

He'd feel better in a couple of months . . . or years.

* * *

David had almost run out of childhood memories to share with Tom before the boy finally conked out at five A.M.

Running on three hours of sleep, David spiffed up and dragged himself into the Bastion for his induction. In the Judgment Room, with a few canned blessings and prayers, he received the title of Reverenced One.

Thrilling.

"Just don't let your brother influence you, David," Vincent warned. "Only the Glorious Ones need to know about the contents of the Book of Light." He gestured to the doors. "The more people know, the harder it is to govern them. The more people know, the less they understand. It's unnecessary trouble, stirring up the pot. Are we clear?"

Who brought up the Book of Light? David hadn't thought much of it since Jade's trial.

"Clear, Glorious One."

Vincent extended his hand. "Congratulations, David. We're happy to have you on board with us. I recommend that you spend the evening in prayer. It is essential to clear the mind and soul of past trauma and vices as you enter into this new relationship with your god and country."

"I'll consider it. Thanks."

Vince's gold chain bracelet quietly jangled as they shook hands, and, for the first time, David allowed bitterness to have its place. Shaking the hand that killed his wife was like making peace with murder. Peace with murder was getting kind of annoying. He drew his hand back and smiled. "Have a good day, Glorious One." Overtired and annoyed, he needed a smoke.

Outside, he leaned against the Bastion and lit his cigarette, then he slipped the lighter back into his pocket.

First, letters of resignation must be written and sent to the gate boards in Sections Twenty-One through Thirty, abandoning the oversight of the small-scale responsibilities for his part in legislation and governance of Theocracia as a nation.

Second—what was second? How was Hesper? How long would it be before she was sterilized or executed?

Hesper was Cole's darling now, and even if she weren't, David had never been the type to make a woman his world or get overly protective. He enjoyed what little freedom he still had.

She delighted him, though, and it would make his heart sick to see her wind up as another unrecorded statistic. Some days, he truly wished he hadn't given her away. She deserved to be taken care of and kept safe. Not every woman needed that, but she did. She would deny it, but only because of the things she didn't know about life with the Kyrios.

Nevertheless, she wasn't his, she was Cole's—zealous, high-energy, bulldoze-you-over Cole's. And now that his position had been elevated from that of an honored senior officer to successor, the potential for getting into real trouble skyrocketed. David had to start behaving when he became a successor, Cole would, too. It was time he believed whatever the Kyrios told him and lived life with a clean conscience. Sometimes it was best not to know the full extent of corruption you could do nothing about. Especially when you had a wife to care for.

Cole had accused David of cowardice for years, but why bother to defend himself when it was clear that Cole couldn't understand why passion wouldn't fix anything? Not a single thing.

David snuffed his cigarette on the Bastion wall and dropped it. Blowing out the smoke, he stuffed his hands in his pockets and went inside.

Crossing the red carpet to get to his office, several stopped him with congratulations on his promotion. Numb, he nodded and faked a smile as he thanked each one and did the polite things he was supposed to do.

He stopped at the stairs to the Judgment Room.

The normal noise of the Bastion carried on as people passed this way and that, but for David, the surroundings were fading to black, and his heartbeat fluttered in his chest like little more than a dying butterfly.

Was he shivering or trembling?

He'd never trembled before.

Braced against the staircase's balustrade for support, his body quivered, but at least he'd remain standing.

Maybe.

He closed his eyes and took a few breaths. Perhaps stress and too much alcohol were getting to him. Dehydration?

Opening his eyes, he looked up to the Judgment Room doors and a noiseless scream forced itself from his mouth. He couldn't feel his heart. Or his toes. Or his face.

Several naked, genderless people, with flaming shocks of hair and eyes that shone moon-white, stood in a row before the entrance to the Judgment Room. Hot-iron bones glowed through the ghostly pallor of their flesh, covered with beautiful, unique designs, like tattoos. One had an eye on its chest, another had a hand on their face, a vine wrapped around the waist of still another.

Together, the beings opened preternaturally large mouths to reveal roiling fires, hungry for space to grow. The flames licked at their lips and curled around their faces until, writhing, they rose into the air.

A blast of hot wind threatened to knock David over, drying his skin and stinging his face as he clung to the balustrade to keep himself upright.

An oddly musical dissonance of terrified screams of men, women, and children poured from the flaming mouths, growing in intensity the longer they screamed.

They stopped abruptly, closed their mouths, and looked at David.

Synchronized, they thrust out their hands and a light appeared over his head. When they moved their hands up, it went up, when they moved them down, it went down. Involuntarily, his own arm released the balustrade and jutted out. The light moved with his hand's motions, too.

The strange beings lowered their arms and retreated single-file through the Judgment Room doors, leaving the sparkling light still hovering above David. The orb, alive with the appearance of swirling smoke and gas—a thing of beauty—offered glimpses of jewel-like colors that made his heart leap each time they tapped at the orb's barrier with muted clicks.

It would be so warm and comforting. Clean. If he . . . could just . . . hold it.

Without warning, it expanded and flooded the area with blinding light. All was as it had been before. The familiar ink and paper smell of the Bastion returned. He hadn't even realized it was gone.

Laughter startled him. Two officers walked by, chatting. Hadn't they seen that? Heard it? Was he the only one? He had to be. How could he be? Something tripped his trigger, set off his brain, traumatized him. That must be it.

He locked his office and made a premature departure from the Bastion. Someone would give him guff about it tomorrow, but they could shove it. At home, David left Tom in Lorelei's care and returned to bed for the afternoon. It would be unwise to diagnose himself, but it was a real possibility that he might need someone else to.

He tossed about on his bed, trying to relax and calm his racing mind and heart. He wasn't *that* tired. Not drunk. Not out of his mind.

What remained?

Maybe this wasn't a hallucination. Maybe, for the first time in his life, he witnessed a supernatural event. Until now, he questioned the reality of spirits altogether. Like a frightened child, he yanked the covers over his head.

Spirits were real.

If spirits were real, perhaps God was real. God was a spirit, right? Good spirits came from God. Someone taught him that.

Maybe?

Where did bad spirits come from? Did they exist?

For someone destined to God's service, he knew precious little about his deity. He whipped the cover off his face and stared at a moon-silver spot of the blue and black damask bed canopy.

He needed water.

As he attempted to crawl out of bed, terror shot through his heart and up his throat. Too young for a heart attack, right?

He grabbed at the canopy hanging down the bedpost and pressed his cheek to the cool silk. *Breathe. Breathe.*

What kind of man was he, shaking like a super-virgin on her wedding night? He was no virgin, and this wasn't his wedding night. Why was he thinking about virgins? This was spirits and the Kyrios and death and dying and—*screw it!* He scrambled off the bed and grabbed his keys. There were no prisoners in the jail tonight, so the Bastion would be empty. Perfect.

God let him see those things, and there had to be a reason. If that was not the case, well, the Kyrios would catch him, find out he'd lost his mind, and hopefully put him out of his misery or get him help.

He ran for the door.

Shirt. He needed to put on a shirt.

* * *

Shadowy and streaked with angular lines of moonlight from the windows, the Bastion's deserted foyer waited in ominous, too-good-to-be-true silence.

David cursed at the sound of his own feet on the stone stairs to the Judgment Room. If those spirit people showed up now, he'd crap on himself.

He pushed open the well-oiled Judgment Room doors without a sound. A faint light emanated from the staircase that led to the jail. That light always stayed on. Nothing alarming.

He ascended the platforms to the large alcove where the Kyrios claimed they kept the Book of Light and grasped the curtain's edge, feeling the red velvet in his palm—only a curtain—then pulled it aside and stepped in.

He wasn't dead. *Friggin' liars telling us we would die if we went in here. I knew it!*

The dark mysterious sanctum smelled faintly of incense. He swallowed back the rush of longing for Jade and blindly reached for something to hold on to.

"God?" he whispered, too afraid to speak aloud. "God? I saw those spirits. Where are they? What do they mean?" This was ridiculous. Trying to chat with God as if It were his buddy?

He touched the left wall and felt around as he dragged his fingers across it to the center wall, then the right wall, looking for something—anything! Staggering into the darkness of the center of the room, he passed straight through to the other side. It was empty.

Frustrated, he leaned back on the hard stones to collect his thoughts. What could he tr—*scra-a-a-a-pe.*

He froze.

What was that? What was that? What was that? Heart pounding, he turned toward the sound.

Scra-a-a-a-pe. Then voices. Judging by the tone, someone was arguing under the floor?

He swallowed his heart back into his chest. Nope. Not happening.

All awareness of his surroundings failed, and before he came to his senses, he had passed through the Judgment Room into the foyer and out of the Bastion. Stiff with terror, he slid into his vehicle, gently closed his door, and coasted down the road with his headlights off. At home, he pressed his car door shut and dashed for the back entrance. Once inside, he made for Lorelei's quarters. A light rap and whisper of her name at the crack of the door brought her to him.

"Sir?" Lorelei peeked out.

He whispered, "I've been home all evening. Sick."

"Right, sir. If you say so, sir."

"Okay. Good." *Dear, dear, Lorelei. I could kiss her.*

After several cigarettes, twenty push-ups, a glass of ice water, half an hour of swinging and banging his *gada* around, a few cups of Earl Grey tea, and a reluctant shot of the spiced rum he purchased in the east a few years ago, David had rational thoughts.

A room under the Bastion—under the place where the Book of Light was said to be. *Said* to be but wasn't. This was big. He couldn't ignore it.

Yes, he could. He could ignore it and go on living like a well-fed slave until they pecked off every wife he had. Cheerfully!

Perhaps he should tell Cole and let him decide what to do. Most likely, Cole would come home to visit someday and use that time to sneak into the Bastion and have a look.

He poured another shot of rum. God, it smelled like Dulce. Down the hatch.

Why couldn't he do it himself? Why throw it on Cole's lap? This had more to do with him and Jade than it did with Cole, really.

Do it! Just do it, you pantywaist! Trembling, he opened his dresser drawer to dig out black street clothes and change into them.

This was crazy.

He slid a cigarette from the pack on his bed-stand and planted it firmly between his lips and lit it, puffing away as he searched for his flashlight. Half a cigarette later, he found it in the bed-stand that used to be Evelyn's and clipped it onto his belt. He checked his watch. Three A.M. The Bastion opened at six.

Time to go.

Time to quit smoking.

He never used to smoke this much. As a matter of fact, this was disgusting. Maybe Hesper knew an herb that would help. It was considered sinful in the eastern countries to do harm to others, even if his own religious leaders didn't seem to think so. Smoking harmed others around him, didn't it? Mayb—he was distracted, rambling to avoid what he dreaded. His feet wouldn't move. Another drag at his cigarette and a moment resting his forehead in his shaking hand and he would be—*crap*—not ready. Never would be.

Had to be.

Also had to go pee.

And get a gun.

* * *

Click. The flashlight's strong beam reached across the foyer, and David swept the area with it a few times before proceeding through the darkness to the Judgment Room.

Past the platforms, he pulled the red curtain aside and entered the alcove. Everywhere he stepped, the stone slabs seemed fixed in place . . . but he hadn't imagined it. A room had to be here somewhere. The voices had been too clear and too near to have come from the jail or beyond a stone wall.

Then, under a fortuitous step, the floor moved with an intriguing, quiet grate of stone on stone. Nervous excitement tingled in his fingertips as he fit them into a gap at the edge of the slab and lifted it. The aroma of incense wafted upward from the uncovered hole. David shone his light down a rough staircase of wood, building up courage—well, that was the idea anyway.

A faint noise caught his attention. Human noise. He tilted his head to hear better. Slow, quiet screaming—like the strange spirit people earlier that day.

God, no.

The noise expanded into a chaotic unity of voices, a supernatural orchestra tuning up before a performance. Getting closer. Closer.

Time to run.

He backed away, but the voices rose out of the hole. He could tell exactly where they were and shone a light on the spot as he pressed himself against the wall.

Nope. Nope. Time to go.

As he turned to run, the incorporeal voices exploded with a deafening scream. Someone grabbed and yanked him backward. He opened his mouth to cry out, but the voices were so loud, his own—if it was working at all—couldn't be heard. An invisible force struck his chest, burning hot, violent, and swift. His body vibrated with the impact.

After that, silence.

He was alone.

Panting, his body tense and tight against the wall, ears ringing, he closed his eyes and swallowed, then resumed panting. As he swiped his sweaty forehead with the bottom of his shirt, a whispering sound spoke into his ear. He scanned the area with his flashlight and even peeked out of the curtain into the Judgment Room.

There it was again.

Dad's whisper. *Nepenthe.*

"What do you mean?" David whispered. That voice had been missing for so long . . .

You need it. Accepting it hurts.

"It's in there, isn't it?"

No answer.

It was. It was in that hole. It was a step in the right direction. It was the thing he needed to be able to forget. It wouldn't make life better, would it? Probably not. This was likely to make it worse, but he'd deal with that another time.

Into the hole. With enthusiasm! Or something like it.

The farther into the Bastion's gullet, the less he smelled incense as sulfur overtook the sweet fragrance. At the bottom of the stairs, he paused. Jade returned to his mind, suffocating with his fourth child.

The fourth. One by Anise and two by Jade, but he repressed the thought of the first one most days.

Not today. He never thought of himself as a vengeful person, but a wild hope bubbled up in his mind. A hope for justice, not revenge. He passed the light across the small room before him. To his left, a swath of orange silk covered a narrow, roughly-built table. It hosted a few candles and fresh incense sticks, sprawling out of a green glass bottle like a dead, black tree, void of twigs. Beside the bottle, two gilt-edged wooden incense trays contained fresh ashes.

High-lipped shelves, resembling feeding troughs, had been installed on the cement walls to his right. He shone the light on them for an instant and drew back with a sharp breath and leap of the heart. Recovering from the initial shock, he shone the light on the troughs again. Each one contained human bones, charred in a few locations.

These had to be the people who showed themselves to him that morning—at least some of them. One caught his eye more than the others, though. All the skeletons were intact, but this one had a glaring anomaly: a missing finger. Dad had disappeared years ago, and most assumed Earth People attacked and killed him. Maybe that wasn't true.

As David turned to run, his flashlight caught the face of a visitor blocking his exit. Vincent's grim visage turned David's heart to ice.

Vincent slapped the flashlight from David's hand into the wall, where it landed with a crack, burying them in darkness.

* * *

Hesper awoke to a man's scream, crisp and clean in her mind. The cold terror in the sound shattered her nerves. David? No. Almost, but not quite.

It wanted her and looked for her—a moth to flame—and would keep coming until they met. She just knew.

Cole would not wake. She shook him and called his name—only breathing. He never slept that soundly.

She threw off the covers and fled the room, down the stairs to the glass doors that would lead her to the trees. The sound came from outside, so she opened the door and charged into the yard.

City lights grayed the northern skies, and the fruit trees glowed orange in the beams of the alley's street lamp. Hesper spun around, searching for the person attached to the voice. Then she stopped to listen. Which direction did the screaming come from? She could not tell. "Hello? Hello?"

Only screaming answered.

"Are you hurt? I might be able to help you!" Then, as if cut off with a hatchet, the screaming ceased.

She squinted against the new moon and shadow-mottled light beneath the trees, hearing only crickets and her own hurried breathing. Perhaps she should try to wake Cole again. She turned to the house. Behind her, a *thunk,* a crackle, and a heavy, rapid swishing.

A man, enveloped in flames from top to bottom, ran straight to her. She ran but caught a foot in her nightgown and tumbled to the ground. As she scrambled to her feet, he caught up with her and wrapped her in his arms. The orange glow of his blaze embraced her. Not hot, but a gentle and perfect warmth.

He lowered his voice and whispered in her ear, "I burn, but I never die because I need you." Sobs caught in his throat until, at last, the dam broke, unleashing a lamentable howl that hurt Hesper's ears. A scream rang through her mind, but she could not speak. Confused and emptied of strength, she submitted.

* * *

Hesper opened her eyes. *Only a dream.*

Seated at his desk, the small lamp's light illuminated Cole's face as he studied an old book he'd brought along from the base. A plate with a few crumbs had been pushed aside. He held a glass of wine in his hand but delayed in drinking due to a sudden interest in whatever he read. Hesper glanced at the clock. The short hand pointed to the two.

"Cole?"

He did not look up. "Hm?"

"I had a bad dream."

He frowned. "Again? I didn't know you still had those. The one about Joram?"

"No. Different. I heard something like David's voice and . . . and there was more, but do you suppose he is okay? Should we call him?"

"It's just a dream, Hesper." He smiled. "Get some rest."

He needed to study. He had a Book to find. Mysteries to solve.

She curled up into a ball, cold beyond the help of a blanket.

Twenty-Nine | Post-Conquest: 232

PRE-CONQUEST RELIGION ABSORBED Cole's attention for too long, and his lack of self-discipline kept him up late. It was one of his favorite studies. He purchased the book in the northern country and smuggled it in, so he rarely cracked it open on the base. This was an opportunity to study it freely, but there was no excuse to stay up so late with it. Still, he rose early in the morning to exercise, have breakfast, and head to work.

Alan's office doubled as his home, crowding the place with a mixture of dirty dishes, pot holders, manila envelopes, and books. Fiction stacked with books of law, and biographies lay next to biology—overwhelming clutter.

"Mr. Bandello?"

The old man stepped into sight, a book in one hand and a mug in the other. "Honestly, please, call me Al." He glanced up with a smile. "I'm shocked you've shown up so soon! You're quite a man. Hard worker, I suspect. You just got here yesterday, and you're already settled?"

"Settled enough, sir. What may I do for you?" Cole pushed up his glasses.

"First thing's first, if you'd like, there's kringle and fresh turnovers on the counter in my wee kitchen. Plenty of chicory tea. I don't keep coffee these days."

"No, thank you, sir." Cole smiled. "I'm here to be of service to you."

Alan sipped at his mug. "Right. Well, we don't have much work just now. Only a few things I've taken care of already, but uh . . ." He looked this way and that, evidently trying to think of something.

"I'll organize for you." Cole offered. He might even wash the dishes before the day was over.

"Perfect! Do whatever you fancy. I'm sure we'll have work soon. That lawyer across the gate's taking folks from me with his young age, but they'll see through his capped teeth in time."

"I hope you haven't burdened yourself to show kindness to us," Cole said. "If you haven't the need for an assistant, please, say so."

Alan looked up, distressed. "What! No, no! M'boy! I always have need of help, as you can see." He gestured to the disarray around him.

Cole grabbed up the nearest stack of books and began the categorization process. "Let's see. Fiction, fiction, biography, religion, reference, psychology, law . . ." On to the next stack, and the next, and the next.

The old man waddled about, looking over papers. Occasionally he made comments about "that lawyer." Cole didn't want to be rude, but Alan's interruptions were making him a little crazy. After the third interruption, however, Alan froze in the middle of the room until Cole sensed it and met his stare.

"Brock, you like things just so, don't you?" Alan asked.

"Yes, I do."

"Don't like things or people to get in your way."

"Who does?"

Alan chuckled. "Fair enough. But I think we both know you're a little beyond the average in that area, son."

"I'm just honest."

He'd also blown Hesper off last night. She woke up scared, and he told her to go back to sleep because he was too concerned with his own interests. What good was an honest jerk?

Oh, my god.

"Honest! Are you now?" Alan flicked at his earlobe and looked around the room, entertained by something. "I suppose you are. Overall, you seem to be. You stand like an honest man, and you don't make bones about anything. I think it'll be a delicious experience to get acquainted with you. However, I'll let you make the environment one you feel comfortable in without further interruption."

* * *

Nearing the end of the organization of the first half of Alan's office, Cole grabbed some papers that had been hiding for who-knew-how-long underneath the mess of books on the table and shuffled them into a neat stack. The writing, loopy, long, and jumbled together, was almost illegible. Judging by the format, it was a letter.

He wasn't trying to read them, but the few legible words stood out. Dilemma, civility, Gentles, Book . . . Book of Light. *Book of Light? . . . Book of Light into the hands of . . . something, something and hope in—* Cole shut his eyes. He had begun to read but had to resist the impulse to keep going.

"Al, where do you want these papers?"

Alan's face lit up. "Oh, welcome back to earth! I'll take that." He snatched the papers from Cole's hands. "Goodness, that's an old letter! I had to rewrite it. Lost it in my chaos." He shook with a belly laugh. "Repulsive, isn't it?"

Cole smiled and shook his head. "What kind of cases do you get around here?"

Alan sat in a ratty swiveling chair and propped his feet on the desk. "Eh, a smattering of slip-and-falls, private nuisances." The neat stack of papers splayed out when he tossed them onto the desk.

"You know, the stuff that would be a waste of my mind if they didn't pay me exorbitant fees. Not enough of it these days! My glasses are getting pretty old 'cause I haven't been able to afford new ones in a while. Eh, priorities. I can afford books, brandy, and baklava!"

"Have you ever appealed to the Book of Light?"

Alan's eyes widened with surprise and a bit of humor. "Hm, no. I can't say I have. Since the Kyrios claim they have it, if I were—hypothetically, you understand—to appeal to it, they'd have to ship it across the country, accompanied by a Glorious One to read it for us. Fascinating that you would dare even think of such a thing. You're quite a person."

"Do you know much about it?"

"Oh, a bit." Alan scrunched his face.

Time to hold off. No sense in making the old man nervous. Cole directed his attention to a stack of books in need of sorting.

"Cole, are you very interested in the Book of Light?"

"Why?"

"The speed of your work has increased exponentially since broaching the subject. Seems it's excited you. No one in law circles has brought it up to me before except to recite the blather about it being the 'skeleton of Law.' Did your *alma mater* teach its contents or about the application in a courtroom setting?"

"I went to several schools. None of them did."

Alan clasped his hands together and rested them in front of him. "It's dangerous stuff. Why do you want to find out about it? What has made it relevant to you?"

"Curiosity," Cole said. "I once appealed to the Book of Light with the hope that it would fight against an unjust verdict."

Alan said nothing and stared into the floor for several minutes. Cole pretended not to notice, but if the old fellow had more to say . . . No. This required proper pacing and wisdom, not passionate persistence.

Finally, Alan spoke. "Brock, m'boy. How much can I trust you?"

"Why? What do you know?"

"How much can I trust you?"

What on earth was the man looking for? Alan possessed so much unknowable knowledge as it was, what was he convinced he understood about the Book of Light? Might be worth finding out. Might be a bunch of nonsense, too.

"Completely. You can trust me completely."

"I *believe* you," Alan declared. "I trust my instincts. I fancy myself a good judge of character, and I have, thus far, been wrong only once or twice to my knowledge. I trust myself, and so I trust you." He fiddled with a box of paper clips, cleared his throat, set the paper clips down with a decisive air, and fixed his eyes on Cole. "According to my studies, the Book of Light has been hidden and possibly destroyed. The Kyrios saw it as a challenge and, well, they erased it, metaphorically speaking."

"What are your sources? How do you know this?"

"My father told me things. It's been passed along." Alan swished the list of sources around the air with his hand.

His sources may have been dubious, but Cole wasn't foolish enough to dismiss things just because they weren't written down. "It doesn't exist anymore?"

"Well, now, I didn't say that exactly, did I?"

"What do you mean?"

"Hm." Alan flicked at the tip of his nose with his forefinger, studying Cole. "I think we'll talk about this another time. You know the saying, 'If you play with the death-light you might find the afterlife sooner than you'd hoped?'" Alan waggled his eyebrows. "You get too tangled with the Book of Light, and you're liable to run into the Kyrios and a host of other dangerous people. That's a fearful thing. A *fearful* thing. Even talking about it can be dangerous." A shrewd smile made his face shine. "But I will say that I believe the Book of Light is a powerful force. A holy, mystical relic, perhaps, but it has healed broken hearts and bodies and stirred up dying embers in the soul." He thumped his chest.

"The Kyrios stole the idea and abused it. Over the years, they made it into something it was not and hid it behind a curtain. In time, people came to believe that it had always been that way and that the power now rested in the hands of the Glorious Ones—as if the Glorious Ones could let anything *rest*. They're always squeezing power like a bear trap." Alan clenched his fist and clamped his mouth shut.

Relaxing, he clicked his tongue against his teeth. "Not another word on it. I say I'm done, but I keep going. Terrible habit of mine. I'm a butter-finger with loose lips. I have no fear of death and no fear of the Kyrios for myself. But for you? I don't want you to get hurt, son."

He picked up his stapler and held it to his mouth. "I know you're listening, Kyrios!"

* * *

Cole followed the sound of the shower and leaned on the bathroom's doorjamb, loosening his tie. "I've acquired interesting information today. If it's true, that is."

Hesper called out from the shower, "Oh, hello! What did you learn?"

"Alan claims to know about the Book of Light."

"What? How?"

"Strange, isn't it? Seems planned."

"By whom?"

"That's the question, isn't it?"

Thirty | Post-Conquest: 232

HE WAS ALIVE? It had to be a miracle. If not, the afterlife hurt an awful lot. David groaned. When Ariana joined in the fight, he was done for. Two against one was lame and cowardly, but effective.

David's right eye wouldn't open. He opened his left eye to see white walls and a tin ceiling. The infirmary. The fact that they didn't put him in jail stood as a victory. It meant they liked him.

Despite a corkscrew headache, an aching gut, and sore ribs tossed in for fun, he managed to sit up on the hard cot and push through the pain to put his feet on the floor. His toes shrieked at him. Some, if not all, must've been broken. He probed his teeth with his tongue.

They were all there. "Thank God." If he lost teeth, he'd lose the will to live. Anything but the teeth.

As a Meros soldier, he had endured the most rigorous, oftentimes cruel, military training in the world, or so he was told. Pain was a small inconvenience. Right? Right. He attempted to stand, but the throbbing foot nauseated him, and he lowered himself back to the cot.

"Hello?" A sharp sting scolded his lip. Dry and hoarse, he barely recognized his own voice.

The doors opened at the far end of the infirmary as Vincent stepped inside and strode past row upon row of white cots to sit across from David. He stared at the floor, a triangle of thumbs and fingers hanging between his knees. With a sigh, he lifted his eyes. "I'm here to make a deal with you."

David tried to keep his lips stiff to avoid offending the wound. "What deal? You've got me. You cheated—two against one—but you've got me."

"We need you, David."

"You mean that you don't want *Cole*. You'll keep me alive because you don't want Cole joining the Kyrios."

"Your private convictions are disconnected from your work. We need that."

"You want me because I'll roll over and take it. Cole won't. You've never liked him, even though he's twice the man I am and is the most pious person I know. Why?"

"He's not Kyrios material. He has the blood, but not the goods."

"What are the goods? A weak mind? An unwavering loyalty to *you*?"

Vincent stood. "Here's my deal. You can take it or leave it. You tell no one about what's happened, and I'll spare your life. You'll spare your brother in the process as well. This would set him off like a match." He pointed at David. "And so would we." Their eyes connected. David understood.

"If. . . if I agree to keep my mouth shut, how would you ensure I'm keeping my end of the bargain?"

"Oh, I'm not worried about it. You will. If you think about it long enough, you will."

"Fine."

"I'm sorry. What's fine?" Vincent turned his ear to David. "Your grumble is hardly audible."

"Fine to your B.S. Fine to your—just fine. I agree to keep your secret in exchange for my life and my brother's. Are you satisfied?"

Vincent glanced toward the ceiling as if in thought, then he dropped his gaze to David. "Getting there. Cole would thank you if he knew about this, David. I'm certain his life and his wife are more valuable than the information. Let Cole hang himself if he wants to, but at least you won't be his executioner."

Hesper? Hesper. What would they do to Hesper?

"And his wife," David said. "I keep silent for his wife's life and safety, too, or no deal. I'll fight you 'til you kill me."

Vincent laughed. "I have no interest in killing innocents. I'm interested in maintaining peace so that the Kyrios can focus on what's necessary for the health of our nation. Truly." He reseated himself, his eyes intent on David's throbbing face. "Listen to me, I know things you don't know. Things you'll never know and don't need to. Glorious Ones bear the burden of a truth that requires secrecy. I have nothing against you or Hesper or Cole. Cole impresses me, honestly. He's courageous and sharp and I have always thought well of you two.

"Not everyone is meant to be led or accept authority blindly. I understand that." He smiled. "However, we cannot just smile and nod at your antics. We have to protect the weaker minds from people like you and Cole because they would destroy themselves and our nation by following your example, thinking they're wise."

"I hear what you're saying, Vince, but all I can *hear*-hear is that you're a guy who claims not to want to kill innocents and hopes to protect weaker minds, but you have no qualm with destroying minds and hearts in your bedroom and courtroom."

Eyeing David with a slight smirk and a puff of laughter through his nose, Vincent licked his lower lip and said, "That's what you think I do? Angry housewives tell you their side of things, and you just . . . believe them?"

This conversation wouldn't be worth it. "Maybe I'm a weak mind after all."

The infirmary walls echoed with Vincent's genuine laughter. "You're not weak-minded. That's not what it is. You've got a big heart and strong intuition—not unlike a dog. That's all a part of the mind." He slapped David's knee. "Well, David, I'm glad we've spoken. I suggest you claim you went into the city for a few drinks and got caught up in a fight like the good old days. I'll send Dr. Kratz to bring something for your pain."

David went home to rest, allowing only Lorelei to enter his room with food and drink while he sat at his desk, staring into the grain of the wood for hours, thinking.

He should be with Tom. Poor Tom. But he couldn't. He just couldn't.

In moments such as these, his wine cellar beckoned, but he had a strange desire to be sober.

Aloneness tortured him, but Dulce would be little comfort for this. *Anise, please, come out of that room.*

* * *

Early on the second day of work, Cole accepted Alan's offer of a thin slice of cassata and a cup of chicory tea. Alan leaned against his desk in his conversational pose, nursing a mug in his hands. "So, Brock, tell me about yourself."

"Well, that's a vague question I've never been good at answering." He took a gulp of his tea and sat back, his ankle across his knee.

"Okay." Alan thought for a moment. "Where do you come from?"

"Born and raised in Section One."

"Which gate?"

"Cove Gate."

The base, really, but he sure couldn't tell him he was raised on the base. The situation was risky enough.

Alan gave a devilish grunty laugh. "Oh, dear, Cove Gate. That explains things. You're right in there with the Kyrios. How do you feel about them?"

"Explains things? What things?"

"I can smell religiosity and strict upbringing from a mile away, son. So, how do you feel about them?" He picked at his nose and flicked something off his finger.

"The Kyrios?"

"The Kyrios," he repeated.

"I have no problem with the Kyrios, per se."

Alan sniggered, rubbing his belly. "Ah, I see. You appreciate the positions and loathe the persons."

"I didn't say—"

"HA! M'boy, you say plenty you don't mean to say. It's written all over your face!"

Cole's lips cracked with a false smile as he forked the last of the cassata into his mouth. It unsettled him to be read and interpreted by someone he didn't realize was capable of doing so. Now that he recognized the old man's sharp observational skills—or dumb luck—he'd have to be more careful.

Alan grew serious. "Heard any word on whether the Kyrios are dispatching a purging crew to Pomo Gate?"

There had to be a hefty leak in the Bastion for him to catch wind of that.

"No. No word of a purging crew. The Kyrios usually keep their affairs private. Do they have a reason to send one?"

"Ah! I heard a rumor of reports to the Kyrios that Pomo Gate allows illicit births." Alan flicked at his ear and the tip of his nose before he settled his gaze on Cole.

Cole straightened up, rubbing the spine of the book he held. "Mongrels?"

"Yes, mongrels, as you say. I prefer to think of them as illicit. That's all they really are. Humanity supersedes the laws we create to demean it."

"Interesting perspective for a lawyer, Alan."

"Ha! Naw, m'boy. Not entirely." Alan blew his nose with a handkerchief. "Normal lawyers—not those vacuous lickspittles of the Kyrios—often have a fairly decent grasp on legal versus moral. Unfortunately, vacuous lickspittles are now the ones teaching the up-and-coming lawyers. The daddy of them all being that honored

Senior Officer Cole Chandler fellow." He pointed at Cole. "Born and bred in a Kyrios test tube, living on privilege and maybe a prayer. I went to hear him speak at Sacred Gate University a few years ago. Seems quite bright, knows his stuff, but a coward with strong opinions he won't share. Just toeing the Kyrios line. I smelled it all over him, even from the back."

Must have sat w-a-a-a-a-y in the back. Cole pushed down a laugh.

"I suspect he's religious," Alan said. "But that's beside the point. What it comes down to is . . . I'm wondering, son, if you are for God or the Kyrios?"

"I'm not going to report anything, if that's what you mean, sir."

Alan glanced at his wristwatch. "Well, goodness me, look at the time! I'd say we've worked ourselves silly. How about a break?"

Despite having done next to nothing, the men lounged in comfortable chairs and discussed frivolous things unrelated to mongrels, the Kyrios, or books of any sort. For the remainder of the day, they discussed women, the wonderful world of salmon, and how potatoes grow. Whenever Cole tried to work, Alan distracted him, preferring conversation over having an organized office. So, they talked and twiddled.

Near closing time, Alan let out a great sigh. "Business is down. It's so down. It's that lawyer—good for nothing—he's ruined my reputation."

"How?"

"He spreads rumors. He's just a . . ." Alan shook his fist and clenched his teeth.

"Alan"—Cole smiled and propped his feet on the half-cleared book table—"What else do you do with your life?"

Alan jerked his head backward. "What do you mean? I'm a lawyer."

"It's not busy here. You said it yourself. You've got to have a hobby or something you enjoy. You obviously like books, and not all these books here are about law. What is it? Skydiving? Mongrel rights activism? Vigilante crime fighting?"

Playfulness glittered in Alan's eyes. "I'm a vigilante crime fighter." Hands in the air, he surrendered. "You've caught me. My secret identity is out. With this body and these skills, it's hard to hide." With a grand rub, he presented his poochy paunch.

Cole laughed. A serious answer would be nice, but a friendly relationship was more important. As outspoken as Alan was, he had a secret. Clearly, he wanted to be found out, but it would take time and trust.

As the shadows shifted and the light in the house grew more golden than white, Alan's tales of university exploits lurched to a halt an hour before closing, when Cole's insides struck a match and lit a fire inside of him. The burning radiated through his chest cavity and into his throat.

Alan stopped talking, sat up straight, and looked around as if he heard something. He studied Cole, almost suspicious, but gave it up to look toward the door a moment before it opened.

"Hello?" The strong male voice rode low over a gravel road.

An intimidating figure clomped around the corner in old, dirty boots. His knees showed through the holes in his faded jeans, and a black spiral tattoo wrapped around his left arm from somewhere under his shirt down to his wrist, where a leather glove hid the rest. It appeared he had torn his shirt's sleeves off to tie them around his right bicep. A standard military knife hung off his belt.

When the young man saw them looking him over, he slid his backpack off and set it at his feet as he pushed a smile to his lips.

Cole rose to get a glass of water to cool down the burning in his chest.

Alan stood, his hands resting on his belly. "May I help you?"

"Um. I hope so." The strange man's eyes dodged about as he blew out a few small laughs and dragged his fingers through his black hair. "I heard you give folks a place to stay sometimes."

"Certainly, son." Alan coughed and clutched his chest.

The young man grimaced. "Can I sit down?"

"Sure. Sure."

Cole downed his water. "Are you all right, Alan?"

"I'm always all right, m'boy." With a deliberate knowing look, he said, "How about you?"

"Do you have a needle and thread?" asked the young man.

"Whatever for?"

"Stitches."

"Son, if you need stitches, we'd best get you to a hospital. I can drive. I'll pay for it." Alan stood to lead the way and grabbed his keys off a hook on the wall.

"No! No hospitals. I take care of myself. I've done this before."

"Brock, you can go home for the day," Alan said. "I'll take care of the young man."

Cole eyed the knife at the man's waist. "Are you sure, sir? I would rather stay."

"Looking out for the old man, are we? Admirable, Brock, but this is business I'll tend to alone." He considered the black fabric around the young man's left arm. "On second thought, your wife is Unified, no?"

"Yes, she is."

"They're good with stitches, aren't they?"

"Especially her. She was a medicine woman."

"Would she be willing to assist us?"

* * *

Hesper required a needle and thread, fire to sanitize the needle, warm water to wash the wound, honey to dress it, and a clean cloth. Between the two households, they managed everything.

Dried blood caked the strips of cloth to his skin in a few spots, but they peeled away without much trouble. She examined the wound. "It is wide, but not too deep."

The needle made the sanitizing fire dance as she dragged it through. She cleansed the wound with the water and cloth, then set to the stitching. With a face of stone, the stranger watched everything she did.

"What is your name?" she asked.

"Jesurun. I go by Jes. You?"

Needle in hand, she froze. His voice felt like the glowing remnants of a fire that burned someone's house down. Trouble and destruction? Yes. But the heat of the rubble warmed her. She'd heard his voice before.

He burns, but he will not die.

"I am Hesper. Do we know each other?"

"You remind me of somebody I used to know, but I don't know you."

She finished the stitches in a few minutes and applied honey for a dressing. The job was neat and well done, and it felt wonderful to have done it. Useful in a world that had no use for her beyond pleasure.

Jes inspected her work and nodded approvingly. "I usually do it myself, but it's kinda nice having someone else do it for once."

Cole crossed his arms. "You get wounds worthy of stitches on a regular basis?"

"I'm sure the lad has his history," Alan said. "We probably shouldn't ask about it. Care for a cherry turnover, Jes?"

Thirty-One | Post-Conquest: 232

COLE HAD TO move on with life, ignore what he felt about Jesurun, and enjoy Hesper, whose spirits were consistently low and level these days. They talked about the sweet, simple, non-philosophical things Hesper most enjoyed. For a time, all seemed right with the world as they sat on the terrace and gentle breezes blew citrus scents their way. Eating fruit they picked from their trees, it was as if they were Adahy and Hesper again.

Almost.

He couldn't keep himself from eyeballing Alan's yard four houses down. While Hesper told the story of the doe who ate a daylily from her hand, Cole's wandering eyes caught on the people in Alan's backyard. Black hair and black clothes—Jesurun. Short, thick, and fast—Alan. That was a bit strange. Might even warrant a follow.

"Cole, what do you see?"

He startled. "I'm sorry. Maybe I'm crazy, but I have to go."

"Go where?"

"I need to follow them." He pointed at the men.

"Why?"

She was offended. He was hurting her. He'd brushed her off once, and he couldn't do it again, but . . .

No.

He had to let it go. It wasn't really his business.

312

But what if it was?

"I just do. I wish I were armed, but I haven't the time to run in and get myself together. I have to go."

"Cole!"

"I'll be fine! They're going on foot? Out the back door? How can I ignore that?"

Hesper's face crowded out his scattered thoughts and forced a smile to his lips. "I suppose you have the self-control required to ignore it, don't you? It's important, Hesper."

Why was it important? Was it that important? Her gray eyes begged him not to go, even though her pride never would. He sighed. "I'll be back soon."

* * *

At the end of the alley, Jes and Alan took a road to the south and picked up their pace. Cole maintained a firm follow from a distance, staying in the shadows as much as possible. The journey ended in a rural section on the southern outskirts of Pomo Gate, where several weathered and unkempt homes dotted the area, though only one house showed signs of life. Its roof needed replacing and the broken windows, repaired with duct tape, leaked copious amounts of jazz music. If these people kept recordings in their home, they didn't respect laws concerning entertainment choices—unless they had a jazz band in there.

Cole liked them already.

Jes and Alan stepped into the building without knocking. Cole sprinted for the house and crouched beneath a window. Music overwhelmed the voices within. Shades kept most of the house's secrets, glowing with buttery light interrupted only by passing silhouettes. Bent over, he rustled through the high grass and weeds around the house to look for a better location or—if he was lucky—a way in.

The broken basement window on the north side would do nicely. With a loose hinge and an old-fashioned lock, it would be a cinch. It lifted on the loose hinge side, and the rusty hinge on the left broke off, tearing up the frame's rotten wood. After an assessment of the size of the opening, he scanned the basement with his flashlight. It was only an empty room with stairs leading up to a door. Perfect. He slid past the grassy overgrowth into the basement and set the window against the building to give the impression it was in place should anyone happen to walk by.

Strong, earthy, almost-sweet stench of mold pervaded the dirt-floored basement. Cole crouched to look under the door. The muffled voices and music indicated that the dim room on the other side of the door probably came between the basement and the rest of the house. Perhaps a pantry or closet. He took a chance and cracked the door ever so slightly.

A pantry. Canned goods and boxes lined the wall to his right. Cole entered and crouched at a peeling door to hear the voices on the other side.

Jes' voice stood out, low and rumbly.

This better not be Alan taking his new buddy to a birthday party.

Heartburn crept into his throat and a strong sensation of being watched skittered through his brain and down his spine. He jumped and backed away from the door.

"What's up, Al?" a man's voice said.

Cole crawled back to the door to hear better.

"This here is my new friend," Alan said. "Jes came looking for help this afternoon. He's had a rough life, but he's taken a real turn around due to a fellow who sounds an awful lot like Ansel."

"Ansel's been gone several months," said the other voice.

"Yep. This young man claims to have met him about two years ago while working as a bouncer in Sacred Gate."

"Go on."

"Even before meeting Ansel, he'd fall into some kind of trance. Blazing tattoo. Drawing. You know, different but the same as usual. He's wanted in twenty different sections—Did I get that right, Jes?"

"Yeah. What do you mean different but the same as usual?"

"The LEWs want him dead."

"Do you have the drawings?" the man asked.

"Yes. Right here." A pause. "Give the folder to Seamus, hey?"

Several moments of silence passed before Seamus spoke again. "Son, how does it feel when you draw these things?"

Cole just barely made out the quiet response. "Like fire. It sucks."

"Right. I see. Do you know much about the Book of Light, Jes?"

"Heard about."

"It's disappeared. We've been looking for it ever since. We haven't come across it for a good hundred years."

"We? A hundred years?"

"Our group." Seamus laughed. "We may look old to you, but we're not that old. People have been looking for it in secret for two hundred years. Every time it resurfaces, the Kyrios find and destroy it. They've had three known encounters in our lifetime."

"Who knows how many there've been who no one knows about." Another man's voice spoke.

"Who's 'they?'" Jes asked.

"The Kyrios," replied the new man. "I work with them. I know what they do. They don't get the death-light out of thin air, Jes."

There was the leak.

Alan cleared his throat and spoke carefully. "Jes, this must sound bizarre to you."

"What?" Jes sounded irritated. "You think my writings and pictures are the Book of Light? That thing the Kyrios have? A kids' story?"

"No, Jes," said Seamus. "We think *you're* the Book. The Book of Light is a person. It always has been."

The room grew quiet.

"What did I do to make you think it's me?"

"This won't sound logical to you," Seamus said. "But, throughout history, there have been individuals with a particular sensitivity. Us. If the Kyrios don't kill them first, the Books are drawn to us. We know who they are by the burning sensation in our chest. The symptoms they exhibit are also important."

Jes barked a derisive laugh. "You guys are nuts." A chair slid across the floor. Papers shuffled. "If the Book of Light was a person, everybody would know. I'm just as ready to get rid of those schmucks, too, but I'm not going to throw in with zealots to do it. I mean, really? Heartburn? You decide who the Book is because of heartburn?"

"It's been a long time, Jes," Seamus said. "The people will believe whatever they're taught. Several generations have passed since The Conquest. Plenty of time to erase society's memory."

"Prove it."

"Don't you see how convenient it would be for the Book of Light to be made into something kept behind closed doors for the privileged few alone? No one would ever know. Give it a couple generations, and no one will exist to challenge the Kyrios. Most won't care to risk their hide to do it even if they wanted to."

Cole smiled. If only he could meet Seamus.

"Who are you guys anyway?" Jes said.

"We're just people."

"Sensitive people, huh? With no proof. Nothin'? Just heartburn?"

Another chair slid across the floor. "People who want to see the Book of Light take its place in the Bastion of Holiness. God's power *will* follow you if you trust It."

Thirty-Two | Post-Conquest: 232

CLOSE TO GOD? Nope. Everyone assumed the Kyrios were close to God. David used to have the assurance of his own righteousness, but even that had disappeared long ago. He'd tried to do what was right and help people as much as he could without dying. But cowardice . . . it required a heavy emotional fine in lieu of a courageous death.

And now, his soul lay flat on its back, lost in a rush of trouble, unable to even think of connecting with God. His beloved wife had been murdered, his favored wife had likely gone mad, and the Kyrios had dead bodies under the Bastion of Holiness. One might even be his dad. Why would they ever keep such damning evidence?

Fear.

It started in his gut and worked its way through his body—cold, sweating, fear—an oily, stick-to-your-heart kind. A shadow moved in his periphery. Right. He needed childish moving-shadow fears as much he needed a hole in the head.

Faint voices seeped into his room. He checked his watch. Half past three in the morning. Who would be up and why would there be another man in the house besides himself? Perhaps Cole and Hesper had returned. Careful not to let the door squeak, he peeked into the hall and slipped out. The soft voices came from Dulce's room, so he crept up to the door, wincing with each step, and listened. David hadn't heard her voice sound so silvery since the day she fell in love with him. They were not close at this time, but that was the ebb-and-flow nature of relationships. Nothing he ever worried about.

She belonged to him, and the idea of a woman he was intimate with, took care of, and respected, betraying him and sleeping with another man . . . Terrible images came to his mind. Violent ones replaced them. He was prepared to barrel through the door and bruise that slime ball's kidneys. Screw the pain, he'd do it.

A certain word made the man's voice recognizable.

Vincent. Vincent with "the fat one."

He couldn't take Vincent on when he was this injured. The voices fell silent. Like a whipped puppy, David stepped away from the door and sulked back to his room. He'd have the divorce paper signed in the morning. He had to tolerate Evelyn's affairs to keep the Kyrios out of his hair, but he wasn't going to let a woman pull that again.

* * *

Hesper tried to sew. Cole would be fine, but what about her?

Tried to relax. What about her?

Tried to read. She had to trust that he was doing what he must.

Tried to care. She did care.

It was hard to care when he did not. Where was he? He had been gone all night. The short hand barely touched the four. She growled.

I am going to demand someone tell me how clocks work.

Out on the terrace, the sweet smell of the trees greeted her—a reminder of how much she needed them. The soft grass soothed her swollen feet as she approached a mulberry tree and hugged it, resting her forehead against the bark. It was not quite the same as the forest. Perhaps the closeness of many trees, growing wild—not in rows—gave her the peaceful feeling, but this still grounded her.

Grounding. She was a leaf in the wind.

Grounding. She squeezed the tree.

Why was Cole turning away from her so much?

Cheek to the trunk. Grounding.

He was so focused on everything else, but he did not know . . . he did not know what was coming for them.

The friction of the rough bark burned her palms as she slid to the earth. Strength lived in that bark, years of fruitful service, pruning and growth, disease and treatment.

Give some of yourself to me. Let this experience prune me so I may be useful and not a mere doll to be enjoyed.

The Meros did not need her skills. Even Cole did not need her; he wanted her. Was that not enough?

Let me be useful. She closed her eyes. *But who am I talking to?*

* * *

Challenging Dulce after her lover left was a cowardly move, but the situation required it. David preferred to handle the matter in a civil, legal manner. No fights in the middle of the night. End the thing with dignity.

Before dawn, he took a paper of divorce from the filing cabinet in his office, signed it, and brought it home. He limped up the stairs and through the hallway until he stood at Dulce's door, then rapped gently a few times. Sleepy and unsuspecting, she answered.

Literally biting his tongue between his molars, David flicked his wrist toward her, offering the paper. She frowned, questioning him with her face as she took the end of her safety and security from his hand. After reading it, innocence and surprise tried to make her look pretty.

Innocent? No, ma'am.

Surprise? That he believed.

"Either go get that guy you were with last night to marry you, or I'll have you on the auction block in three days so they can't execute you."

Vincent only hurt the ones he most enjoyed. Clearly, he hadn't hurt her, so he either didn't enjoy her very much or had a deep affection that wasn't merely sexual. For her sake, David hoped it was the latter. He wasn't completely merciless. Most men turned their Gentle wives in for adultery, after all.

"I've done right by you, Dulce, and I don't see you as a toy. You're a woman who's made a choice, and I won't force you to be with me when your heart and body are elsewhere."

The sweet and mild Dulce's face changed. Her jaw set as she shoved the paper into his chest, letting it dip, float, and dive to the floor. The door closed in his face.

* * *

Alone, David sat in the dining room with a bowl of oats drowned in spiced milk. A small glass of orange juice at his right hand, and a soft-boiled egg in a shiny copper cup at his left. Half-way through the meal, Dulce, a streak of pink, rumbled down the stairs, past the dining room entrance, and out the door, which she slammed behind her.

Cool and collected, he enjoyed the rest of his oats and his egg. Lorelei entered the room and began to clear his dishes, so he sat back and watched her work.

"Say, Lorelei, I don't need this big table anymore. You don't suppose we can cut it in half and tip it up in such a way that I can eat my meals in a wooden teepee? Then—Oh, no, let's sell it. I'll get myself a card table. What do you say? I'll live the bachelor days of the ordinary little fellows out in the real world."

Lorelei stood dumbly with a plate in hand. David raised the glass of orange juice, arched an amused eyebrow, and considered her as he sipped. He set the glass down, smiled, and said, "How about you marry me, Lorelei. You've always been my true love."

She blushed and gave him a light smack upside his head.

"I haven't made you blush in ages! It's a sign, Lorelei dear. In the east, red is the color of marriage." He laughed. "You've certainly been my first and truest love, Madam, even if not for wedded bliss."

She shook her head and shuffled off to deliver his dirty dishes to the kitchen.

David leaned on the table and rested his head in his hands, staring into his juice, focused on the pulp at the top. *Damn that man. If anyone deserves damnation, it's Vince.* Or maybe it wasn't. *Maybe it's the idiot staring at pulp.*

Thirty-Three | Post-Conquest: 232

AFTER AN EARLY morning meeting with the Kyrios, David slid his chair back and rose to leave, but Vincent reached across the table and grabbed his elbow—a silent command to stay. After everyone left, Vincent delivered an icy glare and released him.

"So, you're divorcing your last sane wife, hm?" He gestured for David to sit.

Not until you do, pal. "Divorced."

"Why are you doing it?" Vincent sat.

Playing dumb so you can execute her and get her out of your hair, Vince? Turd. David sat back down. "Did it. She doesn't please me anymore."

"How is that, David?"

"Do I have to answer to you for everything?"

Vincent smiled. "It's a far more serious thing when one of the Kyrios divorces a spouse. So, in this matter, yes, I need to know."

David gave a show of thought and, with a saucy squint and smirk, whispered, "I don't think you do."

Leaning back, Vincent crossed his legs and offered a half-smile. "What course of action do you intend to take with her?"

"I told her to find someone else to marry, or I'd put her on the block in three days."

"Harsh." Vincent grinned. "You see, David, I don't believe you. You're too much of a gentleman, too soft, too kind to be able to dump a wife because she's not making you happy anymore. You don't have to be afraid to tell the Glorious One the truth."

"I told you the truth already. Lay off, Vince."

"Tsk. David. This must be addressed. I wouldn't care what you called me if it wasn't for everyone else who won't understand the familiarity. What you practice in private may slip out in public. I'm just Vince, and you know me well, but that was a remarkably reckless statement. Are you okay? Are you suicidal?"

"Forgive me."

"Would you like counseling? I realize you're skilled in this area, but sometimes we need some—"

"Oh, shut up."

"You're just a tad worked up, I see." Vincent laughed. "Listen, the Kyrios can't divorce their wives as common men. You'll notice many of the Kyrios' spouses die or disappear."

David scowled. He'd never thought about that, but as he considered it, he had to acknowledge the truth. His own father, for example.

"Therefore," Vincent said. "I suggest one of two things for you if you wish to be done with your Gentle."

"Oh?"

"She's pregnant. Then she'll be pregnant again. Bring her to Dr. Kratz for confirmation each time. He'll give it. After one or two 'abortions' she will be weakened or dead from the internal arsenic applications we do at the same—"

"The *what*?"

Vincent quirked such an amused, pitying smirk, David could hardly stand to look at him.

"We don't record statistics for a reason, David. We must do something about the Gentle population, and if we can do it subtly without the time and money involved in jailing and official trials, we do. It's a costly hassle by comparison. The arsenic approach is merely a delegation of execution duties.

"The Gentles are inconveniently located in the ever-spreading woods. It's no good for us as a society. We can't afford to control their population aggressively because there are people who would not approve. Plus, they're all turning into Earth People. No Good." He sliced the air with his hand. "This passive-aggressive means has served us well. Long-term plans for a better future."

David's senses drifted away. A thread of humanity and a large conference table kept him from flying forward in a suicide effort to strangle Vincent.

Vincent rested his elbows on the table and folded his hands. "If you wish to keep this private—no doctors involved—conjugal activities are often an effective and covert means of application if you're careful and creative."

David pushed the painful words out through his tightening throat. "Vincent, are you joking with me?" What a stupid question to ask. Vincent never joked.

Vincent burst into disgustingly authentic and charming laughter. "No. You're Kyrios now. You have to know how we handle things, and it may as well be after you've been humbled. Let's get it over with while your arrogance sits by the wayside.

"Get a little sexually creative, and you'll have it taken care of much quicker than if you go through the doctor."

Don't you dare cry, Dave. "Why don't you just do away with the Gentles? Stop toying with people's hearts."

Vincent sniggered. "David, David, David, we've been training you, yet none of the principles stick. There must be 'law', or it will appear to be tyranny. We must have a placid surface and a turbulent undercurrent." Vincent spun a pen around on the table, speaking as if by rote. "Since we began applying the polygamous tactic, so many years ago, we've had less trouble from the Earth People, because we don't seem to be as aggressive as we once were. Without the pressing need to save entire communities, they're sitting back to 'build themselves up' for a big attack somewhere down the road." He giggled—actually, giggled.

David urged his lips to stay level, but they curved downward in disgust.

"It hasn't changed the death toll, but no one is paying attention to or realizes it," Vincent continued. "Polygamy has been a simple method of legislating a path for objectionable necessities. We are operating productively beneath the modern sensibility radar, conditioning the less-enlightened, and using it all"— he cleared his throat—"for God's glory.

"But, when good leaders latch on to one effective method to handle a problem, they become too obvious, and all the passionate, compassionate nuts and saps come out of the woodwork to cause trouble for them." Vincent gestured to David. "I assume we'll change tactics before long." He rolled his eyes as he rolled his pen back and forth on the table. *Slap*. His hand came down on the pen and rested there.

"This is all beside the point. As Kyrios, you must handle your divorces carefully. I suggest you apply this method if you object to a false accusation of adultery. I admit it's good to avoid because it reflects poorly on the Kyrios. Theocracia needs the men in the Kyrios to be strong examples of masculinity, not milksops with small attachments who can't satisfy their wives." Vincent laughed. "We all know—or hope—you're not a milksop at least."

Vincent grew serious and leaned forward with his face as malicious as David felt. "You're treading on thin ice, David. You should have fallen through already, but I've been merciful because you're a mere boy who never grew up. I'll see to it that you . . . mature." He stood. "Keep your nose out of that hole and your wife in your house or there will be consequences."

Oh, the words that itched to pour out of David's mouth. Furious, venomous, well-earned words lurked under his tongue, clawing at his teeth. They scratched his dry throat as he swallowed them.

Go screw yourself.

Kiss my—

Words weren't worth dying over.

Biting, on the other hand . . .

"Now"—Vincent beckoned for David to follow him—"We have an assignment for you. You need to prepare for a flight tomorrow. Here's your opportunity to prove yourself to us."

* * *

The sun's glow exhaled over the horizon and the birds stirred to life. The hum of vehicles passed Cole, and a sprinkler going off added the perfect effect to the perfect little neighborhood in perfect Pomo Gate.

Cole approached his door. *Keys!* He had left without his keys. He knocked in hopes Hesper would hear him. When she didn't open the door, he knocked again. No answer.

Around the back, he looked through the sliding glass door. Hesper lay on the sofa, her lips parted, and her strong arm hanging down, fingers touching the floor. He smiled at the sight of her until he noticed a distinct curve at her belly.

For as long as he'd known her, she always had a flat abdomen. Women's bodies bloated and changed, but this was different. He hadn't seen it this way before. Unified women often experienced no morning sickness, so the lack of misery didn't mean anything. He wasn't in the habit of tracking her cycle, either.

Had he ever been irresponsible when they made love? No. But other thoughts came to mind. None of those thoughts were things she would do, but things someone else would do to her, then silence her with shame and threats.

He rapped at the glass door. Hesper sat up and hurried to let him in. "You were gone so long."

"You tried to wait up. That was sweet of you."

She wrapped her warm sleepy arms around him and laid her head on his chest. Weary and cooled by the night, he welcomed the warmth.

"Did you find what you were looking for?" she asked.

"I'm not sure what I've found. I'm hopping in the shower." He motioned for her to follow him to the bathroom. He'd explain while he scrubbed.

* * *

Cole had only a few hours before he needed to be at Alan's, but a few hours of sleep were better than none. Hesper and Cole laid down together, and he rested his hand on her belly and considered the feeling of it. "Hesper."

"Mm?"

"You said they touched you when you were taken into the base. As far as I could tell, they never . . ." He paused, searching for words. "You were never violated in a violent way?"

She frowned. "They pulled my trousers down and beat on me."

"Who? David?" *I'll kill him. I will, honestly, truly, viciously kill him in the slowest, most painful way I can think up.* "David wouldn't . . ."

"No!" She shook her head. "Trinity."

"That's the extent of their abuse, though? Nothing sexual?" As if that wasn't bad enough.

"Nothing sexual. No."

"All evidence indicated you hadn't been raped, but it's not unheard of." He laid on his back and stared at the ceiling. Encouragement was the word for this moment. He mustn't scare her. If something was going on with her body, she knew. "Things are looking up, Hesper. It will get better."

She turned to her side and touched his face. "We can always look up and keep getting better, even if the rest of the world does not."

* * *

Cole stood at Alan's door, rolling a spicy cinnamon drop in his mouth as he adjusted his tie.

You saw nothing. Heard nothing. Know nothing.

The heartburn scratched its way up from his stomach to his throat. He had to get used to it. The cinnamon drop probably wasn't helping.

The bell on the door jingled, but no one came to greet Cole. He waited in the entrance area, which was also a small kitchen. Pancake batter and syrup scented the air, and fresh-made butter-light shone through the window by the sink. Jes' voice blazed a path down the hallway from the private rooms.

"Bandello, I came for help, but if all you're gonna do is—"

"What? Give you a resolution for your life-long existential crisis? Help you understand why things have happened to you the way they did?"

"Get off it," Jes shouted. "You don't know me."

"Won't you take a moment, Jes"—Alan's voice cooled to mint—"to consider trying to think beyond your—"

"Beyond what, Bandello? My own nose? Gimme a break."

"Proboscis came to mind, but nose works. You glow like an iron from a blacksmith's forge! You must learn how to submit your anger to the One who made you capable of this, or, in time, you will be more destructive than the Kyrio—"

"Just shut the f-f-f-f-f-f-f—" Jes punched something. "Leave me alone. Why can't you guys accept that I might be what you're looking for"—his voice smoothed out—"but *I'm* not what you want?"

"Jes, you are—"

"No, I'm not! I'm not gonna go overthrow the Kyrios and run your country. This . . . this isn't a job for me."

So far, Jesurun didn't sound threatening, just angry, so Cole maintained his distance.

Alan cleared his throat. "Get over yourself, Jesurun."

"Get over myself? Did you miss somethin'?"

"No. I heard and understand completely! Do you honestly think your dreadful life gives you the right to say 'no?' Do you appreciate the number of lives at stake? Do you think you're so special you can flippantly toss this aside—like a lover you've grown bored with—in the name of self-loathing? Looking out for number one, I assume."

A few moments of a ticking clock and dripping kitchen faucet went by. One of them would tromp down the hallway at any moment.

Or maybe not.

"I know about a hard life, Jes. You've had a cakewalk by comparison, but I don't advertise it," Alan said.

Someone moved, but it ended in a minor scuffle.

"You listen here! Don't storm off!" Alan continued, breathless. "I think that when youth and attractive features haven't gotten you what you want, you've used your bulging biceps and sculpted *abdominus rectus* altars to lasciviousness and dominance!"

Cole laughed. *His what?*

"My what?" Jes asked.

"Your muscles, man! You think that anything good in life will come through sex and pummeling! That's not survival, sir. That's mere arrogance most would feel justifiable for your situation. Don't take the excuses people give you. Rise above them! Somewhere along the way, someone taught you that, or you would have killed me for the trouble I'm giving you. Purge the sun of your life as it approaches its zenith, and the setting will be a glorious miracle of gold and tourmaline."

"What are you talkin' about, Al?"

"Don't turn your back on your Maker, Jes. At one time, I fell into unbelief because I thought God a cruel taskmaster wielding inconsistency as Its whip. It's not true. Life is life. God is God. The twain shall meet, but neither is obligated to make things easy for us. No! They teach us, son.

"A spiritual power is at work in you. Your fulfillment depends upon allowing It to have Its way. Your life is about more than you!"

"Whatever. I don't care," Jes mumbled.

"I do. Someone has to." Alan barreled through the door resembling a fresh cinnamon bun accidentally tumbling from the oven. Cole's presence made Alan's face twitch with panic. He fetched a mangled handkerchief from an inside pocket of his coat and wiped frosting-sweat away from his brow. Flushed and anxious, he grabbed his briefcase from beside his desk.

"Cole, Cole, there's a good man." He set down the briefcase and wiped his hands with his handkerchief before picking it back up.

"Are you all right, sir?"

"Plenty all right. As a matter of fact, I'm more than all right," he said, unsmiling. "I am positively popping with inordinate jubilance! Hold the fort. I trust your judgment. If anyone stops by, take down their situation and say I will, most assuredly, ring at them tomorrow or over morrow at the latest. If they don't have a phone, take their address. Most people who come for my services can afford a phone, though. I have a meeting of burning urgency that I cannot miss. Agreed, m'boy?"

It wasn't easy to throw Cole off, but it seemed like Alan managed it at least once a day. Cole stammered, "I . . . uh . . . yes, sir."

"Splendid! Well, Jesurun is here, sleeping."

"Sleeping?"

Alan expressed mock confusion. "I say, isn't that what I just said?"

"Yes, sir. Sorry."

"AH HA! M'boy, no apologies needed. Methinks you think me too severe. Believe me, I am not." Alan wiped his forehead. "Oh, and *Cole*—I mean Brock—whenever you speak to Vincent—Oh, yes, I know Vincent—I suggest you tell him he's too late." Alan winked.

"However, you are not of the same mind as the Kyrios, even though they sent you." Touching Cole's chest, he said, "You're one of us. Can't rest even though you want to, searching, looking, waiting for that glorious thing—whatever it may be—that will finally settle your spirit. I feel as though my young soul stares back at me through you. You feel the burning, don't you?"

"How did you know who—"

The Leak. Of course.

Alan tapped his nose and stepped past Cole for the door.

* * *

Emboldened by Alan's brazen confession, Cole sat at the lawyer's desk and went through the drawers. Half-way through them, finding little more than poorly organized office supplies, benign papers, and candy wrappers, he encountered a bag of . . . *What the—Oh!* He almost laughed. Condoms. Alan's story about faulty prophylactics came to mind. Not courtroom suitable evidence, but enough for Alan it seemed.

With Alan's hypothesis in place, Jade and David's situation made a lot more sense.

He sighed.

Jade.

Her tragic ending would dog Cole's conscience to the grave. He took a choppy breath and placed the bag back in its drawer. Close that memory, tag its toe, forget about it, and move on. The drawer slid in place, a slab in the morgue of his mind. He was after the Book of Light, not an autopsy of Jade's tragedy. He spun the chair to face the room behind him. Work needed to be done. He'd discuss this with Alan when he returned.

Cole began with a stack of mail on a box. He lifted the lid, out of curiosity, and discovered . . . a real record player? He'd seen one in a book before, having studied them during a period of fascination with musical history. The Kyrios banned recordings over a hundred years ago, claiming they provided too much unwholesome entertainment along with the internet, cell phones, and television.

Cole knew a few people, including himself, who kept CD players because they were easy to hide and more likely to work than other electronic devices once used for recorded music. Only the wealthy could get them, though, because it required overseas travel.

He set the mail aside and lifted the tonearm. An unexpected nub under his finger provoked an investigation.

A hidden microphone.

One of the pieces of advanced technology the Kyrios and law enforcement wardens used, but few knew they had. They were expensive and rarely used, though.

Alan was right? It just wasn't in his stapler. Or was it?

How many might be in his own home back on the base?

A cough arrested his attention. He straightened and faced the visitor, pressing his finger over the microphone behind him. Jes shuffled in with a pipe in his mouth, holding up a loose pair of oxblood silk pajama pants to keep them on his legs. Probably borrowed from Alan.

Cole took a good hard look at Jes' tattoo. From the glove, it swirled around his arm and up over his shoulder where it sprouted tiny roots. The roots increased in thickness over Jes' heart and appeared to burrow into his chest. Under his right pectoral, a *café au lait* mark stood out to Cole as well. David had the same tan splotch. Same place, too. Cole almost said something about it, but Jes took the pipe from his mouth and spoke first. "Alan gone?"

Sweet pipe smoke reached Cole's senses now. "Yes. He's gone."

Jes turned away, exposing his back to Cole. The form of a tree began at Jes' waist. Its branches wisped upwards, like a jagged blue-green flame covering the length of his spine, licking at the base of his skull.

A type of Juniper tree? Rich, glistening, cerulean berry clusters dotted the upswept evergreen branches.

"Where'd you get that tattoo on your back?" Cole asked, awe tinting his voice. "I've never seen one so vivid and detailed."

Jes huffed. "I don't know, okay? You people need to give it a rest." He disappeared around the corner.

Now, for this microphone. If Cole removed it, they would know. However, whatever they'd heard, they'd heard. It wouldn't be worth it to make them aware that he'd found it. He'd have to be careful in the house Alan gave them, though.

He lowered the stylus to the record and turned a knob on the front. Much to his surprise, it worked. The player delivered a smooth voice from the past in its beautiful, grainy way. The Conquest had destroyed much of the nation's history, replacing it with the Kyrios' version of it, but they missed just enough to keep fascination and hope alive.

Cole sat back and closed his eyes, listening to the record scratch out the delightful sound of rebellion with the dulcet tone of brass.

Thirty-Four | Post-Conquest: 232

JES CRAVED A safe place to rest for a week, not harassment from religious fanatics. Especially about something so crazy. The story about this Ansel guy came out in a casual conversation with Al, but Al used it to turn Jes into a god or something.

Why'd you go rambling about yourself, moron?

He always left people when things got bad, but maybe that wasn't his luxury to enjoy anymore. Too many LEWs were on his tail for him to use homeless shelters or sex to get a place to stay. And a bed felt pretty good after sleeping in alleys and abandoned buildings for months.

A rough scrub and fresh clothes would help him think. He pulled off his glove and began a hunt for razors in the cupboard near Al's bathroom sink.

After shaving, Jes set the razor down and inspected himself in the mirror. He looked so old next to other guys his age. Scars on his cheeks, a scar over an eyebrow, a scar on his chin. The rest of him was pretty much the same. Really, those were the least of the scars life had given him.

Why me? He laughed. *Stupid question. Why* not *you?*

The whole tattoo thing made his life worse than just that of an orphaned kid on the streets, and it was an inescapable part of his crap-existence. The one on his back almost always stunned his lovers, though. One semi-long-term lover affectionately dubbed it "the tree of life" and kissed the berry clusters every time Jes took his shirt off around him. Jes smiled. It had brought him some pleasure, at least.

His life had been spared fifteen years ago, but sometimes he wondered if his mom was just a selfish broad who couldn't stand to watch him die. From what he knew of good women, he got that it'd be hard to stomach watching a kid get murdered. But was she stupid enough to think that if he survived, he would have a good life? Didn't she think of what it would be like for a little kid when he found everybody dead? Did she think a dad who ditched them would actually try to find him? Did she think at all?

She was just an innocent girl who wanted to save a life—did the best she could—wasn't that enough to write someone down as a hero? What if the hero saved someone who became a monster?

"What are you?" he said. "Not a monster. Am I?"

His arm tingled. He'd learned to control himself, at least, so there weren't any violent, uncontrollable episodes like in his teenage years. Sometimes nothing happened when he was angry, either. The tattoo thing had a mind of its own. When the fire did come, he had no choice but to find something to write with and to write on, or it wouldn't stop.

He left the mirror and bolted for his room where he found that Brock guy digging through his folder. Jes' face sizzled as hot as his arm. "I'll deal with you in a minute!" Jes grabbed his backpack in search of a piece of paper and a pen. Empty. *That son of a . . .*

Brock had it in his hands. Jes threw the backpack across the room with a bear-like roar and ripped the notebook away from Brock.

"Quit staring, and give me that pen," Jes yelled.

Doubled over, Brock gave him the pen and stared stupidly at Jes' glowing tattoo.

Jes finished the drawing and tossed it aside. Fingers wrapped around Brock's throat, Jes lifted his body off the floor and looked him in the eyes. "You mess with my stuff and I. Will. Kill. You."

Brock would kick his butt under normal circumstances. He usually stood straight up and eyed him the way a LEW would, which meant he'd trained in some kind of fighting or another.

Jes tightened his grip.

Hesper's memory, a scent on the breeze, passed through his mind. He liked the Gentle who'd stitched him up, so he chased the scent. Her voice had been cool water, dousing out his mad feelings. She looked something like his dark-haired girl. Wouldn't killing her man do the same thing to her as it had done to him when he lost that girl—he didn't even know her name—and Jones? Those killings weren't just, and this wouldn't be either.

He set Brock on his feet and let the death grip go.

"You're not Alan's kinda people. You get that chest burn stuff, but you're a LEW. I can tell. You stand like one."

"Not a warden," Brock gasped and adjusted his clothing. "I'm on a personal quest." Back to the wall, he tried to catch his breath.

"Personal quest. Right." Jes snorted. "For what?"

"For . . . For peace of mind and a way back to God."

Jes raised his eyebrows. "How'd you plan to find *that* in my backpack?"

"I don't know," Brock admitted. "I wanted to see your folder."

"You were at the house last night."

"Yes, yes I was. You saw me somehow."

"Sure did. I felt you behind the door. New experience for me, but there it is." Jes grabbed the notebook and threw it at him. "Here's what I just drew. Enjoy."

Brock caught the notebook and opened it. Each paper before this had been torn out and placed in a folder, leaving the soft-cornered notebook mostly empty with remnants of the papers' edges bunched up in the spiral.

A simple picture, the latest featured several hands, palms out toward a jagged ball of light, as if holding it in place without touching it. Maybe reaching? Maybe both.

Brock looked up at Jes and closed the notebook. "Thank you."

"Yeah, whatever. I left the water runnin'."

* * *

Hesper could not find the thrill when Cole came home raving about all the things he had seen since the night before. However, she could not ignore the burn on his neck. A slightly raised, pink bear paw print.

"Did he grab you by the neck?"

"What? Why?" He left her to look in the bathroom mirror. "That's the shape of the tattoo on his hand. Wow."

Hesper half-entered the room to see him, fingering the mark, fascinated. The danger did not bother him? Well, it bothered her.

"Why did you omit the part about your neck?"

He shrugged, still studying his burn in the mirror. "Who wants to admit to being picked up by their neck?"

"But he stopped? He did not hurt you?" she asked.

"He stopped before doing any damage. It won't happen again."

"May I see these things you told me about?" She grabbed the tip of her braid and wrapped it around her finger. He'd never agree to this. "Jesurun's hand and drawings, I mean."

"I'd rather keep the two of you apart."

She scrunched her nose. "Why?"

"Safety. He's—" He licked his lips and huffed uncomfortably. "Well, he's. . . he's a low-life and emotionally—perhaps mentally—unstable. You can't trust him."

"I cannot trust *him*?"

"I don't—" In his silence, her words reverberated like a drum. "That's completely different, Hesper."

"I thought you were a traitor until I saw the proof," she said. "Some would argue that you are, even with the evidence I saw. Does he not deserve—?"

"No, absolutely not." Cole swept her logic away with a sharp brush of his hand.

"Okay." She bit her tongue. "I do not agree, but there is no sense in arguing with someone who controls my life. You might put me on the block if I give you too much trouble." She walked away to cool her temper alone.

* * *

Cole stepped onto the terrace for a breath of positive air in which to think. Perhaps he should forget he found Jes, ask no more questions, and request assignment to teach in a university or something. Far enough away from the Kyrios to have peace, but near enough for comfort.

Forget? He couldn't forget. How does one forget this?

They don't.

They can't.

Cole glanced back through the glass door. Hesper sat in the living room sewing some little whatever, but she looked up and smiled at him. The embroidered silver leaves at the neckline of her plum cotton dress caught the lively sparkle in her gray eyes.

His Hesper.

Courageous enough to marry him and live outside of the world she knew, she took what came and handled it. Ever a realist, ever an innocent, ever the little girl who changed his mind about the value of life. If he left her, she would be lost in a world she trusted him to guide her through.

When it came to people, he was never easy to please. He appreciated quality, and there wasn't a lot of that in the world. But she was *nonpareil*. Not a single thing about her displeased him. Besides her personality and heart, he loved her bolt of black satin hair, shapely strong shoulders, and form and figure to be rivaled by none. No, she wasn't still the little girl, she was a woman who made a choice to walk beside a man.

Me.

He wasn't as handsome as David, he wasn't as good with people, he wasn't as romantically skilled, and he cut her heart with deceit. Every Unified person with any sense or desire for true unity craved peace and safety, and his temper and passions kept her from that.

She didn't need him, she wanted him and chose him, not to control her, but to walk with her. She brought him light, while he had brought her only darkness.

If he died, she'd survive, but she wouldn't have the right to choose who took her after him. In his absence, one person would take her, no matter who else wanted her—out of spite. He would treat her as a female and toss her aside. That was worse than the thought of her living alone.

For that reason, he had to live at the expense of justice.

No more rocking the boat. There are too many innocents at stake.

Thirty~Five | Post-Conquest: 232

HESPER AWOKE WITH a gasp. A pleasant breeze agitated the curtain, revealing the darkness outside. Her dream of Joram was cut off this time, but not for any obvious reasons. Half-asleep, she swung her legs over the edge of the bed and trod softly down the stairs to the living room.

At the sliding glass door, she stopped, more alert. Why was she standing here? She could and should go back to sleep. Instead, she opened the door and went outside. Past the terrace, her bare feet sank into the soft lawn and she crossed it to the small grove.

Under a mandarin tree, she breathed in the fragrant citrus air. At one time, it would have inspired her, but she was not inspired now. Her mind was too heavy.

An unprovoked adrenaline zap gave her a start, and as she jumped up to run back to the house, the leaves of a tree rustled and something—or someone—landed on the ground with a dull thud. She swiveled around to look, and a figure, darker than the night, rushed her. Snagging a foot in her nightgown, she fell but quickly clambered to her feet.

This was a bit too familiar.

A scream tore through her lips just as her pursuer grabbed her and covered her mouth with a strong, gloved hand, flooding her nostrils with the scent of leather.

"Shhh!"

She stopped struggling and stiffly submitted to his arms.

Jesurun.

Cole was right? He was a low-life?

* * *

Hesper's assailant released her when Cole flew through the doorway with a flashlight in hand, shouting her name. He approached on silent, swift feet and aimed his gun at the trespasser.

"You touch my stuff and I. Will. Kill. You," Cole growled.

Jes held up his hands. "Listen, I . . . I just had to stop her when I saw her. I . . ." He wiped his wet face and glanced behind him as if he expected someone. The words shot out of his mouth, hard and fast. "It was pure luck she came out while I hid here. I swear. I wasn't gonna hurt her. My arm lit up and I drew trees. It looked like these, so I came here. You're not safe."

Cole pointed the gun to the ground. "Come inside."

Choking on sobs, Jes whispered, "No, no, you don't get it. It's Alan and his group. I let him kill them." He swatted at Cole, eyeing the darkness around them. "Turn out that light, they'll see us."

Cole turned out the light. "Who?"

"One of their people. He had a medallion." Jes swiped his nose and eyes with his sleeve. "He was a spy or somethin'. He'll kill me and anybody here who's met me. I know it. Come with me."

"Hold on. What are you talking about?"

Annoyed, Jes repeated, "I could've stopped it, but I didn't. Someone killed them all."

"The killer has a medallion?"

"Yeah. I don't think that—"

"*We* will be fine," Cole said.

Jes scoffed. "Do you wanna take a chance?"

"I'm not taking a chance, Jes. I'm with the Kyrios."

Jes took several steps back as if he'd been shot with an automatic rifle, prepped to make a run for it.

"I'm not one of them," Cole explained, "but my sister is. I've been sent here with a medallion of justice."

Jes' eyes flew open and narrowed to slits in an instant. "Did you . . .?"

"No, I didn't have anything to do with this."

Jes took in a sharp breath. "He's pulling in over at Alan's. I gotta go."

The tiger-eye headlights shone through the darkness. Despite the claim that he needed to go, he didn't. Postured like a frightened animal, he stared at the vehicle.

If the killer showed up at their house, it would look worse if they had fled. They'd be hunted down and executed for justifiable suspicion of treachery.

No more rocking the boat, huh, Cole?

This was not rocking. This was plugging up holes in the boat, nothing more.

Jes needed help. The guy might run, but where could he go if twenty of the thirty sections were looking for him? What part did Jes have to play in this ridiculous situation? Who really knew? But God was with him. Jes was clearly uninterested in spiritual matters, but God seemed to be interested in Jesurun's matters just the same. What more did Cole need to know to at least stand with him?

"We'll hide you. Come in but be quiet. They've got microphones in Alan's house. They might have them here, too."

As they made for the house, the headlights in Alan's driveway lit up.

"Hesper, to bed," Cole ordered, then pointed Jes toward the basement door.

Cole waited in the kitchen for the traitor. In two or three minutes, someone rattled the door with firm, rapid knocks. Cole waited for a few more before he shuffled over to the door and mumbled in what he hoped was a sleepy way, "Who is it?"

"A messenger of the Kyrios. May I speak with you, sir?"

"Of all the . . ." Cole opened the door.

"Successor Chandler." The hiss of a stiff military uniform came with the salute. The man wore his medallion and the insignia of an officer beside his embroidered name. Clapton. He smelled of wintergreen. A popular scent these days.

Cole saluted. "Successor? Are you sure you have the right Chandler, Officer Clapton?"

"Yes, sir. I'm sorry to be the bearer of sad tidings. Her Reverence, your sister, passed away."

Trinity died? That wasn't unexpected, but the timing was suspicious.

"Is that why you're here?"

"No, sir. The Glorious Ones wanted me to report to you. I've been with Mr. Bandello's group for several years. The mission is nearly accomplished, and I'm tying up loose ends in the next few days. I understand Bandello employed you, so you ought to know that, since he's no longer necessary for my mission, he has been duly executed." He glanced at Cole's hands. "Anything peculiar going on, sir? All's well?"

Alan really was dead. That stung more than it should.

"All's well. Nothing peculiar except for your visit. Are you certain you're supposed to report to me?" Cole leaned on the doorjamb.

He eyed Cole's neck. "Yes, sir, I'm to report to you."

"Anything I can do to help you tie up your loose ends?"

He shook his head. "Just need to locate and execute a couple of Mr. Bandello's associates. If any show up, please, contact me. But if all's well, the Kyrios send this." He presented a long cream-colored envelope, which Cole took from him. "You'll need to pack and prepare for a flight later this morning. Are your hands well, sir?"

My hands? What the . . . "My hands are fine. Why wouldn't they be?"

Officer Clapton's eyes narrowed too deeply for Cole to trust. "Are you familiar with the criminal Mr. Bandello's been harboring?" A quick zip of the eye peeked over Cole's shoulder.

"No, I don't know any criminals. Sorry to disappoint you." Cole scratched at his jaw, regarding the suspicious officer's demeanor with distaste. "You look at me in ways that officers normally wouldn't look at successors, Officer Clapton. You ought to rethink your direct manner."

"My apologies, sir. I meant no offense." Clapton saluted once more and returned to his vehicle. The engine came to life with a purr, quiet as a kitten, and he drove down the road.

They put him on the inside to wait until the Book hunters found their book, then he killed them all. If the Kyrios were taking Alan's theory seriously enough to do this, there might be something to it. Something that scared them.

The letter in the envelope said little more than what Officer Clapton already told Cole.

He'd been tricked. Whatever he was here for had nothing to do with mongrels. Whatever waited for him at home wouldn't be pleasant.

But the concern with his hands?

He opened the basement door, and Jesurun quietly came up the stairs. Cole grabbed a notepad and pen from a drawer and sat down, kicking the chair near him away from the table for Jes. He wrote, "Spill it."

Hesper came down the stairs and stood behind him.

More collected now, Jes sat in the chair and pulled the makeshift folder from his tattered backpack. The latest drawing consisted of basic human forms with no details, seated at a table. One with a medallion for a face held up a gun. A traitor.

Cole handed the picture back to Jes and wrote, "Why are you supposedly responsible for this?"

Jes set the drawing on the table and took the notepad to respond.

"I wanted to stop. I decided to make myself not be the Book of Light, or whatever they say I am. I fought as long as I could, but the burning got bad. Like, it was gonna kill me."

He rubbed at it, then pulled up his shirt to show an angry pink rash around the roots on his chest. He continued writing, "I saw what I drew and ran out there to try to help, but it was too late. I liked Al. He was a cool guy." His letters grew dark and messy. "It's my own friggin' fault! I never killed anybody who didn't deserve it, but I've gone and killed him."

"How did you get here?"

"My arm started burnin' again, so I blew out of there and laid myself out to draw in the tall grass by the meeting house. I recognized the trees I drew 'cause I stole some of the oranges from them on my way to Alan's the other day." The pen clinked on the table. Jes leaned on his elbows and put his head in his hands.

"So, what're you going to do about it?" Cole shoved the paper between Jes' elbows so he'd see his words.

Jes lifted his face and blinked a few times, his mouth slightly open.

Not much of an answer.

Cole brought the paper back to himself. "Tonight, you've gotten a taste of what it's like to know you had the power to stop a tragedy and refused to do it. It won't get better with time."

Jes shook his head, sniffling. He snatched the pen and wrote, "I can't. I tried to do somethin' about this stuff before, and the LEWs came after me. I'm wanted 'cause everythin' in here"—he stroked his tattoo down to his hand—"if I say it out loud, makes the Kyrios and their LEWs 'n crap look bad."

"Maybe it was to chase you here to us. Alan and his friends were here for years, and you just now arrived when we did?"

"I can't—"

Enough! Cole slapped his hands on the table. "Not only can you, you must!" he scribbled. "That officer isn't going to stop looking for you. He can't go back to the Kyrios without your head on a platter. You have a responsibility, and it's time to man up."

Jesurun's facial and neck muscles tightened, and his eyes flared with a dangerous glint. He wrote quick and hard, "I can't draw them to death! Get real, Brock," then tossed the pen and sat back in his chair.

Ooh, he was angry? Good. Far better to get angry than weepy. In the proper hands, anger could be pointed in an appropriate direction.

"Cole. My name's Cole." He underlined it.

Jes rolled his eyes and shoved his things into his backpack, then gave his final words on the last clean page of Cole's notepad. "I have manned up. To reality alone. It's harder to give up on the dream of better days than it is to work for it." He shrugged his shoulders. "Thanks for not turnin' me in." The pen slid across the table and fell off the edge into Cole's lap.

Jes tromped out, backpack over his shoulder, just the way he was when he had come into Cole's life.

The familiar heartburn faded as Jesurun escaped into the darkness.

The shaking boat had steadied, but the paddles had been lost.

Cole let out a hard, desperate sigh and smacked his forehead onto the table. He couldn't promise safety or tell Jes what all of this meant or what would happen if he agreed to stand against the Kyrios as Alan and his friends thought he should.

Really, none of this was Jesurun's problem.

* * *

Hesper rushed out of the kitchen, through the living room, and out the door.

Cole followed.

Something unnatural happened to Jesurun. Based on the information she was given, she understood that some thought the power of their god lived in him and that he belonged in the stead of the Kyrios. No matter the truth, she was willing to give him a chance. She had to.

As she approached the dark figure between the trees, he turned around and waited. About a yard away from him, she stopped, clasping her dress, mangling it, frightened and sure at the same time.

"Jesurun," she said, "do not leave."

"I can't help you guys. I'm sorry."

"Do you . . . Do you know they do not let Unified have children with Meros men?"

"Yeah."

She caught his eyes as they passed over her face and clung to them with her own until he lit up with the message. *I am pregnant. Do you understand? Do you truly understand?*

"Do you care for justice? I imagine you do. Anyone who lives as an outcast must deal with false justice often. It may be within your power to bring true justice for all the children the Kyrios have destroyed. It may be within your power to give the Kyrios wisdom."

"Miss, I don't have that power. Where you all got this idea from is beyond me. Sure, I might've stopped that officer. I can knock one man out, but there are five Kyrios, not to mention a huge army."

Hesper's nerves frayed and unraveled. Part of her wanted to scream and shake him, but the rest of her wanted to crumble to the ground and beg.

"How do you all live separate from each other? We are like pieces of humanity scattered through a nightmare. No one's problem is yours, no one's problem is mine. We are on our own."

Jes took a step forward and put his finger in her face. "I wanna live. I'm not gonna look for trouble when it's hunting for me." His wild brown eyes sparkled with untamed passions. Like Tane.

"Why will you not see your survival as a wonder? Why must you see only the suffering?"

Hands shoved in his pockets, he lifted a shoulder. "Because suffering exists. I'm sorry you're in trouble, but I can't help everybody in a fix. This has gotten blown way outta proportion. No one has proof of anything. All I do is draw and light up." He licked his lips and chuckled. "I'm a friggin' firefly with a pencil! Okay? That's not gonna help you. I help people when I can, 'cause it's just right to do, I guess. But most of the time, I gotta look out for me." He nodded, then shook his head. "This is one of those times. I'm not gonna talk to the Kyrios or try to stand up to them. It'd be stupid."

After a few false starts, she stepped toward him. "Jes, will you let me . . . let me come near to you?"

"What for?"

"I am not sure. The only thing I can think of." She shot a look at Cole. His jealous side popped out at unexpected times. Would he trust her?

Cole nodded.

Jes narrowed one eye and frowned. "Fine."

She approached and placed her hands on either side of his head. "What're you doin'?"

"Tell your story in your mind, Jes. Think about it. Share your pain with me. Press it through your thoughts and let me show you the relief of unity in the face of suffering."

"What?"

"Just try," Cole said.

Suggesting he think on his life required him to have at least a few thoughts, even if he did not want to do it. They stung, hurt, burned. Behind it: water. Somewhere flowed coolness—an undercurrent, rushing in the opposite direction.

Jesurun barked a cry that startled Hesper. Teeth clenched, he grabbed her hands and growled, "What . . . is . . . this?"

Presently, a series of images and thoughts, scents and feelings, colors and lights flooded Hesper's mind.

Sweet vanilla perfume, a dark hole, gunshots, tears. Loss.

Haylofts, old men, murder, blood-stained pajamas. Violation.

A dark-haired girl, nectarines, and a kind old man. Toothpaste.

Love. Love. So much love.

Blood.

Thorns, nettles, stinging. An earthy, spicy tonic with a metallic scent buried beneath it dashed itself against her consciousness. Despite everything, bitterness did not live there.

He released her.

* * *

For the first time, Jes didn't burn with his emotion. A gentle breeze of calm cooled him, starting at the tree on his back. He hadn't felt settled since the night his mother picked him up and hid him. Warm and comfortable, peace filled his little heart as his mother's licorice hair touched his cheek. Now he relived the moment before the safe feelings disappeared.

Pain festered inside of him, but Hesper entered his thoughts and unearthed his hurts like potatoes, showing them to the fresh air and light as she brushed off the dirt and admired the scent of the soil.

Over the years, Jes' lovers got carried away sometimes. He'd charm them, and they'd sleep with him and get attached after the experience. Some folks just didn't get that sex didn't mean affection or loyalty. For the first time in his life, he imagined he might understand how they felt. It was weird and stupid. Old-fashioned. He just wanted to take care of her like his girl in Apple Gate, but even more.

She had opened him up and dug around the inside of his mind. Something he'd never experienced before. As if he was a plugged-up pipe to flush out. At peace now, his good sense did tell him to run, but if he went away, would he go back to burning and anger? Could he feel that way again?

Nah. It was just something that happened. They shared it, but it wasn't going to keep him. Wasn't going to make her something special.

Twitching his jaw up and out, he said, "Does your chest burn, too?"

Hesper frowned. "No."

"What'd you do to me?" Her hands and arms had no special markings like his did.

"Listen," Cole said, "Jes, we'll talk about this. We'll be out of your hair before the day is over, but until then, we can sort out a plan or ask God for guidance in this situation. Maybe It can convince you, or me . . . I mean, I don't know what's going on any more than you do."

Hesper held her face, crying.

Oh, geez. Don't cry.

"You must not leave, Jesurun. None of us know what you can do, but I hope you will wait and see, rather than run. I trust Cole's interest and belief in you. I realize it is not easy to turn to something your good sense tells you is foolish, but life is worth more than pride."

Easy for her to say. Or maybe not. That black "X" always meant something hard happened.

"You're stuck, aren't you?" he asked. "They gave you choices, but they're all fake. Like pickin' which rope to tie you up with. Choices that are worth nothin'. I dunno what I can do for you."

She did not want him to do anything for her. It would content her to see the right thing done, no matter who benefitted from it.

"I have never been sure whether their god exists. However, I do not see a way to explain what they say happens to you." She tipped her head and smiled a little. "You know I had a dream about you? You were on fire and ran from those trees, blazing." She pointed.

"You ran at me, grabbed me—as you did tonight—and you said you burn but could not die because you needed me."

Jes squinted at her. "I want to say you're lying, 'cause it's all nice and easy to tell me crap to get me feelin' a certain way so I'll do what you want." He studied her face. An honest face. She wasn't lying. "And I think that's what's up. I'm not gonna stay and be your personal bodyguard. You're just gonna have to face the pain of thousands of other Gentles before you." He pointed and stabbed his finger at her. "What makes you think you deserve to avoid the suffering of your people? Huh?"

The breeze passed through the leaves above their heads.

"Nothing," she said.

When faced with the question of why they deserved anything from life, people rarely had a good reason. At least Hesper was honest enough not to try.

He tossed his hands up. "There it is!"

"But I do not understand why a trail of suffering cannot be destroyed. I would never say others should suffer just because I have.

"You do not think of my suffering, you think of your own and you put it onto me. If you suffer, why should I not? Why should my pain matter to you? That is what you ask yourself, is it not?

"You may not be bitter, but you are proud, and nothing can break pride except suffering." She walked away, and her husband followed her, leaving Jesurun in the darkness.

Alone again. Always alone.

They couldn't go, but they could. What did he want? He didn't know. No clear answers. No. No. They couldn't go!

"Hang on," he said. "It doesn't make sense, you guys, but I wanna help you have your baby. If there's somethin' I can do, I'll do it. But you gotta convince me there's a plan worth tryin'."

Thirty-Six | Post-Conquest: 232

COLE, HESPER, AND Jesurun sat on the terrace to avoid being picked up by any microphones in the house. Nothing was a guarantee, but it seemed prudent to take a few precautionary measures.

"I know where the group kept their information. Years of study. Interviews n' things. Info from the times they got to the Kyrios' computer stuff."

"C.W.A.S. Computer World Access System." Cole set three glasses of water on the ground and seated himself. "Nothing nearly as extensive as the internet of the past, but quite powerful in a world where only a few can access it."

"Yeah. That's in the toolbox under the kitchen sink in their meeting house," Jes said. "Guess they figured no one would suspect a toolbox."

Cole sipped his water and puffed a laugh. "Discretion was not their strong point. Officer Clapton took it already, no doubt. I'm going to go to the house to see if there's a chance any of the 'loose ends' he's looking for are there or in need of help. It's unlikely, but I can't think of a good reason not to check. They might have information that will assist us, too."

"And I doubt there'll be a clean-up crew. If he's smart, Clapton will try to paint you as the killer. Burning evidence, the way a clean-up crew would, is a sure-fire way to announce Kyrios involvement—

something they'll try to avoid. But even if someone shows up to do the job, I have every right to be there." Cole stood. "I'll be back soon." He went inside to find his bag and dig out the extra communicator. "If you need anything."

Hesper followed Cole to the trees. "Do you think you will run into trouble?"

"I doubt it. Clapton'll lurk about Alan's, waiting for Jes to show up. As for the medallion, I'm wearing it just in case Clapton called the LEWs a little later than I would have. If they show up, and I'm wearing a medallion, they'll have no problem with my being there."

Hesper rubbed her forehead with her fingertips. "So many confident assumptions, Cole. Let them go. These people can take care of themselves, even if they are there."

"Would you just let it go, Hesper? Or would you take the step and help someone even when you were scared?"

Hesper slid her arms around his torso and lifted her face to kiss him, but his cold kiss broke her heart—not in a sweet way. They drew back from each other and he smiled, holding her arms, stroking them with his thumbs.

"I'll be back."

* * *

Indoors with Hesper, Jes grabbed his notebook to communicate.

"So how do you do that?" he wrote.

"Do what?"

He pointed to his head.

"I do not know. I started doing it several months ago, but I am never sure how it will work."

"Do you think it's God? Like, somethin' God lets you do?"

"I have not believed there is a god until today. I doubt It would do anything for me." She handed the paper and pen back to him. Her hand rested lightly on a bookshelf while she looked out a window. She wasn't in a mood to talk anymore. Writing all this was a hassle.

Jes wrote, "I like you. Your guy is all right, too. I know I'm not showing that right. I dunno what I can do, but I'm tied to you." He put the paper in front of her face and smiled.

She smiled politely and nodded.

Quickly, he scribbled, "Since your big thing is keepin' your baby alive, I promise I'll do whatever I can. I wanna stop that suffering road. I wanna make it so that baby has a chance, and give you and your stuffed-shirt husband a chance, too."

That was the reason that sounded good anyway. Really, he'd probably just gone nuts or secretly wanted to die. Suicide by Kyrios.

* * *

Light warmed the windows, and the familiar jazz music skittered through the broken panes. Cole recognized the vehicles from his first visit to the house, so they weren't wardens. With the vehicles still present, the lights on, and music playing, Cole couldn't be sure of what waited inside. He avoided burnings, but now he chose to enter a house of death.

This time, he entered through the front door. Noisy with music but eerily quiet when it came to signs of human life, the house's atmosphere made Cole tense and hyper-alert as he scanned the area. He did have a gun this time, so that was a comfort. It wasn't the idea of being hurt that concerned him, though, it was what it would mean if someone had orders to shoot him for interfering. He was the superior in this situation, but Clapton had not treated him as one. The whole thing was a bit screwy.

Passing through a barren room with matted green carpet, he entered the kitchen, which stank of metal. Some of the victims lay on the yellow linoleum floor, blood pooled beneath them, and a few lay slumped over the table. All of them shot in the head. Life, like saffron threads, had sprayed across the walls and table. Alan and his chair lay on the floor with a half-eaten carrot a few inches from his hand. If Clapton sat where Jes' picture depicted him, Alan saw it coming. Cole cringed at the thought. What a shame that Alan would never see the fruit of his labors. He knelt beside the jolly man's pallid form and closed the blank, unblinking eyes.

Dignity.

This kind of thing ought to have been done in silent darkness and left that way. The lively music and bright lights made the scene more pathetic than horrific.

On a whim, Cole checked under the sink. The toolbox was still there? Excited energy zapped him. He needed to get out before anyone saw that he had it. While it could be empty, if it wasn't, it might be a tremendous help.

* * *

Nearly home, Cole's communicator buzzed. No good. He answered the call and picked up his pace.

Panting, Jesurun began speaking before Cole. "We're running. Don't go to the house."

Cole glanced toward the house as he passed it in the alley. Nothing seemed amiss. "What's going on?"

"That guy. Clapton? He showed up at the door with real deal Kyrios," Jes gasped. "I mean, real deal. Chandler and, uh, Minh?"

"That's . . . that's my brother. Why?"

"Your lady opened the door 'cause she recognized your brother and figured it would be weird if she didn't answer. I hid quick, but Clapton and Minh charged around lookin' for me. I knocked Minh out when she found me, so me and Hesper ran out the door before the other two caught what happened."

If Jes struck a Reverenced One, he was dead. Looking back, Cole caught a glimpse of several unfamiliar cars parked in front of the house.

"We're heading for the market," Jes said. "Should we stop and wait for you?"

"Do you think it's safe?"

"Nope. We'll wait as long as we can."

* * *

Providence favored them. The three met in the closed market and slipped into an empty bare wood booth where cinnamon and cardamom filled the air. It would be a couple of hours before the business owner would arrive.

Cole gave Hesper a quick smile as he crouched beside them, then addressed Jes. "My brother is a good guy. I don't think—"

"Good guy or not, he's Kyrios, and they do what the Glorious Ones tell them. Maybe it's easier to see that stuff on my end of things than yours, cause nothin' can convince me I'm wrong."

"Now that we have run, how much trouble are we in?" Hesper asked.

"Heaps. They'll probably call me soon."

She thrust out her hand. "Cole!"

"Your chip," he breathed.

She stared at her hand. "What can we do?"

"Nothing I want to do. I've heard of them being removed only once. Someone had a severe allergic reaction to the material. But they'll have to dig out the tracking system and turn it on. It's a process that takes at least ten minutes. We've got time."

"You are irrational today, Cole!" Hesper snapped. "You assume too much."

"We will stagnate and die in indecision if we don't make a few assumptions. We don't have a choice."

"We may not have a choice, but I have a knife," Jes offered. He pulled it from its sheath.

"No," Cole said. "Infection. We have nothing to sanitize with or to cover the wound. Out of the question."

"Cole, they will find us!" Hesper hissed.

"We have to go back sometime! The hope for a plan is the only reason to prolong this. Let's get a good head start before the sun rises."

Hesper's chip meant either perpetual motion or surrender. Near the edge of Pomo Gate, they traveled north, down a road to a factory with hundreds of tiny fish scale steel-framed windows of various colors. They ran the perimeter of the building, yanking at every door. Locked. The steel frames made it impossible to fit through a broken window. Jesurun grabbed a rock and bashed the glass until his arm blazed red.

"YES!"

Pressing his hand to the metal bars for several minutes, the steel melted and shriveled away as the panes fell and shattered on the ground. He shook the liquid steel from his hands.

Cole shot a look at Hesper. What would an atheist make of such a thing? *Heck, what do I make of it?* Fixated on the sight, Hesper didn't notice his look.

Jes shrugged and picked a piece of cooled steel from between his fingers. "Sometimes it happens, sometimes it doesn't. I did it in jail once, but another time, it didn't work. I dunno why. Don't bank on it very often."

The three crawled through the opening and entered a cold cement world of dust, cobwebs, boxes, and broken machinery. Above them, metal beams crisscrossed the expanse of the ceiling, and enormous lights, long burnt-out, hung from the rafters.

Cole crouched and opened the toolbox. Empty. Officer Clapton must have taken everything. "Well, that's that. I guess we have to plan according to what we do know."

"I hate to tell you this, but we've been found." Jes pointed toward the silhouettes of unwanted visitors passing by a cluster of cloudy windows ahead of them.

Cole grabbed Hesper's hand and ran, followed by Jes. Voices echoed through the cavernous structure a moment before they burst out of the gloom and into the fresh morning air. The sun peeked over the treetops, stirring the world to life.

Rather than take the main road, the trio followed a country path toward the gate's borders and crossed a field of wildflowers, aiming for the stream that drew up the border of the gate. Across the stream, they passed into the area between Pomo and Canvas Gate and continued running until they disappeared into sparsely wooded terrain and planted themselves beneath a low-hanging tree.

"Cut this thing out of me. Now!" Hesper demanded.

"We can't do that, Hesper. We must—"

She pushed. "They will get us in our sleep. We cannot run forever. We *have* to get it out."

"Blast it all! I know, Hesper! I know!"

"I will do it myself, then!" she roared.

Cole grabbed her wrist as she reached for Jes' knife. She shrank away, eyeing him as if he hurt her feelings. "I will not die. Why are you not letting me do this?"

"Got an itch to be a martyr, man?" Jes asked.

Oh, he did not just say that . . . "Hesper, they're going to get us no matter what we do. Jes and I will die, but you won't. I'm not going to let some ridiculously filthy knife that's been who-knows-where and done who-knows-what get into your bloodstream! While you're breathing, there's still a chance that you and the baby can survive. Somehow. Call me an idiot, but I'd rather sacrifice myself or keep running than take that risk."

As soon as the words were out of his mouth, the stupidity of them struck him upside the head. Still, he would not back down. He wasn't wrong, but . . . but what? *She won't call you an idiot, so you'd better do it yourself. Proud idiot.*

"Cole, I am a woman, not a child. You do not own me. I am making this decision for myself because you clearly love me too much to think for the good of the group. Stress is clouding your judgment. May we have that knife, Jesurun?" Hesper extended her hand, and Jes passed the knife.

She was right. To survive, the Unified way was the only way.

Hesper from the woods mixes with Hesper who's had enough Meros foolishness.

A smile sneaked onto and off his lips quickly as he snatched the knife from her hand and grunted with disapproval. Only a small incision into the barely scabbed-over wound and the tiny chip came out with a spurt of blood, like squeezing a seed from a grape. He held it between his fingers for a few moments.

Thinking more clearly now, a plan got through. Why should everyone surrender? Three of them might stand a chance if they approached this from the right angle.

"Jes," he said. "Will you take Hesper? The two of you should run."

Hesper glared at Cole. "Explain your meaning."

"We can use this to save three out of four. You have a child, and he has a gift. I'm expendable."

Hesper assumed her stubborn face. Anything he said from now on would fall on deaf ears.

"Hesper, look at me." He took her face in his hands. "Don't look at your thoughts or anything else. Look right at me! It's your turn to think rationally and without sentiment. If I surrender, they will stop hunting while I prepare and go to them. It will give you a chance to run."

"I'll do whatever," Jes said. "I'm in this to take care of her."

Hesper clapped her hands. "No, no! You crazy men! I refuse to leave you just because we face something frightening. It does not please me to do, and you cannot make me." Tears trickled from her eyes. "My life may not be my own in your world, but unless you are willing to hit me hard enough, I am conscious, and you will not move me." She cried, "You would not do it, either, Cole. If I am weaker and need your protection, do not give me the guilt that will come with this." She held her face in her hands. "I would bear death better than guilt."

Cole's communicator buzzed. David's name appeared on the small screen. Cole answered.

"Hey, Cole. What's going on?"

Cole laughed, incredulous. "What do you mean 'what's going on,' idiot? Why are you here?"

"Oh, so you're with them, too?"

"What in blazes is going on?"

"Trinity died. I've been promoted. Yay, right? We're assigned to clean up after Officer Clapton's assignment, but Clapton here is suspicious. Thought you were harboring a criminal. Saw weird marks on your neck. We found the criminal in your house with Hesper. Are you aware of all of this?"

"You came across a guest visiting my home. That much is true."

"Listen, I hate this as much as you do. Believe me. I can't leave without you, though. You, apparently, have someone who is wanted by the Kyrios. Dead. He's dangerous."

"He's only dangerous to the Kyrios!" Cole pointed an accusatory finger at the air.

"I was afraid you'd say something to that effect. If you've allied yourself with him, I can't let you guys go." David sighed, weary.

"Get us there alive."

"Yeah. About that. I already have directions from Vince because he anticipated your efforts to make a deal. You guys come out, and you'll all get a trial, rather than Immediate Justice. You and the man you have with you."

Cole could barely talk through the thick anxiety in his throat. "We're done for, aren't we?"

"At this point, we should just throw our hands in the air and scream, 'cause I think we've been set up and we're on the way down."

It wasn't over until they killed him, or was it? Hesper couldn't be allowed to hear what he had to say, so he crawled out from under the tree bough. A brisk walk would eat a bit of his frustration and get the chip to the stream.

"If I'm executed, take Hesper," Cole whispered. "She's to stay alive, no matter what." His voice grew dangerous when he repeated, "No matter what."

With a sudden, sloppy intake of air, David broke the news. "Vincent said he would take her."

"No! Try to persuade Vince to let you have her." He paused and rubbed the back of his neck with his sweaty palms. "She's pregnant, David. If you can get her, you need to let her have the baby. You've made it happen before—once. Make it happen again. Without so many witnesses in your house, you should be able to get her out somehow."

Cole dashed to the stream and tossed the chip into the water to be carried away.

A long pause.

"I'll do what I can, Cole."

"If I die, and you don't make a way for her, I swear I will come back from the grave and haunt your sorry hide until you kill yourself. When you get to the afterlife, I'll dog your soul 'til you beg the spiritual powers to end your existence."

Another long pause.

"That's a lot."

"Promise," Cole said.

"I promise to do whatever I can."

What more could he expect?

Quietly, David said, "I can give you a head start, but we've got a lot of people here, and we're pretty sure we have your patch of trees mostly surrounded. I highly doubt you're running on the river at seven miles per hour. I even hit the tracker a few times to see if that fixed the reading, but . . . ."

"Running isn't the best choice. Vincent keeps his word."

"Knock it off, Cole," David spat. "You sound like me. I hate it. Now I understand why I annoy you so much."

Cole smiled. "It'd feel good to run, but it would be the death of Hesper. You wouldn't let them rape her, but . . ."

"You don't have to explain," David said. "I understand."

Cole hunched his shoulders. "We'll meet you at the gate's western border." He ended the call and kicked at a patch of ferns. He'd punched a tree a few years ago and regretted it for months. His hand still stiffened up in cold weather sometimes. A few kicks at the ferns would have to suffice.

The supposed Book of Light needed to get where it belonged.

Let's see if we've got it right, shall we?

Back at the tree, he crawled under the bough to join Hesper and Jesurun. Hesper lifted her hand, which showed no evidence of a cut. No blood. Nothing. The two looked at him, half-guilty, half-out-of-their-minds-excited.

"What did I miss?"

"Jes touched it. When he took his hand off . . ."

Cole gave his attention to Jes. "That's new?"

Jes rolled up his sleeve. "When I saw what happened, I tried it on me." His stitched wound was gone.

"Maybe you had to stop being angry for a bit, Jes."

* * *

David's black eye and limping gait shocked Cole. A gash on his forehead stuck out like a flash of red lightning. The doctor didn't take care of it properly. Forcing him to travel to the other side of the country at this time had to be Vincent's idea of a joke. Flanked by Reverenced One Minh and Officer Clapton, David's hands filled his pockets, his face grim. Several local law enforcement wardens waited in parked cars, engines running.

* * *

A thousand words hid behind David's face as he watched them surrender. Had his eyes ever been so expressive and his composure so disoriented? To see him in between grief and responsibility made Hesper hurt—wanting to apologize, but unable to, wanting to save them, but powerless. The weight pushing on his chest pressed on hers, and the pressure in his mind squeezed tears from her. David glanced at Jesurun once or twice but zeroed in on Hesper alone.

David had Tom, Lorelei, Anise, and Dulce to stay alive for. They would suffer if they lost him, and it would be selfish for him to abandon them.

Before Hesper got into the car, she reached up and touched David's hand where it rested on the door. "I love you, David," she said. "You will find *nepenthe*?"

He stared at her, lips parted, more uncomfortable than she meant for him to be.

"I intended to give you comfort." She frowned.

His weak smile and dip of the chin said he was not comforted. He whispered, "You know, Kali, the blue lady in my parlor?"

"Yes."

"She's a goddess of destruction, right?" His eyes went in many directions, but somehow his mind and focus were all hers.

"Many believe she brings enlightenment by destroying the evil and negative aspects of a person. In that way, she is compassionate. Sometimes compassion hurts. It provokes a change of heart." He inclined his head to Hesper. "I don't deserve comfort, but I need a change of heart. So, don't feel bad. You're just being like Kali—as I knew you were—a compassionate destroyer of evil. You don't even know you're doing it. I hope, someday, you see it in yourself."

Thirty~Seven | Post-Conquest: 232

VINCENT PERMITTED COLE to stay home, rather than jail him. A benevolent act, at a glance, but little more than a psychological tactic to break him through time with his loved ones. Vincent's method of torture allowed the traitor to think about the cost of his behavior for himself and for Hesper.

If Vincent wanted to kill him, he wouldn't make the effort to break his resolve, would he? Maybe he had a deal. If he stopped being a pain in the rear, Vincent would show mercy. No. This was all a part of Vincent's game, but Cole couldn't keep the thoughts out.

Alone in their room, he took in the familiar sight of his beloved library and breathed in the smell of it. He hung up his coat and set his bag on the floor by the bed and nearly sat in his favorite chair before realizing Hesper hadn't walked more than a few feet into the room. So still, hands limp at her sides, dead inside. She'd never seemed quite right since leaving the woods.

He had hoped their marriage would help, and it did seem to, but this experience took her down. When she learned his identity, she admitted herself to be weak as she apologized to him. Ever since then, self-doubt plagued her more than anything. If he knew Hesper as well as he thought he did, her greatest comfort and confidence for this moment would come from being needed and helpful to him.

He reached for her. "I need comfort from strong, nurturing hands."

Capable arms enfolded and held him like an orphaned fawn.

"I hope to God we're not going to be martyrs, Hesper." He squeezed her and kissed the top of her head.

"Where has your courage gone?" She pulled away to look up at him. "Your god may come through tomorrow. God may do something wonderful. Who can say?"

"Listen to you, my precious atheist."

"I am ashamed that Jesurun is in jail while we are comfortable in our home with each other."

Only Hesper could find a way to consider herself privileged on the night before her husband's execution.

"He's fine. They won't hurt him. I want to close everyone else out and be an encouragement." He placed a tiny, promising kiss on her lips. "May I indulge you?"

Chin raised, she said, "I believe I am entitled to it."

They kissed each other with all the sunlit water they had. No benediction had ever blessed Cole so much. Drawing back to look her over, the emotion on her face thrilled him with its conflicted discontent, warmed by the afterglow of shared sweetness—the loveliest expression known to man.

Some dared tell women to smile, but Cole preferred an authentic countenance of pleasure that he put there himself. No woman should have to fake anything for his sake.

"Hesper," he whispered, "are you able to hurt anything?"

She smiled, confused, shaking her head. "I suppose so."

Fingers tangled in her hair, he closed his eyes and said, "Set the broken bone. Kiss me like you have to hurt me to heal me, like the *aurora borealis* and its sweet heart-breaking. Show me your spirit, woman."

Mere poetry. Stupid talk.

But in a moment, she proved that an idea can be both stupid and inspired.

She'd be okay. Somehow, she'd be okay.

* * *

He wanted her to hurt him to heal him? He was more frightened for her than for himself.

His face, the energy in his stance, the hopeful anticipation in the firm tangle of his fingers in her hair, all expressed sincerity and longing. He ached for something contrary to her nature.

What was her nature?

She was more than her nature, was she not? Life required more of her.

* * *

David made his way through the low-lit, dank hall of the jail. The officer on guard stood in reverence as David entered.

"At ease, Officer Atwood."

The jail's sole occupant sat on the cold, stone floor, knees up and arms resting on them. Eyebrows furrowed with rows of troubled thoughts, he paid no attention to David.

When one of David's teachers explained that he had a "naturally hypnotic presence," he built on it with training and expected to counsel and help others, not realizing that it would take him into the jail regularly. Still, he rather enjoyed watching stormy seas calm under a soothing touch or the power of gentle words, and to hear the truth sing out rapid *legato* without the violent techniques they learned in school. He rarely required any other tactic from his skill set.

However, he didn't visit the jail to calm or draw from a prisoner tonight. He needed to soothe himself and quell his conscience with kindness.

"May I get you something to eat?" he asked.

Jesurun turned his face toward him, absentminded, as though following the flight of a passing fly. He pursed his lips together and lowered his eyebrows. "They're here, aren't they?"

"Who?"

"People like me—whatever I am. I feel them."

Jesurun stared at the wall, though David wished he'd look at him.

"You know about them, don't you?"

Cole had explained Jesurun's situation on the trip back to the base, but David never mentioned the charred bones to Cole or Jesurun.

"Not sure what you mean."

"When I walked in, I felt like I walked into myself. I dunno what I mean, but I knew more of us existed, and they were here somehow."

David came close to the cold bars and whispered, "Are you really what they say you are?" He wanted to ask where he was from, who his mother was . . . But why? It wasn't worth it.

It wasn't!

Jesurun took a deep breath and nodded with a resigned air. "I'm somethin'. I dunno about all this Book stuff. Not really."

"How can you prove it?"

After a few moments, Jes strode over, took off his glove, and reached for David's forehead.

David jerked away.

"It's okay. I'm proving it."

Eyeing Jes, David allowed a touch. A normal, human touch pressed against his forehead, but soon it burned with a scorching heat that quickly cooled. Watching with his good eye, the coolness flowed under the surface of Jesurun's skin like a current of ocean water. He touched David's eye, his lip, and lastly, knelt to touch his toes through his boots.

David swiped his fingers over smooth skin where the gash had been. Split, dry lips transformed into a mouth that was kissier and softer than a grown man's ought to be. The eyelid that had been swollen, opened, and the hot pain in his injured feet faded.

With a sharp puff of breath, he stared at Jesurun, then at Jesurun's hands. A miracle?

Jesurun met David's stare and cracked him open and flipped through his soul like pages in a novel. Strange feelings sprang up in his chest. Flappy-flyers. *Oh, my God.* It was like being with Hesper.

David didn't swing that way, so what was the matter with him? He had to get Anise out of that room. A man had needs, after all, and now might be the time since he had the lips of a baby. She'd be impressed.

"What can I do to help Hesper, Reverenced One?" Jesurun asked.

David tipped his head. "Why? You like her?"

"I promised I'd do what I can to help her have the baby. I don't have a thing for her, it's just that I messed up. I shouldn't have let Cole turn us in. I should've run with her."

I know the feeling, kid. "Don't let that eat you, Jesurun. You couldn't do anything about this. Cole made a prudent decision, considering the circumstance. Trust me on that. I'm the one who forced him into it."

Jesurun leaned his forehead against the bars. "Yeah. I'll try. Haven't trusted a military guy before." He snorted a laugh. "One of the last things my mom told me was that I shouldn't trust anybody with golden buttons and black boots, 'cept for my dad. Never found my dad to trust him. I guess you'll do since I'll probably be dead soon, right? Check 'trusting a military man' off my list of life goals."

"I wish I deserved it, Jesurun." David bounced on the balls of his feet. This sucked. "Well, if you need anything, let me know."

David strode through the hall to the guard's desk. "Officer Atwood, this man isn't going to have a trial." With a glance in Jesurun's direction, he scowled and pulled a wallet from his pocket. The meras whispered against each other as he counted out a thousand. Going over the Glorious Ones' heads required significant remuneration. This was just the start. "I'll get the papers you need from Vincent."

Officer Atwood shook his head. "No, sir. Not worth my life."

"Ten thousand are coming your way if we survive it."

Officer Atwood took the money.

Thirty-Eight | Post-Conquest: 232

WINTER'S FIRST SNOW fell in the night, and the house carried its special tranquil silence. Hesper and Cole picked at bowls of hot buckwheat in the dining room as they suffocated in a somber fog. David scuffled in, dressed in his most flamboyant harem pants and garish orange and silver bathrobe from the East. The robe hung open, exposing David's chest. Cole had forgotten about that *café au lait* mark. David needed to know about that.

David's eyes flitted between Cole and Hesper. He took a long breath, staring at the floor, then he looked to Cole, grim.

"How is Jesurun being treated?" Cole asked.

"He was treated well."

"Was?" Cole straightened up.

David waved his hands in front of him. "Is, is! I talked to him last night." He smiled. "Just a slip of the tongue. I didn't sleep well."

Cole considered David's forehead. "Your face is better. What happened?" Those things don't go away overnight. Jesurun had done something for him. No question.

"I'll see you later," David said. "I have business to attend to."

"Dave, this might seem stupid to mention, but Jes has the same *café au lait* mark on his chest."

David froze. He turned his head a little, his mouth opened, but he said nothing and walked on.

He'd make his own decisions. Cole wouldn't bring it up again. In a few hours, he wouldn't be able to.

* * *

Little Thomas stayed home with the flu. At least, that is what David claimed. Family was required to attend trials, but sickness served as a valid excuse. No one wanted a child to witness an execution.

Dark smoke billowed into a winter-gray sky like color from a bag of herbs in hot water. Fresh snow squeaked and crunched beneath the slow-moving weight of the vehicle. Hesper's feelings seeped from her without passion or even a name. Like that smoke.

In the Bastion, law enforcement wardens escorted them into the Judgment Room. This time, the procession of the Kyrios included David. He would have to make the accusation, agree with their verdict, and stand against his kin. It did not look right. How could he be the person who made Hesper feel fireflies inside? Who had become her friend and would have become her husband under different circumstances? How could anyone separate themselves from their loyalties for the sake of religion or work? It did not bother her so much yesterday, but today? She could not grasp it.

Cole took her hand and squeezed. With a resolute jaw and dry eyes, his mind stood tall in another place. That was his way in troubling times. It protected him while hurting everyone else. It is how he became the educated man he was, how he got things done and survived in this harsh culture. She would let him be there if it gave him courage.

Cole rubbed at his sternum.

"What's wrong?" Hesper whispered.

He sucked at the air and gave her a quick glance. "Heartburn."

Where was Jesurun? A sick, dark feeling twisted her thoughts. She reached behind her and touched the tip of her braid, wrapping it around her finger.

Vincent noticed the same thing, apparently, because he scanned the room, frowned, and whispered to Ariana, who shook her head.

"We're missing someone?" he asked, aloud. "Send the officers from the jail, please."

The officers arrived without Jesurun. Vincent thrust his head forward. "Our prisoner. Where is he? Officer Atwood?"

"We took care of him, sir. We received orders for a quick execution."

They killed him? Vincent had him killed without a trial.

Snake!

Vincent glared at the officer, blinking rapidly. Disgusted, he slowly closed his eyes and pressed his lips together. "You did what?" His eyes snapped open. "Who told you to do this?"

"An official letter signed by you, Glorious One." The officer eyed David, but Vincent did not seem to notice.

Such a silence fell. The only noise came muted through the doors from the foyer of the Bastion as Vincent's gaze swept over the Kyrios, none of whom dared to look at him.

The moments he spent composing himself gave Hesper pause. Maybe he was truly surprised. Cole had said Vincent never wrote his own letters. It would not be hard to fake an inconsistent signature. If that was true, he had set himself up for this.

"Well," Vincent's voice crackled, "Who has forged my signature is a question for later. The matter at hand is that we permitted a grave error. One that speaks poorly of our integrity. I'm truly sorry, Cole." Turning to the guards, he asked, "What have you done with his things, Officer Atwood?"

"We burned them with his body."

The smoke in the sky! Hope reduced to ash in that fire, and in her ignorance, Hesper barely considered it. David had said Jesurun *was* treated well, and Cole had called him on it. David backed out of his slip-up, and they had trusted him to be honest, but now: the truth. She watched David, hoping to read his face, to see an apology hidden there, or something determined and traitorous, but David did not look at her and offered no telling expressions.

"Very well. Nothing can be done now. Moving on." Vincent waved his hand. "What are the charges and against whom are they directed?"

"The charge is treachery, Glorious One," David announced. "Directed against Successor Cole Chandler."

Vincent laughed. "Treachery? Who would have *ever* expected it, Cole? Certainly not me!"

Cole nodded.

"Speaking of treachery, this morning, I ordered the purging of the community you based yourself in during the years you used to cultivate your Gentle sentiments."

Hesper's heart throbbed. Perhaps she misunderstood.

Cole's lips trembled. "Why?"

"It produces too much trouble, and we have solid evidence pointing to that community as the culprit in the attack on your nephew, Tom. It was time to stop that Earth People factory once and for all." Vincent regarded Hesper. "I see we have a Gentle broken heart."

Hesper sneered to overcome grief. Anger worked and looked better. Her situation tied her hands and emotions, rendering her powerless over anything and everything. What was the use of grief? It would not be the last of her losses.

"I no longer have a heart, Glorious One. It was broken long ago, and what remains is not worth your consideration."

Vincent considered her in a manner she'd never seen. A sincere, apologetic, pitying frown. "My mockery was in poor taste. I'm sure this grieves you more deeply than you will show. You are a woman of great self-control, and I perceive by your quivering fists, you demonstrate restraint. I vow to make some restitution for your loss, Mrs. Chandler."

She stilled her hands. Vincent was not a cold person, he was a burning one that left scars with his warmth.

He cleared his throat and redirected his attention to Cole. "You're in trouble, Cole. What do you have to say in your defense?"

Cole coughed and rubbed at his sternum. He cleared his throat. "I appeal to the Book of Light."

Vincent's groan evolved into a laugh. "Oh, sweet mother of pearl, you have to be kidding."

"I insist." Cole closed his eyes and moved his lips in an almost imperceptible way. Hesper had seen him do this before. A whispered prayer.

"I half-hoped you were the Book." Vincent shook his head in mock disappointment. "That group of chest-burning conspiracy theorists draws them. We've monitored those people for years. They have cells all over the place. Most of the time we got to the Books before they ever reached a 'chest-burner.'

"You've been such a nuisance and your father had peculiar traits that required extra attention, so I thought sending you to one of their groups might awaken something. I tried to hurry things up a bit." He shrugged. "But what excellent timing! You got the truth you wanted, and you've tasted the thrill! At least you'll die happy, right?"

* * *

That Reverenced One, David, told Jes he was free to go, but Jes' loyalty to Hesper got in the way. A few days ago, he would've taken him up on it, but a chunk of Hesper was stuck in his brain. She dug around to see his grief and left herself there. That's how it felt anyway.

He wouldn't change it, though. She lit up his world. Not just in his mind, but through his actual eyes. Almost as if he had been wearing sunglasses and Hesper took them off for him.

David had been leery of Jes' suggestion that he hide behind the curtain in the Judgment Room instead of escape. Jes had to get a little tough. Convinced that David had a thing for Hesper, Jes used her potential fate and all its possibilities to convince David to agree to the idea.

David offered Jes a gun, but he didn't want one. Why insult God like that? If It wanted this to work, it'd work, if It didn't, it wouldn't. He'd learned a thing or two about biting the hands that fed him, and he wasn't diggin' the idea of biting a god's hand.

Stuck in this dark room for hours, Jes listened to Vincent's pompous crap as he mocked Hesper, insulting powerless people living the last hours of their lives just to make it sting.

Friggin' jerk. I'd love to break his neck.

He grabbed the curtain.

God, if you're real, now's not the time to ditch me, okay? 'Cause this is all I got. Me. Light me up and do what you want. I'm dead if I do, I'm dead if I don't, but goin' this way might make a difference for that girl out there. Give the kid a good chance, hey?

The next step? Dying.

In his experience, he stood a better chance if he acted like he'd never lost a fight. He smiled. Showtime.

Cole saw him first, and the wide-eyed, tight-jawed terror on his face made Jes giddy. The Kyrios twisted in their seats to see him. Red and orange blazed through his arm and chest, and his legs buzzed with energy.

"Hey, I got some wisdom from your god. It says you suck and you're due for a hefty whoopin'."

The Kyrios leaped from their seats as if bitten by their chairs. Reverenced One Minh toppled over. Ariana tore a knife from beneath her tunic and yanked David to herself. Pressing the knife against his throat, she screamed, "Someone grab the Book! Do you really have to be told?"

* * *

David submitted to the petite arm wrapped around his lower ribcage—she couldn't reach any higher. Her small size tempted people
to underestimate her, but her knife, now scratching his skin, wasn't
to be trifled with. One intentional twitch of her hand would do him
in.

Honestly, without him in the way, held as a hostage to keep the
marionette strings dictating their actions, Jesurun and Cole would be
free to act without reservations. Even if they didn't take out the
Kyrios, they would at least stand a chance.

What did *he* have to live for? Perhaps he should go out with a
bang—or a slice, as it were—and give Hesper a chance to live and
have a baby.

Otherwise, after a wedding night with Vincent, she'd set his bed
on fire and he'd execute Immediate Justice. Someone ought to warn
Vincent about Hesper and old Kali beforehand perhaps. The woman
was pretty and reserved, but she'd give an untrustworthy crap like
Vincent the fight of a rabid wolf. He'd win the fight, but she'd leave
scars. Scars on his memory more than his body, most likely, but
still . . . scars.

Reverenced One Minh pulled a gun on Jesurun.

Vincent shouted, "Put the gun down. If we can keep him alive, we
should. It will simplify the process."

Simplify what process?

At a standstill, everyone waited for Jesurun to surrender to save
David. That settled it. Death might actually be a relief. *Nepenthe*, at
last? All the mistakes, all the things he'd seen and wanted to stop,
but didn't, or couldn't. All the pain he turned to pleasure to hide
from and forget never became *nepenthe*. This would be, though.
Even if he preferred to find it in life, this would have to do.

"Jesurun, surrender," Ariana said. David took that moment of
distraction to move his fingers enough to unsnap his gun holster.

Cole's eyes, shining and angry, screamed a warning. He wouldn't understand right now, but if Ariana didn't panic and cut David's throat, Cole might be able to thank him later.

Cole used to be a good catch. Hopefully, that was still the case. David whipped out his handgun and tossed it to his brother.

The fatal twitch.

* * *

Cole spotted David's smooth move with distaste. David wouldn't think to try to use the gun himself. He'd toss it and hope for the best because he was overwhelmed. He was going to die, but he might not have to if he'd think things through! David's hand crept down to his gun and tossed it in Cole's direction. Cole caught it.

Still a good catcher, thank God.

Ariana dropped David's bleeding, gagging body to the ground. Now that the worst had happened, Cole had no time to think about grief. David intended for this to increase the odds of survival. That had to come first.

Cole aimed the gun at Vincent. If Ariana threw the knife, Vincent would receive a loving, thoughtful bullet. Hesper rushed to attack Ariana but Reverenced One Pierce reached out and grasped her arm in a hard-locked grip. She kicked him between the legs and carried on. Quint Pierce had never been a remarkable person, and he proved it again and again.

A thick, odorless cloud appeared in the middle of the room, steadily pouring in as if through a window in the air. The cloud expanded, flashing with radiant bursts of bright blue, topaz, crimson, and sparks of purple.

Minh's voice echoed off of the stone walls. "My God! Oh, my God!"

Ariana shrieked and ran for the doors. The cloud issued a flash of azure lightning that dropped her to the floor. The strike left a smoking black hole in her back, sparking with purple. Thunder growled low and long, building up until it filled the room with its resonating power. A strange quivering hum tore Cole's eyes away from the cloud. The Kyrios were shivering, holding themselves, teeth chattering as they looked on at one another in dumb, frozen terror. Then, within moments, sweat saturated their clothing and some began to disrobe to escape a scorching heat Cole could not feel. Comfortable, cool air surrounded him. Jesurun and Hesper appeared to be unaffected as well.

Jesurun broke free from the quiet hysteria and planted a blazing fist into Vincent's chest. The blow tossed Vincent like a wave, then brought him crashing to the floor at the bottom of the platforms. The sizzling-hot stone fried his skin, and his perfect hair melted in the puddle of boiling blood beneath his broken skull. The Kyrios lifted their blistering feet up onto the chairs and gazed in helpless horror as the cloud claimed the room from wall to wall.

Jesurun dropped to his knees, face to the ground. Hesper stood across the room, watching in the way of a wild animal. In a few moments, the haze blocked Cole's view and muted the cries and screeches of the Kyrios until it suffocated them. Several minutes later, in silence, the lightning decreased as the cloud disappeared the same way it came.

Seeing that Hesper and Jesurun were okay, Cole hurried past the bodies of the Kyrios to his brother and dropped to his knees.

That fat head coward.

For the first time since he was eight, Cole cried in public. Hesper's strong arms lay over his back, and her head rested against him. Elderberry wine, oil, and tears bled out of her spirit and into his own.

* * *

Jesurun crouched beside David's body. He owed this guy. If he could do something for him, he would, but what? He touched David's throat to heal the gash. While he left no sign that David had ever been wounded, the guy was still dead. What could he touch that would make this okay?

Would God care? That was the better question. What would God be willing to do?

He rested his hand on David's heart. No fire burned down his arm, and only coolness flowed from his back. The image of an unfurling pink flower bloomed in his mind like a dream. The flower pulsed, and a faint thudding tapped at his palm.

A heartbeat.

Life radiated through David's face, pushing the paleness away. Just as Jesurun touched the cold lips, an intake of breath drew cool air through his fingers. Hesper and Cole sobered and jumped back, startled. David's chest surged upward. His lids opened, and tears poured down the side of his face and into his hair. Blinking, he stared at Jes a moment before a wild laugh burst out of his mouth. "I didn't expect that."

Hands to his face, he rolled to his side and released a long, mournful wail until he had lost all his breath, took in fresh air, and repeated the same, hoarse, wavering cry.

Jes stood to back away and give the family time to figure out their feelings, but strong, lady-arms wrapped around him.

"You have my gratitude," Hesper said. Her body shook with tears as Jes patted her back, giving several furtive glances to Cole. The threatening glare never came.

"Yeah, no, it's . . ." *Well, it sure wasn't nothin', Stupid! Don't say that.* "It's pretty amazing. I'm glad it worked."

Thirty~Nine | Post-Conquest: 232

COLE COVERED HIS face with a scarf and bundled up to bring Hesper home to Lorelei. She couldn't be left alone, but, for the sake of safety, she couldn't stay with them either.

David and Jes waited for Cole in the locked Judgment Room. It wouldn't be abnormal for a trial of such a nature to take all afternoon. He had time before anyone on the base might grow suspicious. If they were going to make anything like a smart move now, he needed a clear head to formulate a plan.

The reformation of an entire nation wouldn't be easy and might never happen, but Jesurun had allied himself with something bigger than an army. Why would anyone challenge It once presented with evidence of supernatural intervention? One here and there, but after continually failing, it wouldn't happen much. Time would tell, of course. Jes did say that his powers didn't always work. That could be problematic.

Where could he go to be alone with his thoughts? He scanned the base, considering the closed businesses and homes.

Friends.

Beyond the base, the forest called.

Cole came home with a bag full of things from Hesper's community. Her drum, a few wooden boxes, and Theia's betrothal token. Hesper would like that.

After a hasty shower to beat away the chill in his bones and to wash the feeling of death off his body, he whipped out a pair of blue jeans and a sweater and went in search of Hesper. She wasn't in the parlor, so she was probably in the dining room, eating or talking with Lorelei. He didn't have time for a hunt!

"Sir," Lorelei called, pointing out the dining room window. "She's outside. I check on her to make sure she's all right. She's just sitting in that tree. Sir, what's going on?"

"Something big, but I'll have to tell you later, ma'am. She needs to come inside and stay inside. Lock doors. Keep the shotgun with you." He hugged her and turned back to the foyer to grab a scarf and coat.

Wrapped up, he stepped outside. At least Hesper was dressed in a coat and hat and taking care of herself. The cold had steeped her cheeks in crimson, and she shivered despite her warm coat.

"How long have you been out here?" he asked.

Now noticing him, she turned her head. "Awhile."

Cole pulled himself up to the branch beside her. "We need to get through tonight, Hesper. Then we'll take tomorrow and get through that. Life is not over."

"Are you certain Mama and Papa are gone?"

"They were still in bed. Yes, they're gone. Probably went in their sleep. Let's go inside, hm?" He cradled Hesper's shoulders and hugged her. "I brought things from home for you, then I have to go back to the Bastion. We're in a dangerous spot, and we can't waste any more time than we already have." He pulled her closer to kiss her temple.

The rough tree branch scratched at her fingers as she caressed it. "Cole, this has all been built on assumptions. Jes has supernatural abilities, but why do you believe he is what they have guessed he is? Where is the proof? We cannot control this enough to rely on it."

"You're right. We're trying to understand as we go, but this is a step in the right direction. The source of our troubles is gone. That's a good thing."

Hesper shook her head. "I do not think this is the end of our troubles. It is a bad poem about a sickness. The Kyrios were only a symptom. Life is never so easy."

Thank You

* * *

To my fellow readers who complete the art of writing by taking it in and experiencing it.

To fellow writers and beta readers who nourished me and my story, guiding us into a healthy growth of artistic freedom and the development of a stronger craft. If it were not for you, I may never have accomplished this.

Carla Glover, Anne Wheeler, Erin Maruska, Annie Hara, Clay Hardy, Carol Beth Anderson, Her Supreme Reading Magnificence Shannonononon, Caith Esra, Britta Sorenson, Ruth Behnke, Aaron VanDeBogert, Judy Himsl, Eve Cammon, Heather Kam, Meghan Tomlinson, Lia London, Jennifer A. Dege, Anna Lee, Christina Goebel, Lexi Kenan, Sonja Greer.

To Dad for giving me the crazy gene so that I could write a book.

Special thanks to my husband for letting Cole use his poem and for his input, ideas, and time spent reading this with me.

Special thanks to Carla Glover. Girl, after me, you've read this story the most. You saw it through so many stages and you've always been a willing reader and encourager. You have been a BLESSING and a FRIEND to me and to this story.

Friends of the art, family in the art, I salute you.

About the Author

* * *

Sarah Joy Green-Hart grew up in a restauranteur family in the Northwoods of Wisconsin, waiting tables in between reading, writing, acting, petting cows, and dancing with flocks of cats.

After earning an A.A. in Theology and cultivating an adequate taste for the artistic, the eclectic, and the odd, Sarah's family—with a proper advanced warning—released the Sarah-Kraken on a gentleman with an affectionate interest in said Kraken.

Sarah now homeschools four wee wolf cubs by day and howls at the bookish moon in her laptop by night with the charming Earl Grey (and a few of his friends) at her side.

Besides the bits and pieces of her soul found in this book, you can also find her on her blog "Shivelighting."

shivelighting.wordpress.com

38757456R00216

Made in the USA
Middletown, DE
11 March 2019